Futuristic Romance

Love in another time, another place.

PASSION AMIDST THE STARS

Raul dragged Esme back into his embrace, where he hugged her so fiercely she feared her ribs world crack.

Esme's radiant eyes met Thorson's over Raul's shoulder, and she grinned at the look of combined relief and jealousy on his face.

Not now, Thorson, she begged him mentally, still grinning. *Please . . . let me enjoy this reunion unhindered by your jealousy.*

Thorson flushed. Then, without replying, mentally or aloud, he turned away and left the apartment.

Esme forgot about him as Raul raised his head and crushed his mouth against hers. She forgot everything but the well-remembered, well-loved taste of Raul's lips and tongue. His warm, familiar hands roved her body, as though seeking to confirm for themselves that she was real, and she responded in kind, satisfying the long-denied need to touch him.

Daughter of Destiny

JACKIE CASTO

LOVE SPELL ⬧ **NEW YORK CITY**

LOVE SPELL®

March 1995

Published by

Dorchester Publishing Co., Inc.
276 Fifth Avenue
New York, NY 10001

Printed in the United States of America.

Daughter of Destiny

The Master's Prophecy

THUS SAYS THE MASTER. THERE WILL COME A TIME when, because of your disregard for Me and My laws, your hatred of your brothers and sisters, and your misuse and abuse of the Homeland which I gave you, you shall suffer and die in great numbers, and many of you will damage your souls past my recovery.

In the days when your wickedness has reached its peak, the land will be made desolate from your predations, and where once there was plenty for all, there will be sustenance for none. Neither water, nor food, nor peace will you have. Having destroyed your own inheritance, you will then, out of hunger and terror and hardness of heart, turn upon and rend one another, each seeking at the expense of his brothers and sisters to obtain that which is already lost.

Then will I show mercy to those who have sought Me. Into that Valley upon the Homeland which I will keep protected and hidden for the time when it will be needed, will I send a Remnant of My People which I will save for Myself. Male and female, will every race I have created be drawn there, as will those of the lower creatures which My Remnant will need for survival. Their population will not overrun the Valley's resources and among My Remnant will I preserve peace and the knowledge of My truth. And unto the latter days, their awareness of Me and their love for Me and their obedience to Me, will not diminish.

Others will I save also, separate from My Remnant on the Homeland, and these will multiply, fluorish and prosper in the places I will send them. Yet these Others, as did their forefathers and mothers, will come to

follow the enemy. They will make war among them-
selves, threatening their own survival as well as all that
I have given them.

Then will I once again show My love and mercy. I
will send one of Mine to the scattered, and that one will
forge a link which cannot be broken. My two Remnants
will then come together—the one to teach My truth, the
other to learn it and to protect it . . . against the day of
My enemy's wrath.

CHAPTER ONE

For the third time since her arrival on Genesis, Esme rode in a mechanical craft which sped at terrifying speed along concrete passageways among towering buildings. But this time, she did not concentrate on her fear of traveling so fast among these alien surroundings. Instead, she was intent on constructing a mind shield, which she had asked Raul earlier that day to teach her before he had left her to return to duty so that she could resist the insolent mental probes of the man who sat beside her.

She had never needed a shield on her own planet, the Homeland, where a small number of people who regarded their planet as the original homeland of all humankind lived. Nor had she needed one among Raul's people before meeting Laon. It was she who had read other people's minds, and now that her

7

thoughts and memories were being sifted without her consent, she felt shame at having done it to others for so long. But at least, unlike Laon, in her explorations, she had turned away from very private matters, and no one had known that she had roamed through their thoughts, sparing them the discomfort she felt now.

"Is that the best you can do?"

Esme knew Laon's lazily contemptuous question was meant to intimidate her, perhaps even to make her cease constructing her shield. But she was far from intimidated. Should she choose to, she could shatter Laon's mind into atoms, and though she was not yet sure of the extent of his telepathic powers, she did not think he could do the same to hers. His real power over her lay in his position as administrator of the Institute of Training for the Telepathic, which was their destination, and his membership in the High Council of the Empire.

"For the present, yes," she replied to Laon's question, her voice cold. "This is the best I can do. But now that I have the fundamentals, I will build upon them. And before this day is ended, Laon, you will no longer trample uninvited where you do not belong."

Laon merely smiled nastily and shrugged. "Perhaps," he said, unconcerned. "But keep in mind, Esme, you have never been among others who have mind skills comparable to your own and that at my Institute you also will no longer be allowed to trample uninvited where you do not belong."

"I would not do so now except when absolutely necessary in any case," Esme grimaced. "You have taught me how loathsome it feels."

"Ah," Laon mocked, "but sometimes we must do what is necessary, loathsome or not. Have you not already proved you can be a ruthless enemy? How many men did you kill when you destroyed that Rebel ship?"

"I do not know," Esme said grimly. "I only know that I had no choice. It was the lives of those of us on the Condor against the lives of those who sought to kill us."

That incident had happened a few days ago during the journey from Esme's planet to Raul's home Genesis, the governing planet of an empire consisting of many worlds, some of which were in rebellion against the Empire's central authority.

During the journey, the Condor had been attacked by the Rebels' new weapon—a stealth ship that could not be detected, and therefore against which there was no defense. But Esme had detected its presence with her mind, had turned its missiles against itself, thus saving the Condor and destroying its enemy. And as a result of having told the High Council of her feat, she was on her way to the Institute while her beloved Raul, a space captain for the Empire, returned to battle duty. Only now, she was not only to be tutored in her mind skills, but she must find a way to teach other telepaths how to detect and destroy stealth ships, a task she did not know how to accomplish.

Esme stared at Laon where he lounged in a corner of the craft. He was a long, lean, and casually graceful man, and not unattractive with his black, backswept hair, his somewhat mesmeric black eyes, his olive skin, and his aristocratic nose. But Esme was not impressed by his looks; she preferred Raul's large, rugged handsomeness and the unusual clarity of his blue eyes.

"And you, Laon," she said with no inflection in her

voice. "What sort of enemy are you, I wonder?"

Laon smiled, but it was not a pleasant smile. "If you are fortunate, Esme," he said, his smoothly cultured voice tinged with an undercurrent of steel, "you will never find out."

"And if I am unfortunate?" she pressed him.

His black eyes pinned her green ones. "If you are unfortunate," he drawled softly, "you will find that there are worse things than the lack of control over one's physical location, which is what you despise about your current situation, is it not?"

Her separation from Raul was what Esme truly despised, but she made no answer to that effect.

When she said nothing, Laon added, "Believe me, Esme. The lack of control over one's mind and heart can be infinitely more punishing than having no control over one's physical location."

Esme felt a sudden chill run down her spine. Premonition, other than in her dreams, which had foretold that she would travel among the stars and find her life mate in one who was not of her people, had never been one of Esme's skills. But at Laon's words, she felt a distinct warning of impending danger she could not ignore.

In reaction to that warning, she abruptly faced forward, away from the man who held her immediate future in his slim, aristocratic hands. At that moment, Laon somehow seemed to her the personification of the Master's enemy, which meant he was her enemy as well. For her life belonged to the Master, the deity Who had created the People and Who watched over the Remnant of the original humankind who had remained on Esme's planet.

Indeed, Malthuzar, the old high priest had visited

her in the spirit before his death to give her the Sacred Pouch, the most significant of all the emblems of a high priest. Malthuzar had told her the Master had tasks for her which she must fulfill.

Malthuzar had not told her what the tasks would be, but he had known she was to travel away from the Homeland, just as her dreams had always said she would. He had told her to take the Sacred Pouch with her, that it was hers by right now, and to bring it back when she came home again.

Thus, she had kept the Sacred Pouch safe even after Bazil, Malthuzar's treacherous successor, had exiled her from the People. She had protected it as she stumbled across the vast desert which covered most of the Homeland, except for the valley surrounded by mountains which the Master had kept safe for His Remnant against the time when the rest of the Homeland would be destroyed by war and ecological damage as foretold by His Prophecy.

That part of the Prophecy had come true. Esme's people had lived a primitive life in the Master's protected valley for centuries, awaiting the second part of the Prophecy, which foretold that the Remnant on the Homeland would one day be united with another Remnant the Master had saved by allowing them to depart the Homeland before it was destroyed.

Esme might now be among that second Remnant, here on Genesis, though she was not as yet sure. True, the Sacred Scrolls, the record of the Master's laws and the history of the People, said that the Master was the Creator of all humankind, but if that was so, why did Raul's people not acknowledge Him? They did not even seem to have heard of Him, and the whole matter confused Esme greatly.

But she was not confused concerning her feelings for Raul. Whether her beloved acknowledged the Master's existence or not, Esme was sure Raul was the life mate the Master had always meant her to have. Had Raul not been her lover in the dreams that had foretold she would travel among the stars? Had she not known him before she ever set eyes on him as the captain of the Condor? And would she ever have set eyes on him if Bazil had not exiled her from the People?

She had threatened the priest Bazil with exposure and punishment for having sent his spy Marcus after Malthuzar as Malthuzar made his last pilgrimage to the Master's Holy Mountain. Bazil had feared Malthuzar might return with some vision that would threaten Bazil's plans to change things once Malthuzar died, and Bazil became high priest. But Malthuzar had discovered Marcus's presence on the Holy Mountain, where it was unlawful for any but a full-fledged priest to venture, and Marcus, afraid the high priest would have him stoned for blasphemy, had killed the old man.

In her rage over Malthuzar's death, Esme had made Bazil aware of her mental powers. She had also killed Marcus in self-defense by shattering his mind. And then Bazil had threatened to expose her gifts to the People if she did not remain silent and accept exile, which she did for two reasons.

She had kept her gifts secret from her people all of her life because of an inner prohibition Malthuzar had said that the Master had planted within her for her own safety.

The People had mistrusted Esme's mother, Esther, because she was the only one of the People who had green eyes. She had also claimed that a man who was not of the People had come to her on the high meadow, the result of which was Esme's birth. This created the suspicion among the People that Esther was a sorceress.

Esme also had green eyes and since no man of the People stepped forward to claim her as his child, the People had feared her conception was unholy, and that she might be a sorceress as well. Therefore they had ostracized her from birth. Only the fact that a high priest as respected and pure as Malthuzar had blessed her birth had allowed Esme to remain alive and receive normal schooling.

But if the People had known of her mental powers, they would have been confirmed in their belief that she was a sorceress. And if Malthuzar had known of them, he would have insisted she become a priestess and serve the people. Indeed, Esme's mother had once presented Esme as a candidate for seeker, those who were to be trained as priests, and Esme had had to manipulate Malthuzar's mind to keep him from choosing her.

She had done so because her dreams, which had started at an early age, had shown her that she was not destined to be a priestess. Instead, once her schooling was completed, she had gone to the high meadow as a shepherdess to hide her gifts and to ease her loneliness by dwelling in isolation.

The other reason she had agreed to exile was that she had been certain her dreams of traveling among the stars were about to be fulfilled. And Malthuzar had confirmed it in his spirit visit to her. He had also confirmed that she would come home again. Thus, she could extract vengeance upon Bazil when she returned. But if she had denounced him at the time of their confrontation, she would have gone to trial as a suspected sorceress and if convicted, would have had to kill some of her People to escape being stoned.

But Bazil had tricked her. With the help of a young seeker, Baldor, who knew the ancient body disciplines, she had been rendered unconscious and left in the Western desert to die.

But instead, as the Master had planned, she had walked for three nights across that desert and, half-dead, had ended up at the threshhold of the Condor, a royal transport ship, which Raul temporarily commanded on a mission for the high counselor of the Empire to take his son to visit his mother on another planet.

After delivering the high counselor's son, the Condor had been returning to Genesis when it had been attacked by the Rebels' stealth ships. The Condor had been damaged, and after jumping into unknown space, Raul had set the ship down on the Homeland, to make repairs.

When Esme had appeared out of nowhere, Raul had feared that she might be an enemy seductress sent by the Rebels to subvert him and his crew before another attack. Being suspicious of Esme, he had raised his mind shield whenever he was with her. Esme had never before encountered a mind she could not enter, and she feared disclosing her gifts to a man whose mind she could not read. Raul knew she hid something, and therefore, tested her to see if she was an enemy seductress by allowing his crew to use her sexually. No enemy seductress could resist such an opportunity to try to subvert the enemy, but to protect his men, Raul had not exposed them to Esme long enough for her to be successful.

But Esme, hoping that if she was useful to Raul he would take her with him when he left the Homeland, made the men believe that they had used her when they had not. Thereby, she not only proved her innocence, but she also made Raul aware of the powers of her mind. Therefore, Raul decided to take Esme back to Genesis with him in order to have her tutored in her mind skills and to serve the Empire. But before they left the Homeland, Esme recognized Raul as the mate in her dreams, and they became lovers.

On the journey to Genesis, after Esme had destroyed the Rebel stealth ship, Raul knew that no matter how much he loved her, her abilities were invaluable to the Empire. Therefore, upon arrival on Genesis, Raul had Esme display what she had done before the High Council. Then she had been immediately turned over to Laon.

From her first meeting with him, Esme had neither liked nor trusted Laon, and now as she worked on her mind shield she decided that if her suspicions of Laon proved true she would not allow him to interfere with the destiny the Master had decreed for her, whatever that destiny was. If Laon was dangerous, she would be prepared not only to fight him—but to win.

As Laon escorted Esme to his private domain, she saw little of the Institute of Training for the Telepathic other than long, richly carpeted hallways and closed doors. He stopped at one of those doors, opened it, and waved her through.

The room was a luxurious office, and after indicating for her to sit in a chair in front of a magnificently carved desk, Laon sprawled with lazy grace in a high-backed chair behind it. At once he began to explain that she would be evaluated by various tutors, who possessed different mind skills, to ascertain the full extent of her mental powers.

"You will begin that assessment tomorrow morning, Esme," Laon said with crisp authority. "There is no time to waste in finding out how you destroyed that Rebel ship and how you might teach others to do the same. And now," he added, leaning forward to push a button on his desk, "I will have a servant show you to your quarters."

As he leaned back, his smile was almost malicious, and Esme was aware that he was enjoying his position of authority over her.

"You will, I am afraid," he said in a slightly mocking tone, "find quite a difference in the quarters you will occupy here compared to the royal apartment you used on the Condor, or even compared to your Captain Raul's apartment. We have found that telepaths who spend their days in exhaustive mind use require relaxation from any stimulation during their rest periods. Therefore, our student rooms are plainly colored and spartanly decorated. But you will be too busy to spend much time there in any case, other than to sleep, so try not to be too discouraged."

At the moment, Esme cared little about the decoration of her quarters. She was too upset over her separation from Raul, and too aware of her antipathy toward the dark, attractive man seated across from her to worry about such matters.

An elderly male servant in a plain gray robe appeared in Laon's office and Laon gestured at Esme to stand. "Go with Pater, Esme," he instructed. "He will take you to your quarters."

Without bothering to bid Laon farewell, Esme rose and walked to the door of the office where Pater waited for her. But Laon's voice, now the lazy drawl he had used upon first speaking to her mind to mind at the meeting of the High Council, stopped her before she could step through the door into the outer corridor.

"It is customary in our society to take one's leave from a superior with a word of respect, Esme," he said. "Are your people so primitive they employ no manners at all? And did Captain Raul teach you nothing of use outside the bedroom during your sojourn with him?"

Esme checked her fury at Laon's malicious comments. Instead, with deliberate casualness, she glanced at him over her shoulder, the expression in her green eyes coolly dismissive.

She had no intention of replying to his question about what Raul had taught her but she intended to make clear her opinion of Laon's supposed superiority. He might be a respected member of the Empire's High Council as head of this Institute and he might be a talented telepath himself. But he did not command *her* respect, nor did he command her trust.

"My people have manners," she said in a flat, level tone. "We, too, take our leave from our *superiors* with a word of respect." Without another word, she turned and entered the corridor.

Somewhat to her surprise, Laon reacted to her insult with an appreciative chuckle. Pater, however, was obviously appalled by her disrespect for Laon. He uttered a gasp of shock, and as Esme paused to wait for him to take the lead and show her the way to her quarters, she saw that his plain, kindly face displayed dismay.

She mustered a smile for him. "Do not worry," she murmured drily for his ears only. "It does not sound as though Laon intends to take retribution for my barbaric manners. Not that he could if he tried."

Obviously flustered, Pater gestured with his hand toward the right, saying, "If you will follow me . . ." He turned and hurriedly walked away.

He did not speak to her again. After leaving her at the open door of a small room located on a long corridor full of closed doors, he merely bowed and disappeared.

Esme walked into the room, shut the door behind her and stood gazing bleakly at her surroundings. There was a plain wooden bureau, desk and chair, and a spartan couch, which was topped by a gray coverlet. The couch was obviously to serve as both sitting platform and bed. Another smaller room contained a shower, sanitary receptacle, and sink.

Esme had once slept cradled by the solid earth of the Homeland, with the sweet smell of meadow grass in her nostrils, the rich majesty of the very heavens above her, and more often than not the warm body of a lambkin snuggled close. Now, as she inspected her new domain with no enthusiasm, she thought Laon was wrong in his assertion that telepaths required a lack of stimulation during their rest periods. More likely, their minds were further taxed by the barrenness of their surroundings during such times.

Crossing to the couch, she threw herself on it, curled into a ball of misery, and closing her eyes, gave herself up to her aching loneliness for Raul.

It had been no more than two hours since they had

parted after the meeting with the High Council. Yet already, it seemed as though she had been deprived of her beloved for years. Everything in her longed once again to gaze into the clarity of his blue eyes, to feel his chiseled mouth move against hers, to have his strong arms hold her close, and to hear his voice whisper words of intimacy that were for her ears only.

Raul said often that duty had its price. But Esme had never expected to have to pay such a high one as this while seeking whatever task it was the Master required of her.

She had withheld her gifts from her own people, and now it seemed she was going to be forced to use her gifts for Raul's people. Was that really the Master's intention? Why would He withhold her gifts from the true Remnant and give it to those who did not even recognize His name? Could it possibly be that her present situation was the result of an accident rather than the Master's design?

Frowning, Esme recalled that she had once before thought that her situation was not in keeping with the Master's plan. Back on the Homeland, when she had been exiled to the Western desert, she had thought she would die there. She had thought she had somehow failed the Master, and His plan for her was at an end.

But it had not been so. She had found the Condor and Raul and had obtained her dream of sailing among the stars. So what had at first seemed a disaster had turned out to be in exact accordance with the Master's plan for her.

The recollection eased Esme's despondency to some extent, and gave her hope that her present situation was *also* in accordance with the Master's plan, even if she did not understand how and even if it did not reduce her loneliness for Raul. And shortly thereafter, as she lay thinking of how much she missed Raul, two ideas of how her loneliness might be eased, if not completely assuaged, came to her.

She put the first idea into operation immediately. The second, she saved for later that night when those at the Institute, who might have mind powers strong enough to detect her activities, would be sleeping.

CHAPTER TWO

AFTER THE LAST MEAL, WHICH WAS SERVED TO ESME IN HER room where she ate alone, she once again stretched out on her couch. Arranging her body in a comfortable position, she then sent her mind to search the corridors of the Institute, as well as the thoughts of its inhabitants.

Most of the tutors' minds she touched were closed to her, either by sleep or by mind shields, though from those who dreamed, she took what little was there to read. But at the entrance to the other students' quarters, which were at considerable distance from her, she found a telepath on guard who was blessed with acute sensing powers, and she dared not risk brushing the seeking touch he sent on a broad wave. Therefore, she had to withdraw.

Her exploration of her immediate surroundings

completed, Esme then sent her mind above the cluster of buildings of the Institute to seek Raul's mind, so she might find the way to his apartment.

At first, she feared the interference of so many other minds in this heavily populated city would mask Raul's thoughts from her seeking. There was also the possibility that he might have his mind shield up. But at last, she found the faint, but unmistakable, emanations of his thoughts, and she was quickly on her way.

She found him lying naked on his bed. The lights in the room were extinguished, but he was awake. To her horror, in order to ease his need to be with her, he was concentrating very hard on the practicalities of returning to war, on his own ship, the Sesphawk Talon, the following morning.

Raul, no! she cried spontaneously into his mind. *You must not face such danger on your own without my help! The stealth ships might—*

"Esme!"

At hearing her in his mind, Raul lunged to his feet and slapped the light panel by his bed, then stared hungrily around him, searching for her physical presence.

No, beloved, she whispered with pained regret that this meeting could not be conducted as they both wished. *I am sorry. My body is in its own quarters at the Institute. Only my mind is here with you.*

Raul, unwilling to believe that, continued to stare around him. Then, as the emptiness of the room convinced him of the truth of Esme's words, he thrust his hand through his thick hair in a violent gesture of disappointment.

"Esme . . . how . . ." He started to ask how her mind could be with him while her body was elsewhere but then he simply accepted the situation. Backing up to his bed, he slumped upon it, bracing himself with his powerful arms.

I am glad you have come, he said in his mind, his tone relieved. *When I learned I must leave tomorrow, I tried to see you at the Institute to tell you, but Laon would not allow it. He has complete control over his own domain, and only the highest of the council can countermand his orders. He has convinced them that any further contact between us at this time would interfere with the mental stability you need right now. They have gone along with him because they are desperate to learn how to duplicate your success in killing the ship that attacked the Condor. After I left you today, a late report came in that the attacks have resumed.*

Esme's fear for Raul rose again. *And yet they send you back out there?* she asked, horrified.

Raul shrugged. *Apparently the Rebels do not have so many stealth ships that we cannot still inflict damage upon their regular fleet.*

But— Esme was prepared to argue, but Raul cut her off.

Esme, do not waste the time we have together protesting what cannot be changed. I am under orders which I will obey.

His tone did not permit argument, and Esme, though her mind raged with protest, stayed silent.

How goes it with you, little one? Raul then asked.

Esme sighed. *They start evaluating my powers tomorrow morning. I do not know what will happen when they are done.* She hesitated, and then, in a slightly shamed, slightly defensive tone, added, *I tried to find out more before I came here tonight by eavesdropping upon some of the minds at the Institute, but I learned little.*

Esme ... Raul's tone was slightly chiding, but beneath it Esme also sensed a certain amount of amusement.

I am on my own here, Raul, she defended her actions, *and I am not convinced that Laon really has my best interests at heart. I sense an ambivalence in him about me that disturbs me, and he has warned me that he can be a formidable enemy. I do not feel at all secure, and I dislike my situation intensely. And though I now know how it feels to have one's mind invaded against one's will, and though I no longer wish to invade the minds of others without their permission, I have no choice. If I can learn anything that might help me, I must do so.*

Raul frowned, his protectiveness toward Esme prodded both by the disturbing nature of her words and by his own guilt at having been the one to place her in her present situation. He had separated them and had known her happiness would be forfeited to duty, just as his was.

Esme, perhaps you are only unhappy over our separation, he suggested, wanting to believe his own words. *I am. But in a time of war, we cannot think only of ourselves. And though I like Laon no better than you, I cannot see why he would wish you harm.*

Esme would have protested, but she abruptly saw how the poison of her suspicions could add to the guilt Raul felt. That consideration might not have completely stayed her hand, but knowing that he was leaving to face danger on the morrow, where he would need his skills, and his mind free of mental distress, was enough to make her drop her protest.

She therefore phrased her reply carefully to reflect the truth, if only part of it. *Yes, Raul,* she whispered in mingled love and pain. *I am very unhappy over our separation.*

She had her decision justified by the relief that combined with his pleasure at hearing her love for him reconfirmed.

As I told you, Esme, he vowed, his tone thickening with desire for her, *we will not be apart forever. If I had all of you here with me, I would show you in other ways than with words the strength of my intentions.*

His tone and his words provoked a wealth of love and desire inside Esme, and she silently bathed his mind with her feelings.

Her sending made Raul close his eyes, lower his head and groan in response, and Esme not only felt his desire, but saw it arousing him. She realized then, wonderingly, that though the barrier of space separated their bodies, they could still share in their blended minds a part of the ecstasy they had once shared, and Raul, at least, could be eased of his physical frustration.

Without thinking to ask his permission, and without hesitation, she rather forcefully melded her mind with his. Quickly, she wrapped them both in an illusion so strong that it began to matter less and less that their physical bodies remained apart. And though their sharing was not as wholly satisfying as it would have been had they been able to feel with tactility the longed-for touches and kisses, and physical blending that filled their minds, it was all they had, and it was more than either had believed possible.

Afterwards, Raul, lying on his stomach on his bed, raised up on his elbows, shaking his head violently.

Esme, disturbed by his ambivalence searched the complex emotions tangling his mind.

Feeling her there, Raul roughly grated, "Ask me, and I will tell you!"

Startled and hurt, Esme abruptly exited his mind and drew back to hover nearby.

Then, feeling her absence and disliking it intensely, Raul sighed with weary resignation, and turned over on his back to lie with his arms above his head, his fists clenched, his eyes closed.

"Come back," he invited, softening his tone. "It is worse when you are gone than when you make me an instrument of your will."

But Esme hesitated, still disturbed by the turmoil she sensed in him.

Raul then spoke again, and though his voice was still soft, there was a firmness there that Esme took very seriously.

"I can tolerate the use you have just made of me, Esme. Indeed, I would be a fool to believe I had not played a part in instigating what just happened, and I admit I participated most fervently in its fulfillment. But toleration is different than wholehearted acceptance. A man consumed by his own heat and that of the woman of his choice will say and do many things when that woman lies physically in his arms that afterwards, if he cares to recall them, seem foolish and unmanly.

"But no man can be comfortable doing and saying such things while lying with his arms empty, his control absent, helpless under the eyes of another, even when he loves that other. And it is not in my particular nature, as it is in some men's, to be comfortable allowing any woman, even you whom I care about as I have not cared for any woman, to take the initiative in lovemaking from my hands. If you seek me like that again, ask for my permission, do not force my cooperation. Most likely," he finished, his voice wryly cognizant of the strength of the needs she aroused in him, "I will give it."

Then, as Esme was about to approach and offer her apology, he added, "In all other matters, Esme, stay your will from contravening mine for I am not completely at ease with the strength of my feelings for you. The novelty of the relationship we share, though it has its benefits, does not ease the slight discomfort I feel. Therefore, take careful heed of what you do that concerns me. For while my unease does not weigh too heavily against my sense of fitness or my desire for you, it might one day. And I would avoid, as I think you would, a separation between us more serious than what duty imposes upon us at this time."

He took a deep breath, and then in the tone of a gentle command, he added, "Now come to me."

Esme obeyed and returned to his mind, but she was unable to hide her mental turmoil. Raul's words had shaken her badly. Her apology was sincere, but redolent of her fear that she might one day do something that would cause him to reject her.

I am sorry, she said quietly. *I acted without thought. I did not realize you did not really want to act upon what I saw in your mind. I promise I will not again—*

Esme . . . Esme! Raul interrupted, his voice gruffly tender. *My intent in that lengthy explanation was not to create misunderstanding between us, but to bring a better understanding instead.*

He stopped, wishing savagely he had her body beside him, so that he could comfort her by holding

27

her in his arms and stroking her.

He had deemed necessary the warning he had just issued, for it could become altogether too easy for one with Esme's powers to reduce any man's autonomy to shreds. And should that happen, their relationship would deteriorate and perhaps dissolve completely. But he had always placed the value of action above the value of words, and he would rather have taught her, in the intricate language of the body, the lessons he would have her learn about his nature. So also, would he rather now show her physically his need to take the burden his words had instilled within her away, leaving only the lesson.

Esme took these thoughts from his mind and they eased her anxiety.

I take your meaning, she told him softly, letting him feel the decrease in her mental turmoil, *and I will not forget the lesson.*

Raul nodded, relieved. Then he smiled, and a wicked light appeared in his eyes. *Take also my thanks for the relief of my body's tension,* he teased. *It was only your unwillingness to give me a choice in the matter, not the pleasure you brought me, that I resented.*

I was not unwilling to give you choice, Esme responded. *It was in my precipitateness that I erred.*

Raul shrugged then narrowed his eyes thoughtfully. *Did your body receive the same release as mine?*

I regret to say that it did not, she confessed. *My mind only found the pleasure I crave with you. But,* she added quickly when he frowned, *I discovered a thing this afternoon, while I lay resting on my bed at the Institute thinking about you, that I will put to use when I return to my body.*

What is that? he asked, curious.

I learned that if I substitute my own touch for yours when I think of you and our past lovemaking, and anticipate what it will be like when we once again lie together whole and complete, I am able to ease my body's needs a little.

Raul stared into space as though he searched for her face to study, his lips twitching with humor. *How little?* he asked.

Enough to reach that pinnacle you taught me and quiet my body's demands, but not my heart's yearning, Esme sighed. *It does not really satisfy me completely. Afterwards, I felt a great loneliness for the comfort of your arms around me and the sound of your voice praising what I brought you. It is better than nothing, but I will be glad to discard its use for the real thing.*

Raul's smile faded. *Exactly,* he said, very quietly.

Oh, Esme said, surprised. *Do you do the same?*

Not if I can help it, Raul said, his tone dry. *I have learned to submerge such needs in hard work and exercise. In any case, I have a feeling I will often wake from dreams of you while we are apart to find my seed upon my belly or the bedclothes.*

Esme was pleased and said so. From the reaction in Raul's mind, she knew that if he had her body beside him, she would have received a playful slap upon her bottom as a reward for her audacity.

Then Raul changed subjects. *Esme, do these separations of mind and body tire you? Will this visit make tomorrow's work harder?*

My body lies resting now, Esme prevaricated.

Esme. His tone was stern.

Esme sighed. *I will perhaps have to reach a little deeper within myself for the energy I need on the morrow,* she reluctantly admitted. *But I will gladly pay*

29

the price. This visit is worth it.

Aye, it is, Raul agreed. *I, too, will gladly pay tomorrow for what we have had tonight. And if your mind can reach so far, though I would urge caution upon you in picking the time, I would welcome further visits from you while I am aboard ship. I would not welcome such a distracting visit, for instance, while in the heat of battle, but—*

Oh, Raul, Esme interrupted, again devastated by her fear for him. What if another silent, invisible enemy ship came upon him while she was not there to sense it? *I fear I cannot come. I will try, but the distances are so vast in space that—*

Esme, do not worry, Raul cut her off, heartily regretting his thoughtless words. *I am a warrior. Such risks are mine to bear. I accept them. So must you.*

Never. Esme was inconsolable.

Then leave me now and do not come back, Raul said, deliberately making his tone cold and hard.

Raul! Esme was shocked. *Please . . .*

Accept me as I am, accept the life that I lead, or leave me, Esme. There are some things a woman may not ask a man to do. My honor is not subject to your needs nor even to my own.

Esme remained silent for a few minutes, violently reluctant to face reality. But at last, she had no choice other than to say the words Raul was waiting to hear. *Then I . . . accept.*

He let out his breath and nodded. *Is there some way I can let you know when I return?* he then asked. *I would not have you wasting your energy visiting here every night to check, and I do not trust Laon to inform you of any message I give him.*

Merely call me strongly with your mind upon planet

fall, Esme said, dull misery in her tone. *I will hear.*

Esme, do not do this, Raul said with gentle firmness. *I would have a farewell from you more to my liking.*

What do you want? she asked, trying and failing to control her mood.

I would have you wash my mind with your love and your cheerful good wishes for success and a safe return.

Esme complied with the request almost wholeheartedly. It was only the projection of cheerfulness she had difficulty providing.

Afterwards, his voice softened and thickening with need, Raul added another desire to his list, one that made it impossible for Esme to continue to sink into her own misery.

And I would have again that which you gave me a little while ago, Esme. Only this time, I would have you teach me a method of controlling what transpires between us on this mental bed we share.

Esme was delighted. *You need no teaching, my heart,* she said, as she delicately and sensuously merged her mind with his. *It is something else I can give you that you truly need.*

I would have the teaching just the same, he replied, his breath shortening as a result of the pleasurable joining he felt.

You mistake my meaning, Esme whispered throatily. *I will tell you what I started to recognize after you first began to let me into your mind. You, though you have denied it thus far, have mind skills of your own, waiting to be called forth and released. I can help you release them if you will but allow it. Let me show you . . .*

As she unlocked certain barriers within Raul's mind, she was tenderly amused over the recognition she felt beginning in his consciousness.

To no other person than Raul would Esme have given the key to such power as he might have over her when the latent potential inside him fully awakened. And, in truth, because of his streak of ruthlessness which was a necessary part of a warrior's character, she did it now with uneasiness. But there was a counterforce of decency and goodness in Raul that made the risk of what he might do with such power acceptable to her. And there was her love for him which made such risk a necessity. She wanted him to have every protection possible when he returned to battle.

Is it truly so? he asked, frowning.

Esme knew the question was perfunctory. That recognition he had felt earlier had grown to certainty. *Why do you frown?* she asked.

Because I do not as yet know if I truly want the kind of skills you have, Esme, he said, troubled. *It seems to me it might become too easy to depend upon them instead of the ordinary skills I have worked long and hard to develop in myself and have learned to trust. This will take some getting used to.*

Esme did not understand his concern. She would have given much to have Raul's latent skills erupt full blown, in time to protect him should the need arise. But after what he had said to her earlier about being careful not to step over his boundary of fitness, she did not wish to contravene his wishes on such an important matter.

Perhaps you can forget what I just made you aware of, she said reluctantly.

It was a suggestion she hoped he would not heed. Then, to her relief, she discovered that because he desired to feel again the pleasure they had shared he decided to test his new powers.

She felt his mind, tentative at first, probing hers, exerting influence, and when she immediately, joyfully, yielded to his influence, the probing grew stronger, more dominant.

By the time Raul had finished experimenting with his new power and lay quiet, his chest heaving from his exertions, his body temporarily sated, a lazy slanting smile of male triumph and confidence on his lips, Esme's mind had barely the strength left to return to her body.

Go then, Esme, he said, his voice deep and soft. *Take the rest you need.*

His tone was tenderly solicitous of her mental state, but Esme felt no regret in his mind over what he had wrung from her.

He took the thought from her mind and laughed softly. *You gave me the key,* he said, unrepentant. *Did you think I would use it at your direction instead of as I see fit?*

No, Raul, she said, her tone accepting. *I well know that you will always do as you see fit.*

And so I will. Now go, Esme, before your strength fails you. I would have you safe.

As I would have you. Please take care of yourself, beloved, for me, she dared to say. Then she had to leave, for in truth, had she delayed a moment longer, she could not have made the return journey.

Back in her body, she slumped immediately into a heavy sleep, without even the capacity to think about taking for herself the satisfaction she had given Raul.

Raul, however, lay awake until dawn's light touched the windows of his sleeping chamber, thinking long and hard about the possibilities Esme had made him aware he possessed.

Upon rising earlier than he had planned, he bathed, dressed in his formal uniform, and snatched a hasty breakfast, then used the extra time to make a slight detour on his way to his battleship the Sesphawk's Talon. Finally, when he strode up the ramp into his ship, he carried a thick, plasti-wrapped reference volume that was standard reading among the students at the Institute where Esme now resided. He left his other baggage to the subordinate who had met him at the bottom of the ramp.

CHAPTER THREE

Laon decreed that Esme would remain isolated during her evaluation except for her sessions with her various assessors. He picked those who would have contact with her himself and instructed them, on pain of severe discipline, to keep their minds inviolate from her except in the particular specialty for which they tested her and sought to strengthen if she was found lacking in that skill.

By the end of her third week at the Institute, Esme had accepted that she could learn little about her status or about Laon from the tutors, other than from their dreams. Therefore, she longed to visit the minds of the other students training at the Institute. But they were monitored at night by adepts whose sensing was so acute that Esme feared they would detect any attempts she made to enter the students' quarters.

Far from giving up, however, she worked on the

problem at night in her room, when she was alone. She labored at constructing an intricate system within her mind which she hoped would soon be impenetrable and mask her presence from the sensing adepts. Also she had a strong feeling that there was another reason for her constructing this mental system, but she did not know why. At any rate, she had not yet tested the system for fear it was too fragile for her purposes. She did not want to try it and fail, lest Laon was alerted to what she did when he thought she slept.

But one day, in the small exercise room where Esme practiced the integration of her body and mind, her mental and physical fatigue was so great that she knew she could not continue to put such strain on her endurance much longer. Soon, she must take the risk and test her new system. If it was adequate, she could then spend more time resting at night rather than working on it or prowling the Institute looking for open minds. If it was not, then regardless of Laon's wrath, she must work harder at strengthening the system. Because the inner guide that had been with her all of her days had begun to insist that she would need it in the near future.

"Oh . . . pardon, lady. I am looking for Master Geheir."

Esme, clad only in a short, almost sheer, body-hugging exercise shift, was bent from the waist with her palms upon the floor. At the sound of the unfamiliar voice, she jerked her head up to see a young blond man, garbed in the light blue robe of a novice, hesitating inside the plasti-steel door of the exercise room. Her heart leapt. Here was a student she might talk to at last!

As she straightened up, she tightened her mental shield to mask her own thoughts, and prodded the young man's mind lightly to make him willing to do as she desired.

"Come in," she said. "Shut the door behind you. There is a draft."

But the young man took only one step inside before hesitating, and did not close the door.

Esme dared not prod his mind harder. As she tried to think of some other way to make her visitor stay and talk for a while, she noticed how appreciatively he was looking her over. Then, though she had never flirted with a man in her life—with Raul, she played no such games—she immediately smiled directly into the young man's blue eyes and posed her body in a certain way before moving with casual grace to pick up an absorbent rectangle of cloth, lying on a nearby chair. As she wiped the sweat from her body, she moved and twisted sensuously the way she did under the guidance of Raul's hands.

She almost swooned with relief when the young man at last, his blue eyes wide with admiration, reached absently behind him, closed the door, and stepped farther into the room.

"What are you called?" Esme spoke softly in a low, throaty voice.

She felt him try to pierce her shield to find out if she really was flirting with him. But his mind touch was clumsy and inadequate, and he failed.

"I am Chass," he said. Then his eyes widened even more and he said, "And you . . . you are Esme, are you not?"

"I am Esme," she nodded. "You have heard of me then?"

Chass shrugged and smiled nervously. "Everybody has. It is hard to keep secrets in a place like this. Nobody can keep a shield up constantly. And when the tutors became aware that the students knew there was a special student called Esme whom they kept in their own quarters, they told us, very strongly, to ask no questions and not to seek you, mentally or otherwise, else we would be expelled."

"But you did not seek me," Esme pointed out, and began to soothe the nervousness she saw rising in Chass's mind. He was afraid of getting caught speaking with her. But she was also seeing in his mind his tendency toward reckless rebellion when the rewards were great enough, for which she thanked the Master.

"No. I was sent with this message to Master Geheir." He held out a sealed envelope. "But I am new here and have never been in the tutors' personal quarters before. I lost my way."

Esme took a step toward him. "I am glad you did, Chass. I am very lonely and would be glad of the chance to visit with you awhile."

It wasn't strictly true that Esme was lonely, except for Raul. She had been ostracized all of her life, and had grown used to being alone. Except for Maza, a shepherd on the Homeland, and the men on the Condor, she had never had friends. But she now wanted to appeal to the decency she saw in Chass's mind, and not only to his sensual nature.

"You are lonely?" he responded, surprised.

"Yes," Esme said simply. "The tutors share nothing with me. They only assess my skills and instruct me when they see something that needs to be strengthened, and I am kept apart from all others."

Chass frowned, his sympathy aroused, as Esme had

hoped it would be. "I do not understand," he said. "I mean, your assessment is over and it is common knowledge now that your skills are better and more comprehensive than anyone's, even the tutors'. It is said that even Laon is jealous of your powers. So why are you kept isolated?"

Esme was surprised and her expression showed it.

A light of comprehension lit Chass's blue eyes as he saw her expression. "So that is it," he said, startled. "You did not know that your skills surpass the tutors', did you?"

Esme solemnly shook her head. "I told you. They allow me nothing but what they want me to see."

Now Chass was disgusted. "It must be that they do not want you showing them up," he said indignantly. But then he frowned again, and looked thoughtful. "But how could you not know how good you are?" he asked, puzzled. "I mean, you have almost all the skills, and you have them in abundance. Most of us only have one or two. What is it, I wonder, they plan to do with you now?"

Esme sighed and tossed the cloth aside. "I am not from this planet, Chass," she said quietly, "nor from any other planet that belongs to the Empire. I did not know that most students only have one or two skills. No one else on my planet had any skills at all."

She could see the astonishment on Chass's face and she shrugged. "As to what they will do with me since my testing and training are over, I am in Laon's hands, starting tonight. There is something he wants from me that I have so far been unable to give him. He has been trying to get it all along, in between the testing and the training. Now he will try harder."

"What?" Chass was all ears, his curiosity rampant.

Esme hesitated. "I cannot tell you that, Chass," she said gently. "I am forbidden to speak of it with anyone other than Laon."

Chass looked disappointed, and for a long moment, he studied her and she felt his mind racing. But all at once, he became aware of the danger to himself in speaking to her like this, and he started backing away. "I had better go," he said, his tone nervous.

"Wait!" Esme detained him. "Tell me of the war with the Rebels. How goes it?"

Chass shrugged. "The official reports given to the general population are optimistic. But we sense it will go badly soon. At least, that is what those among us whose talents lie in sensing the future say."

"You have such?" Esme was surprised.

"Of course," Chass shrugged. Then he frowned. "Ahael and Halen are such among the tutors. Did you not know this?"

Esme shook her head, trying to keep the fear for Raul that was ever present in her mind from rising to panic proportions as a result of Chass's news. "But now that I think of it," she said, "the tests they gave me must have been designed to see if I have such skill."

"You do not, do you?"

"Once I did," she said drily, "but only in my dreams, which left me the moment my eyes opened in the morning, and they only concerned my own future."

Chass nodded, and then, his anxiety rising again, he said, "I need to go, Esme. If I am caught speaking to you . . ." He grimaced meaningfully.

Esme realized he had figured out with his intelligence rather than through any mind-reading skills that she was holding him against his will.

"I am sorry, Chass," she apologized. "One more question, and then you may be on your way. Has there been any word of a ship called the Sesphawk's Talon? Captain Raul commands it."

"Everyone knows of Captain Raul," Chass nodded. "But I have heard nothing about him or his ship recently."

"Oh." Esme was disappointed.

"Please. May I go now, Esme?" Chass was starting to sweat.

Esme realized Chass's nervousness was well-founded. If Laon learned that Chass had been speaking to her, Chass might lose his place at the Institute. Then she cursed herself for the recalcitrant thought. She could erase this meeting from Chass's mind and thereby save his place here, as well as herself the trouble of facing Laon's displeasure if he discovered that she had violated her isolation.

She looked into Chass's eyes and froze him momentarily, then dipped into his mind, and neatly capped what she wished him to forget. Then she turned him and made him open the door and step out into the corridor, closing the door behind him before he could turn and see her.

She eavesdropped for a moment on his mind, and smiled as she saw him standing there, confused, looking at the message in his hand. Then, with a very light touch, she started him walking in the correct direction.

As she continued her exercises, Esme kept her shield tight, and behind it thought about what she had learned from Chass. In some ways, it had been a very fruitful conversation, giving her ammunition to use when she met with Laon. In other ways, it had been frustrating and it had released the fear for Raul she normally kept under tight control.

She went through the rest of her routine absently, using her control to fight down that fear and lodge it tightly in a corner of her mind where it could not hinder the process of thought she sorely needed now. For when she dined with Laon in his quarters that evening, she was certain she would need all her wits about her.

"You look lovely, Esme," Laon said, his black eyes sparkling with the sexual hunger he took less and less care to conceal from her these days.

Esme had been surprised and alarmed when she had first become aware that Laon wanted her. But she had not been surprised to discern that his desire was like Bazil's. Laon's sexuality encompassed a desire to control her as well as to satisfy his lust.

"Thank you, Laon," Esme said in a level tone. She was sorrier now than she had been earlier that the tutor who had brought her to Laon had made her exchange her school robe for one of the prettier gowns Raul had given her.

Esme was fairly certain that Laon's hostile ambivalence toward her lay in his sexual hunger for her, a hunger he had not as yet tried to slake, thank the Master! Probably, he had made no overt advances because he knew of her feelings for Raul. How could he not when he had witnessed their impassioned farewell, and had prowled most of her mind like a stalker on the kill? Therefore, his overweening pride would not allow him to place himself in the position of being rejected where Raul had succeeded. And her obvious preference for Raul also made him hostile toward her.

"Come sit," Laon invited, taking her hand to draw her with him to one of the sumptuous couches in his private apartments.

Esme used her curiosity to distract herself from the unwelcome touch of Laon's hand. Laon did not deprive himself, she thought cynically. His apartment bore no resemblance to the stark barrenness of the students' cubicles. Instead, he treated himself to a rich display of art and finely crafted furnishings.

Laon picked the thought from her mind, that part which she allowed him to see. She was finally able to hide from him those thoughts which she did not care to share.

"Jealous, Esme?" he teased, drawing her down to sit much too closely beside him on the couch.

"Aye," she nodded amiably. "I hate my own gray room."

"Yes, it doesn't suit one of your beauty," Laon smiled, and reached for the golden carafe on the small, exquisitely carved table in front of him. He poured wine for himself, and when he started to pour wine into another matching golden goblet for Esme, she stopped him.

"I do not drink wine, Laon," she said with firmness."

He stiffened, and when he turned his dark face toward her, she saw that he was angry. "You will sip it then," he said harshly. "It is only polite to do so, and if you are going to live in this society, you must learn to comply to its demands."

Some hint of danger brushed Esme's mind, making her cautious. "If you insist," she said, but she had no

43

intention of allowing any of the wine into her stomach.

Laon relaxed, smiled, and handed her the goblet.

Esme tilted it until the clear red liquid touched her mouth, made a swallowing motion with her throat, then handed the goblet back to Laon as she licked her lips clean of the wine that had splashed against them.

As Laon took the goblet, a satisfied smile upon his saturnine face, Esme became aware of why she had felt danger. There was something in the wine, even the small amount she'd tasted, that was making her body flush with heat, her limbs lethargic, and her mind spin with erotic illusions.

"What have you done?" she asked, staring at Laon through a haze of artificial lust that appalled her. It had no connection to her emotions, but was purely physical.

Laon, all pretense of playing the polite host now gone, leaned back and grasped a thick handful of her copper-colored hair in one hand, and her chin in his other hand. He brought his face close to hers, and in his dark eyes, Esme saw things that made her close her own.

She tried to draw back, but her body's lethargy prevented her from breaking Laon's tight hold without using the power of her mind, which was unwise to use against Laon unless it became necessary. He controlled her eventual fate, after all.

"I have reached the limits of my patience with you, Esme," he said. His voice was a sensuous murmur, twining through her heated veins and her racing imagination, sparking the heat in her belly into a higher flame. "Now, I am going to force you to give me the information I want."

"I have tried my best to give you what you want," Esme protested. "It is not that I do not wish to, but that I cannot . . ."

She broke off and moaned involuntarily as Laon touched his mouth to the unbearably sensitive shell of her ear. His body pressed against hers, and wherever they touched, she felt her senses flame into life.

"I have come to believe that is true," he said in that sinuous whisper that trilled through her body and mind. "If for no other reason than to save your precious Captain Raul, I think you would reveal voluntarily the method you used to kill the Rebel ship if you could. Since you have not, I can only assume that you really cannot tell me what I must know, and I have decided to take other measures to retrieve the information."

"This way?" Esme gasped, writhing now, completely unable to stop her body from seeking his. "How can making my body want yours help?"

Laon drew back, and the look in his eyes was so heated, Esme took fire from it, drowned in it.

"The drug I have given you to dispel those inhibitions you have long felt where I am concerned is one part of the process I have in mind," he said silkily, touching his mouth against the corner of hers.

Esme, her mind wailing in protest at her body's actions turned her head, her mouth hungrily seeking his.

"No, Esme, not yet," Laon said triumphantly, drawing back a little. "First, I want you to understand fully what is going to happen between us. And I want you to be as convinced as I am that this is the only way to extract the information from your mind that will save your beloved Captain Raul and many more warriors like him from the Rebel stealth ships. I want you to know, without doubt, that it is absolutely essential, in order for you to be of help, that you give me what I have long wanted from you and which you are desperate to have from me at this moment."

"No! I do not want you!" Esme cried out.

Laon laughed. "Do not be absurd, Esme. I have not seen a woman so consumed with her own heat since the drug I gave you was outlawed."

"Outlawed?"

Beneath her lust, panic welled inside Esme. She fought to still it, to ascertain if Laon spoke the truth. Desperately, she looked into his mind, and when he felt her probe, he made no effort to hide his thoughts. He let her see his absolute conviction that what he proposed to do was the only way to obtain the information she had so far been unable to give him. She felt despair at his conviction, but she did not doubt its sincerity. She also saw that he had kept her isolated so that her loneliness was at a peak when he offered himself to ease it.

Laon shrugged, his smile confident, as he responded to her question about the drug's being outlawed.

"The drug was previously an aid to a sexual ritual we in our society call Daccall," he explained. "This ritual is normally practiced when a man and a woman make life bond. But the drug was outlawed because in sufficient quantity, it can make a user exhaust his mind and body in seeking satisfaction again and again, and the strain can be fatal. But do not worry. Ahael foresaw that you would not take enough for that to happen to you, and his seeing was true. The small amount you licked from your lips is exactly enough for my purposes without putting you in any danger.

After all, we would not want to lose one with your skills."

Then his eyes narrowed and he said, "But you do not want to keep those skills only for yourself when they can benefit the man you love, do you? Therefore, you must share them with me, and also with others."

"Laon, please . . . I still do not understand!" Esme wept now, her physical need unbearable. "How can this Daccall give you what you want?"

"It is very simple, Esme," he said, taking her searching hands in his own and stretching them behind her, forcing her body to arch. Then, holding her wrists with one hand, he withdrew metal cuffs from a pocket in his robe with his other hand.

"I can undo those with my mind, Laon," Esme pointed out between bitter sobs. "You know that."

"Yes, I know," he said, his smile indulgent. "But they are part of the ritual, and therefore you will *not* unclasp them. You will do *nothing* to inhibit the ritual. Ahael foresaw such."

Esme momentarily quieted, and Laon snapped the cuffs into place. Was Ahael's forseeing true? she wondered dazedly. Was she condemned to go through with this unholy ritual *voluntarily?*

Laon interrupted her thoughts. "A man and woman who undergo Daccall," he explained, "share not only their bodies, but their minds as well. They can deny one another nothing. We have used the ritual before here at the Institute, unconnected with the life-mating celebration, in order to release resistant minds. But yours is so unusually resistant that I added a mind drug to the sexual one. Therefore, you will release your mind more completely to me than is usual in the Daccall ritual. You will give me access to things that you yourself are not even aware of knowing, one of them being, hopefully, the method by which you destroyed that Rebel ship."

He chuckled over the new consternation he saw in Esme's eyes.

"Oh, yes, my dear. You should fear me. The Daccall sexual ritual is not a gentle one, and I would not have it otherwise. Your fear excites me." Then his expression turned coldly calculating rather than heated and excited. "But I think there is another reason why you look so fearful. Did you think I did not know you were hiding something else from me, Esme?" he grated. "And did I not warn you that I would make a bad enemy should you try to thwart me?"

Esme was alarmed that Laon somehow knew she hid something other than her destroying the Rebel stealth ship from him. She hid the mental system she had been constructing in her mind but she was determined even now not to give it up if she could help it. Her inner guide insisted she must not.

Laon's eyes narrowed as he studied her condition and his voice was satisfied as he continued speaking. "It will take awhile for the drugs I gave you to be expelled completely from your system, Esme. I have left word that you and I are not to be disturbed for any reason for three days and three nights, which is the normal period for the partaking of Daccall. And most of my people think that is all I plan to do—instruct you in Daccall. Most of them do not know about the drugs I gave you and would be horrified if they did know. But I prevailed upon three of my closest colleagues to concur with my decision to use the drugs, because of the dire urgency of the present battle situation. So do not think, when this is over, that you will be able to bring me to account for breaking procedures. I have the needed signatures to give me the legal authority to do this."

Esme sobbed now, torn by inner conflict. If Laon was right that this was the only way to obtain information which would help Raul and other warriors, she was obligated to go through with what Laon planned. But the thought of betraying her loyalty to Raul, even though such betrayal was in order to help him, made her sick at heart. When he knew about it, would Raul forgive her or would she lose him? Furthermore, would the Master forgive her? Betraying a life mate was against His law.

"I want to give you what I know, Laon," she sobbed. "But Raul is my life mate! How can I betray him like this?"

Laon snorted. "You will betray him more if you continue to withhold the help he and the Empire need," he asserted. "Our losses grow. The Rebels have more of those stealth ships than we thought, and without your help, your precious Raul may die, and the Empire may fall. Besides, you and he have taken no vows as yet, and he is therefore not your life mate . . . not officially. It may be the custom on your world to regard yourself as life mated before the vows are spoken, but it is not so here. I assure you, your Raul was not celibate before you came into his life, and he will therefore have no right to condemn you for what you do with me, especially not when you do it for his sake."

Esme couldn't answer. She had felt the first barrier of her mind breaking under the drug Laon had administered. There was no more time. She must prevent the unraveling of the system she had so carefully built over the past three weeks, and which she was now so certain had a special purpose beyond what she had first thought.

She cared not if Laon took everything else from her mind. Indeed, she realized Laon was so determined in his purpose that she would have to kill him to escape what was about to happen, which would then likely result in her own execution for murder. His persuasive arguments had also convinced her that she must endure anything to save Raul, even the loss of her beloved's regard for her.

But at the same time, all her instincts told her she must withhold knowledge of her new, impenetrable shield, for a time of need was coming. Therefore, as Laon picked her up in his arms to carry her to the rich silken cushions of his bed, she was unaware of what he did. Ignoring her body's raging need as best she could, she sent the knowledge of her new shield behind its own barrier.

As Laon took up a small, bejeweled dagger and cut the gown she wore from her body, she tested if the knowledge was safe. Only when he tethered her ankles to two posts at the foot of the bed did she come back to herself, as certain as she could be that she had protected her new shield and that neither the drugs nor Laon could release it.

Though she could have blasted Laon's mind into a million particles, she allowed him to uncuff her wrists and refasten them in loops that matched the ones holding her ankles. And to overcome her revulsion for what was about to take place, she deliberately allowed the sexual drug's potency to work on her body. But as she deliberately sped the drug's progress, she became aware that she could also negate the sexual drug's effect and the mind drug's effect as well!

As Laon came to the bed, naked now, and straddled her body, Esme lay still, testing what she had just discovered. The lust raging through her body began to fade, and the torn barrier within her mind began to heal, and joy over her resumption of control rose within her heart.

An instant later, however, as she realized she was obligated to continue with the ritual to save Raul, her joy died.

With utter sadness, she forced herself to stop inhibiting the effect of the sexual drug and sped it on its way. This disloyalty to Raul she would commit for love of him, she thought in despair as her body began to throb with lust again, a lust enhanced by Laon's skillful hands upon her breasts. Yes, this and more would she do if it would save her beloved.

With that thought, she allowed the second drug to dissolve all the barriers in her mind until it reached her special shield, where she stopped its progress. Then she thought no more as she submitted her mind to the ravaging probe of Laon's, and her body to his use.

Esme groaned with pain as Laon withdrew from her and rolled onto his back to rest. As she lay too tired to use her mind to alleviate her physical hurts, she reflected that Laon had spoken truly when he had told her Daccall was not a gentle ritual. For two days now, she had taken instruction at Laon's often brutal hands and body, and her own body's resources were almost at their limits.

But as she lay dozing, trying to recover her strength, she felt no regret over what had happened during these past two days, even though Laon had not obtained what both of them wanted and now knew he never would. He had not said it to her yet, but she knew, just as she knew he kept her with him because he had become more her captive than she was his.

She did not regret what had happened because she had learned much from Laon about her own skills and his and she intended to learn the secret she knew he carried deep within him, and which she had not yet been able to wrest from his mind. She could not even guess what the secret might be. She only knew, in that quiet, certain place inside her, that it was vital that she find out what he hid.

As she drifted between sleep and waking, Esme considered what she had already taken from Laon's superb mind these past two days, and what she had learned about herself and her powers as well. She had, for instance, in reaction to what he did to her, learned how to lessen pain so it did not consume her whole being, and expanded her knowledge of healing her own body.

Had she not learned how to turn aside her pain, she would have gone mad. Had she not learned further how to heal herself, she would have been unable to escape permanent injury. In the first stage of Daccall, upon being thwarted in gaining what he sought, Laon had thought she deliberately withheld what he wanted, and in releasing the ritual brutality had gone overboard and sought to break her will. In the process, he had lost control of himself and had almost broken her body instead. Esme had learned that the submission she gave Raul voluntarily could also be coerced from her by force, and with it, bring a sort of twisted parody of pleasure.

While Laon was recuperating from his exertions during that first stage of Daccall, she had sobbed and pleaded so convincingly, that she had finally convinced him that she did not deliberately withhold what he sought. So he had abandoned the first stage of Daccall, where he had lingered overlong and violently, and entered into the next stage.

Esme had at first much preferred the new stage, until she'd seen the trap that lay within it, of becoming bound to Laon emotionally as well as physically because of his sexual skills. She would never have credited him for possessing them if she had not felt the overwhelming pleasure he wrought.

She had remembered then what Raul had told her when she had sent her mind to visit him that night before he left for battle. She understood now why he had disliked feeling helplessly embroiled in his own passion under the storm of hers without first inviting her to use him. And she had used that knowledge to escape, at least partially, the bonds Laon almost succeeded in placing upon her.

In the process she had learned to distance herself from what was happening to her body while her mind still remained within it, and she had learned that not even to save Raul's life was she willing to hand over her own life completely to Laon. She would die for Raul she knew but she would not become a helpless slave to another man for him.

Still, she knew that her escape had not been total. Her body now knew a man's body other than Raul's, and her body would not forget the drugging pleasure/pain that Laon had taught her. In fact, it was her body's response to Laon's that she forced herself to use to stay with him past the time when they both knew they were not going to gain what they had originally sought. She must stay with him now to take his secret from him.

The third stage of Daccall, where Laon deliberately gave her almost absolute power over him and forced her to use it, had lessons for Esme as well. In that stage she had learned her own capacity for cruel use of another human being and she had shrunk from the knowledge, only to find another trap awaiting her, the trap of guilt and responsibility for a human she had misused. Laon tried to bind her to him that way, too, and it had taken all her will not to let the trap close completely, past breaking.

In that stage, she had not been anymore successful than she had been in the first two. But she had learned all that Laon had in his mind except for the one thing—the most important thing—she was certain he still withheld. Because she somehow knew that whatever he hid was vitally important, she considered the sense of responsibility she felt for him worth the cost.

"Here, Esme," Laon said.

She had not noticed he had risen from the bed, but he now sat beside her, forcing two small pills into her mouth.

"No!" She spat the pills out.

"It is only a stimulant," Laon said gently. "Look, I will take these myself and give you the two I was going to take. Look into my mind and take the truth from it."

She did so, as Laon took the pills she had spat out and placed them in his own mouth, handing her two others. She also remembered that it mattered not what drug he gave her. She had learned to negate the effects of such drugs on herself.

She relaxed then and swallowed the stimulant. She would need its help in maintaining the energy to extract from Laon what remained to be learned.

Then Laon lay down beside her and cradled her in his arms. Esme sped the stimulant through her blood, knowing she would soon need the strength it carried. Already, Laon's body was reacting to hers though he had to be almost as fatigued as she was.

"How much longer will you keep me here?" she asked drowsily, though she already knew from her inner clock.

"Another day."

Laon stroked her breasts and the tiny residue of the sexual drug within her, along with her body's conditioned response to Laon's, brought heat rising in her senses. Her nipples rose to his touch.

"But we have failed," she pointed out, unnecessarily.

"Do not play games with me, Esme," Laon sighed, bending to kiss her forehead. "You know why I keep you here and your body does not object."

"And when the time is up?" Esme did not respond to his latter statement. Her body provided Laon with all the answer he needed.

"I would discuss that with you," Laon murmured, sliding down to turn her to face him. He kissed her, and Esme allowed her tongue to respond to the curl of his, while she let her body do as it wished and press against the swelling heat of his manhood.

"What would you discuss?" she asked when he released her mouth.

"Daccall leaves a bond in the participants past the time of its fulfilling," Laon murmured. "And though I know you did not succumb completely, I also know

55

you could not entirely withhold from me what Daccall is designed to impart in its participants. Your mind and body will always respond to mine now, just as I will always respond to you. And I want that bond between us to become permanent."

Esme's eyes flew open and her gaze became entrapped in the dark heated sincerity of Laon's.

"I have never taken a life mate," he went on, stroking her body with his possessive, intimately roving hands. "I would now . . . I would have you beside me, Esme, from this time forward."

Esme shook her head, her mind whirling under the stimulus of the drug, her body on fire for Laon's.

"I am Raul's," she said distinctly. "I love him. *He* is my life mate, and I can never have another."

As though he did not wish to hear her words, Laon closed her mouth with his own, and kissed her deeply, and turned her on her back, stretching full length upon her, pressing her down into the bedclothes.

Esme's body leapt with anticipation to receive what he still withheld from her. When he released her mouth, she whispered her need. Laon entered her immediately, but did not begin the movement that she craved, and he would not let her hips begin their own rhythm.

"Laon . . ." she whimpered. "Please . . ."

"In a moment," he whispered. "But first, listen to me. I would not deprive you of Raul completely but he is away most of the time. When he is home, I will step aside that you may have one another. All that I will require is that you give me yourself the rest of the time."

Esme twisted her head wildly in a negative gesture,

while she struggled to release her hips from Laon's maddening restraint.

"He would not permit it!" she gasped. "And I would not want him to. It is obscene and unlawful. And I do not love you, Laon."

His laugh came from low in his throat as he drew back and then plunged into her, once, bringing a moan of pleasure from her mouth.

"Is love necessary when we can share this?" he asked, his voice low and possessive. "Can you do without this for months at a time while Raul is away? I do not think so, Esme. I think you will try, but I think I will not let you succeed. You know that if I come to you and touch you, you will not be able to deny me. And I *will* come to you and touch you like this when Raul is away."

"I will not be your mate!" Esme cried out.

But as she did so, she let her body work for her and take its own pleasure separately from her mind, and she led Laon carefully down the path she wanted him to take.

"Perhaps not immediately," Laon allowed, his voice husky. "But in time, you will. Each time Raul is gone, I will come to you, and you will greet me with a protest when I arrive. But you will always end beneath me like this . . ."—he drew back and plunged into her again, and Esme's body arched to meet his as it had learned to do—". . . taking the pleasure I can give you as greedily as you do now. And soon you will not protest when I arrive. Soon, you may even come to me first and beg me to give you—"

"No!" Esme opened her eyes wide and met Laon's black gaze full on, her green eyes scornful under the glaze of sensuality. "I will not give myself to one who withholds from me what you do!"

Laon abruptly went still, frowning at her. She felt his probe in her mind even before he asked, "What do you mean?"

"You know what I mean, Laon." Esme suffered his probe, and allowed him to see what she wished him to believe—a possible love for him cut off by his deceitfulness. She let him think she would accede to what he wanted if he would tell her what he hid.

Laon abruptly withdrew from her mind and from her body, and rolled over onto his back, in turmoil over the choice he faced.

But Esme followed his movement, and began to use, with a vengeance, the skills she'd learned while he had lain subject to her will under the third stage of Daccall.

Laon tried to resist her, but he was more a victim of Daccall than Esme, and he soon writhed under her hands and tongue.

Tell me, Laon! she entered his mind and lashed it with her demand. She did not want to release him from the pleasure/torture of her mouth long enough to speak aloud. *Tell me or you will never have me completely!*

She whipped him with her mind and with the exquisite pain of her hands and mouth upon him. At the same time, she prevented the release he desperately sought to free himself from her demand that he give her what he most wished not to.

Had Laon not taken her through Daccall before this encounter, Esme could never have sustained the cruel subjugation she practiced upon Laon with diabolical skill now. She would not even have known—and in truth she would have preferred not to have known—that she had it within her to do such things.

But she closed her ears to his screams and sobs and maintained her hold on him until at last she had what she wanted. His last shield dissolved from his mind, and when she saw what was behind it, Esme was so shocked she almost refused the reward he begged from her. Finally, she collected herself and gave him the small mercy of spilling his seed upon his own belly. Her cruelty did not stretch so far as to deny him that much.

Afterwards, she sat back on her heels and stared at Laon in mingled disbelief and horror as he panted and retched and tried to recover.

When he could at last hear her, Esme whispered the question uppermost in her mind. "Laon . . . how could you?"

The look that came onto his face made her back away from him. But he seized her arm in a brutal grip and threw her to the bed, straddling her and pinning her long hair with his knees, her wrists in his hands, so that she couldn't move.

"What do you know of anything, little savage?" he snarled, the look in his eyes vicious. "Do you think I would give up my prestige and power for the sake of patriotism? Not only would the Rebels have ruined me, they have promised me even more honor when they win! This way, I will not lose, even for a moment, that which I must have!"

His shield was down so tight, Esme knew she would have to kill him to pierce it and she was not ready to do that.

"What do they have on you, Laon?" she demanded. "What could make you—"

"Cease speaking!"

The rage and fury Esme sensed in him silenced her. She knew he would kill her if she did not obey him completely now. The alternative was to kill him first, and if she did that, she wasn't sure she would be given time to prove her justification for it before she was killed by those he controlled. She decided, at the moment, that unless she had absolutely no choice but to defend herself, she would endure whatever punishment Laon was intent upon wreaking.

Laon hauled her off the bed and dragged her by her hair into the living quarters of his apartment, where he caught up the bottle of wine containing the drugs he had used before.

"I will make you wish you had never seen my face," he snarled, forcing her head back. "When you lie dying, slick with your own unfulfilled lust, your skin clawed in strips by your own hands, remember that you had the chance to be my mate!" he hissed at her. "And you chose instead to pry where you do not belong, and die for something you do not even understand!"

And with that, he brought the carafe of wine toward her lips, intending to pour its contents down her throat.

CHAPTER FOUR

Afraid to strike out at Laon's mind for fear she would kill him, Esme instead directed the force of her mind to the carafe he held, and after wresting control of it, she slammed it against the side of his head. In the process, both of them were drenched with the red wine.

"Ahhh!" he cried, and an instant later he slumped unconscious on top of her.

Esme lay for a moment, panting and thanking the Master that her instincts had served her when she most needed them. But then she became aware that the drugs in the wine were being absorbed through her skin because she felt them working inside her. Impatiently, she began to counter the effect with her mind even as she struggled out from beneath Laon's body and got to her feet.

Glaring down at Laon, she saw that he was more

spattered with the wine than she was, and, as much as she would have preferred to be on her way, she found she didn't have it in her to let him die the way he had intended to kill her. So she dragged him to his shower and turned on the water to rinse them both free of the wine and the drugs. Then she went into his body with her mind and negated the effect of the small portion of the drug he had already absorbed through his skin.

Leaving him slightly sedated so that she might have time to get away, she slipped naked, wraithlike, through the corridors of the Institute to her own quarters to dress and retrieve the Sacred Pouch. She might leave all else behind, but not that. Malthuzar had said she must bring it with her when she returned home, that it would be needed.

At the rear exit of the Institute, she paused, thinking of how to get past the guard, who was a sensing telepath. Fortunately, however, he was also very weary, and Esme decided to use his own weariness against him. Thus, she sent him to sleep with his head on the plasti-steel desk where he sat. Then she slipped past him, turned with her mind the tumblers of the lock that held the heavy door closed, pulled the door open, and, breathing deeply of the fresh night air, stepped out into a small open courtyard surrounded by high walls.

She almost forgot to relock the door. But after taking one step, she recalled the minor detail and impatiently took care of it. Then she went to the gate in the high wall, undid its lock, stepped across the opening, and soon stood outside on a wide stretch of hard paving.

It was a long way to Raul's apartment, and she was so physically weary Esme dreaded the thought of walking. But there were none of the mechanical crafts in sight to use, even if she'd had the proper Genesian coinage to pay for such transportation. Too, she did not have Raul's thoughts to use as a reference point to show her the way. But she remembered the physical objects her mind had soared over when she had visited him on the night before he had left for battle, and with those to guide her, she began to walk.

Dawn stalked the sky by the time Esme arrived, trembling with exhaustion, outside the complex of buildings wherein Raul's apartment was. She had started the ritual of Daccall already tired. Then there had been two days of almost unremitting physical exertion, followed by this long walk in which she had had to use her energy to blank the perception of her presence from the minds of those few Genesians out at such an hour. And the stimulant Laon had given her had long since passed its usefulness.

She leaned against a building to rest as she searched with her mind for any hint that Laon had recovered and had alerted guards to seize her should she head for Raul's apartment for sanctuary. But there was only the sleepy mind of one guard at the door to Raul's building, and Esme sighed with both relief and the weary knowledge that she would once again have to excise from someone's mind the memory of her passing.

There was no choice but to walk straight across the wide street and the smaller strip of paving in full view of the guard, who straightened at the sight of her. Esme noted the quickening of interest in his mind and thought she must, indeed, provide an interesting sight. She wore the first gown her hand had touched in her quarters, the formal one she had worn to the conference attended by the high counselor, and since the bodice was too tight to insert the Sacred Pouch under it, she wore it around her neck. But she wore no skin paint, and had not bothered to straighten the wild tangle of her thigh-length copper hair, and she knew her eyes were sunk into two deep, darkened pools of exhaustion.

"High Lady," the guard said uncertainly in greeting, eyeing her hair and the pouch with surprise. But those were the last two words he said, and Esme made certain he would remember nothing about her appearing in the early hours of the morning at his post. Then she walked straight past him and into the mechanical box that swept up to various levels of the building.

The effort of excising the guard's memory took almost the last of Esme's strength, however, and she leaned, eyes closed, trembling against the mirrored walls of the mechanical box as it took her to the level of Raul's apartment. When it came to a stop and its doors opened, she stumbled as she exited the box, and she walked unsteadily to Raul's door, hoping fervently he had not excised her prints from the panel that controlled access to the apartment.

He had not, and Esme lurched across the threshhold, barely able to close the door behind her and make it to Raul's bed and fall upon it.

As consciousness left her, she prayed the Master to protect her as she slept, for she knew she would sleep a long while, and that Laon, if he thought of it, would send to check for her here. If he did, she knew she did not have the power, and would not for some time, to defend herself.

Then she slipped heavily into a dreamless sleep that lasted one full revolution of the hands on the face of the plainly functional timepiece on the small table beside Raul's bed.

Esme dreamed that Raul called her name, and she stirred in her sleep, wanting desperately to go to him. But she was unable to slip the bonds of exhaustion that still held her chained, and after a while the calling stopped, and she slept dreamlessly once more.

When next she stirred, she was much restored, and she brought her eyes open to blink for a moment, uncomprehending, at the unfamiliar bedclothes upon which she lay face down.

Then she sensed Raul's presence all around her, and she smiled with relief and forced herself to sit up. For a few moments she merely sat cross-legged upon the bed, silent and at peace. She looked around and let the memory of the few days she and Raul had spent together here upon first arriving on Genesis, and that last mental meeting they had shared here, float gently through her mind.

Then, looking down at herself, she grimaced and, pulling the thongs of the Sacred Pouch over her head, went to take advantage of Raul's sanitary chamber.

Half an hour later she left the chamber naked, her skin glowing with clean warmth, her hair washed and tidied, even her teeth scrubbed. Her gown hung clean in the shower to dry. From Raul's closet, she fetched one of his silk robes and wrapped it around her.

In Raul's small, functional kitchen facility, she searched for something to quell the gnawing of her stomach. There was nothing fresh in the cold chamber, but she found a number of already prepared frozen meals, one of which she popped into the quick heater to warm. And soon, clean and fed, she sat on the midnight-blue couch in Raul's sitting room, thinking about what to do.

She had no idea how much longer Raul would be away. Though there was enough food in the apartment to last her for a while, she wondered how much longer the Master would protect her from Laon's finding her. Should she fall again into his hands, she knew her choices would be limited. Perhaps he would not kill her right away, though she much doubted whether he would risk letting her live long enough to talk to anyone about what she knew. Perhaps though, if his rage had subsided, and if he craved her physically and mentally, and there was some way he could spirit her to a prison of his choosing, he would not kill her at all. But Esme somehow doubted he would think that the benefits of keeping her alive outweighed the threat she represented to him.

"Raul . . ." she whispered forlornly. "Come to me please . . . quickly."

Silence greeted her plea and Esme sighed. She was on her own, with no help forthcoming, no place to go. She had no choice other than to stay where she was and to wait.

She then thought to distract her mind by writing in the journal she had started shortly after her arrival on the Condor. It contained her personal history, her people's history, and some of the Sacred Scrolls she had copied from memory. But when she searched the apartment, her journal was not to be found.

She shrugged in defeat at last. Perhaps Raul had taken it with him, but she could not see why he would. It was written in the language of the People, after all, and he did not know that language.

Finally, having nothing else to do, she reclined on

Raul's bed again and sought sleep to relieve her boredom and further restore her body's well-being. And when next she woke, it was to the sound of voices in the adjoining room.

Esme sprang to her feet beside the bed, every sense straining to assess the danger she was afraid she faced. But her mind found Thorson, the Condor's medic. He had treated her after her sojourn on the desert, and then had become her teacher, instructing her in Genesian customs and culture. He had also experienced much pain when she and Raul had become mated because Thorson loved her himself. She also found Raul, and her heart soared with joy!

As she stood, trembling with happiness, she heard Thorson, his voice coming closer, say, "But, Captain, you said yourself that if she was anywhere near, she would have answered your mind call. And the guard swore she hadn't been here. If you ask me, we should—"

Then Raul's huge form filled the doorway to the sleeping chamber, where he froze as his haggard eyes found her there awaiting him.

"Esme . . ." Her name was a whispered sigh on his breath, and the sound vibrated with his relief.

Esme ran and threw herself into his arms, then yelped and jerked backward as her bare breast came in contact with the sharp edge of one of the decorations on his shoulder.

"What . . . ?" Raul, frustrated at having her in his arms one instant and pushing herself away from him the next, looked down. As understanding hit, he reached up and ripped the decoration away, then dragged Esme back into his embrace where he hugged her so fiercely, she feared her ribs would crack.

Esme's radiant eyes met Thorson's over Raul's shoulder, and she grinned at the look of combined relief and jealousy on his face.

Not now, Thorson, she begged him mentally, still grinning. *Please . . . let me enjoy this reunion unhindered by your jealousy.*

Thorson flushed. Then, without replying, mentally or aloud, he turned away and left the apartment.

Esme forgot about him as Raul raised his head and crushed his mouth against hers. She forgot everything but the well-remembered, well-loved taste of Raul's lips and tongue. His warm, familiar hands roved her body, as though seeking to confirm for themselves that she was real, and she responded in kind, satisfying the long-denied need to touch him.

She was not surprised, only immensely pleased, when he backed her into the room and closed the door behind him, then backed her further to his bed where he seemed to force himself to push her down upon it and release her so that he could undress.

Esme gazed at his beloved, rugged face, noting the weariness carved there, the light of immense relief and desire in his clear blue eyes. She then let her eyes lovingly roam the rest of him as he peeled out of his formal bodysuit.

He has lost weight, she told herself, *but he is as magnificent as ever.*

Raul gave her no time for further thought. Lifting her with his strong hands to lie flat on the bed, he came down atop her, and without even the slightest nod to foreplay, entered her immediately.

Esme sucked in her breath as she felt the slight discomfort of friction, but it was gone almost immediately as heat and desire welled within her, providing the moisture needed to make the hard, driving strokes of Raul's manhood easy and slick.

Dimly, beneath the rising spiral of exquisite pleasure, Esme understood that Raul's need at this moment was to assure himself of her living presence, reclaim her for his own and release the tension of the fear he had felt for her safety.

She was more than happy to be alive and to assure him she was completely submissive to his claim of possession, and anxious to obtain for herself as well as for him the momentary release from fear and tension that he sought for them both with his driving use of her.

She timed her explosive release to match his, wanting synchronicity in everything between them at this moment. And when he lay quiet upon her, except for an occasional shudder, she cradled him in her arms, her love for him brimming full and running over.

At last he raised himself above her and studied her face with a thorough intensity Esme didn't really notice because she was studying him in the same way. He rolled to his side and ran his hand over her from shoulder to knee, kneading and touching, and as he did so, Esme's hands traced his shoulders and chest and arms, then returned to his face.

"Thank the saints you are safe," he whispered at last, his voice shaken and husky.

"And I thank the Master that you are the same," Esme responded softly. "I have worried much that I would never see you again."

Raul's eyes caught hers and he shook his head. "As long as I live, you will see me, Esme. Often enough, I expect, that you will tire of my face and my use of you."

Esme grinned at him. "Do not speak such nonsense to me," she chided. "I will never tire of either."

"Let us hope not, because I will not release you in any case," Raul said, his tone so fierce that Esme's grin faded and she could only look into his eyes with all her love in hers, until he relaxed and a slanting smile curved his lips.

"Now," he said grimly, resting on his elbow. "Tell me what has happened to cause Laon to flee the planet and searchers to seek you everywhere, fearing for your safety because it is known he put you under the influence of an outlawed drug and then through Daccall."

Esme's eyes opened wide. "You know then?" she whispered, her relief and gratitude immense as he seemed not to view her negatively because of her experience.

"I know," Raul said harshly, "and I will not again discount your suspicions of anyone. I have much self-blame over what happened to you, and much disgust that I did not sense Laon's treachery sooner. I had suspected before that someone on the council was either talking out of turn or was a traitor because Rebel ships found us on the way home from our secret mission to take the high counselor's son to visit his mother, and one of their stealth ships inflicted the damage that sent us to your planet to make repairs. I thought there had to have been a leak. But I didn't suspect Laon. His reputation was too pristine. And when I voiced the idea of a leak to my admiral, he dismissed the idea out of hand, so I had to let the matter drop."

He paused, and his eyes on Esme were fiercely warriorlike, but also ablaze with love for her.

"I vow to you, Esme," he grated, "if I had come back to find you dead from the effects of the drug, your body disposed of by Laon to hide his treachery, as was feared by those who informed me of what happened, I would have sought the shedding of his blood first and then my own!"

Esme gasped at the violent truth she saw in him, and then she raised a hand to stroke his cheek to calm him and shook her head. "Then," she said with soft fervency, "though I am very glad on my own behalf that I live, I am doubly grateful to know that you will continue to live. I do not want to exist without you, Raul."

"Nor do I wish to lose you," he echoed, his tone ragged. Then he turned purposeful. "Now, Esme, come into my mind and show me exactly what happened. I have not the patience to listen to you tell it."

Esme shrank back. "No!" she shook her head, her eyes wide with anxious apprehension.

"Esme," Raul said gently, "I do not want to take you back through such things, but it has to be done. Do it quickly so the pain of reliving will not linger overlong."

"You do not understand," Esme gulped, averting her eyes and sitting up.

Raul rose up to sit beside her. "Explain then," he said, puzzled by her attitude.

Esme bit her lip. She would have forfeited much not to have to tell Raul about what had happened. But she couldn't even contemplate showing him! How could she stand letting him see her own degradation at Laon's hands.

"Esme!" Raul was gentle, but he was also growing

increasingly impatient and he was very firm.

"My heart," she whispered, hanging her head, her voice softly miserable, "the regard you hold for me is most precious. I would not lose it by . . ." Her voice faltered.

Raul understood then, and he took her shoulders in his large hands and turned her to face him. Esme still could not look into his face, fearing to see his condemnation.

"Look at me, Esme," he ordered, and again he was gently firm.

Esme shook her head.

Raul took her chin in his hand and forced her head up. She had her eyes tightly closed.

"Open your eyes and look at me, Esme," he said softly, "and tell me what there is to fear about what you see."

Slowly, reluctantly, Esme opened her eyes and saw nothing but compassion and love and continued possessiveness. But she had not as yet told him what he wanted to hear. Perhaps when she did, all those things she saw in his eyes would change to contempt and rejection.

"No, Esme," Raul shook his head. "I will not hold you in contempt, nor will I reject you. I have not undergone Daccall, but I know enough about it to understand that you are not to blame for anything that happened while you were under its influence."

But Esme knew she did bear blame for part of what had happened, and the prize she had sought at the time no longer seemed worth the price she might be about to pay.

"I will tell you," she whispered, begging him with her eyes, "but please do not make me show you, Raul.

I would not have you see me like that."

Raul shook his head, and his gaze was steady and unyielding. "We cannot have such a thing between us, Esme," he said quietly. "What I do not see, I will imagine worse. Now do not delay further, but come into my mind and show me what I need to see. And I warn you, hold nothing back. I will know if you do."

Esme did not even think to question how he could know such a thing, any more than she had thought to question how he had known earlier the source of the guilt and fear she felt. She took his word as fact.

Slowly, hesitantly, she began, starting with a skimming rehearsal of how she had spent her weeks at the Institute before the time in question. She felt Raul's interest, but realized also he would prefer to see those things at another time in more detail. Now he wanted only one thing from her, and sighing with resignation, she gave it, starting with her arrival in Laon's apartment.

She found ease for her agonizing guilt and embarrassment by employing what she had learned at Laon's hands. She stood aside, in her own mind, almost impassive, and let the scenes roll sequentially into Raul's mind, giving him not only the pictures and words exchanged between herself and Laon, but also the thoughts she had had during the experience. As she did so, she noted his various reactions and dampened her pain at those reactions to a bearable level.

There was anger and self-blame as he watched her writhing helplessly under the influence of the drug, and there was deadly rage as he watched Laon practice his brutality upon her during the first stage of Daccall. Not even the twisted pleasure nor the lessons she had learned from that brutality dampened Raul's fury.

She was almost relieved to go on to the second stage, though she feared the unbridled pleasure she had taken from it before realizing the trap it embodied would arouse Raul's contempt. But she could scarcely believe Raul's reaction to what had occurred during the second stage of Daccall. He watched almost impassively, his jealousy there but muted, and she was amazed as she realized he was noting the sexual techniques Laon had employed upon her with much interest—not with the degree of anger or contempt she had expected!

When she was done with that stage, she spoke Raul's name aloud, her distress and indignation quivering in her voice.

He looked at her steadily, and he was unrepentant. "When we have the time," he said softly, "I will practice Daccall upon you myself. Do not, as you did with Laon," he advised, "seek to avoid the bonds I will place upon you then."

Esme took a deep breath, uncharmed by Raul's intention, as she thought he would be uncharmed when he saw the next stage!

"The bonds you already have upon me seem sufficient," she said, her voice and eyes sullen.

"I will be the judge," Raul said firmly. "Now continue, Esme. The hour grows late and we have much to do when this is finished."

"Very well," Esme said, her voice containing a hint of grim anticipation. "But I think you will change your mind about the benefits of Daccall by the time I am done showing you the next stage."

She could read nothing of Raul's reaction as she unfurled scenes from the third stage of Daccall for his benefit, a fact which puzzled and annoyed her. She would have hesitated before going to the end of what had happened between her and Laon and posed a question or two, but Raul, noting her intention, commanded her to finish.

She did, morosely at first, and then with more impassivity. When she was done, Raul nodded, satisfied.

"Good thinking," he approved. "If you had killed him, his guilt would have been more difficult to prove. His fleeing the planet will help to confirm it."

Esme would have gotten up from the bed then—her bladder needed relieving—but Raul held her arm. When she looked into his eyes, she saw a stern thoughtfulness that puzzled her.

"As to the question you wanted to pose earlier concerning whether I will still seek Daccall now that I know all that it entails, I knew already. And as to whether the risks of undergoing the third stage outweigh the benefits, I have not as yet decided. I will let you know at the time. But, Esme," he added, holding her gaze in a vise of blue steel, "should I decide to allow you to practice such things upon me, I do not think you will find the pleasure in your own brutality that you did with Laon."

Esme nodded, her gaze solemn. "I think you are right," she agreed quietly. "In fact, I do not even think I can attempt that third stage—not with you."

Raul shrugged, his smile lazy and, to Esme's eyes, somewhat mysterious. "You will attempt whatever I instruct you to attempt," he said simply and before she could even think to protest, however feebly, his arrogance, he pulled her close and kissed her rebellion away.

"Also," he said, "I will not be as brutal with you as

Laon was during the first stage of Daccall. Now go and attend to yourself," he added, getting to his feet and picking up his discarded bodysuit. "Then dress. We will be leaving shortly to attend a conference."

The mention of a conference made Esme uneasy, but she shrugged the feeling away. Raul would not, she was certain, force her to show an audience what she had just shown him.

In fact, Raul did almost exactly what she had been certain he would not do. He did not make her show everything to the High Council, except her and Laon in bed and how she made him confess his guilt and his attempt to kill her.

She could meet no one's gaze. Her cheeks were aflame with humiliation and her body shook with it by the time the high counselor pronounced her innocent of any blame and allowed Raul to escort her out of the room.

Raul noted the stiffness of her carriage and her unwillingness to suffer his touch, and he stopped and turned her to face him in the corridor, his hands firm upon her shoulders. Her furious gaze studied his face, but it also contained her lack of understanding of his motive in forcing such things from her, and the hurt her lack of understanding caused her.

"Esme, stop this," he said with gentle firmness. "Most of those people in there"—he gestured with his head toward the door of the council room—"have undergone Daccall themselves. It is a common way to spend the first days and nights after vows are taken to mate for life, though the use of the drug you had is not a part of the process anymore. Too many people were careless and were ending their lives instead of sealing their commitment to one another."

Esme was eased very little by Raul's explanation. "But it is a private matter, is it not?" she said, her voice trembling.

"Normally, yes," Raul admitted, "and it will be for us when we take Daccall. But what happened between you and Laon was evidence of his crime, and therefore necessary to share with his judges."

"I could simply have told them," Esme whispered, miserable with shame.

"No, Esme." Raul pulled her resisting form into his arms and held her tightly against him. He kissed the top of her head. "Believe me, it would not have served. Laon was held in too high regard by the council to be convicted for his crime without such incontrovertible evidence. And the only shame you should feel concerns the discomfort you caused those of the council who sensed the agony of humiliation you felt. It struck them as strange. We are not so modest on Genesis as your people must be. I will show you, at some time, what takes place in some of our arenas of entertainment, and I promise you the art of some of our performers will make what you showed the council seem tame in comparison."

Esme's bruised feelings were still not totally soothed, but she found the protection and comfort of Raul's body against hers of some help.

Later, back in his apartment, upon his bed, she allowed him to soothe her further with his body until her humiliation was driven far from her mind. When they lay spent and temporarily sated at last, she asked him of the war and whether he had found the enemy upon his last search.

"Some scattered encounters only, of not much

consequence," he said, puzzlement in his voice. "I like it not, Esme. It seems to me they wait for something major and do not wish to risk their regular fleets at this time. I like even less the knowledge that Laon must already have informed his masters that their stealth ships have little to fear from us."

Esme felt the familiar brush of fear tracing her spine.

"Raul, I would go with you the next time you venture among the stars," she said, her voice trembling with her fear for him.

Raul gathered her into his arms and held her close. "You will indeed go with me," he agreed, making Esme's heart leap with gratitude, "but not into battle," he added, dashing her gratitude, and her hope along with it, into nothingness. "I am going to take you home, Esme," Raul finished, his voice quiet and firm.

He cut off Esme's indignant protest by putting his hand over her mouth. When she would have sought his mind, his shield was up.

"I will have you safe," he said, unyielding to the plea in her eyes, "and your planet, tucked into unknown space as it is, is the only place I can think of to keep you that way until I am free to come for you."

Her eyes told him what she most feared, that he would never be free to come for her, that his life would be lost in the battle to come.

"I think not," he said, shaking his head. "I am not any longer without weapons of my own, Esme, and I will use all I have to protect my ship, my crew, and myself. It may happen that the Rebels will win. If so, when I do come for you, I and my crew will have to stay there with you instead of bringing you back here. But the fact that I will come to you is not in doubt."

He let her speak then, and Esme did so in a doubting wail. "How can you know that?" she demanded. "You are not precognizant and neither am I, and I cannot stand the thought of living my life without you!"

Raul sighed and held her closer. "You can stand it, Esme," he said gently. "We all stand what we have to. But I do not think either of us is going to have to live our lives without the other, and I would rather have your trust rest in me than have you make yourself miserable like this. Will you spoil the joy of this time we have together with your wailing about what the future might hold?" he chided.

Esme held back the wail that trembled in her throat.

"That is better, little coward." He chuckled and turned her to face him, pressing her nakedness close to his by rubbing his hands from her shoulders to her thighs. "Now let us practice for the ritual of Daccall we will soon undergo," he murmured against her mouth. "I feel a great need to be well prepared for that particular undertaking."

Esme looked into his eyes, her own asking a question.

"Aye, Esme." Raul nodded. "It will be done to seal the vows of life-mating we will take. You did not think, did you, that I would ever be willing to let you go?"

"I did not know," Esme whispered. "You said, before you last left for battle, that I might spoil things between us, that you were uneasy with your feelings for me."

"And so I was," Raul murmured, his mouth nibbling at hers. "But since then I have discovered a thing or two that makes me content with what we share."

"What?" Esme asked, but at that instant, Raul's hand parted her thighs and she forgot to listen for an answer. It was a long while, in another place, before she remembered to ask again.

CHAPTER FIVE

For THE TWO DAYS BEFORE THEY DEPARTED FOR THE Homeland, Raul was occupied in conferences with his superiors and checking on the resupply of the Sesphawk Talon.

Esme, because of an Institute request to the High Council which she heartily resented, spent those days back at the Institute from which she had fled. But at least they sent one of her favorite tutors, a sweet-natured precognizant called Halen, who was bent with the weight of her years, to fetch her.

In the private car in which they rode to the Institute, Halen held Esme's hand in her two aged ones and peered at her kindly through filmed blue eyes. "Accept my sorrow, daughter," she said without preliminary, "for your treatment at our hands. It would have been otherwise had Laon not ordered it thus."

Esme held no grudge against this woman, who had

treated her with gentle kindness while she assessed Esme's precognitive skills.

"I do not bear you any ill will," Esme assured Halen. "I know well how hard it would have been for you to go against Laon's wishes."

"Aye," Halen answered. "But still, had I not had other reasons for going along with him, I might have disobeyed. The treatment one such as you received was scandalous and brought me much unhappiness."

"Put it from your mind," Esme said gently. "It is over now."

At that, Halen brightened. "Yes, it is," she said with much satisfaction, her aged voice quavering, "and one good result from it is that no longer will Ahael, with his inferior forereading and his craven submission to Laon, be my superior. When his suspension from duty is over, I will check *his* conclusions as carefully and contemptuously as he always checked mine."

"Ahael has been suspended?" Esme asked, surprised.

"Aye. He was one of the three who signed the authority to give you the drug. He has been sent to one of our retreats to be reminded of the duties and responsibilities of one of his kind to those he serves."

Esme stared at Halen. "Laon," she said grimly, "told me Ahael had foreseen that I would not take enough of the drug to harm me. Are you telling me that Ahael's seeing was not always clear and that he often twisted what he did see in order to serve Laon's purposes?"

Halen sighed, a breathy sound that denoted her age. "Often it was thus," she agreed, "but Ahael is not so bereft of integrity and caution that he would risk the life of one sponsored by the High Council so carelessly. He checked his seeing with mine. And I, seeing much more than he did, knew you would eventually bring about Laon's downfall as well as the strengthening of the Empire. Therefore, I allowed what happened to proceed."

Esme was startled by Halen's words, then saddened by them. "Perhaps," she said gently, "you may also, upon occasion, be wrong. For while it is true that because of me we are all free of Laon, the drug and the Daccall ritual did not work. I was unable to provide an answer as to how to teach my gift to others so that we might abort the threat of the Rebel stealth ships."

Halen snorted, then smiled mysteriously. "Of course, you could not," she said matter-of-factly. "I have known all along that would be the case, and so I told Ahael. Your gifts are unique. In any case—and this knowledge, I have kept to myself—your contribution will not lie in placing adepts on each of our battleships to counter the Rebel stealth ships. But, of course, it did not suit Laon to take it as truth when I said as much to Ahael. He insisted upon putting you through what he did to make sure. Now, we know why. He wanted to reassure his secret masters that we do not threaten them in that way."

Esme was puzzled, then became excited. If there was some contribution Halen foresaw that she was supposed to make, perhaps it was one of the tasks the Master intended her to fulfill.

"Where does my contribution lie then, Halen?" she asked. "If you know something, you must tell me and the council. Raul thinks the Rebels prepare for something big."

Halen seemed unconcerned regarding the Rebel

threat, nor was she inclined to enlighten Esme further. "It is useless to tell the council anything," she said, waving a trembling hand dismissively. "Between the lies of Laon and Ahael, my reputation is so diminished, I would not be believed."

"Then tell *me*!" Esme begged. "If I know, I can . . ."

But Halen shook her head and the car stopped in front of the impressive entrance to the Institute.

"It is forbidden me to tell you, Esme," she said simply. "The Master has decreed you will walk in faith, rather than knowledge, and you must also undergo a testing. The Master cannot be gainsayed."

"The Master!" Esme had not once heard anyone on Genesis acknowledge the existence of, or even knowledge of, the Master. "Halen, you are aware of the Master?" she asked joyfully.

But Halen said, "Be silent, Esme. All will be fulfilled in time."

Then the elderly precognizant was helped out of the car by a guard, and Esme, of necessity, had to follow.

As they walked at a slow pace, due to Halen's age, toward the conference chamber where Esme was to meet with all the rest of her tutors, she tried to gain the knowledge she wanted from Halen's mind. But all she got was a swirling mist, in the midst of which rose the peak of the Holy Mountain on the Homeland.

"You know of that, too?" Esme whispered, and Halen merely gave her a smile and told her to ask no more questions.

As they entered the conference room, Esme hesitated. All her tutors were arrayed around a circular table at which there were two empty chairs. Then Esme was stunned as the tutors, moving as one, bowed from the waist to her, as they did only to one another, not to a mere student. Halen, too, from where she stood beside Esme, bowed from the waist.

Esme stood, her eyes widened to their farthest width, staring, while the tutors remained bowed. Then Halen whispered with amused impatience, "Release us, child. My back will freeze into this position if I have to hold it much longer."

Esme gulped. "How?" she whispered back. "What do I say?"

Halen quickly told her and Esme, her voice displaying her own amazement, said to the tutors, "Greetings, one and all. You may rise."

They did so, Halen most gratefully, and then the old woman escorted Esme to the place of honor at the table. "Seat yourself," she whispered to Esme.

Esme sat, and the rest of the tutors, with a rustling of movement, sat as well. Halen did so, uttering a sigh of weary relief, and when she was settled, she glanced at the faces around the table, an expression of calm dignity on her aged face. Finally she settled her gaze on the strikingly kind countenance of a man in his mid-years whom Esme had only seen at a distance. He was not one of her tutors.

"Will you speak to Esme on behalf of all of us, Jaheel," Halen invited, and there was no question in her voice, merely satisfaction.

As Esme watched, Jaheel rose to his full height, which was impressive, and spoke directly to her in a voice so pleasant that she felt an involuntary smile curve her lips and a sense of well-being suffuse her body and spirit.

"I am Jaheel, High Lady," the man said. "You do not know me. I am one with the gift of healing the body and easing the troubled spirit. It was decided that I should address you because it was felt your spirit might be troubled at having to return here, that you might be angry with us because of the treatment you received here."

He paused in order to give Esme an opportunity to reply.

She didn't know what to say. Finally, she spoke the simple truth. "It is true I was not happy while I was here," she said quietly, "and I did not relish returning. I did not see what you could want with me."

Jaheel nodded. "It is to answer that question, and to offer our sincere apologies and to establish a rapport —late, but we sincerely hope not too late—between us, that we requested the council to permit us this audience," he said. "To begin, Esme, we humbly request that you grant us each, one by one, the chance to greet you privately by mind and share with you the warm feelings we have had all along, but were not, until now, permitted to express to you."

Because of the sincerity of the emotions Esme felt among the tutors, she could not do other than agree to the request.

Jaheel smiled. "We are most grateful. I believe Halen will begin."

Opening her mind, Esme found Halen within it immediately. *We have already spoken, child*, Halen said, *and you are already aware of my warm feelings for you. I will add only a sincere welcome to our midst. And were circumstances different, I would wish you could agree to another request that will be made of you. But you will not, and it is for the best. Farewell.*

Before Esme could reply, the tutor sitting next to Halen, the one who had tested her skill at moving objects with her mind, had replaced Halen's presence in her mind and spoke with warm respect. *I greet you, sister, with love and awe. Never in my long years at the Institute have I met one of your power, and I know, because of your fear, you did not show me all of which you are capable. Perhaps one day you will grant me the privilege of a more voluntary demonstration. I would be honored if it came to be. Welcome to our midst.*

Around the table it went, with each of the tutors expressing such warmth for her and such respect and awe for her abilities that Esme was much moved to have offered to her that which she had long been deprived—friendships among those who understood and accepted and revered her as she was.

Her green eyes glittered with tears by the time the last tutor had withdrawn from her mind, and she sat for several minutes gathering her composure before she said the words which all of them awaited. "I am honored by your feelings for me," she said, with sincerity and warmth vibrating in her soft voice. "I return them. I am proud to be in your midst."

They all then smiled with relief and pleasure and nodded at her and spoke aloud to her for a few moments, reiterating their welcome.

Then Jaheel rose to his feet again and went to a small cupboard behind him and withdrew from it a bundle of dark blue material, the color which Laon wore as administrator at the Institute. Returning to the table, Jaheel held the bundle out to her and addressed her briefly. "We would also be honored, Esme, if you would accept the role and the robe of he whom you are most qualified to replace," he said.

Esme was stunned, then flustered and alarmed. Friendship or not, she had no desire to remain at the

Institute. Regardless of her skills she felt unqualified and was unwilling to take on Laon's duties and responsibilities.

"But I am leaving with Captain Raul the day following the next," she stammered. "And I do not know when I will return, if ever. I therefore cannot—"

"If you will indulge us a moment," Jaheel broke in hastily before she could complete her refusal, "I am sorry I failed to explain clearly. You need not stay here with us at present to accept this honor, Esme. We offer it because it is so richly deserved we cannot do otherwise. But if you must delay in accepting, together we will appoint someone to fill in for you until you can."

Esme felt overwhelmed. This was exactly the sort of thing she had sought to avoid on the Homeland. She felt a pull as though she sank into sucksand. The daily, draining responsibilities beckoned like a possessive specter. And now, no more than when she had manipulated Malthuzar into refusing to accept her as a seeker, did she feel that such service was what the Master intended her to embrace.

Suddenly, Esme remembered what Halen had said to her, and she turned her head to seek support from her aged friend. Halen's filmed eyes were twinkling, her crinkled lips smiling. Esme sent a brief, heartfelt mental plea into the ancient mind so close to her own.

Halen nodded and turned to the others. "Esme has other concerns for the moment. She is not ready for this," she said simply. "Can we not instead offer her the position of intermittent tutor with permanent status guaranteed until she is free to come to us?"

There was a buzz of consternation around the table,

followed by a silent consultation, from which Esme deliberately excluded herself. Then Jaheel faced her again.

"If that is your wish, Esme, then we will postpone the matter until you are ready to give the matter your consideration again. If you would, when you are upon Genesis, consent to come here and aid us, we would be most happy to have the benefit of your services. We would give you the robe of full tutor for the present, with the understanding that you would serve only intermittently for as long as you desire."

Esme hesitated. She could not foresee accepting the honor they wished to bestow upon her even if the Empire won the war and Raul permitted her to return to Genesis with him. The Institute was in need of a full-time, fully committed administrator, someone who could fulfill Laon's heavy responsibilities without Laon's divided mind. And even if the Master had made it clear to her that she was to serve in such capacity, what about her life with Raul? How would she have the energy and time to lead two separate lives?

Suggest they appoint me as interim administrator in the meantime, Halen's mind said privately to hers. *I will not live long enough to be in the way should you come to need the appointment for yourself.*

Alarmed that Halen had used the expression "need," Esme silently demanded, *Halen, do you see such for me in the future?*

I see nothing to alarm you. Halen shrugged mentally. *I do not speak as a seer but as an old woman who regrets a time when I had no alternative but to do that which offended my sense of rightness, even though I knew that what I did was foreordained. You need not ever take up this burden, but I would have it available for you should you ever need or want to do so, both for your sake and for the sake of the Institute. There is no one other than you or me at this time qualified to fill Laon's shoes. In the future that may not be so. There are one or two who show promise among the students.*

Esme hoped Halen spoke the truth. The thought that the old woman might be speaking as a result of having read the future disturbed her.

She turned and addressed those at the table. "I will take the robe of tutor only at this time," she said firmly. "And I propose Halen for the permanent, not temporary, role of administrator."

A murmur of surprise went round the table, and all looked at Halen. But after a moment, seeing her aged countenance and feeble body, they realized the benefits of Esme's proposal and most began to nod their approval.

A vote was quickly taken, and only two voted against Halen. Then there was a brief, moving ceremony, where Esme was appointed tutor and given the robe appropriate to her new status.

"Tomorrow," Jaheel said when all had finished embracing their new member, "if you will return, we will take you on the tour of the Institute which you would normally have been given as a student."

"I will return," Esme agreed. Her curiosity, if nothing more, would be satisfied by the tour, and she would welcome the opportunity to see Chass again and extend her thanks to him for his help.

When the meeting was over, and Esme and Halen were once again in a private Institute car being driven back to Raul's apartment, Esme asked, "Who were the two who voted against you?"

Halen grinned, revealing teeth yellowed and stained with age. "Two who had no hope of being named administrator over you, but who would gladly have taken the honor from me with the hope of entrenching themselves sufficiently that they might be able to fight you for it if you should ever wish to take it up yourself," she said humorously. "Do not worry about them," she added, patting Esme's hand. "They have not near the talent that Laon did, who would have been a notable administrator had his loyalties not been compromised."

Esme was curious. "I did not learn how his loyalty was suborned," she said. "Do you know how the Rebels controlled him?"

Halen sighed. "The specific incident does not matter," she said sadly. "For it was not the real reason he split himself in two. It was merely an excuse. Laon, though he was not precognizant, has a remarkable ability to see how the political winds blow. He is convinced that the Rebels will win this war."

"Will they, do you think?" Esme inquired anxiously, thinking of Raul.

"I do not think so." Halen frowned, obviously puzzled. "When I look, I do not see either side winning a conclusive victory. Sometimes, precognition can be very frustrating. Often, what I see is muddled. I am not sure what the final result of the war will be. All I know is that tremendous change is on the way and that you and your captain will be the catalyst which sparks that change."

Esme was surprised. "You did not say before that Raul would be involved in what happens," she protested.

Halen blinked at her, as though coming out of sleep.

91

"Are not your destinies entertwined?" she replied matter-of-factly. Then the car stopped in front of Raul's apartment and Halen leaned forward to kiss Esme's cheek. "Go, child," she said firmly. "Pretty yourself for your man. Take what moments of joy you can. They are ever too few in everyone's lives."

Esme, seeing she would get nothing further from Halen, did as the old woman bade her. Before Raul returned to the apartment, she bathed and tidied her hair. Then she donned the prettiest of the gowns he had bought her—other than the one Laon had destroyed—before fixing a meal to welcome her captain home.

Her body and mind temporarily sated and purring with contentment, Esme was almost asleep when something occurred to her.

She lifted her head from Raul's shoulder. "Do you sleep, my heart?" she asked softly, her eyes tender upon his relaxed face.

"Almost," he murmured. Then his blue eyes blinked open, and Esme saw a teasing light amidst the sleepiness in their blue depths. "Do not tell me I have not yet managed to satisfy that voracious hunger of yours?" he complained. "I have had a hard day, Esme. Leave me be."

"It is only a question I would ask you," she chuckled. "I would not wear out what I intend to enjoy for a good many years to come by overusing it in the beginning."

The arm Raul had around her tightened, and suddenly he flipped her onto her back and he hovered threateningly over her. "Do you think I am so weak that you *can* overuse me?" he growled. "Perhaps, in

the interest of disciplining a certain impudent female,
I should abandon my need for sleep awhile?"

Esme chuckled again. "Whatever you wish shall be
done," she said demurely. "You are the captain. I am
merely a civilian."

Raul nodded. "That is a wiser attitude to take," he
said in a falsely superior tone as he rolled over onto
his back. "Now what is this question you would ask?"

"Do you know what has happened to my journal?"
Esme inquired. "I cannot find it, and I would like to
take it with me on our journey and record what has
happened to me here on Genesis."

Raul shrugged. "I gave it to one of our historians,"
he said. "If you wish so much to have it with you, I can
retrieve it tomorrow."

"My thanks," Esme agreed. "I would like it."

Raul sighed. "Very well," he said long-sufferingly,
"but it will cause me undue time and trouble in an
otherwise very busy day."

Esme took him seriously at first. "I am sorry," she
said sincerely. Then, with some reluctance, she made
an offer she did not really want to make. "Perhaps,"
she sighed, "I can do without it. It is just that—"

"On the other hand," Raul interrupted, "when one
does a favor for someone, there is usually reciproca-
tion to be had of one sort or another."

Esme still did not take his meaning correctly. "Of
course, I will do anything you wish, Raul," she said
earnestly. "How may I serve you?"

In the dimness of the room, she saw his white teeth
flash in a grin. "Well, as I mentioned when you woke
me," he said in a tone that was much more solemn
than the grin, "I am weary."

"Yes, dearest, I know," Esme said sympathetically.

"Too weary," Raul said as though she hadn't spoken, "to put much energy into satisfying that which you woke when you woke the rest of me."

Esme was silent a moment, making sure that this time, she took his meaning correctly. When she had, she controlled the smile which wanted to curve her lips.

"Oh," she said obtusely. "And what might that be that I awoke within you?"

"Esme," Raul said in a drily humorous tone, "do not try my patience. If you would repay me for the service I will render you on the morrow, get about it so that I may sleep at least a part of this night. Otherwise . . ."

"Otherwise?" Esme's tone was innocent and curious.

"Esme!"

Laughing, she bestowed a much subdued, much changed approximation of the third stage of Daccall upon a man who had protested he was too weary to engage in anything, a man whom, when she had finally ceased her labors upon him and he was at last again capable of speech, bestowed a gift upon her in return that pleased Esme's heart greatly.

"I think," Raul whispered sleepily into her ear as he cuddled her close, "my ambivalence about participating in the third stage of Daccall has just been resolved. A man would be a fool to deny himself such an experience for the sake of preserving a little useless dignity."

"And you are many things, my heart," Esme replied lovingly, "but a fool is not one of them."

"That is truth," Raul agreed. "And you, my love?" he then asked. "Has your ambivalence about practicing it upon me been resolved?"

Esme smiled, nestling closer to his warm body. "You said I would have no choice, regardless of how I felt about it," she reminded him in a whisper.

"That is truth as well," Raul allowed sofly. "But I would rather you were happy with my decision than resentful of it."

"Then," Esme said, her voice warmly amused, "I think I might, if I set my mind to it, find ways to do your will which will not cause either of us too much distress or loss of dignity."

"I am confident you will." Raul smiled and kissed her temple. "Now sleep, little one," he added, settling back and yawning. "Tomorrow night, we will sleep upon my ship or at least you will. I may not have time for sleep."

But Esme, though she lay still and silent in Raul's arms so as not to disturb him, did not find sleep for a long while that night. She was unable to subdue her perplexity and a certain amount of anxiety concerning her future. What test had the Master decreed she must undergo? She was also not nearly as convinced as she wished to be that Halen's insistence that she keep open the option of serving as administrator of the Institute was based on practicality rather than Halen's foreseeing something in the future Halen knew Esme would not like.

But Halen had said the Master required her to walk by faith and not by certain knowledge. And since that same admonition was also contained within the Sacred Scrolls as a directive to all the People, Esme at last stilled her quest for answers and rested quietly.

CHAPTER SIX

THE INSTITUTE WAS NOT TERRIBLY LARGE. IT SEEMED THAT even the Empire, with its many habitated planets, did not boast a great number of citizens whose gifts justified bringing them to the Institute for training.

Esme enjoyed the tour now that her status had changed, and especially since Jaheel had been appointed to serve as her escort. In the company of such a beneficent soul, Esme doubted anyone could remain troubled for long. Still, as they made their way to the students' quarters—which Esme had requested be last on the tour, intending to share mid-meal with them in their communal dining room—she sighed, regretting lost opportunities. She could have enjoyed her time here had her status been that of a regular student. Instead, she had been miserable.

"Where would you sit, Esme?" Jaheel inquired as they stood in the doorway to a large room where most

DAUGHTER OF DESTINY

of the tables were already occupied.

Esme sought Chass with her mind and found him across the room, sitting at a table positioned under large windows which overlooked an enclosed garden. Across from him sat a comely young woman whose looks were spoiled by the haughty expression upon her face.

"Over there," Esme said, gesturing with her hand and starting to walk in the direction she had indicated.

She was aware that a silence descended upon the room and that many eyes traced their progress as she and Jaheel made their way down a passageway between the tables. Her own curiosity was as much aroused by the students as theirs was by her, so she looked from side to side, smiling with a friendly warmth and nodding as she walked. Some of the students smiled back. Some seemed too awed to respond.

Then she stood by Chass's table. He gradually became aware of Esme's presence as he had been longingly gazing with such intensity at the beautiful young woman across from him to notice what else was going on. Awkwardly he scrambled to his feet. As he rose, Esme deftly removed the cap on his memory that had kept remembrance of their former meeting out of his mind.

"Esme!" he said in a startled tone, a smile appearing on his handsome face. Then he noticed that she was wearing the robe of a full tutor, and the smile faltered. "I mean . . . greetings, Mistress . . ." he stammered, and glanced at Jaheel as though expecting a reprimand. Jaheel looked surprised that the young man had spoken so familiarly to Esme.

Esme didn't enlighten Jaheel as to how she had made Chass's acquaintance. "I think, upon this occasion," she teased the young man lightly, "that we can dispense with formalities and use first names. May we join you, Chass?" she asked, indicating the table with her hand.

"Of co . . . ah . . . certainly!" Chass stammered, glancing nervously at the young woman who had now risen to her feet and stood with her hands folded and an expression of attentive curiosity on her face.

"Please, sit down," Esme spoke to both Chass and the young woman as she sat upon the bench Chass had occupied. She patted the bench beside her for Chass's benefit and nodded at the young woman.

Chass hesitated until the young woman had reseated herself and Jaheel had sat down beside her; then he awkwardly sat down beside Esme.

Esme looked with friendly inquiry at the young woman, though, in truth, she did not care for her haughty expression much.

"Ah . . . this is Niah," Chass interpreted Esme's look to mean she wanted an introduction.

"Greetings, Niah," Esme said graciously.

"Greetings, Mistress." Niah nodded her head, atop which rested a crown of golden braids, respectfully but there was a regal pride in the gesture, and Niah's blue eyes, as they inspected Esme, bore a tinge of jealous resentment.

Esme's dislike of Niah firmed. She did not show her reaction, however. Instead, she turned to Chass. "How goes it with you, Chass?" she asked fondly.

"It goes well." Chass nodded. "My studies progress."

"Good," Esme said sincerely.

Then two servers hastened to the table to dish the food in the serving dishes onto plates for Esme and Jaheel. After they had poured fruit juice into goblets for the two of them, the servers departed, bowing respectfully, and Esme nodded at Chass's plate, then the young woman's, upon which their food was growing chilled.

"Please . . . continue eating," she said. "This looks too tasty to waste."

Both of them, however, as did Jaheel, waited until Esme had picked up the tined utensil lying by her plate and taken a bite of glazed fowl on a bed of cooked white grain, before they resumed eating.

"Tell me, Chass," Esme said when she had swallowed her bite. "What is your specialty?"

Chass hastily swallowed whole the bite of food in his mouth. "Moving objects with my mind," he got out, sounding choked.

"Then we have something in common," said Esme smoothly. "We must compare methods one day." Then she politely turned to Niah. "And you, Niah? What is your specialty?"

The haughty, regal expression on the girl's face was pronounced. "I am a problem solver," she said proudly. "I take diverse facts and make sense of them when others cannot."

"Indeed," Esme murmured. Glancing at Chass, she saw on his youthful face as he stared at Niah the hopeless expression of a young man in the first throes of infatuation who knows his affections are not returned. Esme felt impatient with him. Though it was true that Niah was beautiful, Esme felt certain Chass would be better off pursuing someone with less pride and more human sweetness in her character.

"Aye." Niah nodded. Then she boldly asked a question, and her eyes were again jealously resentful. "I have heard that you have almost all the skills," she said, omitting Esme's title. "Is problem-solving one of them?"

Esme debated voicing the retort that came into her mind. She had no real wish to humiliate this chit, no matter how irritating the girl's attitude. But then, it might do Niah good to have her arrogance pricked. More important, it might do Chass good to see his beloved slip a little from the pedestal upon which he had placed her.

"Yes, I have such abilities," Esme said, though she had never given the matter much thought and was actually unsure of how far her talents extended in that direction. Then she added, with calm dismissal, "But it has always seemed to me that *everyone* does to some degree. And I have found that such an ability, without the leavening attribute of wisdom, is a much over-rated commodity."

Niah's fair skin flushed a bright red and the look in her blue eyes became venomous for a moment as she stared at Esme.

Esme stared back at the girl, her green eyes suddenly cold, and sent an unarticulated sense of warning into the girl's mind.

Niah immediately dropped her eyes. Then, as though needing the boost of Chass's regard to soothe her frayed ego, she glanced up at Chass. But Chass was staring at Esme with a puzzled, but admiring, look in his eyes, and Niah flushed again, then put her utensil down with a clatter beside her plate, upon which there was still a goodly amount of food.

"With the Master's and the Mistress's permission,"

she said stiffly, looking at no one. "I would be excused. I have preparations to make for an afternoon class."

"Certainly," Esme said, glad to be rid of the girl's disturbing presence. The encounter with Niah and Esme's discomfort at her own petty behavior were threatening to spoil her pleasure in the day.

"Permission granted," Jaheel said gently, and Niah, moving with stiff dignity got up, bowed at Esme and Jaheel, and walked stiffly away.

Chass watched her go, his expression thoughtful, and still, to Esme's disgust, filled with longing.

"Esme," Jaheel murmured and when Esme looked at him, he sent her a chastizing look from his warm eyes. But there was a reluctant humor there as well as he said, "Niah is a daughter of the high counselor. She is having a little trouble adjusting to the democracy we impose upon our students."

Esme grimaced and for Chass's benefit, said, "Well, I suppose I should regret causing her embarrassment, but I found her attitude annoying. I hope she will one day add to her surface beauty and her minor talent by learning a degree of humility and simple human kindness I find lacking in her now. Otherwise, whatever poor male falls into her clutches will be in for much unnecessary trouble and unhappiness, when if he would only search a little further, he could find the more rewarding sweetness of another sort of mate."

Jaheel sighed, disapprovingly. Chass looked at Esme in wide-eyed astonishment. Esme ignored both of them and ate her food, and as she did soon became aware that Jaheel was sending her the ease of spirit which was his gift. She looked up, grinned, and nodded.

Jaheel smiled back, then proceeded to engage Chass in gentle inquiry as to his history. As Chass answered Jaheel's questions, Esme learned that he was from a prosperous mining family on one of the cold outer worlds, and was one of only half a dozen from that planet who had ever shown sufficient talent to be accepted at the Institute.

As they finished eating, Esme looked at Jaheel, and said, gently, "If you would not mind, Jaheel, I would have a private word with Chass before you escort me to the gate."

Chass looked startled. Jaheel nodded. "As you wish, High Lady," he said respectfully, and got up to walk slowly to the door, stopping to speak to various students he had treated as he made his way forward.

Chass stared at her with curiosity when she turned to him. Esme smiled. "You have heard, perhaps, that things have changed for me since we last met?"

Chass glanced at her robe, which was of a blue only a shade lighter than that which Laon had worn.

"I would say things have changed a great deal." He grinned. Then his grin faded and he looked puzzled. "Why did you turn down Laon's position?" he asked.

Esme shrugged. "Because something calls me elsewhere," she said. Then her eyes softened upon him. "I wanted to express my thanks for what you did for me," she said quietly, "and to tell you that if ever there is something I can do for you, you have only to ask."

Chass blushed. "I did nothing really," he said. "You kept me there, answering your questions. Left to my own courage, I would probably have run away."

Esme shook her head. "You were nervous, yes. And it is true that I exerted certain . . . pressures . . . upon you. But had it been another who came to me that day, I would have had to use much more pressure. You are a brave man, Chass, a man of integrity and strength. I value you."

Chass's blush deepened, but there was a pleased, prideful look in his blue eyes now as well.

Esme was glad. She thought Chass would need all the pride and strength he could muster should he continue to pursue Niah.

She picked a sense from his mind and asked, "Is there something I may do for you now?" Then, before he answered, she knew what he would ask and was annoyed.

"Not unless you can somehow convince Niah to look upon me with favor." He sighed. "I have despaired of convincing her to do so on my own merits."

"That I will not do!" she said sharply, causing Chass to look at her startled. She softened her tone then, and said, "Ask me something else, Chass. Anything but that."

He studied her face, his expression curious and thoughtful. "You truly do not like her, do you?" he asked quietly.

Esme sighed. "No," she said flatly. "I do not. And if you would take advice on the subject of one female from another, you will abandon your pursuit of her. She will take from you more than she brings you."

Chass's smile was slanting, resigned. "Nevertheless," he said, shrugging, "I have a fever for her that I think will not depart until I have had her. The only other female for whom I have felt such interest is unavailable to me."

Esme took his meaning immediately, but since she was not prepared to go to the lengths it would take to distract Chass from his interest in Niah, she remained silent. She did, however, lean over and kiss his cheek, a gesture which brought a sharp intake of breath from him and a muted gasp of surprise from those students watching.

"I must go now, Chass," she said softly, smiling as she sensed the sexual and emotional turmoil her kiss had aroused in him. "Remember, if I may help you and I am here on Genesis to know of your need, I will. Meanwhile, may you have good fortune in your studies and in your life, and may the Master guard your spirit."

With that, she rose and walked away, feeling Chass's eyes on her back with the same longing expression in them as he had earlier directed at Niah. She grimaced to herself, hoping Chass would one day fix his affections on someone more suitable than either she or Niah was for him.

The Institute's private car took her to Raul's apartment to gather her few possessions, then transported her to the guarded docking facilities where the Sesphawk Talon stood, sleeker and trimmer than the Condor.

Raul was unavailable so Thorson met her at the ramp. After she hugged and kissed him, he escorted her to the captain's cabin, a much smaller one than Raul had had on the Condor.

Interpreting her look of surprise, Thorson shrugged, smiling. "This is a battleship, Esme, not a royal transport such as the Condor. The Condor could fight for its protection if necessary, but fighting is the Talon's whole purpose."

Esme shrugged. "No matter," she said, taking the

small carrybag containing her possessions from him and tossing it on the double bed. "I was once used to no such comforts at all, and in any case, as long as I am with Raul, I care not about the luxury of the accommodations."

Sensing Thorson's discomfort at her statement, she swung around, put her small hands on her hips and looked at him sternly. His expression, however, did not turn repentant, and she sighed at last and went to him to place her arms around his waist and lean her head on his chest, bathing his mind with comfort and affection.

But her gesture did not entirely subdue the turmoil inside him and Esme stepped back and shook her head at him.

"Am I never to be allowed to show my affection for you and other male friends without causing them discomfort?" she asked plaintively.

At that, Thorson smiled. "Do not ask the impossible, Esme," he teased. But he then brought his arms around her for an affectionate hug. Then he held her shoulders in his hands and looked down into her face as she turned it up to him.

"Who else do you hold in as much affection as you do me?" he asked.

Esme looked at him chidingly. "A young man at the Institute," she said, "and once there was a young shepherd upon my own planet, as well as an old priest. And it is my hope that there will be many more men, as well as women, who will come into my life for whom I feel friendship and affection." She gave him a wry look and asked, "What would you do with me, I wonder, if I were yours instead of Raul's? Lock me up in a chamber to which only you had the key?"

"Aye, I might." Thorson nodded, looking teasingly shamefaced by his attitude.

Esme shook her head. "It would do you no good," she said simply. "Locks are no barrier to me. The only way I can be held, Thorson," she added, "is by the sort of bonds Raul has put upon my heart. Then I am truly bound, more so than others are held by locks and walls or anything else."

Thorson sighed, but accepted her words. Then he said, "When you are settled in, Esme, there is someone who is impatient to speak to you."

"Who?" Esme asked curiously, going to the bed to unpack her bag.

"A historian to whom Raul gave your journal. It seems that the reading of it has caused him much excitement and he has prevailed upon the council to allow him to accompany us back to your planet. Raul, when he learned of it today, was not particularly pleased to have the man underfoot, but he had no choice."

Esme turned, a puzzled expression on her face. "But why should my journal interest him so?" she asked.

Thorson shrugged and turned away to leave the cabin. "Ask him yourself," he said. "I will bring him to you in a few moments."

Esme used the time to put her things away. She was just finishing when Thorson came back with a small, plump man who seemed to bristle with excited energy.

"Esme, this is Jemiah, Master of history. Jemiah, this is Esme."

"My dear Esme! This is such an honor!" Jemiah

106

strode forward to seize one of Esme's hands and bow over it, touching his forehead to its surface. When he raised his head, his eyes darted over her with a consuming, curious intensity that made her feel uncomfortably like an object in a museum, and he talked nonstop.

"Oh, I have longed to talk to you ever since I broke the code of your ancient language and was able to read your journal," he said excitely. "If what I suspect is true, this is the biggest discovery made in years. Please, my dear"—he gestured to the dining table in the small cabin—"let us sit and talk. I have a thousand questions to ask; my mind is consumed with them. Please."

Esme glanced helplessly at Thorson, who shrugged, grinned, and turned to leave.

"Thorson!" she called after him while resisting Jemiah's tug upon her hand. "When will Raul be free?"

Thorson turned his head to look at her over his shoulder. "I have no idea, Esme," he said. "He is always exceedingly busy on the eve of a launch. You may not see him until we are in space tomorrow."

Esme was disappointed. "Very well," she said, and Thorson left the cabin. Esme then allowed Jemiah to drag her to the table.

"Now," he said, quivering with eagerness. "Let us begin."

Two hours later, Esme was weary of Jemiah's endless questions about the Homeland and its history. He had read her journal after all and though she hadn't had time to copy all of the Sacred Scrolls into it, the ones she had transcribed from memory gave him the same information he insisted she repeat for him verbally.

"Jemiah, what is the point of all this?" she sighed. "Why insist that I repeat for you what I have written and you have already read?"

Jemiah's twinkling blue eyes and mischievous smile gave him the appearance of one of the small animals that roamed the high meadow. Indeed, his charm was such that Esme could not be angry with him, but he was sorely trying her patience.

"I merely wanted to ascertain that you did indeed write from memory that portion of the journal detailing your planet's history," he said.

Esme frowned. "And how else would I have done it?" she demanded.

Jemiah gave her an apologetic look. "The art of forgery is not unknown in such matters," he said.

"Forgery?" Esme had never heard the term.

"Never mind," Jemiah said, looking satisfied, and he bent to rummage in a carryall he had with him. An instant later, he withdrew a sheaf of papers, which he tapped upon the table to straighten, then placed carefully in front of Esme. "Can you read our language, Esme?" he asked.

Esme nodded absently as she looked at the machine script on the first page. Then her eyes widened as she realized what she was reading. It was a part of the Prophecy she had known all of her life but it was not part of the scrolls she had copied in her journal. She hadn't gotten that far before arriving on Genesis. Now she read the words slowly.

"Beware. There will come a time when, because of your disregard for Me and My laws, because of your hatred for your brothers and sisters, and because of your misuse and abuse of the world which I made for you, you shall surely suffer and die in great numbers, and many of you will kill your souls as well so that your spirits will be forever separated from Mine," the Prophecy ran.

"In the days when your wickedness has reached its peak, the land will be made desolate from your predations, and where once there was plenty for all, there will be sustenance for none. Neither water nor food nor peace will you have. Having destroyed your own inheritance, you will then, out of hunger and terror and hardness of heart, turn upon and rend one another, each seeking at the expense of his brothers and sisters to preserve that which is already lost.

"Then will I show mercy to those who have kept faith with Me. Into that valley upon the Homeland which I will keep protected and hidden for the time when it will be needed, will I send a Remnant of My People which I will save for Myself. Male and female, will every race I have made be drawn there, as will those of the lower creatures which My Remnant will need for survival. Their population will not overrun the resources I have put at their disposal, and among them will I preserve peace and the knowledge of My truth. And unto the latter days, their awareness of Me and their love for Me and their obedience to Me, will not diminish.

"Others will I save also, separate from My Remnant, against the day of need. And these will multiply, fluorish, and prosper in the places I have made ready for them. Yet these, as did their forefathers and mothers, will come to follow the enemy. They will make war among themselves, threatening their own survival as well as all that I have given them.

"Then will I once again show My love and mercy. I will send one of Mine to the scattered, and that one will forge a link that cannot be broken. My two Remnants will then come together—the one to teach My way, the other to learn it and to provide the means to protect it—against a day of need."

Esme looked up at Jemiah, her eyes wide. "Where did you get this?" she asked wonderingly. "I thought only the People—"

But then she fell abruptly silent as she began to understand the implications of Raul's people having the Prophecy. She had wondered if they could be the other Remnant. But the fact that not one of them other than Halen had ever acknowledged the Master had made her doubt such a conclusion. She had failed to take into consideration that the Prophecy stated they would forget Him, and she was saddened that they had. She was further saddened, and then outraged, at what Jemiah said next.

"It is an ancient myth, Esme," he said gravely, "long since known only to the few like me who preserve such trivia."

"Myth?" Esme repeated. "Trivia?" she added, indignant. "This is no myth, Jemiah, nor is it trivial! This is the hope and the purpose of the People, and when we arrive upon the Homeland, I will show you these words in their original language, not as they have been reproduced by some machine! Among mine, such *truth* has been passed down from generation to generation!"

Jemiah was excited. "Then you do recognize the words?" he asked.

"They have been written in my mind and engraved

upon my heart since my earliest childhood!" Esme declared. "I could not fail to recognize them."

Jemiah nodded, smiling with satisfaction. "Then, your planet, this Homeland, as you call it, must have been settled by one of the early colonization parties which somehow lost contact with Genesis. They must have had a copy of this myth and decided to use it as a basis to form a civilization. By the saints, it will be fascinating to see how they have evolved!"

Esme shook her head, her eyes stern. "We are not a colony of any other planet," she stated firmly. "We are the Homeland! It is you who came from us, not we who came from you!"

Jemiah shook his head in turn, his eyes kindly, but firm. "No, my dear, that is impossible," he said. "The planet which our ancesters called Earth and which spawned us all was devastated and made uninhabitable by war and ecological damage many thousands of years ago. It is no longer even known where in space it lays. If the saints hadn't foreseen what was going to happen and sent out the ship which eventually deposited our ancestors on Genesis, there would have been no humans left, and you and I would not be sitting here discussing the issue."

Esme was impatient with him and tapped a finger upon the pages of the Prophecy in front of her. "Does this not say that such would happen, but that the Master would preserve His Remnant in the valley he held back from destruction while He sent others elsewhere? The Settlement lies in such a valley, Jemiah, and all else upon the Homeland is desolate. I know. I have seen my planet from space."

"There is only the one habitable valley on your planet?" Jemiah broke in, his tone disbelieving.

"That is truth," Esme nodded.

"But it can't be!" Jemiah scoffed. "The population would long since have overrun it and overused the resources necessary to keep anyone alive!"

Esme shrugged. "Our population is stable and has been for years past counting," she said simply.

"But I thought Raul said you were a primitive people," Jemiah protested. "Too primitive to have developed birth control! So how do you explain this stability?"

Esme held out her hands in a gesture of ignorance. "I do not know," she admitted. "I only know that it is so. Each mating couple produces two children only, without use of this birth control you speak of and without denying themselves the use of one another. It is their duty to replace themselves, and that they do and no more." But then she had a thought and added, "Unless one of our high priests and some of the seekers opt for celibacy, that is. Then, it always happens that someone else opts for polygamy and the missing children are restored in that way."

And then she remembered her mother, and she frowned.

"Aha!" Jemiah seized upon her expression. "What are you thinking?"

"I was thinking that my own birth does not fit the norm for my people," Esme said. "You read in my journal, I am sure, that my mother was visited one night on the high meadow by a man who was not of the people, and I was born of their union."

Jemiah grimaced. "I am sure there was nothing mysterious about your conception, Esme," he said. "In a primitive society like yours, it is not surprising that no man came forth to claim responsibility for impregnating a woman everyone thought was a sorceress simply because she had green eyes." His tone denoted disgust at such thinking. "If your mother was as beautiful as you are, there must have been many men who were tempted by her, yet were afraid to own up to it, and one of them was your father."

Esme stared at him with level steadiness. "It is clear you know nothing of my people," she said quietly. "No man of them would have failed to claim me if he had fathered me. And anyway, if that had been so, my mother would have told me," she added. Then she gave a resigned sigh. Jemiah's expression told her he did not believe her, and she saw no sense in belaboring a point he could not accept until he had been among her people and seen the truth for himself.

"Who are these saints so many of you swear by?" she asked, changing the subject.

"I told you, the ones who got some survivors off Earth before it was destroyed." Jemiah shrugged then, seeing Esme's curiosity, he added, "They were not actually saints, Esme. Their descendants called them that because it was they who saved us all. Over time, people deified them. But in actuality, they were the scientists who had the knowledge to build the ship that took a small group of people off Earth in time to avoid destruction. In the group were men and women who controlled enough wealth to build and to supply the ship, and certain government officials who provided the secrecy needed to hide what was being done from the general population. Of course, none of the original saints was still alive by the time the ship found a suitable planet upon which to land. It was

113

their grandchildren who arrived upon Genesis."

"Genesis," Esme said the word, smiling at Jemiah in a telling way.

He waved a pudgy hand in dismissal. "The name is only a relic of one of the primitive religions that was once practiced upon the original Earth," he said, shrugging. "It was chosen because it was the name of the ship that brought the survivors' descendants to their new planet, and for no other reason. It only signifies a new beginning."

"I see," Esme said, her tone dry. "So it could not be that the Remnant resides upon the original Earth, and the Empire represents the other survivors the Master saved, and my people have nothing to offer yours? After all, we have been at peace among ourselves for centuries. You might want to learn how we have managed that."

"Don't be foolish, Esme." Jemiah smiled, kindly but with a superior air. "Though we in the Empire could certainly use something or someone who could bring us peace, I doubt that we will find that something or someone among your unsophisticated kind. You don't war because there aren't enough of you to do so, that's all. Even you, with your gifts, were unable to help us concerning the stealth ships."

Esme stared at him, suddenly astonished. For upon his mention of someone of her people who might bring peace, she remembered that portion of the Prophecy regarding one who would forge a link between the Master's two groups of survivors, and she realized that though she had not brought peace to the Empire and the Rebels, she *had* forged such a link.

She had thought about this matter once before and decided the Master wouldn't possibly use someone as lowly as she for something so important. But the facts were plain. He had and the realization of the role she had played in fulfilling the Prophecy imparted both a feeling of exaltation and of humbleness within her.

But was forging the link all she was to do? she wondered. Halen had said she, Esme, had a task to do for the Master. But surely that task was not of such a grave and grandiose nature as bringing peace to a galaxy-wide empire torn asunder. Surely, her next service to the Master would be something less exalted than that!

But Esme accepted that she would have no choice in the matter if the Master truly had something so awesome for her to do, and if it came to be that such a task was hers, she would try to fulfill it to the best of her ability. She could do naught else. But she could not yet believe that such a responsibility would come to rest on her shoulders, nor that she could carry it if it did. However, even the possibility of it made her feel heavily burdened and worried.

"I am tired now, Jemiah," she said quietly. "I would like a meal and then my bed. Will you please excuse me?"

Jemiah looked disappointed, but he reluctantly nodded. "May we speak of this again upon the morrow?" he asked as he stuffed the papers back into his carryall and then stood up.

"I suppose," Esme said wearily, "though I do not see why you wish to talk to me when you discount what I say."

Jemiah hesitated, then came around the table, and patted her shoulder. "I do not discount everything you say, Esme," he said gently. "Merely those things I know cannot be true. It is just that you have been reared on myths and I have long searched out truth. And while I would not wish to deprive you of your myths if they give you comfort, I cannot but speak the truth as it is and not as you would wish it to be."

Esme smiled faintly, almost bitterly. "You have no idea what I wish, Jemiah," she said softly. "Aside from my love for Raul, I am not sure I know myself. I am not sure of much of anything at this point."

"Of course, you are not." Jemiah nodded agreeably. "How could you be, growing up so ignorant and deprived? But your ignorance has already been very much alleviated, Esme, as has your deprivation. And as you continue among such people as myself and your captain, so will your knowledge grow."

"Will it?" Esme asked thoughtfully. "And even if it does, I do not desire knowledge so much as I desire wisdom. I have pondered more than once this question of the difference between knowledge and wisdom. And it seems to me that while your people have a great deal of sophisticated knowledge, your wisdom is deficient in many areas. Otherwise, why do you war against one another? And why do you no longer acknowledge the Master, who gives peace to those who do acknowledge Him?"

Jemiah said nothing, merely looked impatient with her, and Esme got up and escorted him to the door of the cabin. She was anxious to be free of his narrow-minded reliance upon his own small corner of the truth.

When he was gone, reiterating that he would be back after first-meal the following day, Esme leaned her back against the door of the cabin. She stared blankly into space, mulling over what her conversation with Jemiah had caused her to wonder. What would her role be in events to come? And whatever that role was, would she fail in it or succeed?

After a while, she whispered aloud that which lay heavy upon her heart.

"Master, I ask only one thing," she softly begged. "If You would use me and Raul, please do not separate us forever or even overlong for my peace of mind. I will obey You, yes. I will do whatever You ask. But please do not take from me that which has brought me the only joy I have ever known, and the lack of which will surely kill my desire to remain in the flesh."

Then, without ordering the meal which her stomach craved, she lay upon Raul's bed and cradled in her arms the pillow upon which he must have lain his head during previous journeys aboard the Talon. The sense of his presence gave her much comfort amidst her many fears.

CHAPTER SEVEN

SOME HOURS LATER, THE DEMANDS OF ESME'S HUNGRY stomach awakened her. She yawned and stretched and looked at the empty place beside her with forlorn disappointment. Raul had not yet sought his bed, nor her.

She was traversing the short distance between the bed and the sanitation chamber, when a sense of danger swamped her so strongly it buckled her knees and threw her body to the floor, even as her mind soared outside the ship of its own accord to face the threat.

When she arrived in the darkness outside the hull of the Talon, and had the rest of Raul's squadron in sight, she knew that this time, her powers could save no one. Nor could the added protection provided by Raul's squadron be of help. As far as her mind could see the limned shapes of the enemy stealth ships were too many to count. The missiles they commanded would come in such quantities she could not hope to turn all of them back.

She also sensed something else, but her urgent need to act left her no time to wonder about it. Instantly, she sent her mind to the control room of the Talon, where Raul sat relaxed in one of the launch couches.

Jump! she almost screamed into his mind. *Order the squadron to jump! The enemy is here and unseen and there are too many to fight!*

Raul did not even bother to question her assessment. He shouted one code word before his feet hit the deck of the control room, and just as quickly did his men obey it. His communications officer tapped a button that sent the code through an open channel to the other ships of Raul's squadron, while his navigation officer hastily set the jump controls.

"Go!" Raul roared, and the navigator started the jump before the echo of Raul's voice ceased reverberating around the chamber.

Esme's mind vaguely noted the streams of light on the view screen that meant the Talon was jumping, but most of her attention was elsewhere. Just before the jump, she had felt the collision of two of the stealth ship missiles into the hull of one of the other ships Raul commanded, and her mind still shuddered from the impact of the death screams she had heard.

Oh, Master, how many were killed? she wailed.

Her outraged grief made her forget to shield her thoughts from Raul, and he winced, then swung around to face the direction in the control room from which Esme's thoughts had seemed to emanate.

What is it, Esme? he asked.

Esme did not want to burden him, but it was his right to know. *One of your escort was hit,* she answered, her tone verging toward hysteria.

Just one? Raul's tone was quietly grim.

I do not know, Esme wailed. *I felt only the one, but—*

All right, little one, all right. Calm yourself. And now Raul's voice held a soothing quality overlying the grimness. *Be silent now,* he added. *We will know soon enough how many we have lost.*

But once the ship had settled into another portion of the vastness of the universe, there was little time to assess damages. Raul had just ascertained that one of his ships hadn't made the jump with the Talon when Esme, incredulous, detected that they had been followed.

The Rebels have followed us! she cried. *Raul, they are coming!*

After two more jumps, Esme felt as though she had stumbled into a nightmare. Each time the Talon and its escort jumped, the stealth ships followed and inflicted damage. The squadron had lost six ships by the time Raul, in the middle of another jump, his face a terrible mask covering his inner rage, sought Esme's mind.

This should not be happening, Esme! he said harshly. *They are fixing upon us in a way they should not be able to. Can you tell me how?*

Esme, confused and frightened, sought the inner calm she needed to think. *Give me a moment, Raul,* she begged.

By the saints, Esme, we have no more moments to spare! he declared angrily. But then he held his silence and merely stood, feet planted apart in the middle of the control room, his expression terrible to contemplate.

Esme raced through a mind-clearing exercise she had learned at the Institute and used the resulting calm to focus her thoughts. The answer, when it came, was so simple, and so devastating, she felt numb with despair.

It is Laon, she whispered. *He tracks* me.

What can we do to stop him? Raul was more interested in a solution than an explanation.

They were settling into the clear again, and Esme knew she had only moments to find an answer to Raul's question. It took only that long before the stealth ships followed them from jump to jump.

I must go into his ship, she finally said, *and kill him.*

Raul's head jerked up. *No!* he thundered and then, more calmly, he added, *It is out of the question. The danger is too great. Laon might somehow prevent you from getting back here. In any case, by the time you had accomplished your task, the rest of us would most likely be blown into atoms, because I would not jump again until you returned. I doubt even your powers would help you to find us again if I did.*

To Esme's despair, Raul meant it, and it would take precious moments to convince him to change his mind, moments she did not have.

Raul, I must defy your order to stay, she said urgently. *There is no other way than for me to go to Laon's ship. And you must not wait for my return. You must go ahead and jump again! Perhaps I can track you, as Laon has been tracking me. Nevertheless, I can stop Laon from tracking and killing you and your men, and I must do so!*

Esme, no! Raul ordered again as he sensed her about to leave him.

Call me strongly, Raul, Esme begged. *Give me what*

I need to track you . . . But there was no time to say more. She sensed the first of the stealth ships, undoubtedly the one which carried Laon, entering their area of space, and she was gone without even taking time for farewells.

Raul had seldom fallen victim to a choice as painful as the one he had to make then. If Esme could not track him, he would lose her. But if he failed to jump, his men might die.

"What are the coordinates for the next jump?" he demanded of his navigator, who quickly rattled them off. As he did, Raul sent them to Esme, and very, very faintly, felt her abstracted acknowledgment. Then he said what he had to. "Go," he ordered his navigator. "Jump!"

And a second later, they were away, with only Esme's vacant body lying in Raul's cabin accompanying them.

Esme had only an instant to seal the coordinates Raul gave her behind the special shield she had constructed while at the Institute. Then Laon became aware of her presence and their minds clashed boldly across the width of the Rebel stealth ship's control cabin.

Laon sat at the navigator's position, his hand resting upon the jump lever. *I wondered when you would figure things out*, he snarled mentally. *What took you so long*?

"Laon!" The captain of the Rebel ship called out, his tone impatient. "They have jumped again. What are you waiting for? Follow them!"

"Not yet, Captain Ivvor," Laon said abstractedly. His eyes were turned inward as he tried to catch what Esme's mind was up to. She was employing some shield he hadn't known she possessed!

As Esme resisted Laon's violent probe, she was dismayed to discover within her an unexpected reluctance to kill him. Furthermore, she knew she had to do more than kill him. She had to also find some way to neutralize the Rebel force because if she did not rejoin Raul, he would come looking for her, and would again put himself and his men in danger. So ignoring Laon for the moment, she searched the minds of the Rebel captain and his crew, seeking information that would help disable them.

"What do you mean, not yet?" the captain roared. "Do you expect them to wait tamely for us to catch up? We've almost got them, man! Hurry!"

"I assure you they will wait for us," Laon said with grim distraction. Though he couldn't detect what Esme was doing from reading her mind, he deducted the truth and he shouted aloud, "Shield your mind, Captain! Everyone, shield!"

"What?" The captain, confused, took a moment to obey Laon, as did the crew, and it was in that moment that Esme decided what to do.

"Just do it, you lowly son of a dirt farmer!" Laon roared. "Esme is here with us! She is searching your mind and everyone else's!"

The captain looked around him, even more confused at seeing nothing, but he at last obeyed Laon and put up his mental shield.

Esme was now uninterested in what else the captain's mind held, nor did she care what his crew thought. She was occupied in deciding how to force Laon to use the knowledge she had already obtained in her interest. To that end, she allowed her mind to meet Laon's directly again.

He was now on his feet, staring at nothing, and though it was clear to the captain and his men that Laon was engaged in a silent battle, it was no battle they understood or could help him with. So they merely sat or stood where they were, their eyes locked on Laon. Only the voice of the communications officer, who was busily trying to answer the confused calls of the rest of the Rebel squadron as to why they had stopped, echoed softly in the confines of the control room.

Coming here may help your lover and his men temporarily, Esme, but it will not save them ultimately, and it will surely kill you, Laon snarled. *Raul is gone, jumped to safety like the coward he is. Thus, your mind cannot return to your body. It is only the bond of Daccall you and I forged between us that allowed me to track you, and you cannot track Raul in the same way because you and he have undergone no such ritual. You had not when you came to me, and I do not see it in your mind now. So what do you hope to accomplish here other than a delay of Raul's death and your own certain demise?*

You see only what I allow you to see, Laon, Esme replied, keeping the combined revulsion and attraction she felt for him tucked safely behind her shield. She spoke in a calm, flat tone that showed no emotion, only absolute confidence.

True enough, he allowed, his voice confident and insinuating for all the uncertainty Esme sensed he was feeling. *But had you brought your body along with you on this visit, I would soon prove to you the truth of what we formed together during Daccall.*

But I did not, and you will prove nothing to me,

Laon, other than that my powers are superior to yours, she answered with surety.

And how will you do that? he sneered. *If you think you can control me, think again! I have a shield of my own that once before proved sufficient to withstand that powerful mind of yours, remember?*

Laon, I will tell you only this, Esme said, tightening her voice into a weapon. *It is true that upon our last meeting, I allowed you to keep your shield impenetrable. To have done otherwise would have killed you, and I did not then want to do that. But this situation is different, and I am not reluctant to do it now, Laon. You will do as I say or I will smash your mind into the separate atoms of which it is composed.*

Laon's face paled, but he did not give in. *I do not believe you,* he said flatly. *You cannot kill me. We have shared Daccall. And in any case, should you do such a thing, it would gain you nothing. The navigation lever is keyed to my hand. No other can use it. If you kill me, no one on this ship will go anywhere again. We will float, indefinitely, right where we are.*

Esme sighed. *I am not as ignorant as I once was, Laon,* she said chidingly. *Think you that I am unaware that these on this ship can transfer to their sister ships?*

Laon looked disconcerted for a moment. Then he shrugged, both mentally and physically. *But you still cannot follow Raul,* he reminded her, his voice silken with malicious satisfaction.

Can I not? Esme said calmly, and an instant later, she locked Laon's flesh in a vise so that he could not move or speak aloud.

Laon's face would have reflected the astonishment

125

he was feeling had Esme allowed him that much freedom of movement, but she did not. She also ignored his mind's protests and threats as she removed part of her attention from him and turned it on the captain.

The captain, his inadequate shield disposed of with one deft blow from Esme's mind, suddenly looked as astonished as Laon could not.

"Send your other ships away, back to their base," Esme ordered, applying enough pressure to the captain's mind to cause him to break out into a sweat and clench his muscles in pain.

The captain was a brave man, however. "I will not!" he gasped aloud, causing his men to switch their fearful, amazed attention from Laon, who stood frozen and unmoving, the expression in his dark eyes frantic with rage, to their captain, who was obviously in a great deal of pain.

Aware that the captain could not be moved on his own behalf, Esme switched tactics. *Very well*, she said, making her mental voice harsh and unyielding, *then I will demonstrate what will happen to your men as a result of your foolishness. Which of these men do you wish me to kill first, Captain? Tell me whom you will sacrifice to your misguided idea of bravery and duty and I will smash his mind into a million separate particles.*

At her words, the captain, unable to help himself, unwillingly provided her with an answer to a question more important to Esme's purposes. He thought not of whom he would sacrifice, but of whom he would most wish to save if he could.

Ah, Esme said, satisfied. *I see. All right. Now watch, Captain. Watch as I destroy the mind of your son, the one whom you helped create and who bears that resemblance to you of which you have always been so proud.*

Abruptly, she left the captain's mind, and his whole body sagged in relief at feeling her absence. But his muscles immediately tensed again as he saw the handsome young man for whom he had such love and such high hopes, stiffen in his chair, while his face contorted in pain.

"Stop!" he roared, and Esme, who disliked intensely what she had been forced to do, immediately released the pressure she had been exerting upon the captain's son's mind. The young man slumped in his chair and clutched his head against the pounding ache Esme's attack had left in its wake.

"I . . . I will do it," the captain spoke into the air, and his crew, turning their heads from side to side, seeking vainly to sense or see the presence of the woman all had heard of, eyed him warily. "Gorgson, order the rest of the ships home!" the captain ordered, his voice a snarl of resentful frustration.

"But . . . but, Captain . . . we are upon the point of success," Gorgson said, daring to question his captain's order. "We almost have them—"

"And she has got us!" the captain roared at his subordinate, making the dark-haired man jerk back in his chair in a startled manner. "Did you see what she did to my son?" Ivvor snarled at his crew, turning his fierce gaze upon each of the men in turn. "She was going to destroy his mind! Tell them, son!" he ordered his boy. "Tell them what you felt just now!"

The slender, youthful brown-haired captain's son, raised his head, and his gray eyes stared disbelievingly around him at the others. "My head felt as if it were in

127

a vise," he stammered. "My eyes blurred . . . I could not see. And my head aches now as though someone had slammed it with a pounding tool."

"And she can do the same to any of us!" the captain bit out, his eyes the color of the storm clouds that roiled often with thunder upon his home world. He glanced contemptuously at Laon, who was still frozen in place, still babbling mental threats at Esme, though no one else was aware of what his mind held. "Obviously, that one cannot help us," the captain sneered. "So we will do as this woman says and send the rest of the ships home. Contact them now, Gorgson, and relay the fact that I will brook no challenge or question to the order."

Gorgson, convinced now, did as he was told, cutting off one by one the protests that echoed in the room through the communicator.

Esme stayed quiet until the last ship had acknowledged the order, at least verbally. Then she said to the captain, wryly, *Forgive my lack of trust in you, Captain, but I think I will check to see that some secret word of Gorgson's did not alert these other ships to pretend to obey.*

With that, she abruptly released Laon from the hold she had on him, and he collapsed just as abruptly onto the deck of the control room, where he lay, panting and wretched, trying to regain control of his limbs.

Esme soared outside the Rebel ship, searching for its companions, and she stayed there as each jumped out of sight, leaving only the command ship behind. Then she came back into the ship and into the captain's mind. Laon still lay where she'd dropped him, and upon checking, she saw that he was still incapable of full control of his own body.

Is it true, she asked, *that only Laon can control the jump lever?*

It is true, the captain said, his voice flat and cold.

Then I suggest you order him to do so to my specifications, Esme ordered.

I cannot. The captain shook his head. *Laon is only nominally under my control. He will do as he wishes and I cannot stop him.*

Esme sighed. She knew the captain spoke the truth. But before she tackled Laon, she made another request of the captain.

Demonstrate for me, she said softly, *the sequence which turns on and off the stealth mechanism of this ship.*

She felt his mind begin to close up in protest and she stopped the movement. *Do not be absurd, Captain,* she said, her patience fraying. *I already have the sequence from your mind. I want it demonstrated only so as not to waste my time performing unfamiliar actions. Now do it!*

The captain, grudgingly but thoroughly, obeyed, as did his men. They first turned off the mechanism, and Esme, upon darting outside for a quick look, saw the skin of the ship revealed. Then they turned it on, as she ordered them to do from outside the ship, and the sleek skin of the ship began to waver and then to disappear, until there was only that limned shape of energy that could not be concealed from anyone of Esme's abilities.

When Esme was sure that she had the whole process committed to memory, she ordered the captain to turn the mechanism off again, and when she was certain the ship lay revealed as completely as would the Talon when they jumped to join it, she then turned her attention upon Laon again.

Get up! she ordered him.

Laon, his eyes burning with frustration, tried to comply, but in the end, Esme had to support him. She put him in the chair which he had occupied when she had first arrived upon the Rebel ship.

Laon, I will no longer dally with you, she said firmly. *If you wish to die without chance of retaliation, choose so now. If I do not appear where Raul is soon, he will return for me, and I, after rendering this ship inoperative, will join him and my body on the Talon. Then we will blast this ship out of space.*

You are lying! Laon spat, still defiant. *You might risk everything for him, Esme, but the man you love will not risk his men's lives by coming back here for you, of that I am certain.*

Esme was afraid Laon was right, just as she was afraid he was right that she could not track Raul across space. More important, she could see that Laon was convinced he was right and therefore would not budge.

Then, she said simply, *I must destroy your mind and this ship as well and then attempt to track Raul as you did me. I have never tried it before, and it may not work. But then I had not tried many things before I fell into your hands and discovered my powers extend farther than I ever realized.* She then showed him a few of the things she had learned at his hands, and she could tell the viewing shook him. *Think about it, Laon. Are you certain I cannot reach where I set out to go?*

She saw he was now uncertain where before he had been convinced. She only hoped he was uncertain enough not to want to put the matter to the test. And as she watched him, she knew the instant when Laon, though he hated his weakness, was ready to listen further.

On the other hand, she said reasonably, *if you jump to join Raul, it will save me time and effort, and I will keep him from killing you and this ship. You will be taken prisoner, but you will live. And a man of your abilities can surely find some way to turn his hand to more than mere survival,* she added with dry appreciation of his considerable talents.

As she had hoped it would, her proposal found acceptance with Laon. He was always a man who would take a chance rather than choose his own death and thereby cause the end of his ambition and hopes. He liked his own life too well to spend it unnecessarily, and his confidence in his ability to wring a victory upon another day was only dented, not destroyed.

Very well, he said, his tone sullen and harsh. *Give me the coordinates.*

One moment, Laon, Esme said softly. *Do not think to try to trick me. I can kill quickly, and I will not hesitate if you threaten either me or Raul or any of his. Do not mistake me, Laon. Please, for your own sake, do not mistake my intention.*

But though Esme knew she would do as she had said she would if it became absolutely necessary, she was also aware that she was still ambivalent about killing Laon, a lingering result of the Daccall ritual they had shared. She only hoped she was hiding that ambivalence from Laon well enough to fool him.

I do not mistake you, he said surlily when she was done. *Now give me the coordinates. I would rather be at the mercy even of your cowardly captain than subject any longer to your control.*

Esme was surprised by his statement. *You think I will release you to try your talents upon Raul?* she asked, scoffing.

I think you will do exactly as he tells you, he said with soft malice, *for fear of losing his regard which means so much to you. And I am certain that his overweaning ego will insist you give me to him for return to Genesis so that he can garner the glory of your actions.*

He paused, and Esme let him see her contempt for his deductions. Then he smiled, his black eyes glittering with bitter amusement.

Think you I did not pick from your mind during Daccall the nature of the relationship you share with Raul? He laughed, a low, harsh sound that grated in Esme's mind. *You would have been better off accepting my offer of mating, Esme. At least, I would not have insisted you obey my every order like a puppet as your captain does. I would not have threatened you with the implied loss of my regard as he has. I would have accepted you, and valued you, for what you are. Your captain cannot. He insists upon controlling you because he fears you and does not truly understand or like your gifts. And one day, if you overstep his sense of fitness, he will cast you aside, or you, tiring of his tyranny, will cast him aside instead. Either way, Esme, you will be left alone, and now that you have experienced the full joy of mating companionship, you will not be able to do without it. And there is no one in the entire universe who will then be as acceptable a mate for you as me.*

Do not count too much on that happening, Laon, Esme said with dry dismissal.

Laon laughed again, maliciously. *Ah, but I do count*

on it, Esme, he said, uncowed and unrepentant. *But I will not be such a fool as to be as gentle with you then as I would have been had you accepted my first offer. I will take a leaf from your captain's book then, but my tyranny will be of a different sort, and you will revel in it rather than cast me aside. To whom would you go if you lost me? What man would dare mate with a woman who can blast his mind over some minor disagreement or other? No one but me, Esme. No one but me.*

Enough, Laon! Esme said, impatient with his demented dreamings. *I would be off. We have wasted enough time.* And she put into his mind the coordinates Raul had given her.

Without another word, Laon turned and punched them in, then operated the jump lever. Within another few seconds, the Rebel ship arrived in the portion of space where Raul and the remainder of his squadron waited.

As Raul's ship and his squadron were on their way to surround the Rebel ship, Esme felt the familiar fatigue that accompanied such an effort as she had exerted over the past hours creeping up on her, dimming her mind's power. But it had to last a little longer, she knew, and she called Raul with part of her remaining strength.

Come to me! he ordered in response to her call, his tone furious.

When you have docked the Talon beside this ship, I will come to you, Esme said, making her tone gentle in order not to anger him further. *I must not leave Laon yet or he will be up to mischief again. Ask Thorson to bring along a strong sedative when you join us. It is the only way I know of to control Laon.*

Raul did not bother to answer, and when Esme stopped waiting for his reply and glanced at Laon, she saw upon his handsome face a look of amused, contemptuous knowledge she would have given much to deny him.

He is very angry with you, is he not? Laon drawled. *Ah, I see,* he added, at picking from Esme's fatigued mind the knowledge of how she had defied Raul to come to capture the Rebel ship. *Poor Esme,* he mocked. *Damned if you do and damned if you do not. And you are not even given any appreciation for your efforts as a reward from he whom you would please above all others.*

Cease this, Laon, Esme snarled, her tiredness thinning her patience almost past control. *I know what you would do, and it will not work. You will not succeed in driving a wedge between Raul and me. I will not allow it!*

Oh, you might not, Laon chuckled nastily. *At least, not yet. But I wonder if Raul will cling as stubbornly to such a determination. You have already cost him much, you know, in the tender of pride and ego, and he may one day start wondering if you are worth it.*

Esme abruptly turned away from Laon and surveyed the crew of the Rebel ship, who were nervously fondling their hip weapons as they watched on their view screens the approach of Raul's ships.

Do not even think it, she said grimly, broadcasting her message firmly into all their minds. *Captain, inform those of your crew who are not here in the control cabin that they are to surrender quietly and make no resistance when Raul's crew boards us. Meanwhile, all of you, remove your weapons and place them over in the far corner behind the cabin door.*

Sullenly, reluctantly, the captain of the rebel ship and his crew obeyed her. When all was accomplished, Esme heard Laon's nasty chuckle in her mind's ear again.

You do not know much about men, do you, Esme? he asked in a pleasant, conversational tone. *At least, not the sort of men who make death their occupation. These men,* and though he spoke to her silently, he gestured with his head to indicate the Rebel captain and crew, *if they should ever have the chance, will kill you without a moment's hesitation and even less regret. You have humiliated them, Esme, beyond forgiveness.*

Esme did not bother to reply. She was by now exerting all her strength to conceal from Laon how hard it was to maintain her presence here until Raul's arrival, while her body's call grew ever stronger. That portion of her which could not survive without her mind and spirit was frightened. And her mind and spirit were frightened as well. Should her strength give out before she was able to slip back into her body, she was not certain the union would ever again be possible.

At last, when she was becoming terrified over the delay, the control cabin door slid open and Raul stood there, holding a hand laser, his ice-blue eyes as cold as death. Some of his men crowded in behind him.

Esme? His mind called her, its tone harsh.

But Esme was already soaring back to her body in the adjoining Talon, and all she could manage in reply was a faint, weak reassurance.

I live, Raul, but I am weak and cannot stay. Seek me later in your cabin.

Raul's concern was only slightly diminished by Esme's reassurance. But his anger was further stirred by her abrupt departure and the deafening silence of her absence, and he had no choice but to accept his duty and secure the enemy ship which she had brought into his hands.

Before he could take Captain Ivvor's formal surrender, however, Laon startled everyone, Empire and Rebel warriors alike, by filling the cabin with the sounds of his triumphant, excited laughter.

But the laughter stopped, abruptly, when Raul slowly turned his head and fixed a stare upon Laon that made the Rebel warriors fear their comrade was not going to be given the option of surrender. After a long, silent moment, however, during which Laon's black eyes opened wider and wider, and his expression of triumph faded to one akin to terror, Raul broke his stare and turned unhurriedly back to the Rebel captain.

"Ivvor," he acknowledged his peer with a nod and an impassive look.

"Raul." Ivvor nodded back, his expression grim.

"I had thought that if we ever fought again," Raul said quietly, "it would be as in the old days as companions, not enemies."

Ivvor shrugged, his gray eyes bleak. "Life does indeed take strange twists," he said just as quietly.

Then Ivvor lifted his head and adopted a proud, stern expression. He straightened his shoulders and stood at attention, waiting for Raul to address him with the formal demand for surrender.

"Captain Ivvor, in the name of the Empire," Raul said, quiet and sure, "I claim your ship and demand the surrender of you and your men."

"Let it be so," Ivvor replied, his voice as steady as his gaze.

136

CHAPTER EIGHT

It TOOK SEVERAL HOURS FOR RAUL TO ARRANGE THINGS SO that the journey could resume. He left most of Ivvor's men at their posts aboard their own ship, but placed them under the guard and supervision of his own crew. Ivvor, he took aboard the Talon and placed under guard.

To the Rebel crew's astonishment, since they had not thought Laon would give up his trump card, Raul took Laon aboard the Talon after forcing him—by some means which no one understood—to unlock the navigation and jump levers of the Rebel ship, so making them operative again. Laon remained under Thorson's gruff care, drugged to a safe level.

By the time Raul started toward his cabin to have a long-delayed confrontation with Esme, he was forced by his near total fatigue to stop by sick bay himself and get a few stimulant tablets. He did not take them right away, however. His impatience to make a few things clear to Esme was too great, and he did not want the drug in his system when he did so for fear it might work too strongly upon his already formidably aroused temper.

"Keep him under until I tell you differently," he said to Thorson, giving Laon's flaccid, drugged body a cold and deadly look.

"That I will," Thorson answered, glancing at his patient in a way that Laon, had he seen it, would have known that this particular medic did not hold Laon's best interests at heart.

Had Esme been awake to see the expression on Raul's face when he crossed the threshhold of the cabin, she might well have sent herself into a self-induced catatonic state. But she still lay on the floor in the same position she had fallen into upon first sensing danger, and she was far from recovered from the tremendous exertions she had endured during the past few hours.

Raul did not see her at first, and upon finding his bed empty, his thunderous expression clouded further. But as he headed toward the sanitation chamber to see if she was there, he almost stumbled over her body, and as he quickly knelt beside her, his expression turned like lightning to one of fear and concern.

Lifting her in his arms, he carried her to the bed, but he did not call Thorson. Instead, he performed an examination of his own, and when he saw that her pulse was steady and her sleep seemingly normal, if exceptionally heavy, he let out a shaky breath of relief.

Moments later, his sweat-drenched bodysuit as well as the stimulants he'd gotten from Thorson set aside, he lay beside Esme, cradling her in his arms, his eyes

138

closed against his own exhaustion. But before he slept, he muttered a few of the words he had to say to her that couldn't wait even for her ears to hear.

"Esme . . . Esme . . . " he said heavily. "You must learn to trust and obey me if not as your mate, then certainly as the captain of this ship which carries you home."

And then, he finally admitted to himself that his anger at her earlier disobedience was as much from his fear for her safety as it was from his accustomed and necessary expectation that his orders would be obeyed immediately and unquestioningly, especially under battle conditions. He also finally accepted that his reaction had perhaps been overly harsh.

He also had to consider the fact that Esme did not as yet have certain information concerning him that might, when she learned of it, make a difference in her future willingness to grant him the obedience and trust he required from her. He had been waiting to test himself before informing her of the changes he had undergone during his last tour of duty in space, where the lack of battle activity had given him much free time for study and practice.

Raul smiled, with weary triumph, as he reflected that his recent confrontation with Laon had satisfied the test he had set himself.

"When we wake, little one," he mumbled against Esme's temple, "I will show you a thing or two." Then he pressed his lips against her warm skin before allowing his body and mind the rest they craved.

A few hours later, Esme came slowly awake, feeling a contentment which made her smile. When she fully awakened, her smile widened as she realized the source of her contentment. She lay spooned into the curve of Raul's body, her buttocks against his loins, and his arm imprisoned her against him with a possessiveness he displayed even in his sleep.

For a long while, Esme didn't stir as she went over in her mind the events that had occurred during her last waking. On the whole, she was satisfied with her performance. But she knew that Raul had not been pleased with her when he had at last appeared upon the Rebel ship, and his displeasure saddened and frustrated her.

While she was not prepared to admit that Laon's assessment of the relationship she shared with Raul was totally accurate, she did have to admit that Raul's insistence upon her obedience to his orders caused her some inner turmoil. She had no problem submitting to him in bed, of course. She had long since learned the secret joy of allowing him to dominate her there. And under normal circumstances, she would never have challenged his authority aboard his ship.

The situation that had existed before she last slept, however, had not been normal. And Raul had asked for her help. Why, then, did he resent her taking the small liberty of deciding *how* she would help?

Raul stirred, mumbled in his sleep, then removed his arm from around her and turned onto his back, freeing Esme to move if she wished. But she did not move, though her mind and body wanted fiercely to turn and press up against Raul, and thus regain the warmth and strength she received from him. Without that contact, she felt cold and bereft and alone. But those feelings stirred her fear that Laon had been right when he had said that she would do anything to keep from losing Raul's regard.

Would she? she wondered miserably. If Raul, upon waking, made her promise that she would never again defy his orders by doing what she considered necessary, would she make him such a promise? And if she did make such a promise, and kept it, would she come to resent him?

Raul's voice suddenly echoed from behind her, startling her.

"Those questions, nor your answers, need not trouble you much longer," he said, his tone dry.

Esme froze as her mind offered the most negative conclusion to his words.

Raul sighed aloud. "Esme, for one whose courage is, at times, awesome," he said rather impatiently, "you can be remarkably cowardly at other times, and with little reason. Now let us attend to ourselves, and when we are more comfortable, we will talk and see if we cannot ease your worries and the residue of my temper."

As he got up from the bed and strode naked to the sanitation chamber, he did not look at her. But Esme's eyes charted his progress, and the expression in their wide green depths was not sanguine.

When he returned to the bed, she remained silent, unable to meet his glance, and took her own turn at the sanitation chamber, but her mind chattered at her the whole time, expressing the worries that so tried Raul's patience.

When she returned, he was lying on his back, his hands behind his head. Esme settled herself crosslegged at his side, her head down, trying to still the turmoil in her mind.

At last he spoke. "I am not sure the benefits of my new talents outweigh the irritations," he said with wry

141

impatience. "If you cannot make your mind cease its chattering, Esme, then shield. Such female nonsense makes my head ache."

At that, Esme dared to look at him, and her green eyes were wide with curiosity as well as a certain amount of resentment. But she did calm herself and Raul nodded.

"That is better," he said, and his eyes upon her were clear and steady and held a considering look that was too objective for Esme's taste. But she held her mental tongue as well her physical one.

"Seek Laon with your mind," Raul invited calmly.

Esme was startled by Raul's unexpected request. But she obeyed, not knowing whether she would find Laon dead, or beaten into submission, or still filled with his brand of malevolent and spiteful courage and rebellion. But when she did locate Laon's mind, she was startled even more.

He was in the state between wakefulness and dreaming, and he was reluctant to wake fully for the simple reason that he feared to face Raul again! Fascination followed Esme's initial reaction of disbelief, as she picked from Laon's mind the nature of the silent confrontation that had occurred between Raul and Laon aboard the Rebel ship.

"You would truly have killed him?" she whispered aloud, her eyes on Raul's calm expression.

"Without hesitation and without compunction," Raul answered, his tone level and assured. "I might still do it if he gives me the least trouble."

"He is aware of it," Esme said, her tone wondering. "He fears you as I have never seen Laon fear anyone else. He did not fear me like that when I threatened him with death."

"Because he sensed your ambivalence, Esme." Raul shrugged, his eyes cool. "If you are going to threaten a man's life, you had better be serious about it if you want to be taken seriously. I meant my threat and Laon knew it."

Esme spread her hands. "But I did mean it," she protested.

"No, Esme, you did not," Raul said, his tone quiet. "When you have shared Daccall with a man, you *cannot* wish his destruction. Laon knows that better than you."

Esme stared at him, wanting to object but then she dropped her eyes to hide the dismayed shame and acceptance they held.

"You are not to blame, Esme," Raul said, reaching a hand to squeeze her bare thigh. "It is clear you still do not understand the nature of the bonds Daccall places upon its practitioners. Nor do you want to understand, do you?"

Esme shook her head. "I would," she said miserably, "if I could, erase from time what happened between Laon and myself. I do not want such a connection with him. I do not want such a connection with any man other than you."

"I know, Esme," Raul said, his voice husky and kind. "And in time, you will be free of Laon. But I would not erase from time what happened between the two of you."

Esme jerked her head up, her eyes brilliant with disbelieving shock.

"He would still be upon Genesis practicing his duplicity otherwise," Raul explained. "And in the long run, it is of no consequence."

"No consequence!" Esme flared at him.

"No consequence," Raul repeated, smiling. "Because when you and I go through Daccall, and you give me wholly what you only partially gave him, your connection to Laon will be severed."

Esme went still, her eyes widening with hope. "That is truth?" she whispered, her longing for it to be so in her voice.

"It is truth," Raul responded wryly. "And the fact that you had to have my words confirmed as truth rather than accepting them as so upon first hearing brings up the next question we have to discuss."

Esme quickly dropped her eyes again. But after a moment spent gathering her courage and her sense of justification in her own rightness, she proudly lifted her head, and the gaze that met Raul's was as steady as his.

"I did the only thing I could," she said firmly.

"No, Esme, you did not," Raul disputed, speaking more firmly than she had. "You acted precipitately. Had you waited only one moment more, I would have firmed the plan already forming in my mind and you would not have had to take the risk you did of not being able to return to the Talon. You most likely could not have returned in any case if I had not thought quickly enough to send you the coordinates of our next jump."

Esme nodded. "Thank the Master you did think quickly enough," she agreed, "for it is true that I am not sure if I could have found you again, using only my mind." Then she frowned. "What plan?" she asked, unable to keep her doubt from her tone.

Upon hearing that doubt in her voice, Raul's eyes turned to ice, and Esme, alarmed and shamed, hastily

144

offered an apology. "I am sorry, Raul," she said. "I only meant that when you asked me at the time what could be done, I assumed you had not been able to think of what action to take."

Raul softened, but not appreciably. "And when you left the Talon to go to the Rebel ship, was your plan wholly formed?" he asked, his voice hard.

Esme, upon thinking about it, had to admit to herself that she had had no clear idea of what she would do even after her arrival upon the Rebel ship. She had felt her way through the sequence of events that had resulted in eventual success.

Taking the thought from her mind, Raul nodded curtly. "Aye, but you had no more than left my presence when my plan was formed. Only it was too late to put it into effect, for you were already gone, and you were essential to its success. I knew I could not, given your stubborn insistence upon having your own way, explain to you the details quickly enough and wait for you to mull them over and graciously accept them, before we might be fired upon and destroyed, so I was forced to let things progress your way, not mine."

In her distress over the clipped sarcasm in Raul's last sentence, Esme could not meet his eyes.

Raul did not relent. "Are you interested in hearing what my plan was?" he asked.

Esme nodded.

"Had you stayed with me, where you belonged," Raul said coldly, "I would have had you fix upon Laon in your mind, and I would have taken that fix from you and directed my missiles thusly. Deprived of his help, the rest of the Rebel fleet would have been unable to follow when we jumped again. And we would not then be still troubled by that traitor's presence among us!"

The lethal tone in Raul's voice brought Esme's head up, and her expression clearly showed her dismay at having underestimated him. Her stricken shame and guilt at not having deducted sooner the importance of Laon's presence among the Rebels, and her resulting failure to discern how they had been able to follow the Talon and her sister ships from jump to jump, was also in her expression. If not for her stupidity, several of the Empire ships that had been destroyed, and the men who served on them, could have been saved!

"Oh, Raul!" she whispered, agonized. "If I had realized earlier than I did that Laon tracked us through me, you would then have thought of your plan in time to use it. All those men . . . their deaths are on my hands!" She burst into sobs of such intensity that Raul immediately sat up, reached for her, and cradled her in his lap.

In her hysterical grief and guilt, Esme fought him at first, thinking she was not worthy of his comfort. But Raul's hold on her would not be dislodged, and she subsided eventually, lying slumped in his arms, her tears wetting his bare chest, her sobs shaking her body.

Raul stroked and soothed and murmured comforting words for a while, until it became obvious that Esme could not be consoled—at least, not yet. Then he merely held her tightly until she was too drained and exhausted and numb to cry.

When he was sure she would listen to him, Raul took her chin in his large hand and tilted her face up to his. Esme's eyes were closed, and without asking, he used the power of his mind to open her lids.

Esme stared at him, unable for the moment to comprehend that what he had just done should not have been possible. Besides, she was distracted by the love and compassion she saw in his eyes. How could he look at her like that, she wondered dully, when she had been responsible for the loss of so many of his men?

"You were not responsible!" Raul told her fiercely. "The Rebels fired the missiles that destroyed those ships and killed my men!"

But Esme merely continued to regard him with dull, listless unacceptance.

Raul made an impatient noise through his teeth, then went into her mind so strongly that she had no choice but to give him her attention.

Esme, I have explored your mind at length, he grated, *and within it I have found the belief you hold in a Master Who controls your destiny. Could it not be His intent that things happened as they did? Perhaps we were supposed to take Laon captive rather than kill him.*

Esme frowned, half wanting to listen now, but also afraid she merely wanted so much to be absolved of guilt that she was prepared to accept unjustifiably what Raul was trying to tell her.

"It is likely there is a reason for everything that happened," Raul went on, speaking aloud and convincing himself now. "Certainly, we would not have a Rebel stealth ship to take back to Genesis for study had we done things my way. And do not mistake the value of such a prize, Esme. Our people can learn more from the construction of that one ship than they could by years of the type of study they are engaged upon now."

A slim ray of hope dawned in Esme's eyes, and Raul seized upon it.

"And if your belief that there is a spirit world that awaits all of us upon our deaths is correct—and even a great many of my own people, though they know not of this Master of yours, believe the same—then none of my men are truly lost, are they?"

"On–only from this life," Esme whispered.

"Aye," Raul nodded. "And consider this, Esme. If you persist in feeling as you do now, you negate the faith and belief you have had all of your life. You negate your Master's reality. Do you really want to do that?"

Esme shuddered and slipped her arms around Raul's neck. "No," she whispered faintly. "No . . . I would not lose Him. It is only that I am accustomed to thinking of Him in terms of his infinite love and mercy and kindness. It is hard to believe He would allow the sacrifice of so many just for one small ship or for some other reason we have not thought of."

Raul shrugged. "That one small ship may make the difference in the war, Esme," he said quietly. "Or if there is some other reason things happened as they did, perhaps it is equally important. And as to sacrifices, do you not believe my men have merely passed to another life?"

Esme didn't answer, but her growing acceptance was obvious.

"In any case, Esme," he said with quiet conviction, "those men were warriors, as I am. And those of us who adopt this warrior's life from conviction, accept all that goes with it, including the possibility of our own premature deaths. Death comes to all, but the savoring of life is not universal. It is for most of those in my calling, however. When you court death the way we do, the value of life is all the clearer and the living of it all the more sweet."

He let her close her eyes then, and as Esme blinked at the stinging sensation that resulted from having them open so long, it finally dawned on her what he had done, and she straightened and gazed at Raul in astonishment.

"Raul?" Her question was hesitant, testing.

His smile was almost jaunty. "Since you opened my eyes or rather my mind," he said with light mockery, "I have made much progress on this matter of using one's mind to the fullest." Then his smile turned to a grin. "Would you have a fuller demonstration?"

Esme, as wide-eyed and awestruck as a child, nodded eagerly. But she was truly not prepared for what happened next.

Suddenly, within the blink of an eye, after experiencing a sensation much like the one that she felt when the ship jumped, she and Raul were across the room. He stood by the dining table, still holding her in his arms.

Esme clung to Raul's neck and looked around her in disbelief. "It is not possible," she murmured in shock. "Even I cannot do that."

"Can you not?" Raul asked innocently, and when Esme looked up into his face, she saw the expression of a small boy, filled with mischief and unconscionably pleased with himself, in his clear blue eyes.

"No," she said in awe, shaking her head. "I cannot. I have tried before but the method escapes me."

Raul laughed and hugged her close, then set her on her feet and held her in front of him with his large hands on her small hips. "Then perhaps," he said, gravely teasing, "I will, at some time, instruct you in the proper method."

"But not now?" Esme was somewhat indignant. She craved immediately to know the secret Raul withheld from her.

"Not now," he said, amiably sly. "It affords me too much pleasure to know something you do not."

"Raul!" Esme stamped her foot and glared at him. "If it were not for me, you would not have found this secret on your own!"

He raised an eyebrow at her, his gaze mocking. "But I did find it on my own, Esme. You gave me the key, true, but I unlocked all the doors myself."

Esme opened her mouth to dispute his assertion, but then the truth of it hit her, and she sealed her lips again. But the gaze she fixed upon Raul was not friendly.

"I will tolerate no pouting," he warned, but she saw no real sternness in his eyes, so she did not change her expression.

Then Raul sobered. "I would have us work together from now on, Esme," he said seriously, "and not at cross purposes. But there is something you must realize before we can. There is also a certain amount of independence you must give up as must I."

The last three words eased Esme's resentment somewhat.

"What do you mean?" she asked, more curiosity than resentment in her voice now.

"I mean that in a battle situation, there can only be

150

one commander," Raul said, gravely stern. "And most times, because of my position and experience, I will command."

He studied Esme's reaction closely, and she thought he looked much relieved when she did not show by word, gesture, or thought that she resented what he had just said.

"At other times, if your expertise is more called for than my own, I will accept your lead," he went on quietly. "But I will be consulted henceforth before you act, Esme. We will agree together, if there is time for consultation, upon the best course to take. But if there is no time for such consultation, you will obey me as my men do. It can be no other way on a battleship, or in battle. Otherwise, there is only confusion, which could result in disaster."

He paused, again studying Esme's reaction. Then he asked the question she had feared, upon first waking, that he would ask. Now, however, she no longer feared hearing it, nor did she resent the response she would give.

"Though I will try not to misuse my authority over you, I would have your promise of loyalty and trust, Esme," Raul said, his voice formal and grave. "I cannot have you setting an example for my men that may one day result in disaster for all of us. I ask you to give me, freely and willingly, the same oath I require of the rest of those who serve me, the same oath I myself gave to those who hold authority over me."

Esme, feeling as though a great burden had been lifted from her shoulders, sighed and nodded.

"I give you that oath, freely and willingly," she responded with soft sincerity, but as she felt Raul's pleasure and relief come over her in a strong wave, she knew she had to make clear to him the one condition she could not abrogate. "Only will I put that which I owe my Creator and Master before what I owe you," she said, her tone regretful but firm.

Much to her relief, Raul accepted the condition. "I am not so sure as I once was that any of us are free of that particular obligation, Esme," he said quietly as he pulled her into his arms and rested his cheek against her hair. "I could not believe in the deity of the saints, as most of my fellows do," he admitted. "But what I have seen in your mind concerning the one you call Master calls forth more response within me. It remains to be seen whether I will ever accept Him as totally as you do, but since meeting you, I have learned there is a great deal more possible than I had ever thought to be the case."

Esme smiled, her contentment full and running over again.

"And now," Raul whispered, raising his head and bending to lift her into his arms again. "Duty comes stalking, but it has not yet knocked upon our door today. Until it does, I would have an oasis of pleasure to sustain me through its next demands."

He carried her to the bed and put her down, then came down atop her.

"It has been my experience," he murmured against her willing mouth, "that danger averted adds spice to loving."

"And it has been my experience," Esme whispered back, "that the spice in our loving is never lacking no matter what the circumstances."

"Hold that belief," Raul said, his smile slanting and wicked, "and let us see who is right."

"I think we are both right . . ." was all Esme had the chance to say in reply before Raul's mouth covered hers.

But the things she said to Raul thereafter, and the things he said to her, would lie treasured in both their hearts and minds from that day on.

CHAPTER NINE

WHEN RAUL INFORMED HER THAT HE WOULD INVITE Jemiah and Ivvor to have last-meal with them in the cabin, Esme doubted the success of the occasion would be great. Ivvor, she thought, had he any choice in the matter, would most likely rather dine with an asp than the woman who had humiliated him in front of his men. And Jemiah would most likely try Raul's and Ivvor's patience with his incessant chattering about matters in which the two warriors likely had no interest.

She said nothing to Raul about her doubts, however. Harmony between them had been restored by their talk and their loving, and she had no desire to spoil it by arguing about such a minor matter.

When Raul, Ivvor, and Jemiah arrived at the cabin for the meal, Esme politely stayed out of their minds, but then she didn't need such help to discern what each man was thinking. Jemiah's desire to resume his much postponed talk with her had him quivering. Only his wary respect for Raul kept him silent past the first pleasantries of greeting.

On the other hand, it was clear that Ivvor had nothing he cared to say and would like nothing better than to get the meal over with and be remanded to his guard again. His rugged face bore a stern, almost surly, expression.

Raul, whom Esme had never seen play host before other than to herself and Thorson, was so smoothly gracious and urbane that Esme blinked at him, regarding him almost as a stranger at first. She hoped, rather resentfully, that her manners had improved to the point where she did not embarrass him.

But as the four of them sat at table and satisfied the first pangs of hunger, she was grateful for Raul's ability to put the rest of them at ease. But when he started reminiscing about his and Ivvor's younger days together at the Military Space Academy, she was fearful Ivvor would react negatively. Instead, he began to thaw, and finally even to smile.

"Those were good days," he agreed, somewhat sadly, after Raul had finished telling a story about a prank the two of them had perpetrated on a rather prissy and proper fellow student.

"Aye." Raul nodded, but something in his voice and eyes alerted Esme that the conversation was about to take a different, more serious, turn. "In those days," he went on, "had anyone told me that you would one day turn Rebel, I would never have believed it."

The substantial muscles in Ivvor's thick arms immediately tensed, and his jaw firmed. But when he met Raul's steady gaze, the look in Ivvor's gray eyes did not falter, nor did it bear any shame.

"In those days," he said quietly, "I would not have believed it either. But I have traveled far and learned much since that time. Enough to see that the council grows ever more tyrannical and exploitive against the weaker members of the Empire. They have forgotten, it seems to me, the democratic dictum upon which the Empire rests."

Jemiah, Master Historian of the Empire, nodded his head and spoke up for the first time. "Of course, they have," he said reasonably. "It has ever been thus throughout our history. This is not the first civil war to tear us apart, nor will it likely be the last."

Raul and Ivvor looked at the little man, and to Esme's surprise, the two warriors viewed him with respectful attention.

"But the last war," Raul said quietly, "was the one which replaced Landor's dictatorship with our present democracy. And despite the Rebels' belief that they cannot accomplish the reforms they seek through the democratic process, I believe they are mistaken. I also believe," he added, returning his steady gaze to Ivvor, "they had a duty to try to do such much longer and harder than they did before they began killing their brothers and sisters."

Ivvor scowled, his temper rising. "What do you know of the injustices perpetrated against the weaker worlds?" he asked Raul scornfully. "You were born of an influential Genesian family, pampered and respected all your life. I was born on Holcroft, a world scorned by Genesis as nothing more than a breadbasket for their bottomless bellies. I grew up on the land that fed such pampered, sophisticated ones as you.

And if I had not shown potential to the recruiters when they deigned to visit my world looking for warriors, I would still be there, slaving from dawn to dusk as my parents did all their lives, and getting nothing in return but the privilege of retaining only enough of what I grew to keep on slaving."

It was a long speech for a man Esme was certain was not inclined to talk so lengthily, and when Ivvor fell silent, his skin was flushed with temper and his eyes sparked with indignation over the injustice of which he spoke.

Jemiah, rather than Raul, responded, speaking so matter-of-factly that it was impossible for anyone to take offense to his words. "Yes, there is no doubt that the stronger worlds of the Empire exploit the weaker. Those of us who make history our lives saw the cycle repeating itself and expected a Rebel faction to develop long before it actually did."

Raul spoke almost curtly. "I do not deny that such is the case. I merely point out that there are devices in place in the system to right such injustices without resorting to war against one another." He looked at Ivvor again, his gaze harsh. "You have access to the same information I do, Ivvor. You know what the probes have found in the Miian Galaxy. Should that alien race of reptiles come against us someday, we will have all the war we can handle. If we are already torn apart by our own petty squabbles, what chance will we have?"

Ivvor's jaw firmed and his eyes remained stubborn. "Those probes are not conclusive," he said curtly. "And even if the danger exists, it is likely far in the future. Meanwhile, we live our lives day to day and there are those who find that day-to-day life intolerable. When the Rebels win, there will be time to reform the Empire into a more just alliance, one that can meet any threat more successfully."

Esme felt Raul's impatience with Ivvor's thinking before he spoke. "The probes are not inconclusive enough to take the risk. The time frame may be shorter than any of us realize. And I repeat, the system already provides a process for redress of wrongs. Why do the Rebels not use it instead of killing their brothers and sisters?"

"We tried at first to work within the system," Ivvor retorted with sullen grimness, "and were foiled at every turn by those in power whose only wish is to cling to their own privileges. They delay and manipulate and spy and distort. It might take centuries to accomplish what we want their way. This way, as distasteful as it is, is much faster and therefore worth the cost."

He glared at Raul, and Esme sensed the turmoil within him, the pain his course had cost him.

"If you think I like killing my brothers and sisters," he said bitterly, "you are wrong! When the order came to seek and destroy you, I would rather have—" But he stopped before finishing what he had been about to say, and after a moment, added, less heatedly, but more grimly, "Following orders is not always easy. But you are a warrior as I am. You, as I, have always expected to die while at your duty. And you, no more than I, would destroy his conscience by abrogating his duty."

As he fell silent, Ivvor pushed his plate away almost violently. Then he sat back and folded his massive arms over his chest, and stared into space, his face set and unyielding.

A silence fell at the table, and in the face of the violent emotions which Esme felt emanating from both Ivvor and Raul, she dared not break it. She was much distressed.

Jemiah, however, speaking in a mildly contemplative way, seemed less cautious, casting his opinion into the atmosphere that had fallen between the two warriors. "It has always been thus," he sighed. Turning to Esme, he shrugged, blinking his blue eyes in which there was no hostility, only contemplation.

"You say you have not seen war upon your planet, Esme, but you have just seen the basic cause of it at this table. Here are two strong individuals who can agree only on the fact that change is needed. Those who control the Empire are not even willing to admit that much. Those who control the Rebels are not willing to exercise patience in attaining their goals. These two men"—he nodded at Raul and Ivvor, neither of whom was looking at Jemiah or at anything else as far as Esme could tell, but who were listening, for which she was glad—"cannot agree upon how to bring change about. Change is inevitable given human nature, Esme. It is even necessary. But when you have this kind of basic disagreement among strong men— and these two men stand as representatives in microcosm of their differing sides, men of action whose honor rests in defending their convictions— negotiation is seldom possible, and therefore change will come about in a violent fashion. Then it comes down, as it always has, not necessarily to which man, or which side, is right, but to which man, or which side, controls more strength and resources. It will be interesting to see the result of the present confrontation."

Jemiah's last sentence brought him a look of disgust from Ivvor. "Have you no personal concern then, Master Historian, which side wins?"

Jemiah took no offense from Ivvor's tone or his question. "No," he said mildly. "I cannot say that I do. I am accustomed to being an observer of history, not a participant in it except," he added, looking at Esme with a twinkle of anticipation in his eyes, "when it comes to the discovery of something entirely new, such as Esme, her planet, and her people's culture. Then I can get excited and be as involved as anyone."

Esme felt Ivvor's attention switch to her, and she wished Jemiah had not brought her into the discussion.

"Aye." Ivvor nodded, his gaze upon her hard and piercing. "I have had occasion to appreciate Esme's qualities."

He spoke drily, and Esme did not fool herself that he really did appreciate her qualities. But her pride would not permit her to avoid his gaze, and she returned his look steadily, though she allowed no personal hostility to taint her regard. Indeed, from what she had seen of Ivvor's character, she found him a man to admire. Also, she thought Raul's respect and his affection, muted though it now was, for his old friend and new enemy well justified.

Ivvor studied her for a long moment, then turned to Raul. "You are a lucky man," he growled perfunctorily.

"I am that," Raul acknowledged.

"Would that we had had her instead of that asp, Laon," Ivvor added with a snort of disgust.

Esme was relieved that, contrary to Laon's prediction, Ivvor seemed not to hate her. Perhaps Laon had been wrong also in predicting that she would obtain no forgiveness from Ivvor for her treatment of him and especially his son?

She set out to see if such was possible. Clearing her throat, she spoke for almost the first time since the meal had begun.

"Ivvor . . ." She spoke gently to get his attention. When his gray eyes rested upon her, she spoke sincerely. "What I did, I would like you to know I took no pleasure in it." She could tell nothing of his reaction from his impassive expression and she would not invade his privacy by taking it from his mind. "Especially," she added quietly, "did I take no pleasure in hurting your son."

Ivvor snorted then, and his voice was harsh. "Are you telling me you would not have killed him if I had not given in?"

Esme hesitated but she could not avoid the truth. "No, I do not tell you that," she said, quiet regret in her voice and eyes. "I would have killed him. It is merely that I did not wish to. He is a good man, a son to be proud of, as you are a good man, a father to be proud of."

She did not expect her words to find a place in Ivvor's heart. She had merely been expressing the truth. Therefore, she was much surprised when, after continuing to study her without any expression for a long moment, he suddenly smiled at her. He looked at Raul then, and the smile became a laugh.

"I repeat you are a lucky man," he said between chuckles.

Raul merely grinned back.

Esme was relieved, but confused. "Is it possible that you can forgive me what I did to your son, what I would have done?" she asked Ivvor in a puzzled fashion.

Ivvor sobered then and gave her a steady look. "My son is a warrior," he said simply. "And you, though you certainly do not have the appearance of one, are a warrior as well. You showed that by being willing to do what the situation called for, whether your actions were repugnant to you personally or not. I could not respect you had you done otherwise. Nor could I respect you had you taken pleasure in your power to kill. For my part, I would have let you kill my son had I thought it would result in victory for the rest of us. But it would not have, and it made no sense to continue fighting when we could not win. If the saints are kind, I will face you and Raul on the battlefield again one day. On that day, expect no mercy from me. Nor will I expect it from you."

Ivvor fell silent, but his words had shaken Esme. She decided Ivvor was wrong in terming her a warrior. She was not. In fact, she did not truly understand the breed. She could not imagine, should she one day be granted the privilege of bearing Raul a son, sacrificing him to duty as Ivvor had been ready to sacrifice his own son. The very idea appalled her.

She looked up and found Raul's eyes upon her, their expression comprehending. Then she heard his mind in hers, his tone gentle yet firm.

Do not condemn Ivvor, he said. *It might have broken him to do as he said he would have had it been necessary but he would have done it. And do not pretend I would not do the same. I would.*

Esme felt sick. *To our son?* she asked, unwilling to believe such of him.

Raul sighed. *If it were necessary*, he admitted, quietly but firmly.

Esme abruptly closed her mind to him then. Nor would she look at him for the remainder of the meal, which, for the most part, was conducted in silence.

Afterward, she accepted Jemiah's and Ivvor's farewells with only the barest minimum of her attention and she was glad when Raul left with them to conduct his evening rounds. She needed time to inspect the damage to her heart Raul had inflicted, time to see if repair were possible.

She had reached no conclusion by the time Raul returned to her. She had been too numbed to think clearly.

While he undressed, she was silent, verbally and mentally as was he. She was unresponsive when he then undressed her and held her in his arms upon the bed.

Then he leaned on one elbow, hovering intimidatingly over her, the expression on his face thunderous.

"And if your Master required *my* life, would you not give it?" he demanded harshly. "Why then do you condemn me for obeying my own master?"

"My Master cannot be gainsayed," she said, holding Raul's icy gaze, her own gaze coldly remote. "He is the Creator of us all. Our lives are His to use and spend as He sees fit."

Raul clenched his jaw. "If that is so, I do not yet see it," he replied grimly. "And if it comes to be that I one day meet this Master of yours, and He is all that you say He is, then will I grant Him the fealty you do. But until that time, I will grant such fealty only to that

163

ideal of loyalty and duty and the right of the many to prevail over the needs of any one person, even myself, even you, even those children we may one day have to love and protect, that I have served all my life!"

He paused, breathing hard, searching her eyes for something Esme didn't know whether she had within her to give. Then, more quietly, but with no less conviction, he added, "We are not at odds on the question that fealty must be granted to something, or someone, Esme, or that we have no choice but to give, should it be demanded of us in the interest of upholding a higher power than our own, what we hold dearest and would rather not give. What you do not seem to accept or understand is that if it ever came to that—if I had to give you, especially, or our children secondly, as a sacrifice to higher duty—I would do what I had to and then join you, willingly, on the sacrificial altar. I would not survive that. And it is not just that I would not wish to survive it, it is that I could not survive it."

He fell silent then, but he had no need to say anything more. His words had healed the breach between them, as well as the tear in Esme's heart. Her eyes softened to love upon his face, and her voice was quietly tender as she gave him her answer.

"Yes, I do accept it," she whispered. "I understand now. I feel the same. And I am sorry that my temporarily injured feelings caused me to doubt eternal truth."

Raul continued to stare at her for a moment, searching her mind, allowing his own feelings to subside to a manageable level. Then, without another word, he swept her under him and kissed her as he might have had they been separated for a long while and had just been reunited.

Esme returned the kiss in full measure, as she returned his lovemaking in full measure afterward. She was with him in every sense through every second of their reconciliatory coupling.

And when it was over, both of them, throughout the rest of the night, held one another even in sleep with a fierce possessiveness that was a result of their residual fear that they could lose one another should their separate masters be unkind enough to require it—or even, more unforgivably, should they each not take enough care to protect their precious union of body, spirit, and mind.

When they arrived in orbit over the Homeland, Raul sent his escort squadron back to duty. Now that he had Esme safely home, he saw no reason why the fighting ships should be taken out of battle for the days he intended to remain on Esme's planet. They were needed elsewhere. Besides, he thought there was a better chance of getting the Rebel stealth ship safely back to Genesis with only the Talon as escort than there would be with a whole squadron accompanying it. Two ships might slip through undetected, whereas a large number of ships would most likely be spotted.

As Esme stood in the control cabin of the Talon, staring at the globe of the Homeland spinning beneath her, she wondered, for perhaps the thousandth time, whether Raul's insistence that she tell her people of her gifts at last would result in their accepting her. He was adamant that the People no longer be allowed to think she might be a sorceress.

"You will tell them clearly that you serve their Master, not some evil force that they fear," Raul had decreed. "And you will show them what you can do and make use of your talents in their behalf while you await my return."

But Esme was not certain it would be as easy to overcome her people's suspicion about her as Raul thought, not when Bazil would do his best to fuel the flames of their fear. But Raul had decreed what was to be done about Bazil as well.

"This Bazil of whom you have told me," he had said, "because he could have killed you directly rather than leaving you in the desert merely in the hope that you would die, which action resulted in you and I finding one another, must be allowed the opportunity to confess his treachery to your people, and to accept your ascendancy over him and keep his life. If he shows that much sense, and if we find that he is deserving of it, we may even return his power to him when I come back for you. But if he behaves foolishly, or threatens you in any way, then you will have to kill him, Esme. I will not do it for you. This is a personal matter between the two of you involving your own honor, and it is fitting that you handle it yourself. My men and I will only serve to assure that it remains a fight between the two of you only, with no interference from anyone else."

Despite the fact that Esme had always known she would one day return home, she was resentful of being forced to return at this particular time and be separated from Raul while he faced danger. Also was she resentful of Raul's highhandedness in laying down the rules of how she would behave.

"I am surprised you give me that much freedom," she flared at him sullenly. "You have already dictated what else I will do. Why not tell me exactly how I am to kill Bazil—with my mind only or should I use a shepherd's stone? Which do you prefer?"

Raul had ignored her outburst and merely stopped her restless pacing in front of him by absently pulling her, using his mind only, onto his lap. And while she sat there filled with resentment, her body stiffened against his hand stroking her back, he had added another instruction to his already long list of them.

"However you kill him, do not make the mistake of showing him mercy, Esme. I have taken his measure from your mind, and I know his kind. He deserves a chance but I do not expect he will be sensible enough in the long run to accept his downfall with good grace. His ambition means more to him than his life."

Esme had remained silently fuming and Raul's impatience with her had led him to force her attention when she would not give it willingly.

"Esme," he had then said with quiet sternness, "why do you feel this reluctance to accept the responsibility that goes along with your gifts? You did not want to be a seeker, nor did you want to be a priest. Even if it is true that your Master, as you say, did not wish you to be such, I think you were a little too relieved that His wishes coincided with your own. You did not want Laon's vacated position either, and not just because you wanted to be with me. There, too, your relief was out of proportion, and one day I hope you will reconsider the offer made you."

At that, Esme had looked at him in horrified confusion.

"It will give you something worthwhile to do while I am about my own duties," Raul had explained gently. "We will be often separated during our life-mating, Esme, and you cannot just sit and miss me while I am absent from you. That is not healthy."

Esme had glared at him then, and Raul had frowned and gone on, his tone curt. "I do not like this selfishness I see in you, Esme," he had said disapprovingly. "When one is blessed as you are, the blessings should be shared. Yet you resent the fact that I ask you to share them with your own people even for a short while. I realize they did not treat you well when you were among them, but they did not understand. And you did not help them to understand, did you, little one?"

Esme hadn't answered. She didn't feel it necessary. She had explained to Raul already why she had not tried to make her people understand. The Master had implanted a prohibition against revelation of her gifts within her, and for good reason. There had been a chance that if she had revealed them and been put on trial for sorcery, even if Malthuzar had supported her, the trial might have gone against her and she might have been stoned. And Raul also knew why she was reluctant to go home at this particular time but he persisted in misunderstanding the situation.

"Esme," he had then asked, his puzzlement evident, "why do you feel this way? What makes you so unwilling to give yourself to others when you are so generous to me?"

Because he asked his question gently, Esme answered. "It is not that I am as reluctant to share my gifts with my people as you seem to want to believe," she had said tartly. "It is that you *force* me to do so."

But then she had realized that Raul was at least partly right about her finding it difficult to share with others, and she had confessed such to him.

"But you are not entirely wrong," she had said quietly. "It is true that I was supposed to hide my gifts from my people. And it was easier to do that in isolation, which is why I became a shepherdess. And all the time I tended my flocks, I had only my dreams of sailing among the stars with you who loved me, and occasionally the company of Maza, another shepherd, to comfort me. Maza would have taken me as mate despite the fact that the People would then have ostracized him just as they ostracized me, but I could not accept. I had to wait for you."

"This Maza is a man to admire, then," Raul had commented with a remarkable lack of jealousy.

Esme had nodded, then continued. "I was almost always alone," she explained. "And though the loneliness was burdensome in many ways, such solitude also permits a kind of freedom that does not exist in the midst of others, especially when those others watch your every move in a hostile fashion. So perhaps I came to overvalue that freedom. And perhaps I still resent that hostility. Or perhaps it is only that I have developed the habit of solitude. All I know is that I prefer being unaccountable to anyone other than you and my Master. Neither you nor He has yet asked anything of me I could not willingly give except . . ."

"Except what I am asking of you now," Raul finished for her.

Esme nodded, her expression momentarily resentful again.

"And are you going to give me what I ask of you, willingly or unwillingly?" he had then asked, his tone serious.

Esme had then sighed in resignation. "Yes, I will give it," she had agreed with grudging reluctance. "But I hope you do not insist that I like giving it."

169

Raul had smiled then. "No, I would not ask the impossible," he had teased her lightly.

Now, as she watched her homeland spin beneath her and contemplated the awful loneliness that would descend upon her once Raul had seen her safely ensconced among her people again and left her to go about his duties, she was filled with dread.

She had tried to keep from her mind the question that plagued her more and more these days, but now she let it come. Had her capture of the Rebel ship been all that the Master required of her? When its secrets had been plumbed by the Empire scientists, would it be enough to stop the war between the Empire and the Rebels so that she and Raul could be reunited? Or was there something else the Master was going to require of her? Something harder? Wasn't it enough that she must live out the days of her and Raul's separation terrified that he would not be able to come back for her?

True, he had skills almost equivalent to hers in some ways and exceeding hers in others to protect him now. But such skills had their limitations, as she had found out on their journey here.

Esme was unsure whether she was glad or sorry she had no precognizant skills. The dreams she had had from childhood had gone only so far as to show her traveling among the stars in an alien ship with a man she loved more than life itself. And those dreams had already come true. What else awaited her, good or bad, she did not know. And if what awaited her was bad, she did not want to know.

But Halen had said she had something important to do and a testing to endure, while Malthuzar had said the Master would reveal her *tasks* as they were upon her, not her *task*. He had used the plural, not the singular. And Malthuzar had given her the Sacred Pouch and instructed her to bring it back to the Homeland. Did that fact, plus the fact that Raul insisted she was to serve her people now, mean she was to replace Bazil as high priest? She did not want to be high priest! She wanted to be with Raul!

Suddenly, she was desperate to have every possible moment with her beloved before their impending separation, and she sought him out.

"I have a request," she said, when she found him.

"Speak it," he said gently, aware that she was distressed.

"Whatever else happens upon the Homeland, I would spend a night with you upon the high meadow before you leave me," she said.

Raul paused before answering, and Esme feared he was going to deny her. Instead, he gave her such joy as she had never before known.

"It has been in my mind that we would exchange vows while upon your Homeland, Esme," he said with quiet sincerity. "It seems only fitting since that is where we met and first loved. And afterward, we can experience Daccall together wherever you like, upon your high meadow if it pleases you."

Esme closed her eyes and bathed his mind not only with her heartfelt affirmative reply but with all the emotion that went with it. As a result, Raul took her to their cabin to deal with the emotions she had felt so strongly herself and which had aroused his own.

CHAPTER TEN

CONTRARY TO HER EXPECTATIONS, ESME FELT A LIFT OF her heart as she stepped from the ramp of the Talon onto the sands of the Homeland. Here, near the oasis where Raul had set the Condor down for repairs all those weeks ago, and where she had crawled half-dead into the water early one morning, she had come to know the first real happiness she had ever experienced.

But it was more than that. This was home. The familiar stars circling overhead were those she had viewed most of her life. The sand she trod, if not as dear to her as the sweet grasses of the high meadow, was part of the planet which had seen her birthing and coming of age.

One of the early scrolls said that man's body was made of dust and when the spirit departed, the body would return to the soil from which it sprang. In her ignorance, Esme had never understood how man could be made of dust. Her education with Thorson had taught her that not only did man and dust have elements in common, but star stuff played its part in man's makeup as well. But that had been only an intellectual understanding. As she stepped upon the Homeland, she understood with her heart.

As she stood staring up at the early evening sky, Raul took her under his arm. "You did not expect to like being home this much, did you?" he said companionably.

"No, I did not," Esme admitted. "But like it or not, I would leave again immediately with you if you would but permit it."

"Esme . . ." Raul chided.

Esme sighed. "All right. I have to admit, I feel within me that the Master is allied with you in this matter of my coming home and letting my people make use of me at last, so I suppose I must accept that I am well and truly trapped. But I repeat I do not have to like it."

Raul didn't reply, merely tightened his arm around her and held her close for a moment. Then he said, "Esme, let us be about it. Time is short. I would take care of necessity and get it out of the way, then have the joy we promised ourselves before duty calls again."

Esme, her throat too tight to speak, nodded instead.

Half an hour later, she was in a hovercraft heading for the Settlement with Raul, Jemiah, and six warriors Raul had handpicked to make the journey. All but Jemiah and Esme were armed with hand lasers. As they passed over the peaks of the Barrier Mountains, Esme's gaze, as she looked down, was dispassionate. But her heart was racing, as was her mind.

She had no clear idea of what she would do upon arrival at their destination, other than confront Bazil, of course, and convince him to make a confession to the People. But what if he preferred death to the loss of his prestige and power? He had said at their last confrontation that such was so, and now that he had had a few months of tasting victory, he might be even more reluctant to lose that which he had gained. And without his confession, it would be that much harder to convince the People to accept her.

"Esme," Raul said. "It will be all right. You will find the right thing to do upon the moment."

Esme sighed, and her breath was shaky. "I hope you are right," she replied.

Then they were circling the Settlement, and Esme forgot what she would or would not do, for things were not as they should be. Instead of only a few night fires burning outside the mud-brick homes and the caves surrounding them, the center of the Settlement was ablaze with many fires and half the People cavorted around them.

"I do not understand," she muttered.

"What do you not understand, my dear?" Jemiah asked with absent interest. His face was pressed to the window of the hover, and he was fairly quivering with excitement over the chance to explore a new culture.

Raul didn't give Esme a chance to answer. "Where do you want Pirson to set the hover down, Esme?" he asked.

Esme thought a moment. "There is a level space to the east on the way to the high meadow," she answered absently. "We will have to walk a little farther, but we cannot put down where I intended. There are too many fires, too many people."

She frowned as Pirson sped the hover to the area she had indicated. For the first time in her life, she doubted her own power to read minds for she could not believe what she had felt and heard from the minds of the People clustered around the central fires. It was simply not possible. The People could not have, would not have, abandoned centuries-old rules and beliefs to practice such lawlessness as would endanger their very souls.

One man stayed with the hover, and Esme, silent and tense, led Raul and the others along a well-used track with which she was familiar and which she needed no light to traverse, other than that provided by the full moon. Jemiah attempted to question her at first, but at receiving no reply from her, no acknowledgment of any kind, he finally shrugged and fell silent. Before long, he was too breathless to talk anyway, for Esme set a fast pace.

The Settlement was in the middle of the long valley surrounded by mountains which had sheltered the People for centuries past counting. A wide circle of cave-pocked hills edged the level area in the center. Bordering the level area, beneath the occupied caves, were mud-brick homes, outside which trade was conducted. The People had no currency, but bartered among themselves for their needs.

The very center of the level area was clear and served as a gathering place for the children to learn lessons, and at other times, for ceremonies and announcements. Now in that gathering place a circle of fires had been lit and at least half of the People, mostly youthful, cavorted drunkenly or indulged in activities hitherto conducted in privacy.

In the shadows outside the fires, Esme came to a

halt and, as her eyes and mind and ears took in the scene, she was forced to accept that her senses did not lie. The Master's Chosen—or at least half of them— had forsaken truth for self-indulgent heresy Esme could hardly credit.

Though he did not truly understand the reason for the rage he felt building within Esme, and was made uneasy by the strength of it, Raul did not attempt to interfere. He merely motioned to his men to spread out around the group, while he stayed by Esme's side, alert and watchful. His clear gaze never stopped moving from the scene in front of them to the glitter of righteous fury shining in Esme's wide green eyes. He shielded slightly from the intensity of feeling in her mind, but he did not cut himself off entirely from the emotion that was almost drowning her ability to think.

Jemiah sensed something wrong as well, and he wisely held his tongue as he gazed fascinatedly at Esme's people, and occasionally spared a glance at her.

Suddenly, Esme's rage reached a peak beyond which she could not contain it. Then she startled all of them—Raul, his handpicked warriors, and Jemiah (none of whom understood the language in which Esme began to speak) and most of all her own people, both those in front of the fire and their elders who crouched in their huts and caves, too shamed to watch the dissolution of their children's morals. Bazil, too, who had instigated the dissolution of morals that was taking place, but who still preferred the privacy of his cave for his own debauchery, jerked his head up from the delectable body of his latest conquest, his pupils dilating with stark terror.

Esme broadcast the words of the beginning of the Prophecy in the language of the People, both verbally and mentally, on a wide band indeed, and the rage within her added to their stunning impact.

"Beware. There will come a time when, because of your disregard for Me and My Laws, your hatred for your brothers and sisters, and your misuse and abuse of the world which I made for you, you shall surely suffer and die in great numbers, and many of you will kill your souls as well so that your spirits will be forever separated from mine!"

She paused to catch her breath, and as she did, the result of her attack became evident. There was an instant of frozen silence, followed by pandemonium as the People tried to figure out who had spoken to their minds as well as their ears in such a terrifying fashion.

Esme would tolerate no escape from the scathing denunciation she intended they hear. Reaching deep within herself, she drew such energy as she had never before found there and a strength that was surely not only just her own. When she had it, she froze the entire frantically milling and caterwauling bunch in front of her. Only, with exquisite discrimination, did she exclude Raul and his men, and Jemiah, and those people who crouched in their homes. She was as yet too incensed even to seek for Bazil, who was dragging on his robe even as he ran toward the gathering place.

"In the days when your wickedness has reached its peak, the land will be made desolate from your predations, and where once there was plenty for all, there will be sustenance for none!" she went on, drilling the Master's words into the unwilling, but helpless, ears and minds of her victims. "Neither

177

water nor food nor peace will you have. Having destroyed your own inheritance, you will then, out of hunger and terror and hardness of heart, turn upon and rend one another, each seeking at the expense of his brothers and sisters to preserve that which is already lost."

Esme, looking like a copper-haired, green-eyed, black body-suited avenging angel, then strode wrathfully into the firelight. The People, their bodies frozen in all manner of contortions, could not even open their eyes wider in acknowledgement of the fear her sudden appearance stirred in them.

"The beginning of the Prophecy foretold events I had thought were long since passed and done with," Esme stormed at her captives. "I would not have believed the Master's Chosen could so forget their history and their special place within the hollow of His hands that they would court His wrath in this manner! Do you feel no shame at all practicing your wickedness in the very shadow of His Holy Mountain?"

Breathing hard, Esme, with a flick of a finger, imperiously freed one of her captives, a man of her own age whom she had taken lessons with as a child. They had not been friends, however. Esme had had no friends among the other children. She had had no friend in all her life until she had become a shepherdess and Maza had taken her into his heart.

Kneeling him in front of her, she jerked his head up and freed his throat for speech. His brown eyes bore a look of sheer terror.

"I appoint you spokesman for this group of betrayers, Addam!" she snarled. "Now explain to me, if you

178

can, how such an abomination has come about? Justify, if you can, the abolition of the mating rules and the violence toward one another I have sensed in many of these minds, and the fact that the fields are being too slowly harvested by the elderly these days instead of stripped quickly of the Master's bounty by those young and strong enough to do so!"

Addam swallowed thrice before he could speak. "Bazil . . ." he got out, his voice a quavering wail of fear. "Bazil said he'd had a vision . . . that we were free from the old ways . . . that new laws had come to him from . . . from—"

But Esme, her lip curled in contemptuous disgust, cut him off. "If Bazil ever had a vision in his life, which I am certain he has not, it came from the enemy who has found a home within him, not from the Master. Or do you no longer even believe in the Master, Addam? I do not see how you could and behave such!"

If Addam could have lowered his head in shame, he would have. "I . . . we . . ." he stammered, ". . . we have waited so long for the fulfillment of the Prophecy, Esme!" he finally wailed his protest. "We tired of waiting and living our lives in subjugation to rules Bazil claimed have now changed!"

"As you no doubt tire the Master with your lack of faith and your easy forgetfulness of His laws!" Esme said scathingly.

Then Bazil's voice, screaming hysterically, came from behind Raul, who had been watching Esme with a pride in her magnificence that had held him almost spellbound. But at the violent antipathy toward Esme he felt in the man who was coming at a dead run from his rear, Raul pivoted and placed his hand upon the butt of his laser as he pinned the new arrival with a deadly cold gaze.

"Seize her!" Bazil screamed. "Seize her! She is a sorceress! I have had a vision!"

"Let him come, Raul," Esme said, her voice cold and contemptuous.

Raul nodded, but as he moved aside to let Bazil race into the open space where Esme stood, he voiced a warning. "Remember, Esme, no mercy."

"I will remember," Esme vowed, and the revengeful glitter of her green gaze rivaled the beam that could issue from the laser on Raul's hip.

Out of breath, panting the words, Bazil still screamed, "Seize her!" as he skittered to a stop directly in front of Esme. Then he abruptly fell silent, his black eyes opened to their fullest width as he stared at her standing there in her black, off-world bodysuit, with her hair in a braid down her back.

"Greetings, Bazil," Esme said, her smile deadly.

Without answering, Bazil jerked his head around, searching desperately for help. What he saw made him stiffen into a stillness that rivaled that of those Esme had frozen into place.

"Look at me, Bazil," Esme invited, her tone softly menacing. "Since you do not believe in the Master, and your minions are presently incapacitated, I am your only source of help."

When he obeyed, Bazil blinked in dazed shock. "How?" he whispered disbelievingly.

"It is a long story, Bazil," Esme said grimly, "and you yourself will now tell the beginning of the story to the People. You will tell them your part in the death of Malthuzar and why you had me exiled."

At that, Bazil's vision cleared slightly, and Esme saw and heard his mind scratch frantically for a means of rescue. She stopped that search by inflicting a degree of pain upon him that buckled him to his knees and brought a howl of agony from his lips.

"Not this time, Bazil," Esme said in a deceptively pleasant tone. "This time, you will not find a way out." She jerked him to his feet and turned him, like a puppet, to face those he had misled, then paused to make sure she and Bazil had the attention of every person there.

When she was certain such was the case, she put into the People's minds a willingness to hear the truth, before she forced Bazil, word by halting word, by means of the judicious use of pain, to make his confession.

He told about setting Marcus as a spy at Malthuzar's heels in order to find out if the old high priest had any inconvenient visions on his last pilgrimage to the Holy Mountain. He told how Malthuzar had discovered Marcus's presence on the hallowed slopes of the mountain, which had provoked Marcus into killing the priest so as not to have to endure stoning for his crime. He told about how Esme had killed Marcus in self-defense, and how she had wanted to bring Bazil to justice, but he had tricked her into accepting exile by threatening to reveal her gifts to the People.

Afterward, he stood with tears of agony rolling down his cheeks while Esme searched the reactions of his listeners. She was gratified by what she found, but she did not yet release them. Instead, she allowed them to watch as she spun Bazil around and dropped him to his knees in front of her. She then bent at the waist and rested her hands on her knees as she stared into his upturned face.

"My mate says I must give you a choice, Bazil," she said so all could hear. "You may choose to serve me or you may choose death. Do not tarry overlong in making your choice, Bazil. My patience has already been strained past its limits by your blasphemy."

Bazil, his eyes streaming tears, looked at her and found nothing of comfort in her cold green gaze. Then, as Esme and his people watched, he slowly gathered his tattered dignity around him like a cloak. Then he made one last bid to have his lies prevail over the truth. "I choose death over service to a sorceress," he said, his voice ringing waveringly across the gathering place.

Esme viewed him with amazement. Then she reached inside the bodice of her bodysuit and withdrew the Sacred Pouch. Straightening, she held it up for all the People to see. No one could fail to recognize it.

"Malthuzar came to me in the spirit and gave this to me, declaring it was mine by right, before he was murdered by this false priest's minion," she declared. "Does anyone here believe that Malthuzar would do such if I were truly a sorceress?"

She waited long enough to ascertain that Bazil's final defiant lie had found no welcome in his listeners' ears. How could it, when he had just confessed the depths to which his ambitious treachery had led him.

Then, her eyes fell upon Bazil again, and her gaze was very firm and clear, if a little sad, as was the tone of her voice. "So be it," she pronounced Bazil's doom. "May you find more mercy at the Master's hands than you have found at mine." With one deft, incisive blow of her mind, she destroyed those functions in Bazil's that controlled his life.

He arched backwards, his disbelieving eyes rolled under his lids, and then he toppled at her feet, and lay there, a lifeless lump of useless flesh, thoughtless mind, and corrupted spirit.

With his death, a wave of fatigue swept through Esme, and under its impetus, she allowed her hold on the People to fade.

"Go to your homes!" she called to them fiercely. "Go repent of what you have done and ask the forgiveness of your parents and your Master! When we meet at this place on the morrow, I would see you clean of mind and heart once more, or I would see you not at all!"

With that, she swung on her heel and went to Raul, who gathered her into his arms and offered silent comfort, while he watched her people quietly, hastily stumble from the scene of their chastisement.

At last, there was only Raul and Esme, Raul's men and Jemiah, and Bazil's lifeless body, in the gathering place.

Jemiah was the first to speak, and his voice was excitedly awed. "I could not catch all of what she said to them, Raul, since she spoke in their language, and I have only just recently learned to read it, much less understand it spoken. Do you know what angered her and what she told them?"

"No, not entirely," Raul answered, his voice quiet. "I know only what I took from her mind, not the precise content of the words she spoke. And you will wait until she is ready to tell you before you ask that question again, Jemiah."

Without another word, he picked Esme up in his

arms and carried her to the cave that Bazil had only recently left. When she was settled on Bazil's couch, he knelt beside her and fixed his quiet gaze upon her anguished face.

Esme opened her eyes and gazed back at him with sadness in her green eyes. "I am all right, beloved," she said. "It is only that I am devastated that my people could lose their faith and behave so contrary to the Master's laws. Also, did the killing of Bazil distress me greatly. I would much have preferred he took the chance he was offered to remain alive. But my physical strength is not depleted by what I did. I think this time, my strength was augmented by His Who gave me my gifts in the first place. I do not think I could have held so many for so long on my own otherwise."

"Perhaps not," Raul allowed. "But no matter whose strength you used, your own or another's, my pride in you is not diminished."

He spoke with level, unwavering sincerity and Esme's eyes suddenly welled with tears. Raising herself, she leaned her head against his shoulder and while he held her, quietly wept away the emotional residue of what had just transpired.

When she lay quietly in his arms, Raul whispered a question into her ear. At receiving her reply, he put her away from him temporarily and rose to go and tell his men and Jemiah to seek lodging wherever they found it for the remainder of the night. No guard would be necessary in front of the cave he and Esme would share, he informed them, for there was no one among the People who would dare to harm them now.

Upon returning to Bazil's cave, he slid down beside Esme on the former high priest's couch, and before the two of them sought slumber that night, they performed, together, by use of the fire of fully realized love, a cleansing of the residue of unredeemed lust Esme's predecessor had left upon his bed.

Baldor strode toward the Settlement. He led a beast-burden, and drove before him several ewes that he intended to trade for salt, wheat flour, and wine.

Maza would have taken care of this chore, of course, as he had done before taking Baldor on as partner. But it sickened Maza to come into the Settlement these days.

It sickened Baldor as well, but though he was no longer a priest, having resigned because of Bazil's desecration of the laws, he had set himself the task of being the lone voice crying out against the blasphemies Bazil had introduced into the lives of the People.

No one, other than the few elders who were so close to returning to the soil that they had no fear of Bazil, and a few very small children who were too young to fear much of anything, listened to Baldor's protests, of course. And he knew that if Bazil hadn't succeeded in making him such an object of ridicule that his words were treated with laughter and contempt, he wouldn't be permitted to speak at all.

But he felt compelled to continue his so far unheeded warnings. He might no longer wear the robe or carry the staff of priest, which had been given him as reward for leaving Esme in the desert, but he was as committed to the Master's principles as ever. In his heart and mind, he considered himself the only true priest left among the People as the priesthood, practiced by Bazil, had become corrupt.

He concentrated so hard upon what he would say to the closed ears that awaited him at the Settlement that he was almost upon the squat, black alien craft sitting beside the track before he became aware of its existence. When he saw it and stopped short, his mouth open in amazed disbelief, he thought he had somehow passed from wakefulness into a dream or vision.

Then a large, fair-colored man wearing a strange black garment that clung to his body like a second skin climbed out of the craft and stood with his hand on an object at his hip and spoke a curt question to him in a language Baldor didn't understand. Baldor merely stared at the man in shocked disbelief while the sheep milled around the stranger's legs and caused a frown to appear on his stern visage.

The stranger hesitated, shrugged, then climbed back into his craft. Baldor closed his mouth, and considered, shakenly, what he should do. If this was a vision, he surely didn't understand its import. And though he'd never had a vision, surely one didn't feel as awake and in the present as he did at this moment, while at the same time one was being blessed with a spiritual insight.

Looking down at himself, he saw the familiar rough wool of his singlet. Beneath the singlet, his strong bare legs reached down to his sandaled feet. Under his feet was the familiar brown earth of the track to the Settlement. Reaching across his chest, he pinched the skin of his upper left arm with the fingers of his right hand. He pinched hard enough that it hurt, and he grimaced.

Then his head came up as the stranger climbed back out of his strange craft, and this time the man carried a small black box which had tangled cords dangling from it.

Baldor held fast to his courage and stood firm as the

stranger came up to him. If this was a vision, he wasn't going to disgrace himself by running away from it, though he surely did want to break and run when the man reached up and placed two cuplike objects in Baldor's ears.

"Greetings, stranger," the man's voice came through the cups, and Baldor, badly startled, jumped back, pulling the cups out of his ears in the process.

The stranger sighed and stepped forward and replaced them.

Baldor was trying mightily not to show that his limbs were trembling now, and to negate this show of weakness, he held his ground this time when the voice echoed in his ears again.

"Do you go to the Settlement?" the stranger asked.

Baldor swallowed, decided not to trust his voice, and merely nodded.

"Are you friend or foe of Esme's?" the stranger then asked, his eyes narrowed suspiciously.

At the sound of Esme's name, Baldor's heart gave a great leap inside his chest. "Es–Esme?" he queried, his voice shaken.

The stranger nodded. "Yes, the woman who once lived among you. She is back."

A light of joy sprang up in Baldor's eyes then and, unthinkingly, he reached to grasp the stranger's shoulders in his large hands and shook him. "She is truly back?" he demanded. "You do not lie?"

The stranger had stiffened as though expecting an attack, but the look on Baldor's face and the eager joy in his voice changed his initial alarm to a smile.

"Yes, she is back from traveling among the stars. We brought her here last night."

Baldor didn't take in the part about Esme traveling

among the stars. He was too alarmed to hear that Esme was in the Settlement—at Bazil's mercy!

"But she is not safe there!" he cried, his joy turning to rough concern in the flash of an eye.

The stranger grinned. "Oh, she is safe," he said, unconcerned. "Even if she did not have Captain Raul and five of his best men with her, I expect she can take care of herself. Anybody who can turn Rebel missiles around using mind power only can surely handle a few upstart primitives."

Baldor was impatient with the man's apparent sanguinity. Also he didn't understand half of what the stranger had said.

"I must go to help her!" he said, reaching to jerk the cups from his ears and thrusting them at the stranger.

The stranger opened his mouth to say something else, then realizing he wouldn't be understood, merely shrugged and motioned Baldor to continue on his way. Baldor did, at a run, with no thought for the beast-burden or the sheep under his care. He merely dashed through them, scattering them in all directions. He had to help the woman whom he had come to care for during their trip in the desert and whom he knew had been innocent of Malthuzar's murder.

He was breathless and had a sharp stitch in his side by the time he topped the rise on the track that continued downward to the center of the Settlement, and as he paused to catch his breath, he searched with his eyes. Then, he abruptly went still as he realized the whole population of the Settlement was at the gathering place, surrounding a small figure with copper-tinted hair who stood in the center.

"They are going to stone her!" he gasped, and

ignoring his own pain, he started off again, running as fast as his legs could pump beneath him.

Raul did not really expect any trouble from the people Esme stood addressing. All were hanging on her every word, the adults as wide-eyed and awestruck as the children, as she patiently explained herself to them and told them what their future held.

But out of habit, his eyes scanned the crowd, looking for any sign that Bazil might still have a disciple or two who had no intention of accepting Esme's explanations and leadership peacefully. Though these people had no modern weapons whatsoever, death could come from a thrown stone as quickly as from the deadly beam of a laser.

Then his attention was caught and held by a disturbance at the outer edge of the crowd. He watched, frowning, his hand on the butt of his laser, as the crowd began to ripple apart and let someone pass through it, someone moving with rough disregard for those who might impede his progress and who was shouting—nay, *roaring*—Esme's name. But when Raul searched the mind of the oncomer, his grip on his laser relaxed and he smiled.

Esme had stopped speaking as she became aware of the disturbance, and as she sought with her mind for the cause of the uproar and found Baldor and what was in his mind, she grinned.

But when Baldor finally burst through the crowd and dashed forward to where Esme stood, he caught both Raul and Esme by surprise. With a strength that shocked even himself, Baldor caught Esme by her nape and shoved her roughly down on the ground so that she ended flat on her stomach. Her breath issued from her chest in a swoosh when her stomach slapped hard against the hard-packed earth.

Then Baldor straddled her body and shook his clamped fists at the crowd in fury, while his look scoured his people with the fire of his righteous indignation.

"Would you add unjustified murder to the rest of your abominations?" he roared. "If you would stone someone, stone the man who has brought you to such a pass! Kill your new high priest if you have murder on your minds! That false prophet deserves it! This innocent woman does not!"

The crowd made not a sound. The People merely stood, mouths open, and stared at Baldor as at a ghost.

Into that silence, Esme's voice rose, sounding drily amused and a little pained and breathless. "Thank you, Baldor," she said, "but I have already dealt with Bazil, and no one here any longer wishes me harm. If you will let me up, I will explain."

It took a moment for Baldor to understand fully Esme's words. But as he looked around, he realized that no one held stones and no one's face held the killing look. He also realized that another of the strangers, this one bigger, more handsome and with an aura of power about him, had left the fringe of the crowd and was walking toward him and Esme with a smile on his face and a look of friendly comradery in his unusually clear eyes.

His face showing the confusion he felt, Baldor nevertheless slowly unclenched his fists. When the stranger reached him and slapped him lightly on the shoulder, seemingly in approbation, and said something in that language that Baldor didn't understand before pushing him lightly away from Esme, Baldor allowed himself to be moved. The stranger then bent, lifted Esme to her feet as easily as though she were a small child instead of a full-grown woman, looked her over with a grin on his face, and asked her a question in that foreign tongue.

Esme replied in the same language, smiling ruefully, and the stranger kissed her temple. Then he placed his arm around Esme's waist, and they both turned to smile at Baldor.

Baldor's mind was like a humbird, fluttering around so quickly, it could settle on nothing. But out of the confusion filling him, three things stood out—his defense of Esme had been unnecessary, she and the stranger were mated, and his shame over leaving her in the desert to die still tore his conscience like a hawkbird tears its prey.

"So it was you, Baldor?" Esme said gently. Moving forward out of her mate's embrace, she stepped closer and stared into Baldor's blue-brown tortured gaze, her green eyes filled with sweetness and acceptance.

He had to clear his throat before he could speak. Then, his tone filled with shame, he nodded, and said, "Yes, Esme, to my lasting shame, I was the one who left you helpless in the desert. That you did not die fills me with gratitude for the Master's mercy."

Esme smiled at him. "But you did not leave me entirely helpless, Baldor," she reminded him. "If you had not left me the water and the food and the beast-burden, I surely would have died. I thank the Master that it was you who left me there other than one of Bazil's closer adherents. You were truly the instrument of the Master's will, Baldor. And you have no need to feel shame at what you did."

Baldor swallowed, wanting desperately to believe her and to relieve his conscience of the one dark blot upon it. "It is true that when I prayed the Master told me to do such," he said hesitantly. "Otherwise, I could not have finished what I started. For though I thought you were a sorceress at the beginning of the journey and that it was best that you be exiled and perhaps die, it came to be that by the time we reached the desert I had changed my mind and did not want to leave you there."

Outwardly, Esme merely smiled again. But with her mind, she reached out to Baldor and gently soothed the last blot from his troubled conscience.

Then, with hardly a pause, she asked, "And what have you been doing while Bazil perpetrated his treachery upon the People, Baldor?"

Baldor sighed and looked around him at the crowd who stood silently watching him and Esme speak together.

"When Bazil came up with his new, so-called vision that we were free of the Master's age-old rules and could behave as we liked, subject only to his direction, I tried to make the People see sense, but only the older ones were willing to listen to me at all, and they were too frightened by their children's unlawful violence to aid me. I thought, at first, that Bazil would kill me for my insubordination. But when I could no longer stomach the mockery he had made of the priesthood and resigned from it, he chose instead to make me an object of ridicule, and thus he stole what little power I had left to be of influence."

Esme nodded. "I am glad there was someone of your generation who was not corrupted, Baldor," she said quietly.

"Oh, there are more than just me," Baldor shrugged. "I shepherd with Maza now, who is of the same mind as I am. And there are a few others but not many who have held themselves back from corruption."

"I am glad about Maza." Esme smiled. "He is an old friend of mine."

"Yes, he has spoken of you." Baldor nodded, looking away.

Esme took from his mind the nature of Maza's words. Also did she take from his mind the fact that he himself was somewhat sad over the fact that she was already mated.

"The Master will provide someone for you if you but ask Him," she said so softly that no one other than Baldor and Raul heard her.

Raul tactfully looked away from the blush that colored Baldor's face, and silently, with wry humor in his tone, he said to Esme, "Should I have second thoughts about leaving you here alone when you have so many admirers to pay you court? If I left Thorson and Laon here as well, I could be assured you would be well protected, unless a small war broke out among your four would-be suitors and they became incapable of protecting anyone, even themselves."

Esme tossed her reply impudently, silently, back at him, without bothering to turn around. "Aye, it might be best if you took me with you, Raul. I would try to bear up under the strain of being deprived of my admirers."

Raul's reply was a simple, lightly reprimanding snort.

"Is it true then?" Baldor asked, bravely meeting her eyes again. "You do have mind powers?"

Yes, Baldor, Esme answered him silently, mind to mind, startling him badly. Then she spoke aloud again. "But I am not a sorceress. And if you will wait until I have done speaking to the People, I have something in mind for you that I think you will appreciate." Then she turned away and finished her speech.

Baldor listened intently as she told the People that she would be staying with them while her mate went away for a while, and that while she was with them, she would serve, temporarily, as their new high priestess while training someone to take her place.

"I already have the Sacred Pouch," she informed her listeners, "from Malthuzar's own hand. May I now have the affirmation that comes with it?"

The People then, as one voice, and without hesitation, hailed her as their new high priestess. And Baldor, without even thinking about it, added his own affirmation to that of the People.

"So be it," Esme said with grave formality. "Then go now to your homes and your duties and over the next few days, reacquaint yourselves with your knowledge of the Sacred Scrolls and the old ways. For under my reign, they shall surely be our guide again."

That served as dismissal, and as the People drifted away, breaking into small groups to talk animatedly to one another, Esme gestured at Baldor to accompany her, and she and Raul led the way to Bazil's cave.

Inside it, Esme poured Raul and Baldor cups of wine and a cup of water for herself. Then she and Raul showed Baldor how a toast was made. After he had touched his cup to theirs, somewhat awkwardly, his face a mask of puzzlement, they each took a sip.

Then Esme fixed Baldor with her green gaze.

"Where are your priest's robe and staff, Baldor?" she asked.

Baldor shrugged. "In the seeker cave, I imagine. That is where I left them."

"Then go and get them," Esme instructed firmly. "You are going to be a priest again. And when you are, your first service to your new high priestess will be to conduct the mating ceremony for her and the man who owns her heart."

She looked at Raul, her eyes filled with love. Raul gazed back at her with a small smile on his lips and a look of quiet anticipation in his clear gaze.

Then she returned her eyes to Baldor's face, and saw his joy over his opportunity to serve again in the office which he had been meant for by the Master.

"I will return in a moment," Baldor said, and handing her his cup, he pivoted and strode away.

When he was gone, Raul nodded at Esme. "He is a good man," he said. "You have chosen well."

"I did not choose at all," Esme said with quiet acceptance. "Baldor belongs to the Master. I could not do other than affirm the Master's choice."

Raul shrugged, and held her gaze, and drew her to him. When she was in his arms, he tilted her face up with his hand on her chin.

"Is there anything I should know about this ceremony we are about to undergo which will bind us together for life?" he asked softly, his eyes a caress as they moved over her face.

"Only that, unlike on your world, the People do not allow dissolution of such vows," she said softly. "So that, if you would ever leave me, you might do so on Genesis, but upon the Homeland, you would still be bound."

"I am bound in any case," Raul murmured, "vows or no vows, regardless of place or circumstance. And though my body may not always lie by your side, my heart is ever yours, Esme. That I vow to you now, with no need for witnesses to attest the truth of my words. You may take it from my mind."

"I have," Esme whispered. "And do you take the same truth from mine."

They sealed the most important vow they would make that day with a kiss and a lingering touch of minds, rather than by speaking words in the presence of a priest and witnesses and by sipping wine each from the same cup, as they would later during the legal ceremony that would bind them as life mates in the eyes of the People.

CHAPTER ELEVEN

THE LAW OF THE PEOPLE REQUIRED THAT ESME AND RAUL each have two special witnesses for the mating cere-mony. Therefore, Raul had the warrior who had remained at the hover send a message to the Talon requesting that Thorson, Jase, the Talon's engineer, who had a fatherly attitude toward Esme and whom she viewed with affection, Ivvor, and any other of the men who could be spared from guarding the crew of the Rebel ship, come to the Settlement. Then he sent the warrior in the hover to search out Maza on the high meadow and pick him up.

Maza arrived much shaken and confused at being approached by a stranger, hauled into an alien craft the like of which he'd never imagined existed, and taken for a terrifying ride in it.

At seeing Esme, however, his terror was forgotten and his eyes lit with joy that she lived. From what

Baldor had told him, he had long since given her up as dead.

After embracing him, Esme stood back with a grin tilting her lips at the astonished questions she saw in his mind.

"I have been among the stars with these strangers you see, Maza," she said in an attempt to explain.

But Maza's confusion was merely heightened by her words, and Esme laughed and hugged him and told him to be patient, that he would know all eventually.

Then Baldor called her aside, and when she stood beside him, he looked at Raul.

"With your permission, Honored Sir," he said formally, "I would take Esme now to the seeker cave and prepare her for the ceremony."

Esme was suddenly saddened. She had forgotten that she had no wedding garment to wear prepared by loving female family members, no one to give her the ritual instructions as to her wifely duties.

"Baldor . . ." She started to tell him that such a visit would accomplish nothing, but he stared sternly down at her in a way that made the words die on her lips. She shrugged, hiding a smile. Baldor—as she should have recalled, since his character was the reason for his being chosen by the Master—was a stickler for adhering strictly to the rules. And on this day, she was not the high priestess with the authority to overrule one of her priests, but merely a woman of the People, about to embark upon a ceremony older than recorded time.

So Baldor left a reluctant Maza to instruct Raul via a translator of his part of the ceremony to come, and of his duties to his mate in their life together, with

Jemiah a fascinated eavesdropper on a third set of earphones, while he took Esme with him to the seeker cave.

Esme had not been in the seeker cave since her testing for the priesthood, yet it looked just the same; only now it was empty of young seekers. Baldor had sent everyone away, planning to institute, with Esme's help, a new search for those worthy to serve. The outer room was for dining and studying, the inner room for sleeping.

She had not much time to look around, however, for only a moment after she and Baldor arrived, a tiny, elderly woman, whom Esme recognized as one who had been kinder to her than most, arrived. She was followed by a younger woman with gleaming black skin and wide, innocent black eyes, who carried a bundle in her strong shapely arms.

"Peace to you, Ana," Baldor said. Esme merely nodded respectfully.

"Peace to you, Baldor," the elderly woman said in a voice that was firm and much stronger than her frail appearance would lead one to believe was possible. "Leave us now," Ana instructed Baldor in a no-nonsense tone, gesturing at him with a gnarled hand. "Help Maza instruct Esme's chosen mate. We would not want him to disgrace her."

Baldor nodded meekly, turned, and left the cave.

"Now, daughter of the People"—Ana fixed Esme with a gleaming look in her dark eyes that was both kind and firm—"if you will permit it, I will serve in your mother's place and prepare you for the ceremony."

Esme felt a welling of emotion inside her that brought tears to her eyes. It was a moment before she could speak. Then, with respectful humility, she said, very gently, "I would be honored to have you stand in my mother's place, Ana, and I will attend your wisdom with open ears."

Some time later, Esme emerged from the bathing pool at the back of the seeker cave, her body glowing and her hair in tangles from the scrubbing Ana's assistant, Dallia, had performed. After Dallia had dried Esme's body, the girl picked up a comb, obviously intending to comb the tangles from Esme's hair and then braid it in the traditional wedding style.

Esme debated the matter a moment, then shook her head and held up a hand to stop Dallia. While the girl watched, her eyes widening ever larger by the second at what she saw, Esme used her mind, first to create a strong wind to dry her sopping hair and then to untangle it and leave it gleaming in soft waves around her face and down her back to her thighs.

Ana came into the bathing chamber at that moment and at seeing the look of terrified amazement on Dallia's face, frowned. "Why do you stand there with that silly look on your face, child?" she said impatiently. "Get about the braiding of my daughter's hair!"

Esme shook her head and smiled at Ana. "My mate does not like my hair braided, Ana," she said with gentle firmness. "Nor do I."

Ana was not pleased. "But it is tradition, child!" she protested.

"And I have been about the breaking of some traditions all of my life." Esme smiled. "This little one is not really so important, is it?"

Ana grumbled mightily, but at last, when she saw

that Esme was not going to give in, she accepted the inevitable and went on to another matter.

"Get the gown, Dallia," she told the young woman, who scurried to do her will.

Esme sucked in her breath when she and Ana met Dallia in the sleeping chamber for in the girl's hands, held out for inspection, was a wedding garment in which to take pride.

Spun of the best wool, then whitened and softened almost to the color of the dasflower and the softness of silk, the gown was ankle-length and had long wide sleeves. Around the simple, slightly scooped neckline Ana had embroidered a line of golden dasflowers and there was a long golden tie belt of wool to match. Under it was to be worn a short singlet of spun cotton.

"It is beautiful, Ana," Esme whispered, reaching to touch it lovingly. "I had thought I would have to go to my mating in my foreign bodysuit, for I did not bring one of my pretty gowns from the ship to the Settlement."

"Aye, it is the best I have ever made." Ana nodded, a glint of tears in her eyes. "It was for my daughter. But she fell away with the other young ones and adhered to Bazil's blasphemy, and now there is a breach between us it will take long to heal."

"But, Ana . . ." Esme started to protest.

Ana shook her head. "If it comes to be that she mates one day, I will make another for her," she said in a tone that permitted no argument.

So Esme subsided and did as her heart wished in any case. She allowed Dallia to slide the short singlet over her head, and then the mating gown. When the belt was tied, she looked down at herself and stroked the material and was tremulously pleased that she would not have to go to Raul looking less than her best.

"Now leave us, Dallia," Ana told the younger woman, who bowed her head in respect, then hurried away. "Come, daughter," Ana then said to Esme. When they were seated on one of the stone ledges, which was softened by antlop skins, the old woman began, slowly and with much solemn joy, to tell Esme the duties she would owe her mate and the secrets of keeping both of them happy with one another.

Esme, who had already taken from the woman's mind all of the instruction she was now hearing with her ears, listened to every word without showing other than complete, respectful attention and wholehearted acceptance.

Esme walked slowly with her hand on Jase's forearm down a corridor the People made for her to the center of the gathering place. There, Raul and his two witnesses, Ivvor and Jemiah, who was absolutely delighted, for professional reasons, to be taking part in such an ancient ceremony, waited with Esme's two witnesses, Thorson and Maza, neither of whom was delighted about taking part in *this* particular ceremony, but who had put their personal feelings aside for Esme's sake.

As many of the Talon's crew as could be spared to witness this mating were scattered among the crowd, smiling with affection and pride as Esme passed them. Only those of the crew with whom Esme was not especially bonded had been left to watch the Rebel captives, who were not likely in any case, without their captain, to cause trouble.

Laon, of course, had been excluded from the celebration, and Esme could not fault Raul for decreeing that his enemy be left on the Talon, drugged and bound. In any case, she imagined Laon, had he been allowed to attend, would feel nothing but pain at having that which he himself had desired be taken by another. And Raul, she knew, would not wish to be reminded on this occasion of that which she had shared with another man.

Then she was face to face with the man she loved, and all else fled from her mind. Raul had had Jase bring him a formal uniform, and he looked magnificent in the black bodysuit, but to Esme, he would have looked magnificent in a ragged, tattered shepherd's singlet. Would not his thick hair have framed his handsome face as fittingly, and would not the blue of his eyes have resembled the sky as clearly, and would not his powerful, altogether masculine body, which she knew as well as her own, have called to hers just as strongly?

On the other hand, she was well pleased by the look in his eyes when he took in her appearance. The mating garment of the People could not really compare with the fine gowns Genesian women wore. But apparently, Raul was not, by any means, disappointed by the way she looked in it.

Jase stepped back as Raul stepped to her side and joined their hands. They held one another's eyes for a long moment, and then smiling, they turned to face Baldor.

Baldor began the ceremony with the familiar words that would always ring in Esme's heart. "We of the People are filled with joy, for one of our daughters and one of our adopted sons have found their true mates in one another and have asked to have their union

203

blessed in the sight of all."

From there on, Esme's mind recorded the words and steps of the ceremony, but her attention was more upon the silent communion and the perfect understanding she and Raul exchanged in their minds.

When Baldor pronounced the final words, "Go you on together then as you have started, of one mind, one heart, one body, one purpose and may your union be blessed by the Master and your joy in one another never dim," she was scarcely aware of the uproarious noise that erupted from the crowd around them. For following Baldor's words, Raul said, "I love you, Esme, now and forever," and she had echoed his words with all her heart.

It was necessary that they stay for the feasting and to receive the customary congratulations, but Esme was aware of Raul's impatience to get on with another, more binding, ceremony to be conducted in private, and she was impatient as well.

Finally, when the sun dipped behind the Barrier Mountains, they were able to slip away. Raul sent his own men back in the hovers they had brought from the Talon, while he piloted the smallest at Esme's direction to the high meadow. He set it down near the cave which she had considered her own and where she had stored her few private things.

"I doubt we will find it very habitable," Esme apologized as she and Raul carried clean skins and food supplies given them as mating gifts up to the entrance. "It has not been occupied for a long while, and mayhap the wild ones have made it their own by now."

"And I doubt we will care, before too much longer,

what condition our surroundings are in," Raul responded with a low, teasing laugh that shivered Esme's skin with anticipation.

"Doubtless, you are right," she agreed, her eyes soft upon him.

But when they entered the small cave, Esme stopped short in surprise. It was clean swept, with no cobwebs and had wood already laid in its pit, ready to be fired, just inside the entrance. She sensed with her mind, then smiled.

"Maza and Baldor," she said to Raul. "They have used this place and kept it in habitable condition."

"We must remember to express our thanks to them." Raul nodded, looking around interestedly.

"Put the food over on that ledge." Esme pointed to a stone extension near the cave entrance as she went to pull the old, tattered skins from the stone sleeping platform carved out of one side of the cave and replaced them with the new, sweet-smelling skins she carried in her arms.

She then sent Raul with a pouch to the Pool of Stones to fetch water while she set the wood afire and browned mutton strips and warmed grain cake for their supper. Neither had eaten much at the mating celebration, and she thought they would need to be well nourished before they began Daccall, for she was certain such nourishment would be forgotten once they were embarked upon the ceremony which would seal their bonds beyond breakage.

Raul did not protest the delay when he returned, but merely sat beside her, munching the unfamiliar food which had nourished Esme most of her life, his thoughts quiet and much contented.

"Would you have us exchange Genesian vows when

we are next together upon your own homeland?"
Esme asked softly.

"Perhaps it would be as well, if for no reason other
than to assure the legalities of our mating there," Raul
said lazily. "But it will not be necessary to make me
feel any more bound, if that is what is in your mind."

"But you know what is in my mind." Esme smiled.
"It is open to you right now and has been this entire
day. And since you do, you know I asked the question
only to ascertain if you felt the need to obey your own
customs."

"What is shortly to come would take care of that."
Raul grinned. "But, Esme, I do not constantly prowl
your thoughts, even when you leave your mind open
to me," he added more soberly. "And I do not think it
a good idea for you to prowl mine uninvited either.
Even ones bound as closely as we are need some
privacy. And I have never been accustomed to hearing
the minds of others, so I seek such communication
only when I need to."

"I seldom prowl your thoughts uninvited, Raul,"
Esme assured him. "I bear in mind always that you
have a distaste for it, and I recall often how appalled I
was when Laon dug in my mind and I could not stop
him."

"That is well." Raul nodded. "I exclude you from
nothing important in my heart, Esme," he added
softly, reaching to draw her against him. "And mayhap as we grow old together, the matter of our
individual privacy will grow less important, and we
will come to share our every thought with one another
as a matter of course."

Esme smiled up at him. "I am not sure about that,"
she said. "I have a feeling you will always have a need

for *some* inner privacy. As most likely will I. But perhaps you are right. Perhaps the reasons I have now to keep my thoughts to myself will dissipate over time."

Raul raised an eyebrow, and his voice was stern, but the look in his eyes was not. "And what reasons are these that you have now for wanting to keep your thoughts to yourself?" he asked.

Esme shrugged, her eyes twinkling. "Oh, it seems to me that when I am angry with you, when I disagree with you, when you are being too stubbornly male for my taste, that it is just as well you do not know *all* of the thoughts that cross my mind, lest your temper be roused more than necessary."

"Enough!" Raul held up a finger and pressed it against her mouth. "If you go on, you will force me to admit that you are at times too stubbornly female for my taste, and then we will be having our first disagreement before we have even sealed our mating properly."

"Then I will be silent," Esme said, teasing him. "I would not spoil what is to come for anything."

Raul's eyes became heavy lidded then, and rather than seal her mouth with his finger, he lightly stroked her lips with it. Esme parted her teeth and touched her tongue to his finger, and that was the beginning of Daccall for them, a very different Daccall from that which Esme had shared with Laon and which would, as Raul had said, wipe her previous experience from her mind forever.

Raul carried her to the skin-draped stone couch and gently stripped her mating gown from her body before laying her down upon their new mating bed. Then he shucked his own clothing, and when he was beside her, Esme looked into his eyes, her love for him brimming in her own.

"I will not hurt you too much during the first stage," he told her softly. "But neither can I be gentle."

"I would not have you do other than as the ceremony demands," Esme responded with utter sincerity. "And during it, I will withhold from you nothing you wish me to give."

"Neither would I have you do other than as the ceremony demands," Raul responded meaningfully. "Do not restrain yourself other than as your respect for yourself and for me dictates during the third stage, which is how I plan to conduct the first one. I have decided I want it all."

Esme's eyes widened, but she could not protest what she saw in Raul's steady, loving gaze. "Then, begin, my heart," she whispered softly. "For I would have it all as well."

And by the third moonrise, they both, indeed, had had it all. Their love truly sanctified and binding past breakage, they slept for almost the first time since exchanging their mating vows, in utter peace and fulfillment and exhaustion, in one another's arms.

The summons came before first light, and it was so powerful that Esme found herself upon her feet without knowing how she came to be there. Before her eyes had even adjusted to the dim light thrown by the dying fire, she was reaching for her mating gown to clothe herself.

She could not disobey, but even as she gathered up a water pouch and the Sacred Pouch, she voiced a gentle, respectful protest at the necessity of leaving Raul without a word. He would worry when he woke to find her gone. Could she not have permission to spare him that worry?

The words formed in her mind of themselves, but they were not her own thoughts, and though the Master had never spoken to her thus before, she knew their source. *The enemy hastens about his work. So must you hasten about Mine. I will bring your mate when we have need of him.*

So Esme left the cave without a backward glance, and before Raul had taken his first look at the morning out the cave entrance, thinking Esme had gone without him to the Pool of Stones to bathe the aches and traces of their loving from her body, she was climbing the foothills of the Holy Mountain.

His grief over the loss of Esme had Thorson so distracted that he was tardy in administering Laon's latest dose of sedation. That, and the fact that Laon's body had adjusted to the medication for some time gave Laon the strength he needed to overpower his former keeper, mind and body, and reverse their positions.

Before Laon dealt the final, killing blow to Thorson's already-battered body, the medic knew that his carelessness was going to cost more than his own life. In his shame at what Laon had taken from his mind, and in his horror over what the man planned to do with that knowledge, he was unafraid as he watched Laon point the barrel of the laser pistol at his head. Death would be much preferable to living with such dishonor.

"Forgive me, Esme," were the last words Thorson uttered before his mind exploded within his skull and he was forever freed from his own guilt.

Laon did not waste time exulting over his victim. There was much to do and little time to do it. In a few moments, he successfully anticipated and avoided the few men of Raul's crew who paced the corridors of the Talon, and made his way to where Ivvor was held. At Laon's hand, the drowsy crewman guarding Ivvor quickly joined Thorson in the spirit world, and Laon and Ivvor conferred hastily and violently.

"Leave her be, man!" Ivvor hissed, not bothering to hide his dislike of Laon. "We have no time for such a delay, and she is too dangerous to toy with. In any case, she is life-mated to Raul. They are even now engaged in Daccall. You cannot break such bonds without her agreement, and she will not give it, you can be sure of that. So what joy will you have of her even if you manage to bring her back, and what makes you think you can prevent her from losing us all we might gain if we act sensibly and leave here now?"

"With such lack of imagination as you show, it is no wonder the Rebels have not yet gained victory," Laon replied with contemptuous impatience. "And if I did not need your help, I would not deign to explain myself to such as you."

Laon ignored the look his words evoked in Ivvor's hard gray eyes, as he also ignored the cold fury in the man's mind. Knowing Ivvor was as addicted to duty as Esme's hated new mate, he did not expect the man's disgust and dislike of him personally to result in anything but a certain grudgingness in the obedience he would unquestionably give.

"Death can break the bonds you speak of," Laon said, his black eyes cold as death themselves. "And they can be reforged with another. Such is my intent. Only do as I say, and I will have the means of forcing

Esme to grant me what she is now intent upon granting her beloved captain. And this time, I will not tolerate the slightest withholding of that which I intend to have. When that is accomplished, we will have her talents on our side. The defeat of the Empire will no longer be delayed, and with the power that Esme and I control between the two of us, the Rebels will have such victory as they never dreamed of obtaining. And they will have it without having to spend the necessary years it would take to condition the Empire's servants to obey their new masters."

When he paused and searched Ivvor's mind, he smiled with grim satisfaction. There was nothing but concurrence there now, which was exactly the reaction he had expected.

"Time is short!" he said, handing Ivvor the second laser he had picked up from the guard he had killed. He moved to the cabin door. "Let us get about the recapture of your ship without further delay."

It took less than a quarter of an hour to make their way by stealth out of the Talon and it cost the Talon's crew only one more death, that of the man on guard at the ramp. Then they crossed the distance over the sand to the Rebel ship where they killed the guards without even having to use Ivvor's crew to help them.

As Ivvor roused his men to ready the ship for takeoff, Laon took a hover and set off to accomplish his private part of the plan he had explained to Ivvor. Dawn was just lightening the desert over which he flew when he heard the faint roar of the Rebel ship's power source and smiled. Ivvor would soon be in orbit over this hellhole of a planet, his missiles trained first on the Talon to destroy it, and then on the Settlement where Esme's people dwelled.

211

When he was close enough, Laon would take the precaution of sending a message to Esme mind to mind before he even saw her face. After she realized the cost of saving her lover and herself, he doubted it would be necessary to give her a small taste of the destruction Ivvor had been told to visit upon her people should she choose to defy her fate.

Esme, moving with a speed and strength that was not entirely her own, was halfway to the Sacred Ledge when Raul searched and sensed that Esme was not merely re-exploring her homeland. She was nowhere around.

He lost no time boarding the hover, and his face and eyes were grim with concentration as he set out to find her with his mind as well as his eyes. But it was slow going, and he went in every direction but the right one before he finally realized where she must be and upon Whose business.

The sun rode high in the sky, but Raul's eyes were as cold as a Homeland winter sky by the time he set the hover down upon a level area among the foothills of the mountain Esme had pointed out to him on their flight to her cave and called "Holy." Another hover had already discovered that there was no place higher to land, and even before Raul paused to sense who had brought it here, he knew by instinct whose hand had been upon the controls.

"Will you blast the Talon now, Father?"

Ivvor's son had spoken eagerly, and Ivvor frowned as he heard the bloodthirstiness in his offspring's tone. When peace eventually came, he wondered, would his boy be able to put aside the thirst for the kill and take up the tame position Ivvor had been promised on his behalf?

Suddenly, Ivvor's mind was upon the mating ceremony Raul and Esme had shared. Despite their present status as enemies, Raul had honored him, for the sake of old friendship, by asking him to serve as one of his witnesses. And Ivvor, moved by the request, had been glad to do it.

He had also been moved by the glow of love that had been upon Esme's beautiful face, and the happiness he had seen in his old friend, Raul's, clear blue eyes. Ivvor wished such happiness to come to his son someday. But without the restraint of compassion in his offspring's soul, would such be possible?

"Father?" There was just a touch of impatience in the young man's voice as he prompted his sire to action.

Ivvor turned his gray eyes upon his son then, and in his gaze was an expression the youth had never seen there before. "No, my son," he said, his voice firm with his decision. "I will not demean myself and my friendship with Raul by shooting his ship while it and the men within it lie helpless upon the ground."

"But—but, Father!" the son protested. "You have always said to give no quarter in battle!"

"And I still say the same," Ivvor spoke curtly. "Should Raul come against me on the battlefield, I will fight him with everything in me. But not in this cowardly manner. Nor," he added even more firmly, "will I any longer follow the directions of an asp like Laon. He will not succeed with Esme, of that I am sure. And should he get around her, he will still have

213

Raul to deal with. With two such as them against him, there is little hope his plan can succeed. And meanwhile, there is a more honorable fight to conduct than blasting helpless civilians into dust!"

As his son stared at him in surprised shock, Ivvor turned and roared at the navigator whom Laon had once displaced. "Prepare for jump!"

And within a few moments, the upper atmosphere of the Homeland was free of any threat.

Esme ceased her prayers and sat cross-legged upon the Sacred Ledge, her mind and body composed and ready. Beside her the Sacred Pouch was now empty. Upon mental instructions from the Master, before starting her prayers, she had withdrawn from it the Sacred Feather, signifying the frailty of human life, and put it in a crevice, where, despite the torrential winds that swirled around the mountaintop, it had merely fluttered gently. Now, as her prayers ceased, so did the wind.

In front of her a candle that had also been in the pouch waited to be lit and a tiny cup, which she had filled with water from a stream at the base of Holy Mountain and blessed, then sprinkled with a powder from the pouch, waited to be lifted to her mouth.

With a flintstone from the pouch, Esme lit the Sacred Candle, and its flame burned steady and bright. Then, with a murmured prayer that if the purity of her spirit be found wanting, the Sacred Drink might kill her, she lifted the bowl of powdered water to her lips and drained its contents.

Then, her eyes fixed intently upon the flame of the candle, she waited. Gradually, as the candle's light grew brighter and brighter and finally filled all of her mind, all awareness of her body faded, and she became spirit only, submissive to whatever the Master sent.

Cursing the slowness of his progress, Laon held his awareness of Esme's presence in the forefront of his mind to guide him, though he didn't really need such guidance. There was only one path, and it rose turning and twisting to the summit of this accursed mountain, which had an aura that Laon found strangely disquieting. It was for that reason that he held Esme's presence in his mind. When he let it fade, so did his purpose fade, to be replaced with a nameless fear he found intolerable.

At last, he topped a rise and saw her a few yards above him, sitting cross-legged and unnaturally still, her eyes closed.

Relieved, but made cautious by the mental powers he knew Esme commanded, Laon hastily gathered his thoughts, then sent his mind boldly across the distance to seek hers, intending to issue his ultimatum. But in the few seconds he had used to gather his thoughts, Esme's spirit had departed, and when Laon sent his mind to hers, it met no response.

Again and again he tried, but there was nothing there to meet his mind touch. Finally, enraged by the prospect that she had somehow escaped him, Laon climbed up to where her body still sat, so very still and empty that Laon's nameless fears had turned to terror by the time he reached her.

Raul had never thought he would curse the limits of such powers as he had come to have. But without seeing where he wished to go, he could not use his mind to teleport himself past the twisting turns of the path. And he could not even sense Esme now to fix upon her. When he had started up the mountain, he had sensed her, but his mind calls had met a barrier he could not penetrate. She was fixated elsewhere, oblivious to all else and then, in the blink of an eye, she was simply gone. One moment her presence had been there, above him, the next instant it was not.

Instead, a fear he had never known, even in the hottest battle, began to fill him, and he sensed another presence. But as he quickened his pace, he deliberately displaced the fear with the cleansing fire of rage. Had Laon killed his beloved, Raul intended to tear the man apart, limb by limb, until there was little left to throw over the edge of the mountain as sacrifice to the Master Whom she must have gone to join.

CHAPTER TWELVE

IN MIND AND SPIRIT, ESME ABRUPTLY FOUND HERSELF INside a cavern behind the Sacred Ledge at the top of the Holy Mountain. Wonderingly, she looked around her. No one of the People, not even the priests, as far as she knew, had ever suspected this place existed.

In the center of the cavern sat a squat black machine, and Esme stared at it, puzzled as to its purpose. But she ceased to think about it when the cavern suddenly became suffused with a penetrating, purifying light. Within that light was the Master's presence, and Esme, bathed in such love and peace as she had never known before, was overwhelmed with joy.

"Your love for Me is pleasing."

He spoke so gently that even though His voice was the sound of muted rolling thunder, Esme felt no fear.

"Had I known what You are truly like, Master," she said with utter sincerity, "I would have prayed from my earliest days that You would allow me to depart my human flesh and come to dwell with You in Your realm forever."

"It is My desire as well to have you with Me when the time is right," the Master replied. "But I have further need of your service in the realm of man, so it is necessary that you continue to dwell in the flesh until your days are full. Also, before you can truly choose to do My will, child, you must undergo a testing."

At that moment, immersed in the Master's presence, Esme could not conceive of choosing other than to do His bidding, nor of failing any test he set her. But then she remembered, with much shame, some things she had done that must have grieved Him, and she was devastated. Perhaps she must be tested because of the lives she had taken. She had killed Marcus, and turned the missiles back against the Rebel ship. True, both of those actions had been in self-defense. But the killing of Bazil had not been. She could have let him live, even though doing so would have resulted in further grief and trouble for the People. And she had also consorted unlawfully with Laon.

The Master knew her thoughts. "You are forgiven for those things, child," He said gently. "All life is Mine, and what I have created cannot be destroyed. Your actions served My purposes. Neither did you act out of hardness of heart, but rather out of righteousness and necessity. Your repentance is accepted."

Esme felt His forgiveness bathe her, and in reaction to her cleansing, she said, with fervent sincerity, "I will always do Your will, Master."

"You will," He responded, His tone compassionate,

"so long as you hold My word firmly in your mind and heart, for a time is coming when that is all you will have for protection. You will forget what you feel for Me now, and the emotions you will have in place of your love for Me will betray you if you do not take care."

Before Esme had time to protest His words, He answered a question that she would not have troubled Him with, for the answer no longer mattered to her.

"Your earthly father was Malthuzar, Esme," He said.

Esme immediately felt a sense of recognition. Why else had she always been so drawn to the old high priest? And why else the strangely personal quality of her grief and desire for vengeance when he had been murdered?

"Why did my mother not recognize him when he came to her on the high meadow?" she asked. "And why did he never claim me?"

"Because I masked such recognition from your mother's mind by presenting Malthuzar to her in a simulation of the form which he inhabited," the Master replied in His gentle voice. "Since she had to give birth to you, I could not erase the incident entirely from her memory as I did from Malthuzar's. But it was necessary that Malthuzar not remember in order to save him pain and temptation. For had he known you were his, he could not have resisted claiming you, and had he known of the gifts I made available to you, he could not have resisted putting you in service to the People. I did not wish his purity to be sullied by rebellion against My purpose for you, which could only be fulfilled if your life developed as it did."

Esme accepted the rightness of the Master's actions from the heart, and the pain of isolation she had endured in her early years now seemed an insignificant price to pay for the reward of being of service to Him.

Such explanations finished, the Master then turned Esme's attention to the squat black shape below them.

"What is it?" she asked.

"It is the means by which I kept My Remnant hidden and their spiritual truth uncorrupted," the Master explained. "Other of My servants in a time long past constructed it and left it here. And now, it is the means by which you, should you pass your testing, will keep the rest of My children from destroying one another as they almost did once before in the past.

"Even now," He went on, "those who feel themselves aligned to what they call the Empire are falling sway to the urgent promptings of mankind's ancient enemy. They debate among themselves using such power as their ancestors used once before to help destroy most of the Homeland I created for them. They are deciding to wipe the base of their warring brothers and sisters clean of life. This cannot be. In the process, they would not only stain their souls beyond My recovery, but they will lose another battle that is coming in the future."

"But why must there be such an enemy to mankind?" Esme dared ask a question that bothered her. "Why do You not destroy him?"

"The enemy was created just as humans were," the Master replied, "and that which is created cannot be destroyed. But though jealousy of Me led him astray and he rebelled, and though he corrupts the power he controls, he is still subject to My purposes. His purpose is to offer choice to humankind. Love for Me must be freely given or it is meaningless. Such freedom involves choice. The enemy is My alternative, and what is between us will one day be resolved, but it is not for you to know as yet the manner of such resolution."

"Then, instruct me as to Your Will and I will do it," Esme said humbly.

So simply and completely did Esme submit that she ventured no other question throughout the remainder of the meeting. She merely listened and heeded, and took joy in the Master's presence. And when He was done with His instructions and left her with a blessing, she was desolated by His absence. But she took comfort in the knowledge that she would one day, if she passed whatever test was coming—and she could not imagine, at the moment, failing to pass such a test—dwell in His presence again without end.

Laon squatted beside Esme's vacant body, shaking it, when Raul saw them. Had he had a laser with him, Raul would not have hesitated to use it. But since he had no weapon but his own strength and wits, he, teleported himself instantly to the ledge.

Laon became aware of Raul only an instant before he materialized upon the ledge, but it was long enough for him to vault across Esme's body and place it between the two of them.

"I had not known you had that trick," Laon sneered as he instantly launched an assault upon the fear for Esme he saw in Raul's mind. He crouched in a fighting stance at the same time, and started to draw his laser.

Raul brushed the attack on his mind aside, concentrating instead on Laon's laser which was the real

221

source of danger. And before Laon could get the weapon fully trained on him, he launched himself across Esme's body, toppling her still figure with his flying legs even as he smashed Laon into the wall of rock encompassing the ledge.

Laon was physically stronger than Raul had credited him, but it was still only a matter of moments before the laser flew over the edge of the shelf. Then Raul, exerting all his strength, tried to throw Laon into the deep chasm on the right of the ledge and to be done with him forever.

Esme's voice stopped him. "Raul?"

She sounded drowsy and distant, but Raul's joy at hearing her voice caused him to stop his efforts to throw Laon over the ledge, though he still held him tightly, and turn to look at her.

Laon stopped struggling for a moment. He, too, merely stared at Esme, his own fate temporarily forgotten.

She was rubbing her head where it had hit the rock when Raul vaulted over her, and her green eyes were as drowsy as her voice had been. They were also cloudy, as though her mind had returned from a great distance.

"Esme, are you all right?" Raul's voice was harsh and breathless, both with exertion and relief.

"I am well, Raul," she replied. Then, looking at the way Raul held Laon, she asked, very calmly, "What do you do with him?"

"I was in the act of killing him when you returned to yourself," Raul said grimly.

Laon at once began to struggle again, and as he twisted against Raul's grip, he addressed Esme, begging her with his dark eyes. "In the name of what we once shared, Esme, do not allow this!" he cried desperately. "You cannot see one with whom you shared Daccall be murdered! It is not possible!"

As he held his struggling prisoner, his muscles bulging and straining at the task, Raul looked hard at Esme over Laon's dark head, his gaze steady and ferocious, his mouth grimly set. Without saying a word, mentally or verbally, he left the decision to her. But it was very clear to Esme there would be a price to pay should she decide against his sense of rightness.

Then, as she took Laon's plan from his mind, her own sense of rightness was violated. But the fact that they were upon her Master's Mountain gave her pause. Would the Master be offended if Raul committed violence here?

"What we once shared is now of no import, Laon," she said, her voice flat and cold. "I have given to Raul what I withheld from you, and no more can you bind those chains about me." She turned her eyes from the agonized fear upon Laon's face then, and looked up at the sky. "And so is Ivvor gone from the Homeland's space," she added.

Returning her gaze to Laon's, her expression turned from cold to sad. "You handled him badly, Laon, as you have handled the care of your own soul so badly throughout your life. Could not one who had your gifts sense the Master's reality at all?"

Laon did not answer. He could not. His mind was babbling as uncontrollably with fear as his limbs were shaking with it.

Esme sighed and looked at Raul then, debating her former question. Would it offend the Master if Raul killed Laon on this mountain?

Before she could make up her mind, Laon called up

within himself every vestige of strength he could
muster and spun out of Raul's grip. He threw himself
forward, intending to escape. But his foot caught the
edge of a small crevice, and he stumbled. An instant
later, he tumbled over the edge of the Sacred Ledge
and fell screaming into empty space.

Esme covered her ears against those screams, but
Raul did not. Instead, he took a step toward Esme and
pulled her almost violently up into his arms where he
held her so tightly, she almost could not breathe.

Esme clung to him, deeply thankful that if it was a
long time before she could be with the Master forever,
He had given her a love more than sufficient to carry
her through the intervening years.

Esme and Raul stood side by side, watching Jase
circle the Master's squat black machine. He alternate-
ly patted it and scratched his head in puzzlement.

"It is not meant to be understood as you understand
things, Jase," Esme said. "It is only meant to be
used."

"Aye." Jase nodded. "But before it can be used, it
must be moved. And I cannot judge its weight to
ascertain if we can take it back with us in the Talon or
if we will have to send a cargo ship for it."

Esme hesitated, glancing at Raul. She knew he
would not be pleased by what she was about to say.
But he had so far listened to all she had told him of the
Master's plan without too much disbelief, if not with
total agreement. And she had so far proved the truth
of her words. Perhaps his patience would stretch just a
little further?

Speaking placatingly so as not to usurp his authority, she told him what was in her mind. But his

reaction, as she had feared it would be, was not a pleasant one.

"What?" His head came up and his rugged face was suddenly creased into a ferocious scowl, while his eyes were narrowed and cold. "You want me to tear the guts out of the Talon and leave most of my men here in order to transport that thing to Genesis?"

Esme put a gentle hand on his shoulder and held his eyes. "That thing will end the war, Raul," she spoke very softly. "Used properly, that is," she added, her tone even softer, for this was the main area of Raul's disagreement with the Master's plan. Raul was not happy with the idea of using what he called "blackmail" on his own government.

Raul clenched his jaw and looked away. "Esme, you stretch my capacity for cooperation to the edge of my tolerance."

"I know, beloved," she said quietly, consolingly, and she leaned against him, and stroked his broad back with loving touches.

"Stop that!" he growled, straightening and shrugging off her hand. "I will not be seduced by your woman's wiles in a matter of such importance!"

Esme sighed and hugged her middle. "It was not seduction I practiced, Raul," she said simply. "I merely offered comfort because I sympathize with your frustration."

Raul didn't answer. Instead he paced a few feet away, his eyes on Jase, who still studied the object on the cavern floor.

Raul had shielded his thoughts from her, but Esme was aware of the turmoil inside him and she did not blame him for it. She was asking him to tear the guts from a ship he regarded with much the same pride and care as a mother might a child. Further, she was asking him to go against the oath of loyalty he had given his government and stand aside while she, a primitive barbarian with no true knowledge of politics or war, conducted negotiations that would decide the fate of many worlds and all their populations. She was asking all this on the strength of a private meeting with a master Raul had no firsthand knowledge of and only half-believed in, despite what he had taken from her mind regarding the power and nature of the Master.

Truly, Esme sighed to herself, she was asking a lot.

Suddenly, Raul looked at her over his shoulder, his expression hard. "If this Master of yours has such power," he demanded, "why does He need us at all? Why does He not just wave His hand and accomplish what He wants?"

Esme shrugged. "I do not pretend to understand everything, my heart," she said gently. "If I were to guess, I would say it has to do with the free will He gives us." She shrugged again, then added, with gentle humor, "Would you truly like it if He waved His hand and deprived you of all choice, of the chance to participate in His plans, and to perform as a puppet instead? I think not."

"And I think I feel much used anyway," Raul grated. "When He put you in my path, it seems He gave with one hand and took away with the other. I have not felt truly my own man, capable of exercising free will, since the day I first laid eyes on you."

"Raul!" Esme was dismayed, alarmed, and afraid. She remembered an occasion upon which he had warned her to be careful of how she exercised her power in her dealings with him, that he was uneasy about the sort of relationship they shared. She had thought he had gotten over such feelings when he came to have mind powers of his own, that since sharing Daccall together, nothing could come between them. But then she realized that the Master could make or break anything, and suddenly she was terrified.

"Esme . . ." Seeing the look in her eyes and feeling the terror in her mind, Raul spoke to her impatiently, but much more gently than he had done earlier in their discussion.

He pulled her to him and held her, but Esme was not wholly reassured. Ambivalence still had its place in his heart and mind, and she knew not how to displace it without abrogating a larger obligation set upon her.

Raul sighed heavily. "Duty, as always, has its price," he said with dry curtness. Then he let her go and spoke to Jase. "See about the mechanism which Esme tells us will open the mountain top, Jase!" he ordered. "We will worry about how to get the thing off the planet after we see whether we can even get it out of this mountain!"

Then he turned to Esme, his expression calm, but distant. "If you are coming with us back to Genesis," he said levelly, "you'd best see about completing your instructions to Baldor. He grows impatient, and I have other things to do which will keep me busy for a while."

Esme stared at him, hurt and angered by his unfairness. But he merely looked away rather than take his leave of her in a more affectionate manner.

It was Esme's anger which made her pivot and walk away without making a further attempt to heal the breach she felt widening between them. But by the time she reached the bottom of the mountain to go in search of Baldor, it was the hurt she felt that brought tears into her green eyes and a heavy feeling of loss into her heart.

The entire population of the Settlement, Esme and Baldor among them, stood at the base of the Master's Holy Mountain, careful not to set foot over the invisible boundary that marked the Master's domain from unhallowed ground.

Every head was upturned, and every mind save Esme's was filled with fear and awe as the Talon's six hovers formed a circle around the now open mountaintop.

Though it was too far to see them, Esme knew that cables snaked down from the hovers into the opened maw of the mountain and that Jase and his men were even now attaching those cables to the black machine that rested on the floor of the cavern and had not seen the light of the Homeland's sun for years past telling.

Esme felt as though it had been years since she had seen or spoken to Raul. She had spent the week instructing Baldor, whom she intended to put forward as high priest before she left the Homeland again. They were both much fatigued, for there had been little time to waste sleeping.

Even the presence of offworld humans among them had not been able to pierce the last tiny core of Baldor's disbelief that the Prophecy could truly be unfolding. His mind could accept it on a certain level. But the habit of unfulfillment was so strong in him, part of him resisted wholehearted acceptance, until Esme had opened her mind to him and allowed him to eavesdrop on her meeting with the Master.

She had done it so the meeting would be recorded in the Sacred Scrolls as well as to convince Baldor. Also she had requested a copy of her journal from Jemiah, who was rapidly learning the People's language and intended to stay with some of the Talon's men on the Homeland when Esme, Raul, and a skeleton crew left for Genesis. She gave the journal to Baldor to be recorded.

Now, as the hovers began to rise and as slowly, gradually, the shape of the black machine appeared, she heard the gasp of the People and most clearly the prayer of acceptance and joy in Baldor's mind.

Esme smiled, wearily. Also from the minds of the People was she taking the determination of some of the young ones to apply as seekers. That task also had yet to be accomplished before she left the Homeland. The Master had instructed that new seekers be chosen. And with her ability to see into minds, it was logical for her to help with the selection process in order to avoid promoting another Bazil into a position of importance.

The black machine was clear of the mountain now, and the hovers, moving in perfect synchronization— which was only possible, Esme knew, because Raul held the minds of the pilots with the power of his own mind—began to carry their burden across the desert to the stripped and gutted Talon.

Esme had learned that Raul would grant her requests from Jase, and not from her beloved. When she had once visited the Talon, where Raul now stayed, with her mind, she had found his shield tightly closed, and she had known, to her despair, that he did not wish to speak to her. Therefore, she had, from time to time, visited the cavern with her mind, and without disturbing Jase, had taken from his mind the nature of the work in progress.

She had learned by that method that the mechanism that controlled the overhead doors of the cavern had been found. But layers of dirt and rock that had accumulated over the ages, had to be removed from the mountaintop and the People would not help. The prohibition against stepping upon the Holy Mountain was too engrained in them. Therefore, the work had to be done by Raul's men, as well as gutting the Talon. Therefore both tasks had taken longer than they would have otherwise.

Though she could spare little time from her work with Baldor, Esme would have helped had she been asked. But she had not been contacted for any reason, by Raul or by any of his men, throughout the whole week she had spent with Baldor. And as each day had gone by, the empty space in her heart had grown larger and colder, and it had taken much willpower for Esme to resist her often frantic desire to go to Raul and attempt to heal things between them.

But she had known, on some deep, instinctive level that had nothing to do with her powers and everything to do with her emotions, that such a visit would do no good. Raul would have to make the first move to reconcile them, or it would not happen. With so much initiative taken already from his hands, Esme knew she must leave this very personal decision to him alone or risk the loss of everything there had been between them.

Now, as the hovers flew out of sight, the crowd knelt at Baldor's instruction for a prayer.

"Esme?" He said her name respectfully, and she

realized with a start as she came out of her thoughts that she was the only one left standing. "Do you wish to conduct the prayer?" Baldor asked.

Esme took in a deep breath and shook her head. "No, Baldor. You do it." She knelt in front of him, head bowed, eyes closed, just as if she were any ordinary member of the People.

While Baldor conducted his prayer of thankful joy that the Master was at last granting the fulfillment of the Prophecy, Esme prayed her own prayer. "Master, I will, as I promised, do Your Will," she said, quietly submissive. "But I beg You please, do not make me pay so high a price for the privilege of serving You. If I must live a long while in this flesh before I come to You in my spiritual body, I ask for a portion of the joy those in the flesh have always sought."

When she rose to her feet again, Esme was not sure how or whether the Master would grant her request. But she felt a measure of calm return to her at having voiced it plainly, and she was refreshed enough to begin, upon the return to the Settlement, the selection of a great many young seekers who would follow in Malthuzar's and Baldor's and their predecessors' footsteps. Esme did not know whether anyone would ever again be asked to follow in her own.

Raul did not come for her. Instead, when the crew who would stay upon the Homeland arrived in the hovers, he sent instructions that she was to come to the Talon on the returning hover. The rest of the hovers would stay with the men and one would be used to conduct Jemiah on explorations where no one of the People had ever gone before.

Baldor had tears in his eyes when Esme said farewell. "You will return?" he asked hesitantly.

Esme took from his mind the knowledge that her departure impressed upon him heavily the nature of the burden he would carry in her absence.

"Yes, I will return, Baldor," she said gently. "But if you would have your burdens eased, there is a certain young woman I have learned would gladly bear them with you as your mate."

Baldor blinked away his tears, his surprise clear to Esme. "Who?" he asked.

Instead of answering verbally, Esme put into his mind a vision of Dallia, the young female who had helped her prepare for her mating.

"Really?"

Esme saw that Baldor's cares began to slip ever so little from his shoulders, and she smiled with affection at him.

"Really." She nodded. "Only you must seek her out rather than wait for her to come to you for she is too modest to assume that the new high priest might be interested in her."

He smiled and nodded, and Esme hugged him before turning to Maza.

"Have you someone in mind for me as well?" Maza asked, not entirely happy. He, too, was saddened by Esme's departure.

Esme didn't hesitate. She had seen the looks of warm regard Maza had been receiving from a certain young lady she knew Maza would never presume to court without encouragement.

"Fresco's girl," she said, naming a stone mason who lived in the Settlement and thought much of himself and little of shepherds.

Maza looked astonished. "She is but a child!" he

protested. "And her father would never permit it!"

"I did not say there was someone for you immediately," Esme retorted humorously. "But in a year or two . . ." She shrugged. "No father can stand between true mates," she reminded him. Then she hugged and kissed him and moved on to Jemiah.

"Esme, my dear," he said fondly, taking her small hands in his own. "I will be ever grateful for this adventure you have propelled me into. I am even beginning to wonder, just a little, if perhaps you could be right about your homeland being the original homeland of all mankind. Perhaps my coming explorations will answer the question once and for all."

Esme grinned at him. "Do not lose all your skepticism, Jemiah," she advised teasingly. "You would seem undressed without it."

He laughed. "Aye, that I would."

Esme hugged Ana and Dallia and addressed a few words of farewell to the rest of the People, who had assembled at the gathering place to see her off. Then she boarded the hover and watched, her eyes filmed with tears, the Settlement fade from her vision until at last the hover crossed the Barrier Mountains and she could see no more.

Then she sat quietly until the pilot set the hover down in front of the Talon's large cargo doors, and she was forlornly sad as she walked up the ramp. For Thorson was not there to greet her this time. He would never be there again until Esme's fleshly body had been forsaken as his had been. As she came through the hatchway into the Talon, she felt the absence of his spirit, and she missed him terribly.

Absentmindedly, she made her way to Raul's cabin. But once inside its confines, thought returned and she hesitated, wondering if he intended her to share his quarters on the journey to Genesis. There was little space for her to stay elsewhere, but perhaps he was not yet ready even to sleep again beside her, much less share with her the sort of intimacy that had once given both of them cause for so much joy.

She shrugged, her expression bereaved. *If he wants me elsewhere or if he prefers to stay elsewhere himself, doubtless it will soon be made known to me,* she decided.

With a heavy heart, she stored away her mating gown, which was all that she had brought with her. She had given the Sacred Pouch to Baldor upon his appointment as high priest, which the People had confirmed, complying with her wishes.

Then she lay down upon Raul's bed for sleep had been too much unavailable during the past week for her to resist any longer the senseless ease of mind and body.

A sense of being watched brought Esme abruptly awake, and she knew in an instant that the Talon was already in orbit around the Homeland. She had slept through lift-off.

She turned upon her back, and then upon her side, and found Raul leaning against the bulkhead, his arms folded across his chest, staring at her with a brooding look of distant concentration.

When he spoke, he did not straighten from his position. "If we run into a Rebel force as extensive as that which stalked us on our way here, will your Master's device provide us any protection?"

Esme was disappointed that he had sought her out only to discuss such practical matters. But her voice was calm, and showed nothing of her feelings, when she answered. "Aye, but I must activate it. It has been inactive since you first arrived in this solar system aboard the Condor, when you set the ship down for repair."

Raul's smile was not amused. "I see. Your Master turned it off to allow our meeting?"

His tone and manner made Esme uneasy, but she did not hesitate long before giving him the truth. Always there would be truth between them, she thought sadly, even if nothing else they shared lasted.

She sat up, swinging her legs over the edge of the bed. But she did not look at Raul while she answered. Instead, she studied with much intensity her own dangling feet.

"No, He did not come Himself and turn it off," she said quietly. "It was set long, long ago to deactivate at the very instant you appeared in this solar system."

Raul stayed silent, his shield tightly down. Esme resisted the desire to look at him and she did not even feel the desire to try to penetrate his shield, for she was afraid of what she would find behind it.

"So I have had no choice at all in anything. We have been bound by your Master's will since birth," he finally said, so softly that Esme barely heard. In any case, it was not a question; it was a statement, and thus required no answer.

He stayed silent for so long thinking that Esme became alarmed. She could tell nothing from his expression, and again, she did not dare try to probe his mind.

When he finally spoke, the interruption of his silence startled her. "Your friends Baldor and Maza informed me that men and women of the People cannot deny one another the use of their bodies," he said with no inflection in his voice. "They say that it is a duty to comply with all such desires either might have."

Confused, Esme frowned. What Raul said was true but she could not comprehend why he would make such a statement. Surely, he knew that she would always wish to mate with him out of love and not out of duty and she hoped he felt the same.

"But perhaps," he mused thoughtfully, "you have become so powerful you are no longer bound by the traditions of your people. Perhaps you are like a Genesian woman now, insistent that her mate has no say about what she will and will not do."

Esme was now alarmed. How could Raul think she had changed so much? She knew he was having difficulty with the knowledge that his meeting with her, their relationship, and everything that had happened recently, and would likely happen in the future, had not been by his choice, but had been instigated by the Master. He was a man of duty, yes. But he was unused to being bereft of consultation in matters concerning his own fate. But how could he think she would ever cease to value his feelings on any matter?

"I am not all powerful, Raul," she said gently. "And I am not Genesian. And while it is true that among the People a man's and a woman's rights and duties concerning life-mating are spelled out, successful matings come about through love and with the use of gentle persuasion rather than insistence on rights and duty. You will never have to wonder whether I mate with you because it is a duty. It will always be from desire for you."

But her attempt to reassure him did not make

Raul's expression change. Nor did he reply. He merely continued to stare at her in a way that she could not fathom his thoughts. And he still maintained his mind shield.

At last, Esme decided to use action instead of words to try to heal his injured pride. She rose from the bed and stripped away her bodysuit.

When she was unclothed, she went to him, and though she received no encouragement from his unblinking stare, and no assistance from him in her task, she stripped his clothing away as well.

Gesturing at the bed, she spoke with gentle persuasion. "If you will lie down, I will show you I have not become a Genesian woman, Raul."

But Raul did not lie down and he did not lower his shield to permit her entrance into his mind, as had become their habit when they made love. Instead, he stood unmoving and said nothing. He merely stared at her.

Esme hesitated but she could no longer bear the distance between them, and after a moment, she went to Raul and knelt at his feet.

But as she performed for him an act that had its roots in her desire to bring them together once again, he failed to participate other than at the end, when in the throes of his release, he wound his fingers in her hair and groaned. And afterward, as Esme remained on her knees, her head down, her heart torn with despair, he paused for a moment and she knew he waited to hear if she required a similar service from him. But Esme did not wish to be serviced. She wished to be loved.

When it became apparent that she would not ask for what she desired, Raul quickly dressed himself and took his leave without tossing a word of love or comfort to her.

It was a long time before Esme got to her feet. She was too numb with despair to move for a different explanation of Raul's earlier words about the rights and duties of mating couples on the Homeland had occurred to her. Apparently, he did not worry that she might allow him to use her body out of duty rather than love. Instead, he intended to allow her the use of his body only because it was a duty he owed her. Obviously, his love for her had not overpowered his belief that his choice of her as a mate had not been voluntary. And now he no longer loved her.

At last she found the energy to rise to her feet. She showered and dressed and went to the Master's artifact to perform the sequence of mind commands the Master had taught her which activated the machine's inner mechanism. When it hummed into renewed life, she returned to Raul's cabin, and though she was not hungry, she attempted to eat out of habit, and almost lost the food lying heavily in her stomach when the ship shuddered on its first jump.

Later, upon Raul's bed, alone in the semidarkness, she struggled hard with her pain and her pride and her love for Raul before reaching a decision. Had it been possible, she would have released Raul from his obligations to her. But she was bound by the vows she had spoken in the presence of the People, and such bonds could not be broken. Also she was even further held by the bonds of mind and heart Raul had put upon her during Daccall.

She had thought at the time that Raul had also taken the same bonds upon himself and she would have sworn he had not held any part of himself back.

But obviously, she had been wrong. He no longer desired to be bound to her emotionally. While carrying out her Master's task, she must somehow have stepped over that line Raul had long ago warned her of that destroyed his pride and sense of control, and she had lost the part of him she most cared to have.

But honor had to be maintained regardless of the cost to her pride and to her pride and to her own and Raul's happiness. No other choice was open to her. She must continue as Raul's mate until the time when he walked away, which of course, she now expected him to do at some point, unless his own sense of duty and honor would not permit it.

Upon making that hard decision, her sorrow was heavier than she thought she could bear. Therefore Esme sent her body to sleep so that she might no longer have to think with her mind and feel with her heart.

CHAPTER THIRTEEN

COME, LITTLE SISTER.

Esme frowned and stirred uneasily in her sleep, coming half-awake. She was vaguely relieved that her movements had not disturbed Raul, for he was not beside her in the bed. Then, in the wake of a deep sadness that accompanied her realization of why he was not beside her, she fell heavily into sleep again, unaware of what had brought her to the point of wakefulness.

Little sister, come!

This time, the chilling, powerful voice in her mind was stronger, and it was accompanied by a surge of power that could not be denied. Abruptly, Esme's eyes were forced open, and in the next instant she focused on a shape outlined in a shimmering glow of light. But the light was not pure and white as was the Master's and it did not warm or comfort her.

240

With a cold chill of recognition, Esme knew the testing the Master had spoken of was upon her. She also knew why the enemy had chosen this particular time to test her. Her sorrow over the loss of Raul's regard had weakened her resolve to do the Master's will.

Come!

Despite the unholy power underlying the command and her present weakness, Esme thought she could still exert her will enough to refuse this testing. And with all her heart, that was what she wished to do, for a coldness lay on her soul such as she had never felt before. The enemy's presence seemed to extinguish every spark of light and warmth within her. She could no longer recall the love, joy, and peace she had felt in the Master's presence. But she could recall His words. He had said she could not truly choose to do His will until she had undergone this testing, and He had said His word was to be her defense. Therefore, the coming confrontation must be necessary.

No sooner had she acknowledged the necessity of the confrontation, and thereby given her tacit consent to it, than she was lifted bodily from the bed. An instant later, under the control of a force she could not resist, she was propelled through the vaccum of space at a speed that left her skin prickling with pain.

Just as she feared her body could not survive another second of the journey, she was dropped, without ceremony, to the surface of a vast, desolate wasteland. The impact drove the breath from her lungs and sent shafts of agony through her. But even as she suffered, she knew her physical pain, added to the emotional pain she felt over the loss of Raul's regard and the bitter, empty loneliness of no longer sensing the Master's presence in her mind and spirit, was part of the enemy's plan.

Her knowledge was confirmed an instant later.

"Let my touch soothe your pain, little sister."

The enemy's voice was deceitfully compassionate. But Esme had learned from the Sacred Scrolls that there was no true compassion to be found in his spirit. He was the father of lies, the ancient, implacable enemy of all her kind. Everything he said, anything he pretended to give, no matter how seemingly innocent, no matter how beautifully presented, would be a trap. She must therefore take care to accept nothing he offered.

"No!" she gasped. "Do not touch me!"

She was not yet looking at him, but she knew he shrugged his shoulders.

"So suspicious!" he chided. "And of your own brother."

Esme did not answer. She concentrated on her body, waiting for breath to be restored to her tortured lungs and the pain of her flesh to ease. Somehow, she knew not to use her special powers to aid the process. She must conduct this confrontation as an ungifted human would, with only the weapons common to humankind as her defense. Otherwise, the enemy could claim the test had been flawed by the Master's unlawful aid.

As Esme lay slumped in physical, emotional, and spiritual agony, panic and terror threatened to engulf her mind. How could she win this confrontation against such power as the enemy held when she was so weak, so bereft of all help?

But before she despaired completely, she remembered again the Master's words, "You will do My will,

Esme, so long as you hold My word firmly in your mind and heart." At that remembrance, her panic and terror subsided to a manageable level.

You are no more bereft of help than any of human-kind has ever been, she told herself firmly. *You have knowledge of the truth of the Master's nature, even if you can no longer feel it. And you have choice. The enemy has no power to compel. He can only persuade.*

When she could breathe normally again, she sat up and looked around her, shuddering in horror at the desolation. The only light on the vast, stark plain came from the enemy, and his light was a swirl of dull, curiously seductive color which she could not name. It was no color she had ever seen before and yet its light allowed her to see clearly and then she froze.

Standing against the backdrop of the desolate plain was such perfection as Esme could scarcely believe. Indeed, the enemy's overwhelming beauty must be the root and personification of all beauty. No one perceiving it could fail to be enthralled with awe and Esme was no less awed than any other of her kind would have been.

Unbidden, the description of the enemy contained in the Sacred Scrolls rose to her mind: "Thou sealest up the sum, full of wisdom, and perfect in beauty. Thou wast perfect in thy ways from the day that thou was created, till iniquity was found in thee."

Esme frowned at that last phrase. She did not want it to be true. It was so deeply, terribly wrong for the perfection she viewed to be flawed in any way that it seemed an offense against the very source of rightness. The beauty that filled her eyes was an end in itself, a unique force, capable of commanding worship in its own right.

243

"Ah . . ." the enemy said with purring satisfaction as he took that last thought from her mind. "You are beginning to understand."

His voice was a seductive force that joined irresistibly with his magnificent appearance so that for a moment, Esme could do nothing but drink him in with every sense the Master had created within her.

But at recalling that it was the Master who had created the senses the enemy was now employing to beguile her, a vague shaft of uneasiness pierced Esme's soul. "Understand?" she absently inquired.

"Yes." He nodded his head, and it was as though the majesty of all the kings who had ever reigned from the beginning of time was combined and enhanced in the gesture. "You are beginning to understand the crime that has been done to me, little sister."

Esme felt confused. Why did he call her "little sister"? And what crime was it he spoke of?

But even as her mind formed the last question, it drifted away from it and focused on the first one. "Why do you call me 'sister'?" she asked.

His smile was seduction personified. Possessive and thrilling, it warmed her womanhood with heat and flattered her sense of her own importance, provoking within Esme a fierce desire to please him.

"Because that is what you are," he said approvingly. "Surely, you are aware of your own divinity by now?"

The thought of being the equal of the one who called her "sister" sparked a feeling of intense pleasure within Esme. But the pleasure was immediately followed by another vague warning in her mind. The Master had not termed her "divine." He had explained that she was the human child of human parents, Esther and Malthuzar. And perhaps His explanation had been designed to counter the temptation of accepting the enemy's unlawful elevation of her status. It was sacrilege for the enemy to suggest she was divine, just as it was blasphemy for her to accept such a designation.

However, she could not seem to hold onto her thoughts, not while gazing into the enemy's luminous eyes, eyes that made her senses swim with pleasure and her heart ache with indescribable longing.

"You have been destined from the beginning of time to rule by my side," the enemy whispered seductively. "Behold our kingdom, sister . . ."

He raised an arm that seemed powerful enough to sweep stars from their orbits, and Esme was suddenly no longer on the stark plain. She was suspended in the deep black velvet of all space and all time, and a rainbow-hued galaxy danced for her pleasure.

Had she not seen this marvel before in her travels with Raul, Esme would have been overwhelmed with awe. But even now, prepared by previous experience for such a sight, the sense of power the enemy created within her made the experience different.

Previously, her eyes had merely delighted in the Master's handiwork. Now, she felt that if she wished, she could stretch out a finger and set the galaxy before her eyes spinning at a faster and faster pace, the way the children of Genesis played with a toy peculiar to their planet. She could make the gases between the stars form into new stars in the blink of an eye, and explode them an instant later. She could make a whole galaxy perform in obeisance to her will.

But hard upon the heel of such thoughts came the

realization that those who peopled the planets of the galaxy she would make into a toy would be destroyed by her careless actions.

The enemy's voice whispered in her ear. "Go on," he said. "Their only purpose in existing is to serve us, sister. See them worship . . ."

And in a flash, she saw vast, uncountable rows of people kneeling at her feet, praising her name. Then the enemy reached out and did what Esme had only imagined doing. He set the galaxy spinning. Stars formed and unformed before her eyes in the space of an instant and the people who knelt before her spun into oblivion and died.

Horrified, Esme turned to look into the fathomless, infinitely seductive eyes of the one who had caused such devastation. He hovered so close, she could almost reach out and touch him. But he did not allow her to touch him, nor did he touch her, and abruptly, Esme knew why. His elusiveness was a trap, for it created within her a savage longing for what she could not have—unless she granted him the fealty and worship he craved.

Smiling promises that made Esme tremble, the enemy acknowledged what she might have if she chose him.

"In time," he said, "when you are completely committed to me, you will have such power and pleasure as you cannot imagine, such pleasure as cannot be described, but only felt."

The choice was before her. Choose the enemy, and she would have such power as no human had ever held. But the power the enemy offered was not as tempting to Esme as was the pleasure. As always, the enemy's temptation targeted the particular nature of the tempted, and Esme was a woman who longed to love and to be loved to the fullest possible extent. Furthermore, she was a woman who was already bereft because of Raul's emotional withdrawal from their relationship.

Thinking of Raul, Esme unconsciously made a comparison between the beauty of the enemy and Raul's merely human appeal. Inevitably, her mate's craggy human handsomeness was nothing compared to the magnificence of the enemy's stunning appeal. Too, Raul did not appreciate her as the enemy did. He no longer loved her while the enemy valued her so much that he offered. . . .

But as Esme poised on the brink of choice, thinking about what the enemy offered, again the words of the Sacred Scrolls concerning his nature rose within her mind: "Thine heart was lifted up because of thy beauty, and thou hast corrupted thy wisdom by reason of thy brightness. I will cast thee to the ground. I will lay thee before kings, that they may behold thee.

"Thou hast defiled thy sanctuaries by the multitude of thine iniquities, by the iniquity of thy traffic; therefore will I bring forth a fire from the midst of thee, which shall devour thee, and I will bring thee to ashes upon the earth in the sight of all them that behold thee.

"All they that know thee among the people shall be astonished at thee. Thou shalt be a terror, and never shalt thou be any more."

"The people you just destroyed . . ." Esme whispered to the enemy. "Did they choose against you?"

She sensed a sudden black turmoil within him. But

then, he gave a contemptuous flick of his hand in the direction of the now wildly gyrating galaxy. "No, they were mine," he smiled.

Instantly, whispering through Esme's mind at the speed of light, sped the designation *"father of lies."* Had those people truly been his? Or did he claim them unjustly, as he had destroyed them so violently?

"But there are always more of them," he went on. "And in any case, their only purpose in existing was to praise my name."

Esme stared at him, trying desperately to fight the effect of his beauty and think clearly. And as she began to try harder to resist, her will strengthened.

"*Your* name," she repeated. "But they were praising *my* name. And if I am your divine sister, is that not as it should be?"

The eyes which had previously fascinated her with undreamed of promises now went slightly opaque.

"That which I just showed you was not the present," he dissembled. "It was the future. Once you have acknowledged me as Lord and become my consort, you will, of course, reflect in my glory, and what you just saw will come to be."

As Esme understood that the galaxy and the people she had seen praising her name and then dying were an illusion, she felt an overwhelming sense of relief. The destruction she had witnessed had not truly happened, and her will strengthened further.

"But if I am your sister," she said, the words coming more quickly now, "why must I acknowledge your superiority over me? And how is it that brother and sister can become consorts?"

He frowned, and his frown was as exaggerated as everything else about him. Esme felt his disapproval as a sharp sword in her heart. Yet at the same time that her heart suffered, her mind noted clearly that the enemy's disapproval sprang from her catching him in his attempt to deceive her. He had counted on her emotions to confuse her reason.

"I could not have a consort who is unworthy of me," he said. "Therefore, you, my divine sister, must be my bride. We are not bound by the same rules that operate with humankind. But naturally, there can only be one who has *complete* power. And such power is mine by right. But in return for your loyalty to me, you will be recompensed beyond your ability even to conceive of it until I have gifted you with—"

"If I were truly divine," Esme interrupted, her strength growing by the moment, "then surely I could conceive of anything. But I am not divine. I am human. Only the Master is truly divine."

It was as though the Name contained incalculable force. At Esme's voicing it, the enemy spun away from her as though struck by an invisible blow, and Esme's will firmed immeasurably.

The enemy staggered, regained his balance, then faced her again across light years of space. But despite the vast distance that separated them now, she could still see his face clearly and the beauty of it had changed. His regal features were now distorted, tragic, shredded by rage.

Esme spoke again, the words tumbling from her mouth. Her salvation rested upon them, and she could not utter them fast enough. "No crime has been committed against you. You are instead the criminal. When you chose to let envy and ambition find a place in your heart, and thereby craved the worship that belongs to the Master, you chose your eventual fate.

You forfeited the purpose for which you were created. And now the Master has given you another purpose. You are His instrument.

"It is out of that envy in your heart that you try to destroy what you cannot create. You have power yes, but only such power as the One who created you gave you upon your creation. It is not of your own making. And when your new purpose is finished, you will have lost not only all you once had and gave up, but all that your envy and ambition led you to seek."

As Esme paused for breath, the enemy's reply came to her across the light years of silence. "I have lost nothing!" he roared. "The final decision as to who deserves worship is to come! And if you will but choose in my favor, it will come all the sooner, and I will give you that for which you long in return!"

But almost all the longing he had previously inspired in Esme was gone now and in its place was such profound pity that she could have cried. She would have wept scalding tears for the loss of all her enemy had once been, and could have been for all eternity, had not his pride and envy been forces as powerful as his beauty.

He took her thoughts from her and could not bear them.

"You fool!" he screamed. "Will you bow the knee to that Other when you could be almost my equal, worshipped as my consort, and bow your knee to no one in the entire universe?"

"Liar!" Esme turned aside his words. "I would have to bow the knee in any case. You would not truly share your power with me. Nor would you share the pleasure you promised. You cannot share anything."

She hesitated for an infinitesimal second, then

asked the question she had to voice, though she already knew the answer. Her pity for the enemy, her agonizing regret over the loss of all that he could have been, would not let her stay silent. "Mayhap it is not too late," she pleaded. "Can you not change course and obey even now?"

"Never!" All his rage, all his envy, all his destructive pride reverberated in that one word.

Accepting the inevitable, Esme nodded. "Yes, I know. And because you cannot, you will lose everything. Indeed, you have already lost."

"I have not and I will not lose!" he roared. "We will count forces when the final battle is finished, and then you will see who has won and who has lost!"

"And the number of souls you win will not satisfy you because they will not be total," Esme replied. "While the quality of those souls you do win will be of such paucity that you cannot take pride in them."

At that, he seemed to swell until he filled all space. But Esme knew it was another illusion, a trick, and she was no longer intimidated by his fury, nor seduced by his beauty, nor tempted by his false promises. As the Master had said it would, His word had saved her.

Then, to her astonishment, the enemy laughed, but his laughter was as much a lie as his words to her had been. It was false bravado. Or perhaps, Esme thought as the force of his laughter brushed against her and sent her body spinning in the blackness of space, it sprang from a merciful ignorance of his eventual fate. Perhaps he could not let himself believe the truth he must know existed, lest his existence be unbearable.

Then abruptly, he disappeared, and Esme was falling through the blackness, falling at the speed of light it seemed. But before she could even worry that she might burst into flame, she found herself once again upon the bed in Raul's cabin aboard the Talon, safe and saved—and very much alone.

Never had she needed more the comfort of Raul's arms around her and the sound of his voice soothing the pain of her heart and mind. She needed his solidness, his warmth, his humanity, his decency— his love.

But his side of the bed was empty, and Esme, bereft of all comfort, wept as she had never wept before.

But as the storm of her tears passed, and she lay exhausted and drained, she heard, as she had heard on the morning the Master had called her to His mountain, the sound of His voice in her mind, and she felt the touch of His loving presence in her heart.

You have met the test, Esme. Now go on to do My will.

And in the next instant, at peace again, she slept.

CHAPTER FOURTEEN

Upon waking, Esme's heart leapt with hope, and desire rose within her, for though she had not heard or felt him join her, Raul lay sleeping beside her.

He slept lightly, in the fashion of warriors, and upon feeling her eyes upon him, he opened his own and turned his head to look at her. At his expression, the hope that had risen in Esme's heart abruptly disappeared. He might have been viewing a stranger.

At his first words, Esme realized he had sensed the desire she felt for his lovemaking. Though her hope had died, her needs had not.

"Do you wish my use?" he asked.

There was no hostility in his voice. Indeed, his tone was punctiliously polite, too polite to contain any of the love and regard for her that Esme yearned to hear.

It was beyond her to lie but it was her intention to reject what he offered. It was too much less than what she was accustomed to receiving, and which she still desired with all her heart.

"Yes," she whispered, her tone bereft. "But . . ."

She was not allowed to carry out her refusal of what Raul offered on his new terms. For the instant the word yes left her lips, his mouth was on hers and by the time he allowed her to speak again, it was too late. Her willpower was gone, fled under an onslaught of desire she could not control. His hands upon her body had sparked her senses into such a flaming conflagration, she was defenseless, unable and unwilling to stop what he did.

But again, there was no mind union to match the union of their bodies and there was no emotional rapport. And when they both had obtained the release of their mutual sexual tension, the rest of Esme was too empty and uncomforted to make the physical satisfaction worth noting.

Afterward, Raul did not hold her close as had been his habit. Instead, without speaking, he rose, showered, and dressed.

Esme still lay in bed, her eyes closed, her mind drifting aimlessly. She did not want to think the thoughts that cried for her attention.

"I will eat with the men," Raul said as he pushed the button that operated the hatch, and an instant later, he was gone.

And such was the pattern of their mating for the rest of their uneventful, rapid journey to Genesis. Raul was mostly absent from Esme's side, and when he came to bed, though he used her body at times, he did not share any other portion of himself with her. Then he would sleep, briefly, before returning to his duty.

Esme permitted the mating not only because it was

her duty, but because once Raul touched her, she could not stop herself from responding. Also, she hoped such intimacies would evolve again into what they had once been. But only on the night before they reached Genesian orbit did she sense anything different in Raul.

As he undressed for bed, she lay watching him, shielding her thoughts as had become her habit these days. She thought about her testing at the hands of the enemy, and how grateful she was that the Master had come to comfort her afterwards, since Raul had not.

Then Raul was beside her, reaching for her. She sensed that he was struggling with something within himself, but his inner struggle was only made apparent to her by the difference in his use of her. For the first time since the journey back to Genesis had begun, did he show any tenderness toward her emotions. But the tenderness alternated bewilderingly with his indifference, so that the hope that flickered at one point in their mating was killed before it could grow into a steady flame.

The next day they were in orbit around Genesis, and Esme's personal feelings ceased to matter. For upon arriving there, she sensed how very little time she had in which to avert the disaster the Master had informed her was coming, and under the impetus of necessity, she went in search of her mate for the first time since boarding the Talon on the Homeland.

She found him in the control cabin, and he looked up as she came through the hatch. She felt his surprise first that she had sought him out, then his withdrawal as he saw the look upon her face.

"How long until we set down?" she asked.

"There is a delay," Raul replied, his voice cool.

"Orbital traffic has been instructed to avoid landing until further orders are given."

Esme would have switched to mind communication to avoid an argument with Raul in front of his men, but his shield was too tightly down to permit it.

"We cannot wait," she said, letting her tone contain the urgency she felt. "The order was given regarding orbital traffic to allow a military fleet access to lift-off. They are to be sent to Synonis where the Rebels have their base!"

When Raul merely looked at her, she realized he didn't understand the import of what she'd just said.

"Raul, those ships carry the banned weapons!" she said tightly. "They will utterly destroy all life on Synonis!"

At that, all the men in the control room gave her their undivided attention, and the looks on their faces disclosed their shock and disbelief.

When the saints had left the original earth, they had carried with them the knowledge of how to construct the weapons which had helped destroy their home. But they had decreed that such knowledge never again be used in war. Even when extensive colonization had made it unlikely that mankind would ever again face the threat of total extinction, that decree had held firm during every civil war that had occurred—until now.

"How do you—" Raul started to ask, his voice grim, and then he fell silent and merely stared at her, his expression denoting his inner conflict.

Esme held her silence as well, awaiting his decision.

Raul was a loyal warrior, and despite the fact that the prohibition against such weapons was as firmly entrenched in him as in most humans, obedience to his superiors was also engrained in him. If the council had decreed the use of the weapons, there must be good reason for their decision. Perhaps such weapons were the last chance the Empire had to avoid certain defeat at the hands of the Rebels. And though Raul might not agree with their decision, he would be defying all of his years of training and loyalty to disobey the Council.

"Are you certain," he finally asked, his voice harsh, "that that which we carry with us will resolve this conflict?"

Esme chose her words carefully. "What we carry will end the war," she corrected him. "It will take awhile for the conflict to be resolved. However, when both sides understand that they have no choice but to negotiate a compromise rather than inflict their views upon the other by force, real peace will occur. Each will lose and each will gain."

Raul continued to study her for another long moment, his expression unreadable, and when Esme began to despair that she had not convinced him, he turned and addressed his communications officer first and then his pilot.

"Identify us and inform Control that we are coming down. Ignore all instructions to the contrary," he told the first. "Implement set down," he told the second.

As his men followed his orders, Raul turned to look at Esme again. But she was already gone.

It was not really necessary for Esme to be in the presence of the Master's artifact to give it her commands, but she felt the need to be there. Her task was fully upon her, and the consequences of failure were too horrendous to permit any mistake.

As Raul's pilot brought the Talon through Genesis's atmosphere, Esme spoke a command to the black machine, making the ship invulnerable to attack. The Genesian military commander had put aside much of his conscience to follow the order to use the forbidden weapons. She did not fully trust the mental state the inner conflict had produced in him. If he could violate a major principle drilled into him since childhood, she thought it possible that he might violate another and fire on one of his own ships and its disobedient captain.

He did not, but as the Talon settled on its pad, Esme knew the ship was being surrounded by a host of guards sent by the commander.

Before she went to join Raul, Esme spoke quickly the series of commands to the Master's device which would not only prohibit attack upon the Talon, but would permit neither exit from Genesis's atmosphere, nor any attack or descent upon its surface.

Then she went to convince the supreme commander of the Empire's forces of what she had done and that he must bring the High Council into session to meet with her.

As Esme stood before the Empire's High Council for the third time, she was sorrowed that she had been unable to force this meeting without casualties. But at least, she had been able to keep the ships carrying the forbidden weapons from leaving Genesis and crashing against the barrier that encircled the planet and polluting the atmosphere with their deadly cargoes. Instead, floating in orbit around Genesis at this moment were several small wrecked ships which had been instructed to try to land in order to prove to the supreme commander that they could not.

As before, Raul stood against the wall behind her,

his face impassive, his arms folded over his chest. As before, the table was circled by the highest scientists, politicians, and military commanders of the Empire. But this time as Esme looked around the table, only Halen, who sat in Laon's place, was friendly toward her. Everyone else seethed with the grim wish to have her destroyed.

Esme understood why. They, as had the supreme commander, had had to go through many mind twistings and justifications to reach the decision to do that which had been always forbidden. The decision made, they did not welcome the delay she had imposed upon them. They would welcome even less being forced to see that their decision was not only an abomination, but was going to be impossible to enforce without her permission, which would not be forthcoming.

"Supreme Commander," Esme coldly addressed the forbiddingly stern man who sat glaring at her as though she were a traitor of a worse stripe than the chief of the Rebels. "Since Captain Raul and I left the Talon to come to this meeting, you have been seeking a way to destroy the ship and that which it contains. Have you yet satisfied yourself that such cannot be done?"

For the barest instant the commander looked disconcerted. Then his face resumed it previous expression.

"I have satisfied myself that it cannot be done in any way which I have yet employed," he said harshly. "I am not yet satisfed that it cannot be done at all."

"And may I ask why you would wish to do it at all?" Esme addressed his scathingly. "The device works two ways, Commander. It protects Genesis from attack as well as prohibiting the sort of abomination you were about to perpetrate when I arrived here. The device makes the Rebel stealth ships seem a child's toys. Can it be that your lust to kill your enemy and protect your privileged position outweighs your judgment concerning the benefits to be had from such a device?"

The commander refused to answer, but Esme felt a stir, half-doubtful, half-rebellious among the council. Most of them were unwilling to give up a decision that had cost them much soul-searching for the dubious benefit of a device that made them prisoners on their own planet.

"How have you come to such a pass?" Esme attacked them all, her voice a whipping lash, her eyes a laser of pure green. "How could it come to be that you value wealth, position, and power more than you value your own self-respect and the principles that make you human rather than animal?"

Agian, there was a stirring of outrage among her listeners. But there was also the beginnings of a faint sense of shame.

"I come from a society all of you think of as primitive and barbaric," Esme went on, her voice a weapon. "And when I first saw the marvels of technology and the sophistication of thought and knowledge that you of the Empire enjoy, I at first held the same view. I *felt* primitive and barbaric and was somewhat ashamed of myself and my kind."

She paused for breath, and saw in the minds before her that they still held such a view of her people, even though they were forced to grant her the hostile respect her present power over their planet justified. Though she did not know if it was possible to change the habits of their minds, she had to try.

"But I have come to feel differently now," she went on coldly. "My people may not journey among the stars in spaceships and they may not attend universities exalted and proclaimed for their depths of learning. My people are indeed primitive in the ways of technology and sophisticated thought. But they are by no means barbaric, *gentlemen* and *gentlewomen.*"

She emphasized her contempt for their titles with the tone of her voice, and was gratified when some of those who understood her meaning had to look away from her stern gaze.

"They would never contemplate doing what you have contemplated," she continued scathingly. "For they possess a wisdom that is far more precious than mere sophisticated knowledge. They understand that in the Master's eyes all are equal. Every life is precious. And any privilege and position granted to one in the flesh is accompanied with responsibilities and duties that cannot be carried out without the tempering wisdom granted only by the Master. And that wisdom rests solely in His admonition to love Him first and one another secondly, as you love yourselves."

Pausing, she saw that these before her were now confused. They did not know who the Master was, and they did not know His commandments. And upon that realization, she almost despaired. But she could not. She had a task to perform for the Master, whom these people did not recognize, and despair was not permitted.

"Would any of you," she asked in furious disbelief, "if you did not have the support of your like-minded companions egging you on to disaster, have been able to come to such an evil decision on his or her own?"

No one would meet her eyes. Many were attempting to use their shields to hide their thoughts. Her fury rising, Esme ripped the shields aside as though they were cobwebs. Halen winced in reluctant sympathy as she felt the blow to the minds of those around the table.

"Do not attempt to hide your guilt from me, or one another, or your own selves!" Esme scolded them with her voice. "I am more glad of my skills at this moment than I have ever been, if for no other reason than that they permit me to force all of you to see yourselves as I do—as anyone would, whose basic humanity had not been corrupted as has yours by thinking that your *privileged position* is of more importance than the millions of lives you intend to destroy!"

A tiny waft of self-justification stirred among the council, and Esme waved it aside contemptuously. "Do you not think to justify what you meant to do by insisting that your purpose was as high-minded as you would like to pretend it was! I see your deepest thoughts and motivations more clearly than you do yourselves. You did not reach this decision merely to preserve the superior civilization to be had under the Empire's system of government and order. Had that been the case, I could have understood your action, even if I could not agreed with it! But it was not to protect the higher good that you endangered your souls! It was to protect what you possess under the empire's system that made you act so abominably, and you merely covered over your own greed and lust and self-glorification with a thin shell of concealing patriotism!"

"Esme!" The high counselor's normally pleasant

voice now thundered at her with condemnation. His face was suffused with the red that signaled his prodigious anger, and his blue eyes had lost all trace of the kindness that had been there when Esme had first made his acquaintance.

Esme merely looked at him, coldly and clearly, and sent into his mind a picture of himself that he had never before allowed to surface to his own conscious mind. But in the interest of future goals, she had the grace to shield from all others in the room that vision, and she allowed the high counselor to know that.

He blanched and involuntarily held up a hand in protest. But there was no protest he could make against the stark truth Esme made him confront for the first time in his life, and gradually his eyes changed from furious negation to agonized realization. Then he used his raised hand to support his bowed head.

"There will come a time," Esme said quietly for his ears alone, "when you will face Another who knows your inner soul more clearly than can I or even you yourself. That One will also have the power to sentence you to an eternity of contemplating the self-loathing and shame you feel now. You are not a young man. If I were you, I would set about at once repenting of and repairing those things in your inner self that cringe under the light of truth. You may make a start of it by supporting from your heart what I am about to propose now, for what I am about to say comes straight from He who controls that eternity you face."

Turning back to the others, Esme spoke with crisp surety. "I am going to give you the chance to absolve yourselves of the crime you were about to commit. If you are wise, you will take that chance. If you are not wise, you will not live long enough to obstruct me."

Into each of their minds, she put what she had learned from Raul. If you threaten a man's life, he had told her once, you had better mean it. Had her task been only her own, Esme would have been unsure of her ability to carry out her threat. But sure of her Master's intention, and the rightness of His power over all of His creation's existence, she meant her threat with all her heart.

The people at the table froze as they took her certainty from her mind and realized their own peril. Only the faces and bodies of those pitiful few who had truly acted out of conviction rather than self-interest remained willing to face what would come, and even those valued their lives enough to be afraid of losing it.

"The machine I have brought with me brings this war, and possibly all future ones, at least among those of our own kind, to a standstill," Esme informed them. "It can be duplicated for use on all the worlds that compose the Empire."

A faint, synchronous gasp erupted from those at the table, and was immediately followed by a few calculating thoughts that Esme viewed with cold disgust. Truly, she thought with weary acceptance, the enemy was always busy upon his work.

"But though its construction can be duplicated by anyone with sufficient engineering knowledge," she scotched those calculating thoughts contemptuously, "the commands which activate the device can only be spoken by me, and those commands are behind a shield I have constructed especially for their conceal-ment. They cannot be extracted from my mind. If you do not believe me, believe Halen."

Turning to the elderly woman who had shown

herself Esme's friend, Esme ordered Halen to put aside such friendship and perform her duty uncompromised.

"Attend me," she ordered Halen.

In full mind view of those in the room, Halen dutifully attempted with all her strength to penetrate the shield Esme had worked upon since her first days at the Institute, before she had even a glimmer of the reason for its necessity. Indeed, though she had used it before for her own purposes, she had not known its true purpose until her meeting with the Master.

"I do not believe the shield she has shown us can be penetrated," Halen said at last, and she was panting with the exertion of trying. "Not even by a full complement of the Institute's best."

Some on the council were visibly disappointed. Some, mostly the scientists, were excited about the possibilities of this new device and a few were still skeptical, though enough were convinced so that Esme could continue.

"Until sufficient devices have been constructed for every world, whether the Rebels' or the Empire's," she said deliberately, "you are all my hostages."

There was nothing tenuous about the gasp and the outrage that erupted then! Esme impatiently cut it off. "Also will you send a message to the Rebel leaders requesting their presence at a peace conference. I will make sure they agree to attend the meeting. And when they arrive for it, they also will I take hostage. And when Synonsis has its device constructed and in place, I will give Rebels and Empirians a choice," she went on. "You may negotiate with one another and re-solve your differences, or each world will be cut off from all others for as long as you remain stubborn—

forever if that is your decision and that of the Rebels."

She fell silent then, and let her listeners erupt into outraged discussion. She sat down, remote from it all. She did not sit to rest, however, for she was not weary and she knew she would remain so until her task was finished. Her strength was augmented by His Who had sent her on this mission.

Esme. Raul's voice came to hers, mind to mind, and she became aware that he had come to stand directly behind her, and that he was tensely alert. *Shield us,* he said. *I would speak with you privately, but I cannot do that and monitor those at the table at the same time.*

We are shielded, Esme replied, her voice uninflected.

You are in danger from some of these, he warned. *They think if you are dead the device will turn itself off.*

It will not.

Then tell them so and make them believe it, Raul urged.

You tell them if you feel merciful, Raul, Esme said coldly. *These who have murder in their minds seem to me unredeemable, and they disgust me so that I would as soon turn the beams from the lasers they have hidden and are contemplating firing at me back upon them as a warning of their own impending deaths.*

Do you have instructions from your Master to do such? Raul bit out, scouring her mind with his condemnation of her hardness.

Esme remained silent, for she did not, in fact, have such instructions, at least not in such clear-cut terms. She was allowed to protect herself, of course. But upon reflection, she realized she did not have dispensation to invite attack in order to give herself an excuse to take out her own anger against others who belonged as surely to the Master as she did herself.

I thought not, Raul said coldly. *Take care, Esme. Power can corrupt anyone. Do not make the mistake of believing that because your Master has set you a task He has given you carte blanche to do as you please beyond His boundaries.*

Raul's words shamed her. And for a brief instant, she felt an approximation of what the high counselor had felt when she had shown him his deepest self.

Feeling her shame, Raul softened. *I will relieve them of their weapons if you wish it,* he said, his voice level instead of scathing now.

I do wish it, Esme said, much subdued. *And Raul . . .* she added when he was about to go about his task.

Aye?

I thank you. She spoke very softly, very humbly.

He knew she was thanking him for serving as her conscience as much as for his concern for her and the simple performance of his duty.

He merely grunted and as he walked on, drawing his laser, he informed those at the table by name who carried concealed weapons what they could expect should they try to use them against Esme or himself.

But Esme's heart lightened at a reaction she had felt arise in him at her words. He felt of use, purposeful, rather than used and truly his reaction was justified. More justified than it was comfortable for Esme to admit to herself, since it pointed up her own human weakness. But she did, nevertheless, admit that she— just as those she condemned had—could make the mistake of coming to believe she was justified in wantonly destroying life when it was not necessary.

One of Raul's military superiors objected physically

to being relieved of the weapon he had concealed upon his person. But Esme was not fearful for Raul as he deftly won the struggle. She was merely proud that he showed no sense of being intimidated by the man's higher rank or by the lethal hostility that erupted in the man at being handled so summarily by a mere space captain, even one of Raul's reputation.

Then did she wait patiently for the council to get their rebellion out of their systems by vehement discussion. And when they had done so, she waited a little longer, until they had fully accepted the inevitable and were resigned to it.

In the silence that resulted, she spoke her question. "Who will you send to the Rebels?"

As though synchronized, all eyes turned to Raul. And Esme, who should have known whom they would choose, but hadn't, felt her heart constrict with fear. It was not at all a safe mission. The Rebels could just as well shoot Raul's ship out of space as heed the call of truce he would be sending out on a broad wave.

As her eyes sought her beloved, however, Esme knew better than to voice the objection that welled in her mind and pushed it behind the shield she had abruptly raised to keep him from feeling her reaction. For his eyes were on her in silent warning, and she knew that to dismiss that warning would end forever whatever chance they might have to reconcile.

"So be it," she said, her voice unsteady. "Compose the message you will send and I will review it. If it meets my approval, then will you all, except Cossan, accompany me to the Institute, where you will remain until the Rebels accept or reject the message. Cossan," she added, addressing the chief scientist, "take from my mind the plans for the construction of more of the devices. You will begin construction immediately, and I will tolerate no delay."

Cossan nodded eagerly. Indeed, Esme had selected him because of that very scientific eagerness which held sway over his political beliefs. There would be no danger of insurrection from such a mind as his, she thought, an opinion which was confimed as she silently put into his mind that which was needed and which he sought with awed enthusiasm, while she took from his mind his deepest intentions.

While the rest of the council debated over the words of the message to the Rebels, Raul came to her, and with a gesture of his head, indicated that he wished to speak to her privately again.

Esme got up from her chair and followed him into a small anteroom which members of the council used for private communications by use of the instrument which resided on a table there.

He leaned against the table, folded his arms over his chest, and instead of speaking, merely studied her for a few moments, his clear blue gaze thoughtful. Esme was unable to interpret what his look meant, and she would not ask. Nor would she probe his mind. Indeed, she had shielded her own thoughts from Raul since the time things had changed for the worse between them.

"I would settle this uncertainty between us before I leave," he finally spoke, his voice quiet.

And Esme's heart immediately flew into her throat.

CHAPTER FIFTEEN

ESME SENSED NO HOSTILITY IN RAUL, BUT SHE WAS AFRAID of what he might say nevertheless. Indeed, though she was unaware of it, she held her breath, and her chest ached under the strain.

"Breathe, Esme," Raul said with a smile. "All plans, whether yours, mine, or the Master's will come to nothing if you lie dead by your own careless lack of oxygen intake."

Esme breathed but she dared not speak. She merely looked at Raul, her eyes wide and, unbeknownst to her, warily apprehensive.

"And be calm," Raul added, in reaction to her expression. "You may not like all of what I am about to say, but I do not think you will find anything to fear in it."

At that, Esme relaxed somewhat. But she was still tense, because she had no idea what Raul would say next and despite her urgent need to know she would not offend him by prying into his thoughts uninvited.

On the heels of her last thought, Raul's clear eyes gleamed with appreciation. "I thank you for your sensitivity in not invading my mind, against my will, these past days to learn more about that which has troubled you so much, and which troubles you still," he said. "Had you done otherwise, I could not feel free to tell you now why I have been so unkind to you and to myself."

He spoke softly and surely, and his voice, to Esme's ears, sounded only faintly repentant concerning the pain he had caused her. More prominent was his thoughtful consideration of his own words and his seeming conviction that he had had no choice than to behave as he had. And since he had said he had caused himself pain as well, she did not worry about that lack of repentance. Rather she eyed him with growing curiosity and hope.

"I was angry at your Master," Raul said quietly. "It seemed to me He had deprived me of my right of choice. And since I had no recourse against Him, my anger spilled onto you, who are the instrument of His will, and also the method by which He deprived me of choice."

Esme had suspected as much and she wanted badly to explain to Raul some things about the Master that might mitigate his feelings. She opened her mouth to speak, but then closed it again, for it was evident that Raul was not yet ready to hear her.

"I have ever given my service and my loyalty willingly, by my own choice," he went on. "But it seemed to me your Master, though you say He gives choice to everyone, gave *me* none at all. He set you in

271

my path, knowing what you were and what would come to be, aware I would be unable to do otherwise than His will because of the bonds you would put upon me. It was as though I was no longer a man, but rather a puppet."

Esme unconsciously shook her head, both over the idea that Raul was merely a puppet, and by his mention of the bonds she had put upon him. He had shrugged off those bonds—at least she thought he had.

But Raul denied her gesture. "No, Esme," he said drily. "I know you have come to believe that my bonding to you, other than in the performance of the physical duties I owe you, no longer exists. But you have never truly understood Daccall, even when you were in its thrall, even though it binds you as relentlessly as it does me. But I understood it. And that, at least, I know I did by choice. Never have I done anything so willingly or so thoroughly," he said, his voice roughening into a husky rasp, "than when I took you irrevocably into my heart and mind and gave my body into your sole keeping. And never have I received anything I valued more than the same I had from you."

In her joy over Raul's words, Esme felt her body pulled of its own will toward his. But Raul stopped the movement as easily as he might have blinked.

"But afterward," he continued, "when I discovered that you belong more truly to your Master than you do to me, I resented His possession of you. And when I discovered He would, through you, use me without asking my preference, I resented His possession of me. I have been dealing with my resentment in my own way."

He paused, took a breath, then went on. "Since my intellect saw and accepted the logic of His plan as concerns the war, despite the fact that His plan strained my loyalties to my own masters, I accepted His plan and set about to do my part in implementing it. But I meant to protect my future autonomy by making sure I can resist the strongest of your many holds on me, and thus He who controls me through you. And I have done such. From now on, if I serve Him, it will not be as a helpless tool. It will be by my choice."

Esme's eyes showed her confusion.

"I do not mean that I meant to vanquish the bonds that hold me to you, Esme," Raul explained softly. "I know that, when you came to think I no longer cared for you, you would have let me go had it been possible to do so under the laws of your people. And you expected me, at some point, to walk away from you, since you could not walk away from me. But I never intended to do that. It was not my desire. My desire was to be able to act according to my own will in *spite* of the bonds you hold upon me. And I succeeded. I proved to myself that I still have free will."

"How?" Esme was becoming more and more puzzled.

Raul's smile was wryly amused. "I did not show the same sensitivity toward your thoughts as you did toward mine," he said.

Esme's eyes widened. "I—but I did not feel you within my mind," she protested. "And I was shielding."

"My skill in such matters increases apace," Raul smiled. "And I have surpassed you in that area as I did in self-teleportation."

"Is it then a contest between us to see whose skills are superior, Raul?" Esme asked unhappily. "I would not have it so."

"No, Esme, it is not a contest. But it is important to our relationship that I have value in it compensatory with yours."

"Raul, that has ever been the case!" Esme declared, distressed.

"To you, I admit, such was always true. But it was necessary for me to know it as surely as you did. And now I do."

Esme took a deep breath of relief. "And what was it you discovered while you roamed uninvited through my mind?" she asked.

"It was not so much what I discovered. I could see what you were feeling without benefit of mind trespass. But I could not feel it with you without entering into your mind."

"Feel it with me?" Esme was puzzled again.

"Tell me, Esme," Raul said drily, "if I were in a great deal of pain, could you stand aside and refuse to help me. Could you indeed inflict more upon me?"

"No. I do not believe I could stand to do that." Esme shook her head.

"But that is what I did," Raul said calmly. "I felt with you all your pain and mine as well. And I found within me the strength not to come to your aid nor to mine, but to hold to my purpose instead."

Esme was silent, unable to comprehend such reasoning.

"I do not expect you to understand completely." Raul shrugged. "It might help, however, if you recall how frustrated and angry you felt when I insisted you return to your home planet and serve your people instead of staying with me. You did not like it that I abrogated your right of choice, did you?"

"No, I did not," Esme agreed, getting angry now. "But I obeyed without subjecting you to a cruel pretense of loss of my regard for you. And in any case, when it is the Master Who requires something of us, it is a sin to rebel."

"To you, it is a sin to rebel, not to me—not yet at least," Raul disagreed. "And I never said to you that I had lost my regard for you. You jumped to that conclusion on your own as a result of my actions toward you. And you were wrong. And I find it strange indeed that you did not have more faith in my love for you than that. I was amazed by how easily you came to believe my regard for you had diminished. Had things been turned the other way around, I would not have reacted in that way. It would take much more reason than I gave you for me to believe that you had ceased to love me. However, though your reaction surprised me, and it added to my pain, it did aid my purpose."

His words sparked Esme's anger higher. When she thought of how she had suffered, and how Raul had suffered, and for no better reason than that he might prove to himself what was, to her, self-evident, she wanted to hit him. Also, his disappointment in her had succeeded in making her feel somewhat at fault for her lack of trust, and she was in no mood to feel guilt. In fact, that tinge of guilt made her anger surge hotter. But instead of dealing directly with the issue, she chose another direction of attack.

"I thought you prized mind privacy," she said, surly now. "And yet, though I shielded from you while you were about your search for independence, you roamed

275

my thoughts uninvited anyway. And now that I think of it, you must have been roaming them again throughout this conversation!"

Though Raul did not admit it, his eyes twinkled at her for a moment in a way that made Esme sure she was right. Then he sobered.

"You will have your mind privacy in the future, Esme. I do not intend to roam your thoughts without invitation at all times. Only when I think it necessary will I be so impolite, and I thought it necessary during our recent estrangement."

"And you think it necessary to be so impolite now, is not that the truth?" Esme demanded indignantly.

Raul hesitated, and then he shrugged. "Yes," he admitted. "But only because there must be no misunderstanding between us in a discussion as important as this one."

"But you have not invited me to probe your mind during this talk," Esme objected tartly.

"Then I do so now," Raul replied, and he released his shield so that Esme could verify the truth of what he still had left to say.

"I learned another thing while establishing to my own satisfaction that I can, if I wish, act independently of you and your Master," he said, his voice now quiet and husky.

"Which was?" Esme asked, still outwardly indignant. But, in truth, her anger had disappeared and was replaced by relief and joy at the renewed intimacy of being permitted access to Raul's thoughts after so long an absence from them.

"I learned the price of my independence," Raul said with simple honesty. "In the past, I was sufficient unto myself. And though I know now that I could be again

276

if I made the choice on my own initiative and was not deprived of you by another's hand, I also know I would find no joy in such a choice. And I cannot imagine a reason strong enough to make me visit again, voluntarily, the depths of loneliness I inhabited while I was about the task of rediscovering my free will."

Esme abruptly felt tears sting her eyes. "Oh, Raul," she whispered a plea. "The feelings I have for the Master do not detract from the feelings I have for you. They are two separate things, and on very different levels. And my feelings for the Master actually enhance what I feel for you. You do not need to vie with Him for my love and my loyalty. The tasks He requires of me, and of you, are for the good of all. Please, surely you understand this. Have you not told me often that the needs of any one person cannot compete with the needs of many?"

"Aye, I have said such, and I still believe it." Raul nodded. "It was only that I did not know Him as you do, and my loyalties were conflicted when He made it clear that I must serve Him instead of those to whom I had previously given my service. But I have come to have reason to thank your Master for something He did in my place, and for that I will always be grateful. Therefore, my feelings for Him have softened to more acceptance than I once believed possible."

Esme frowned. "What mean you?"

"On our last night aboard the Talon before we arrived here on Genesis, I took from your mind your thoughts about the testing you endured at the hands of the one you call the enemy. And I took also the depth of your need for me when you returned from that testing. And had your Master not provided you the comfort I was not there to give, I could not have borne the lashing of my conscience for failing you in a time of such need. But since He eased your pain better than I could have had I been there, my conscience received absolution. But not completely. It was still hard for me not to tell you then what I have told you now. But the very strength of my desire to tell you would have shown that I had not yet found the depth of independence I had set out to find. So I waited until now, when I was sure."

"And what made you sure?" Esme asked, her eyes upon him filled with love and understanding.

"When I had to remind you to get back in touch with your conscience and control your power in that room just now." He nodded his head toward the chamber where the High Council was still meeting. "Having to help you realize that when killing is not necessary it is wrong, I realized that there was good reason for your Master having chosen me to companion you. I have a maturity in certain areas that you lack. And I understood for the first time that my purpose in your Master's eyes is not just to ease your burden with my emotional support and be your servant in matters of transportation and battle. Many other men could do that. But I have qualities that are mine alone and are of enough value to make Him choose me on my own merits, and which have nothing to do with the mating you and I share."

Esme's eyes lit with joy. And in the next instant, though she was not aware of moving under her own power—and perhaps she had not and he had pulled her to him, or perhaps they acted simultaneously— she was in Raul's arms, wrapped against his body so tightly that taking a full breath, had it mattered at the moment, would have been impossible.

"I am so glad!" she gasped against his neck as her emotions broke free and a sob of happy relief welled within her. "I have always known it. And I was afraid that because you did not know it, I had lost you."

"Never."

His voice was muffled against her hair, but she heard something in it that amazed her. Quickly, she drew back and sought his eyes to confirm what her ears and her mind touch told her. But Raul was intent upon seeking her mouth, and she had only a glimpse of the mist in his clear blue eyes before his kiss and the emotions behind it overwhelmed her.

It was a long while before either of them found a measure of quiet within themselves. Then Raul announced his intention, in a tone which Esme would not have dared gainsay even if she had wanted to. "Since you cannot come to me, I will lodge with you in the Institute tonight, and we will make sure you do not feel the lack of my regard, or the lack of my arms around you after our loving, or the lack of my praise for your gifts to me, when we lie together where once you lay alone," he whispered.

Esme nodded, her tremulous smile all the answer required.

Raul kissed her once more, and then he drew back.

"It is time to see what the council has managed to put together," he said. "I believe they are done."

"Raul," Esme chided, falsely indignant. "Surely, you have not been monitoring them while we have been about the latter stages of our reconciliation, have you?"

He grinned. "Somewhat, but my concentration slipped a little in places," he admitted. He allowed her to see in his mind the truth that his concentration had slipped completely, and not just a little.

"And so it should have," Esme said tartly. Then she smiled at him and held him once more. She took another kiss as retribution before they adjourned to the room where the council had just finished composing a masterpiece of hyberbolic redundancy which Raul stripped of all such nonsense as quickly as he had stripped from himself and Esme the barriers to their emotional union.

CHAPTER SIXTEEN

As Ivvor escorted Raul to a meeting with the rebel leaders, he hoped he was doing the right thing. What if the mind tramplers were wrong, and beneath the talk of peace, Raul hid in his mind the kind of weapon his mate Esme was so good at wielding? Perhaps she had taught him her tricks? What if his intention was to slay the leaders of the rebellion upon being ushered into their presence? And Ivvor had pledged to his superiors that Raul was a man of honor!

But, on the other hand, perhaps Raul really had not taken leave of his senses. Ivvor had suspected he had when he first spoke to Raul after heeding the truce call beamed from the small, unarmed ship Raul had brought undetected too close to Synonsis for its protectors' comfort.

Now, sliding a sideways look at his former friend,

Ivvor had to admit that Raul seemed the same as ever, except for the lack of a weapon at his hip. And Esme's part in all this had to be considered as well. Where that female was concerned, Ivvor was prepared to believe almost anything except that she was capable of sending her mate upon a mission of cowardly murder. If she was, and if Raul was capable of carrying out such mayhem under the flag of truce, then Ivvor would never again trust his own instincts about other human beings!

He smiled somewhat grimly as he reflected that if he was wrong about Raul and Esme's intentions, he wouldn't likely be in a position to have to trust anyone again. He would likely be dead.

At the door to the conference room, Raul paused and grinned at Ivvor.

"Rest easy, friend," he said lightly, reaching up to squeeze Ivvor's shoulder in a comradely gesture. "If things work out the way Esme and He whom she serves intend, you and I will cease fighting one another and serve again side by side. And I, for one, will welcome one of your stripe on my right hand."

"Aye, and I would rest easy with you on my left." Ivvor nodded. "But who is this whom you say Esme serves now? Have we a third force at work among the worlds?"

Raul's grin faded to a wry smile. "According to Esme, the One she serves has always been at work among the worlds. According to her, He made them, and us as well."

Ivvor was startled then dismayed. "Ahhhh, don't tell me she's fallen victim to one of those obscure religious cults that spring up out of nothing from time to time and profess that there's some Supreme Being who controls the whole universe?"

Raul shrugged. "If she has, at least this Supreme Being is not all talk. He comes up with some practical ways to enforce His rule, one of which I'm about to explain to your leaders, if you are ready to take me in there," he said levelly, nodding at the closed door in front of which they stood.

Ivvor sighed and shook his grizzled head. "I have the feeling I am going to come to regret the past friendship we shared before this day is over," he said gloomily. "If you had been any ordinary warrior, I would not have sponsored you in this foolishness."

Raul grinned again. "You were ever the pessimist, Ivvor," he said good-naturedly. "It may just as well be that we will be better friends than ever before this day is over. In any case, let us be about it."

"Aye." Ivvor sighed gloomily again. "When one is about to make a fool of himself, the sooner the matter is past and done, the better."

Esme strolled the platform circling the production floor, listening with half an ear to Cossan's eager progress report.

"Another month, Esme, and all of the devices will be constructed and ready for deployment." He paused, and Esme nodded absently. "But surely," Cossan ventured a hesitant question, "you do not intend to go with the cargo ship to every world and activate each device yourself?"

Esme smiled to herself. Did the council really believe they could hide from her that they were exerting pressure upon Cossan to somehow extract from her the sequences which controlled the Master's device?

283

"I have no choice, Cossan," she said mildly. "Who can I trust to withstand the council's pressures should I give the sequences to anyone else?"

Cossan's fair complexion erupted into a blush. Esme pretended not to see it. But still, he went bravely on with the task he had been set.

"But who, if not you, will chair the negotiations that will take place when the Rebel leaders and the council meet? You will still be activating the devices by next Saints' Day, when the meeting is scheduled. And by the way," he added much too casually, "where is the meeting to be held? Have you decided?"

Esme paused in her stroll and turned to meet Cossan's anxious hazel gaze. "Do you not have enough to do, Cossan," she said gently, "without worrying about matters that do not concern you?"

Cossan blushed again, but he held firm. "I was a member of the council until you set me this present work, Esme. And if you permit it, when my work here is finished, I will sit on the council again. So I consider that such matters do concern me."

Esme sighed. She was not physically tired—the Master saw to that—and she had the help of those at the Institute in keeping control of and monitoring the ongoing machinations of the council. But her patience these days was often stretched very thin. And it did not help that the Rebels would not permit Raul to return to her until they saw for themselves that she could do as she had promised and set the devices around the planets they held. They had already ascertained that the barrier around Genesis was impenetrable, but that was not enough for them. Also they wanted to be sure that she really intended the High Council to negotiate with them in good faith.

"Cossan," she said now, holding on to her patience very tightly, "do not force me to be rude to you. Contrary to what certain members of the council believe, I take no personal pleasure in demonstrating my power. Now be about your work and ask me no further questions. I have seen enough to know that you are doing as I have instructed."

Then she turned on her heel and took her leave of Cossan, who stood where she'd left him and gazed after her. Esme was amused to take from his mind the relief he felt that he had done what he'd been told and could honestly report to those who pressured him that his best efforts had resulted in nothing of value.

"Esme, you are kind to want to take some of the burden from my shoulders," Halen gently reproved, "but surely you have enough to do without going personally over these reports of the students' progress with me."

Esme shook her head. "Such normal, everyday tasks ease my mind," she said.

"And your loneliness?" Halen queried, her voice kind.

Esme smiled faintly. "Aye." She nodded. "And my loneliness."

Halen sighed. "It is ever thus for ones who have the power you control, Esme. Few can share the kind of burdens you bear."

"One can," Esme said wistfully, staring out the window of Halen's office at the blue sky over Genesis. The barrier was not visible to the naked eye, of course, but it had come to be a symbol to her, a symbol of separation.

"Why did you not conceive before your captain left

you?" Halen asked curiously. "Would not his son in your womb have provided you with a measure of comfort?"

Esme turned her gaze from the window to Halen's aged face. "I am not all powerful, Halen," she said wryly. "My cycle was not at the proper sequence for conception." Then she frowned slightly. "But even when it has been at the proper sequence when Raul and I have cohabited, I have not conceived. I have wondered if perhaps the Master does not wish me to have a child yet. And I have prayed that it is not true that He does not wish for me to have a child at all."

Halen snorted. "It is more likely that the Master expects you to deal with the matter yourself," she said practically. "If you can heal your own body, surely you can shift one tiny egg to meet its destiny at the proper time."

Esme stared at the older woman, astonished that she had not thought of something so simple. "It never occurred to me to do such," she said faintly. "Do you really think . . ."

"I think if you and Raul want a son or daughter, or a dozen of each, it is a simple matter to accomplish," Halen said firmly. "Sometimes, Esme," she added with a slight touch of humorous impatience, "with all your powers, you behave like a child still. But I have to admit," she added, smiling openly now, "that it is encouraging to see that you truly are not all powerful, and that one with my limited abilities can be of help to such as you."

Esme smiled back affectionately. "Your abilities are not so limited, and you have always been of help to me," she said then added, with a tinge of the anxiety that she could not quite rid herself of, "you are still certain that I will see Raul again?"

"On that, I am clear." Halen nodded firmly. "But if you want to know how many children the two of you will have, I have no such information, nor do I care to look for it. There are other matters to be attended to, such as what you plan to do about Chass and Niah."

Esme grimaced. "She is still about her manipulations on the council's behalf."

"Aye. You may have convinced her father to support you, but Niah has no love for you and she does not forgive you for the humiliation you dealt her personally, nor for stripping the council's power from them. Beware of her, Esme. She is a relentless enemy."

"I do not fear what she can do to me," Esme shrugged. "It is what she does to Chass that I deplore. He is beside himself, torn on the one hand by his affection and loyalty toward me, and on the other by his lust for Niah. She tempts him daily with what she will give him as a reward if he will but report to her anything I say in his company, and his willpower weakens with each temptation."

Halen shook her head. "And you profess to be his friend, yet you let this go on."

Esme flushed a little. "What can I do?" she asked defensively. "I cannot imprison Niah, for fear of losing the support of her father. And Chass desires her so much that he might go over the edge if I deprive him of at least the chance to see her. Besides, I am careful not to say anything in his hearing that might be of use to Niah."

"But his fear that he will one day accede to her demands and receive his reward is turning his self-respect to ashes," Halen said quietly. "And he *may* give in one day. He is fast reaching a point where, if you do not do something to rescue him, you risk destroying his character completely."

Esme recognized truth when she heard it, and she sighed. "What should I do?" she asked simply. "If I refuse him my friendship, Niah will refuse to have anything more to do with him, and he could not handle that."

"You know what you could do," Halen said quietly.

Esme shook her head. "I cannot go into his mind and remove or change what he feels for her," she said. "I have suggested it to him before, but he cannot bring himself to take what I offer. And I will not force such manipulation upon him. He is my friend."

"That is not what I meant, Esme." Halen's tone was stern.

Esme frowned. "Halen, if you mean that I should turn his lust toward me, I cannot do that either. I have undergone Daccall with Raul, and as unreasonably fond of Chass as I am, I could not be so disloyal to Raul. Besides, I do not desire Chass or any other man that way. What you suggest is just not possible."

"But no woman other than you can break Niah's hold over Chass," Halen pointed out gently. "Can you not think of some way to preserve your loyalty to Raul and still turn Chass's affections away from that she-viper who attempts to use him so shamelessly?"

Esme shook her head. "Nothing other than to manipulate his mind to think he is involved with me when he really is not, and that I will not do without his permission, which, as I said before, he will not give me. Besides," she added with a shrug, "what would I do with his affections once I had them? How would he be better off hopelessly enthralled by me instead of

Niah? He might then come to hate Raul, which I could not tolerate."

"Perhaps you do not, after all, have to turn his affection toward you specifically," Halen suggested absently. When Esme looked at her, she saw the elderly woman had the vacant expression on her lined face which was always there when she was forereading. "Instead," Halen went on, her tone flat, "teach him what a healthy mating is about, and perhaps tantalize him with glimpses of a woman who will satisfy his honor, his heart, and his mind as well as his body."

Esme looked away from Halen and sighed. "I grow weary of practicing manipulations upon my fellow humans, Halen. When I have finished with my Master's task, I long greatly to be free of such."

Halen's expression abruptly cleared and she shook her head. "Then I sorrow for you, Esme," she said gently, "for I fear such freedom will be yours only in very brief snatches of time."

Esme frowned. "Why do you say that?" she demanded.

"Think you that the Master fashioned such a tool as you with the intention of using it only once?" Halen inquired softly.

Esme shifted uneasily in her chair, and upon recalling the expression she had seen on Halen's face a moment ago, she was propelled into speech.

"Halen, I beg you," she said almost curtly, "if you have any foreseeings pertaining to such further use of me, keep them to yourself. I have enough to handle as it is!"

"So you do," Halen said, her tone mild. "And Chass's well-being is one of the things on your agenda.

Now look into my mind. I did not see clearly, but I saw enough to at least suggest the image of a woman who is likely to be in his future, and who might solve his problem with Niah."

Curiously, Esme did as Halen asked, and truly, she could not clearly see the features of the female who drifted in Halen's mind. But she saw enough to give her an idea of how to break Niah's hold on Chass.

When she departed Halen's mind, the older woman smiled. "So what is your decision?" she asked. "Will you save Chass's self-respect or let him be lost to himself as well as to the rest of us? It is that simple, Esme."

Esme shrugged her shoulders, her smile wry. "What choice have you given me?" she said rhetorically.

Halen nodded, satisfied. "None," she admitted. "And I suggest you start on this matter soon. Perhaps at dinner this very evening."

Esme grimaced, and then she laughed. In some ways, Halen was a more demanding mother figure than Esther had ever been. But Esme did not resent her for it. Indeed, she treasured the caring behind Halen's subdued bossiness.

Raul paced the small confines of the quarters he had been given, his expression grim. He had not expected the Rebels to try to control him and perhaps later, through him, Esme, by setting a trained seductress upon him. And though—bless the bonds of Daccall! —he was confident of his ability to continue to resist the wiles of the slithering creature they sent again and again to try his mettle, he was not happy with this galling part of his duty.

He would rather have fought a force of multi-missile stealth ships with only a single-manned training fighter than be cooped up in this pen being stalked time and again by a creature who, though nothing like Esme at all except for her green eyes, managed to increase his lonely need for his beloved tenfold!

Though he shielded his thoughts beyond violation, the woman presently in the room with him was trained to sense telepathically a man's need by the way he held his body and by the slight increase in his body temperature. She was beside him in an instant, her pheromoned skin exuding temptation, her artfully draped, seductive body pressing against his.

"I can ease the captain's distress if he will but permit it," she murmured.

The soft, sibilant, seductive voice of Raul's temptress was as sense-scratching as were her fingers upon his bare neck. He took a deep, weary breath and turned a gaze upon her which froze her still for an instant. "Your daily allotted time is up," he said, his voice a cutting rasp. "Get yourself hence!"

The woman's humiliation and fury at her failure of her allotted task showed for the first time in her large, beautiful green eyes. She had been selected primarily for the similarity of her eyes to Esme's, and her thigh-length hair had been dyed to match the copper tints of Raul's beloved. Only her body was different. She was tall and large-boned rather than small and finely made.

"Can you not have at least a portion of mercy?" she hissed at him. "If you refuse me again, my status will be lowered! If you will but agree to take me, I will agree not to enthrall you! You could merely pretend that I have had the desired effect upon you."

Raul's mouth curved into the first natural smile he

had ever given her. "At last," he said with some humor, "by at least *behaving* with an honesty that is uncommon in your kind, do you tempt me at all, even if you continue to lie with your mouth in promising not to try to enthrall me. You could no more keep such a promise than I could break the bonds of Daccall and become enthralled as you wish me to be."

The woman frowned. "They did not tell me you had undergone Daccall with Esme," she said, her tone deflated.

"Perhaps they did not know." Raul shrugged.

Slowly then, the woman brightened. "But then I have not truly failed through any lack of talent or skill," she said happily. Then she immediately frowned again. "But those who count will blame me in any case. Only my immediate superiors will understand, and I do not think they want their own superiors to realize that there are men under certain conditions who even such as we cannot break."

"They will find out soon enough," Raul said, his voice wry.

At his words, the woman looked at Raul, pleading with eyes that were enough like Esme's that when Raul concentrated on them alone, he felt an unguarded shiver of desire go down his back.

"This is my first assignment," she begged. "They gave me this task which they would normally have assigned to another of more experience only because of the color of my eyes. If I fail, they may never give me another chance. Please, though it is true that I lied before about my intent to enthrall you, I do not lie now. I will only ease you and report to my superiors that I am at last making progress."

Raul saw immediately the advantages to be had by

taking her suggestion. If this woman's handlers thought she was making progress, they would send no other seductress against him, which would relieve him of having to endure once again all the tricks of the trade, and they would believe they had him when they really did not.

But in the end Raul set aside his reluctant pity for the woman's unhappy position, as well as the advantages to be had from entering into a conspiracy with her. His loyalty to Esme would not permit the arrangement she proposed. And indeed, he wondered if it came to it, if he could even muster his body to do what was necessary. For he had come to know that there was more to mating than physical attraction, and this woman elicited nothing within him to make him desire her with even an approximation of the desire he felt for Esme.

But he was very gentle in his refusal. "I cannot do it," he said quietly, looking compassionately at her disappointed face. "And even if I could, I find talents such as yours dishonorable when used in battle. Women like you cripple men, you do not kill them cleanly in an honest fight. And if things come to be as I think they will, there will no longer be any use for your kind."

He sighed as her green eyes filled with tears. Then he added a kindly warning. "Even should peace between your people and mine not last, while it is in effect, I intend to abolish the use of seductresses against men at war. I would advise you to take your dismissal, should it come, with good grace and set about finding another, more worthy, trade. If they have not already destroyed all of your capacity to feel true affection for a man, you might even consider finding yourself a protector you can care for. But even if you cannot any longer feel love for a man, you could at least make one very happy if, in exchange for his enthrallment, you gave him real loyalty."

He saw that the woman was halfheartedly considering his advice, but she was in such despair that she was incapable for the moment of reaching a decision. She still had hope that finding another trade would not become necessary.

"Think on it," he suggested, guiding her to the door of his quarters. "And if you can think of some way to fool those above you into thinking you have succeeded with me, I will not immediately disabuse them of the notion."

She shrugged, dispirited. "They will know I have not accomplished anything," she said dully. "They monitor our meetings."

Thus she confessed that everything she had said to him in their interview was a lie, even the part about her superiors' desire to hide from their superiors the knowledge that there were circumstances under which a seductress could not succeed. And certainly, since this meeting had been monitored, the conspiracy between them she had proposed was simply another trick to permit her to attempt to enthrall him.

Raul was not surprised. He had half suspected it, though he had not gone into her mind to confirm it because he had not wanted to. Upon their first acquaintance, when he had explored her secret thoughts, he had not liked what he saw within her mind and wished not to revisit it.

"In that case," he said drily, "if this is the last we will see of one another, think well on the advice I gave you."

294

But she merely shrugged and passed over the threshold without a backward glance.

Raul's next visitor later that evening was Ivvor, who informed Raul with a satisfied grunt that it had been decided to stop this nonsense of sending trained seductresses against him.

"I told them, violently, how I felt about it, that it was dishonorable and most likely useless," he growled. "But the bureaucrats had to test it. I will join with you, Raul, should peace really occur between us, in abolishing such a practice. It makes my skin crawl."

"Aye." Raul smiled sardonically. "But at the moment, you will do me more good by providing a little something in my food that will ease my need for Esme than you did protesting my temptation." He was only half-joking.

Ivvor jerked his head around, startled and at what he saw in Raul's eyes, he roared with laughter, slapped him on the back, and vowed that he could do better than that.

Before Raul settled upon his narrow cot to rest that night, he had the peace of knowing that the monitoring system that recorded his every move had been turned off and that what he did in the darkness to ease himself was between him and his thoughts of Esme alone.

Esme sat in her private quarters, across the dining table from Chass, her compassion aroused by his woebegone expression. He sat lost in thought, consumed by his turmoil over the ignominious position in which he found himself.

"Chass," she quietly got his attention. When he looked up, she held his sad gaze, her own sympathetic.

"There is an answer to your dilemma."

A short laugh expressing his disbelief issued from his chest. "I doubt it," he said, his well-formed mouth twisting into a curl of self-disgust. "I am so besotted with Niah that I cannot even contemplate asking you to relieve me of what I feel for her."

"There is another way, if you will but agree," Esme persisted.

"What?" Chass was still sceptical.

And Esme quietly, calmly, informed him of what she had in mind.

He sat silent when she had finished, blinking at her warily. "But are you certain it will work?" he asked. "At least with Niah, I can see her sometimes, and I can see her in the here and now. But you do not know when this other woman will come into my life. What if I cannot abide the waiting?"

Esme shrugged. "The main objective, Chass, in what I propose," she explained, "is to show you what a healthy mating with this woman in your future can be like, in hopes that when you meet her, your relationship with her will have a chance of succeeding. And, of course, I also hope that what I show you will make you grow dissatisfied with the sort of sick relationship that you and Niah share and that you will at last be willing to put your feelings for her aside and will have the necessary inner strength to accomplish it. I cannot help you with the waiting."

Chass sighed. "I suppose you are disgusted with me?" he asked, quietly shamed.

"No, because you are a product of your upbringing," Esme said. "Is it not true that on your world successful relationships are rare? Are not these obsessive, destructive attachments the norm rather than the exception?"

Chass nodded, not meeting her eyes.

"Then perhaps you can be an example of a better way when you go home again," Esme suggested. "Are you at least willing to try?"

Chass met her gaze then, and the look in his eyes was tortured. "Esme, if you had asked me before, I would have said no. But I am growing sick of myself. Did you know that I have considered taking things you tell me to Niah in exchange for her use?"

"Yes, Chass. Of course, I knew it."

He was amazed. "And yet you have continued to see me?"

"You are my friend, Chass." Esme shrugged. "I did not think you could handle being completely deprived of Niah's company, and she would have refused to see you without the prospect of receiving something in exchange because she has no real affection for you."

Chass's face fell. "I know that is true," he whispered. "I just kept hoping . . ." But then he fell silent before asking, "And why have you decided to take action now, Esme?"

"Because a friend of mine pointed out that it is unkind to allow you to continue in such agony, and also that, should you one day break and do as Niah wishes, your self-respect would be shattered and you would be lost to yourself as well as to those of us who care about you. This friend of mine pointed out that I should, instead of letting things continue on as they have been, attempt to solve your dilemma."

Chass nodded slowly then nodded more firmly. "Yes, it is true," he agreed. "If I should break and give

Niah what she wants, I will be worthless to myself, to my people, to anyone."

"Then you agree to what I propose, Chass?" Esme asked.

"I agree," he said. "And please, Esme, do your best to make it work. I truly do not want to continue as I have been."

Esme smiled. "I will do my best, Chass," she agreed, and immediately, she sent into his mind a blurred vision of the woman Halen had seen in his future.

"But I cannot see her face," Chass objected.

"I know," Esme agreed. "I merely show you the little that Halen was able to see so that you will be convinced that there actually is a woman somewhere whom you will meet one day. It will give you something to hold on to and to hope for. But remember, Chass. The illusion I am about to create for you is only a fiction designed to show you what your future relationship with this woman *could* be like. It will be up to you and to her, at the time that the relationship actually comes to be, to conduct it as the two of you see fit."

Chass nodded and held his peace.

Then Esme created scenes in Chass's mind of himself and his future mate—scenes filled with all the sweetness, and the mutual wish for one another's well-being, and the laughter and the clean passion that was missing from his relationship with Niah.

Chass began to smile.

In his small room Chass removed his clothing in preparation for sleep, feeling much more at peace with himself than he had felt for a very long time.

Niah appeared in the doorway, wearing only the sheerest of sleeping gowns. She came in, shut the door behind her, and leaned against it in a seductive pose. "Are you ready to tell me anything, Chass?" she asked in a throatily promising tone.

Chass, instead of striding eagerly to her side as of old to try to steal a kiss, merely looked at her, his gaze sad. "No, Niah," he said after a moment. "I have nothing at all to tell you."

Niah frowned angrily and straightened. "Then you know I will not stay with you," she said, as she always did.

"I know." Chass shrugged.

Niah was confused by Chass's indifference to her threat.

"What is the matter with you?" she asked suspiciously. "Do not think to play any games with me, Chass. You know my terms."

"I am well aware of them," Chass agreed drily. "And I play no games with you. I simply refuse to accept your terms, as always."

Moving abruptly, Niah started to turn away but Chass's attitude disturbed her enough that she paused and turned back. "You have been with Esme, have you not?" she asked thoughtfully over her shoulder. "Or did she cancel dinner with you?"

"I have been with her," Chass said, and smiled.

It was a type of smile Niah did not at all care to see on his lips. "What is happening?" she demanded. "If you play no games with me, what game is it she plays with you?"

Chass's expression was mild. "Esme does not play

any kind of game with which you would be familiar, Niah," he said wryly. "She is an entirely different woman from you."

Niah was enraged. "Is *she* bedding you then?" she snarled. "Has she discovered that I seek to make you my spy and tries to ensure your loyalty by giving you her body? If that is true, Captain Raul will be incensed!"

Chass merely shrugged again, rousing Niah to further fury. "She has and will do nothing that Raul would object to," he said. "They are bonded in a way I doubt you will ever even contemplate with a man. There is not the sweetness, nor the imagination, nor sufficient submission, nor sufficient love within you to truly mate with anyone."

Niah was now trembling with anger. "Is that so?" she hissed, stalking toward him. "Well, you are wrong, Chass! It is just that I will not truly mate with a lowly miner's son!"

At that, Chass threw the student robe which he had drawn over his head aside, and when he looked at Niah, the expression on his face brought a sudden gasp from her throat. She whirled and made to run away.

He caught her before she had taken a step and taking little care to avoid bruising her delicate skin, held her roughly with one hand while he ripped her thin gown from her with the other. Then he threw her contemptuously down upon his bed and pinned her there. The normal haughty expression on her face had by then turned to one of fear and Chass much enjoyed the change.

"Before I am done with you," he promised, his voice a low, hard threat, "I vow you will have more respect for this lowly miner's son than you ever thought possible."

And before much more time had passed, Esme's work upon Chass had borne fruit. Niah had begun to appreciate the new self-confidence in him, and even to learn the art of submission. But Chass, having succeeded in rousing within Niah feelings she had never had for him before, stopped short of taking what she now offered without the demand of being paid for her favors with information. To his amazed relief, he no longer wanted what she offered on any terms.

Pulling her up from the bed, he shoved the sleeping shift he had torn from her body into her hands, then pushed her to the door of his room. "Go away, Niah," he said with quiet surety. "And do not come back."

Niah fled to her own room, sobbing, humiliated and frustrated, her education in healthy love at Chass's hands incomplete.

One month later, Esme was ready to board the cargo ship bearing all the members of the council and enough of the Master's devices to shield every planet of the Empire. Synonsis would be the first of the planets besides Genesis to be gifted with the device. As she turned to enter the hatchway, Chass called to her with cheerful good humor.

"I value you much, Chass," Esme said, telling him again what she had once told him before.

"And I value you," Chass said sincerely. "I owe you so much that I cannot even begin to thank you. You have given me back to myself."

"No." Esme smiled. "If the rumors I have been hearing are correct, I have given you to a certain dark-haired Genesian woman who is as different from

Niah as night is from day."

Chass shook his head. "I am fond of the woman you mention, no more, and we satisfy one another's need for physical relief and companionship. But she does not desire life-mating with me, and I do not feel that she is the one you showed me in the vision. But then, under your tutelage, I have become very cautious of where I bestow my true affections these days, and I hope I do not miss the right woman because of that caution."

Chass had been joking, but Esme frowned. "Chass," she said, disturbed. "I am sorry. It was not my intention to make you distrust all your perceptions, but only to be wiser in your choice of women."

"And I am that." Chass smiled. "Do not worry, Esme. I was only joking. I will know the right woman when she appears in my life. You can be sure of it. I will know her because she will remind me of you."

Esme's frown deepened. "Chass!" she exclaimed. "You haven't fallen in love with . . . I mean . . ."

"Aye." Chass nodded, his eyes twinkling. "Of course, I have fallen in love with you but not in the way you mean. I can live without you. It is just that I cannot accept too much less than your example, and so far, I have not seen a woman who is only a little less than you. Most of them are far less. But I will meet such a woman one day. You know I will."

Esme smiled then. "Yes, you will," she agreed. But then she hesitated, and added, "But when you do meet her, do not look for perfection. Accept her the way she is, even if she is not exactly as I showed you in the visions."

Chass merely smiled. "As I said before, do not worry, Esme," he said gently. "I am all right now. I am merely choosy. And if you think about it in connection with your own feelings, you will realize that you could settle for no less than Raul. Could you?"

Esme hesitated, bit her lip, then shook her head.

"I thought not." Chass grinned. "And somewhere, Esme, is my own true mate. It may take me awhile to find her, but I can wait."

Esme relaxed. "In that case," she said, "I can only wish you a speedy search. I cannot fault your unwillingness to settle for less than what you want."

Then it was time to go and Chass hugged Esme and kissed her cheek before turning her toward the boarding ramp.

"May the Master bless you and keep you," he called to her as she looked at him over her shoulder.

"He will." Esme smiled back. "And He will do the same for you."

Then she put Chass from her mind and turned it toward the prospect of seeing Raul again, and her smile was lovely to behold.

CHAPTER SEVENTEEN

By THE TIME THE CARGO SHIP, PROTECTED FROM DETECTION by the Master's device, circled Synonsis, Esme was as thoroughly weary of dealing with the council as she was excited about her reunion with Raul, which would soon take place.

First the council members, except for the high counselor, who had been silent and contemplative, had expressed their outrage at being herded aboard the cargo ship without a moment's prior notice. Then they had complained about their quarters and the food. When Esme had ignored their complaints, they had settled to mere grumbling for a while until she had begun her meetings with them concerning the coming negotiations with the Rebel leaders. Then they had once again erupted into complaint.

How could she expect them to include the traitorous Rebel leaders on the High Council? they asked.

Those leaders were not only untrained in governing, they were untrustworthy, as had been shown by their rebelling in the first place. Why not just trust the council to give the Rebels enough of what they wanted to satisfy them?

Esme had not argued. She had merely reiterated her intention. Her refusal to debate with them had infuriated the council members more.

And how could she expect them to take from the solid, entrenched, wealthy supporters of the council as much of their holdings as Esme intended to give the Rebels? Would not those solid citizens then form a rebellion of their own?

Again, Esme had not argued. She had merely informed them that the "solid" citizens would still retain more than enough wealth to satisfy anyone of merely normal, rather than obsessive, greed. She also added that she thought they would see the sense of retaining some of what they had rather than losing as much as they would should their planets be completely sealed off from trade with one another.

One by one she had dealt with the council's objections. And though they were not yet, by any means, happy over the task they faced, they were at least resigned to the fact that they had no hope of changing her mind.

Esme knew that their resignation would dissolve into outrage again, and that the Rebel leaders would no doubt join with their former enemies in feeling and expressing that anger, when all learned where and how she intended the negotiations to take place. But by then, she would have Raul beside her, and with his support, she could face anything the Rebels or the council might say or do.

Now, she was alone in her small cabin, calling Raul mind to mind to alert him that she was here, and to tell him how to come to her and how she would aid him in accomplishing his arrival.

Raul, who had been asleep in his quarters at the Rebel base upon Synonsis, was suddenly wide awake and joyfully returning Esme's loving greeting.

And peace to you, beloved, he said silently, a smile in his voice. *You have arrived just in time. I have been upon the point of exploding with frustration in reaction to the boredom and inactivity the Rebels have imposed upon me.*

And I have had all of doing without you I can take, Esme responded wryly. *I would as soon face, without my skills, a dozen wolfhounds intent upon tearing me limb from limb to get at my sheep as spend another day on my own in the company of the council. They try my patience sorely, and I would have you by my side the next time I have to endure their company and their complaints.*

Raul laughed. *Just give me time to enjoy at least one night of reunion with you before you force me to endure what you have been handling on your own,* he suggested. *Then I will be more willing to help you bear your burdens.*

Surely, Esme responded with fervent agreement. *And now, Raul, if you are ready, you must escape from your quarters and steal a small ship to come to me without the Rebels knowing I have arrived in their space. If they knew I was here, they would try to use you as hostage to force me down to Synonsis. Once you are in orbit, I will guide you by mind to where my ship lies, for it is not visible to sensors.*

Raul was on his feet in an instant, climbing into his

bodysuit, his mind on the ways and means to accomplish what he must do.

Esme, he said when he was ready, *can you mask my presence from those guarding the door of my quarters? Masking is not one of my skills, and I would rather they did not even know I have left than to have to fight them to get out of here. Someone might hear the altercation, or else discover their bodies and raise the alarm.*

I agree, Esme replied. *Besides, it would not be an auspicious beginning to the negotiations if you have to kill someone to come to me. Therefore, certainly I will mask your presence.* And then, worriedly, she added, *But I suppose you will have to use force to take over whatever ship you steal?*

Raul heard the worry in her voice and smiled grimly. *Do not worry about it,* he said. *I will handle things with as little carnage as possible.*

Good. But I hope you do not have to hurt anyone at all, Esme said. *As I said, that would not be an auspicious beginning to the negotiations.*

I will try to stay my hand, Esme, Raul said drily, *but if it comes down to my life or theirs, I presume you wish me to choose my own?*

Assuredly! Esme was alarmed and immediately prayed that Raul would not have to face such a choice.

Sensing her prayers, Raul grinned to himself. *Just do your part, Esme,* he said, his mood lighthearted over the prospect of action. He had had all the enforced inactivity he cared to endure over the past few weeks. *And I will do mine. I assure you, before very much longer, you will be greeting me more personally than by voice.*

It cannot be too soon to suit me, Esme responded fervently, and then she turned her mind to masking

Raul's departure from his quarters from the guards who stood at the doors.

Because of the late hour, the guards outside Raul's room and those outside the building were sleepily inattentive. Esme had to exert very little energy to distract them, and Raul slipped past them like a wraith in the night.

Outside the building, he stole a small mechanical vehicle to take him to one of the gates protecting the launch pads. Leaving his stolen vehicle in the shadows nearby, he then requested Esme to mask his presence from the patrolling guards and climbed over the fence. After locating and stealing another small mechanical vehicle, he drove close to the nearest ship that was small enough for him to operate on his own without a crew.

As he ran up the ramp into the ship, he sensed the presence of only one man in the control cabin. And before the control cabin hatch slid back to allow Raul entrance, he knew that he would have no trouble with its occupant. The man was a young patrol pilot, and this was his first assignment on his own. He was aboard double-checking his ship's readiness for launch the next dawn. And he took such pride in his first ship, that he would agree to almost anything in order to protect it.

Raul was across the control cabin to where the young warrior sat before his pilot board before the man could even turn around. In an instant, Raul had the man's hip laser in his own hand and was pointing it at a youthful face that was so comically startled that Raul had to smile.

"Rest easy, friend," he said mildly. "If you do nothing foolish, you and your ship will remain unharmed. I give you a choice. You can either pilot me a short distance into space, where I will take my leave of you and you can return here with you and your ship undamaged. Or you can stay on the ground, trussed and out of my way while I take your ship where it will remain unmanned when I leave it. It is your choice, but choose fast. I have an appointment with a lady, and I am in no mood to be delayed."

"I . . . I . . ."

While the young man stumbled over his answer, Raul took his decision from his mind and impatiently cut him off. "Start your engines," he said and turned his mind to Esme's presence. He felt her smile at his comment about not wanting to be delayed in seeing her.

Esme, he said silently, smiling himself, *turn your attention from your amusement and anticipation to the control tower, if you please, and convince those on duty there that there is nothing unusual about this ship leaving a few hours earlier than planned.*

Aye, Captain, Esme agreed with humor.

And as the ship which carried Raul to Esme rose into the atmosphere, the ones on duty in the control tower suddenly found their attention on other things besides the untimely departure of a small patrol ship.

Once above Synonsis, Raul issued the verbal directions to the young pilot that Esme silently put into his mind, and much to the young man's confusion, he soon found himself flying at a precise speed that Raul had him maintain which matched that of the cargo ship. The pilot had a sense that something huge flew beside him, but nothing showed on his instruments.

Esme said to Raul, *There is no room inside the ship for you to dock. The machines we transport have taken up all the space. You will have to suit up and come across with the aid of a propulsion device.*

I have not the patience for that, Raul responded, smiling. *I think I will test my self-teleportation in space for the first time.*

Raul, no! Esme was immediately seized with panic. She could not bear to think that he might be lost to her if he misjudged his powers and was left unprotected for so long in space!

Have your people open the nearest small bay to receive me, Raul cut her off, *and be sure they close it quickly once you know I am inside your ship.* Then he simply closed her protest and her emotions out of his mind and turned to the young pilot. "Maintain this speed and direction for five more minutes," he instructed. "At the end of that time, your rear door will be open. Do remember to close it before you return to the base."

He pivoted and strode to the cabin hatch, then paused there to grin at the young pilot who swivelled around staring at him as though he were seeing a man who'd completely taken leave of his senses.

"I thank you for your help, lad," he said lightly. "When you get home, look up Captain Ivvor and tell him of your adventure. Tell him also that Captain Raul says he looks forward to serving with him again when a few other little matters have been taken care of."

Then Raul stepped through the control cabin hatch, closed it securely behind him, and went to the disposal hatch.

Esme? he called, allowing her back into his mind. *Is the bay open on your side?*

Yes, Raul, but please do not do this!

Guide me! Raul ignored her protest, and an instant later he had activated the hatch in front of him and launched himself across the vacuum between the two ships.

The cold was shriveling, the oxygen deprivation severe. And just when Raul wondered if perhaps he should have heeded Esme's warning, he found himself wrapped in a cocoon of warmth and air. He was dragged at instantaneous speed through the open cargo hatch, across the huge space crowded with squat black shapes, and through the hatch that led inside the ship where passengers dwelled in safety.

The hatch behind him slammed down, the cocoon of warmth and air disappeared and as Raul stood, trying to regain his balance, he saw a small female figure running toward him from the end of the corridor.

Esme's mind reached him before her body did, and she was sobbing, furious, so filled with panicky fear that she was almost beyond coherent thought. *How could you be so selfish! Do not ever do that to me again! I hate you, Raul! And if I did not love you so much, I would have left you out there!*

He moved to meet her, and used his mind to speed the closing of the distance between them. When she had slammed into his arms, rocking him backwards, and her sobs were cut off by her resulting breathlessness, his unrepentant laughter filled the silence her lack of breath had left.

Raul gave Esme no chance to regain her breath. His mouth on hers stole what little was left in her lungs, and his joyous, lusty mind speech smothered any further protests and expressions of outrage she might have made.

When at last he let her breathe again, and lifted her into his arms, demanding the location of her cabin, she could only point, and the sounds of her panting efforts to recover oxygen into her lungs mingled with Raul's lighthearted conversation.

"That was a good trick," he said approvingly. "Let me see how you did it, so that I might have the use of the technique the next time I try that."

To Esme's fury, he deftly took from her mind the information he wanted before she could hide it behind her best shield.

"Now, Esme," he chided, grinning, as he strode along, carrying her as effortlessly as though she were a bundle of feathers rather than a furious woman bent on having her caustic say, "you would not want me to be unprepared should I be *forced* to use such means of transportation in space again, would you?"

Esme merely fumed, still silent, still panting.

"Which way now?" he asked, coming to an intersection.

Esme jabbed toward the correct direction with a trembling finger.

As he followed her direction, Raul, with his mind, lifted her finger to his mouth and gently bit it before suckling it.

The result on Esme's senses was more erotic than painful. Her temper slipped, ever so little, from its former seething pitch.

Raul released her finger. "See?" he asked, his tone amiably humorous, his smile teasingly satisfied. "Is it not more rewarding to spend one's energy on other things than arguing?"

"Hmph!" was the first sound Esme was able to

make, and a moment later, they were within her
cabin, and Raul had sealed the door behind him
before tossing her upon the small bed.

As he stood back and began to strip his bodysuit
away, he was still grinning, and Esme found her voice
at last.

"What you did was unforgiveable!" she stormed at
him.

"But you will, of course, forgive me," Raul suggested pleasantly, and added, his voice deepening,
"why do you delay disrobing, Esme? Does your impatience to begin our reunion not match mine?"

"Your *impatience* can go to—"

But Esme's vitriolic comment died into a grating
moan of frustration when she found her arms lifting,
at Raul's will, to strip herself of her filmy gown, a
gown she had chosen especially to please him upon
their reunion.

Her eyes glowing fiercely, speaking volumes of
promised retribution to the clear amusement in those
of her mate, she silently debated breaking his hold
even as her hands accomplished the task he had forced
upon her.

Raul, tossing aside his own garment, silently
warned her about the wisdom of trying it. And in the
next second, the question was moot, for Raul lay
beside Esme's nude body, and his kiss was so hungrily
thrilling that a great deal of Esme's anger fled with her
unconscious response.

She had not yet said all that was in her mind,
however, and she therefore resisted returning Raul's
kiss in full measure. She wanted him to feel shame at
the distress he had caused her and, of course, she

313

wanted him to promise that he would never do such again.

Instead, he raised his head and looked into her eyes, and put a chiding, gentle thought into her mind that made her feel shame instead and brought loving submission to her mind and heart rather than anger and retribution. Quickly, she raised her mouth to his and gave him a kiss that was much more to his liking.

When at last she drew back, Raul whispered, "That is better," and his clear gaze softened and heated to a blazing flame. "Much better," he added, with a groaning gasp as Esme touched him intimately, which invited his intimate touches in return.

And for a long while after that, spoken words, being wholly unnecessary, no longer passed between them.

They lay wrapped together in lazy contentment, waiting for their bodies to recoup from their last reunion so that they could begin another. Meanwhile, they caught up on what had passed while they had been separated. Then Esme abruptly sat up.

"I forgot to tell the Synonsian device to activate the barrier around the Rebel planet!" she wailed.

Raul laughed, pleased that he had managed to distract her so thoroughly that she had forgotten something of such importance.

"I will do it now," she said, and started to get up when Raul pulled her back to him.

"Must you go to it to speak the words?" he asked, stroking her breasts as he spoke.

"N–no," Esme admitted, already reacting to his touch. "It is just that it has become my habit. It is of such importance that I not fail at what the Master has set me to do that I take no chances." Then she had a thought. "And Raul," she added apologetically, "since you do not yet have the same kind of invulnerable shield that I do behind which to hide the sequences, it would perhaps be better if you did not eavesdrop when I say them."

Raul stopped stroking her and raised an eyebrow. He was not pleased.

"Raul, you know how important it is that no one untrustworthy learn how to control the devices," Esme tried to soothe him. "And they have been trying to learn, believe me. Oh, how they have tried!"

"Am I untrustworthy?" Raul's voice was cool.

"No, of course not! But you do not have the proper shield!"

"Then give it to me."

Esme sighed, frustrated by his attitude. Why was he being so obstinate when he knew very well it was not a matter of trust, but of precaution?

"Raul, it took me weeks to construct my own," she said.

"And I, upon occasion, have shown you that our talents differ in some matters," Raul reminded her. Then he relented slightly. "Esme, if I cannot grasp the method with sufficient speed to do any good for the present, I will close my mind when you speak the sequences and work with patience to construct such a shield of my own. Meanwhile, give me the method. It will quickly become apparent whether I can grasp it immediately or will have to struggle to obtain success."

With that, Esme could agree, and she went into Raul's mind.

When he had the required information, he lay back, closed his eyes, and said to Esme, "Attend me while I am about this. If you see that I am veering from the proper path, correct me." Then, his brow furrowed in concentration, he worked inside himself.

While Esme eavesdropped upon the workings of his mind with much interest, she was also amazed, and a little disconcerted, to find that his thought processes worked differently from hers when he was problem-solving. She allowed much seemingly extraneous information into her thinking, which increased her vague intuitive graspings, and while they delayed a direct attack upon the problem, eventually they formed into a whole solution. But Raul went single-mindedly at his purpose. Ruthlessly, he excluded all that might delay or hinder what he sought.

Esme had always wondered how he had accomplished his incredible, breathtaking leap from accepting the possibilities she had shown him were within him to the realization of them. She had not expected that when she had given him a key he would unlock whole universes with it!

Even as she watched him and understood his method, she knew she could not duplicate it. She had been born with her gifts almost full-flowered and had had to grow into some of them more completely.

Raul had been born with such gifts also, but they had been hidden from him for a very long time, and he had to work at accomplishing what Esme had received as a gracious gift. She had not the patience, nor the skill, nor the practice at working within herself and upon herself that Raul had. Her difficulty in constructing her secret shield was evidence of how hard it was for her to do other than what came fairly naturally to her without exerting much effort. She had not relished that task at all, and if her inner guiding voice had not convinced her of the necessity of her work, she would not have kept at it.

Her thoughts departed from her musings abruptly as she suddenly felt and saw an absence in Raul's mind. It was as though a light had blinked off!

"Raul!" she cried, frightened that he had somehow lost part of himself.

Then he was back, smiling, and his eyes held a satisfied gleam.

Esme took a shaking breath. "What happened?" she demanded, angry now that her fear had proved groundless. "Where did you go?"

"Behind that shield you taught me." Raul grinned, much pleased with himself.

Esme eyed him sceptically. "You could not have constructed it so quickly," she doubted.

"Could I not?" Raul's grin broadened.

"Show me again!" Esme's doubt faded, but it was very hard for her to believe the truth before her eyes.

Raul obligingly took her to the very doors of his innermost shield, where he deftly barred her from entering. Frowning, Esme struggled to pierce that which he had constructed, using more force than she had ever used upon anyone before without killing them.

"Enough," Raul grimaced at last when she caused him too much discomfort.

Esme desisted and sat looking at him, her eyes wide. "I would have killed another, using that much force," she said, awe in her tone.

Raul gave her a look that made her blush.

"I could feel when to stop," she defended her actions.

"Indeed?" Raul was disgruntled. "Then why did I have to request you to desist from killing me?"

"You did not ask me not to kill you, for I was not about to kill you," Esme said matter-of-factly. "You just told me you did not wish to be caused anymore discomfort." Then she looked at him admiringly. "You bear pain well, Raul."

He grunted, eyeing her with disfavor. "Which it seems is a blessing," he said pointedly.

Esme smiled and stretched herself along his body to cuddle against him. "You are truly a marvel," she praised him. "I would not have believed it possible that you could do such if I had not witnessed it."

"And you are forgetting once again what it is you need to do," he replied, softening enough to pull her closer against him. "I will attend you while you speak the sequences. Then you may attend me while I tuck them where they will be safe from all but those with powers equal to yours and with the sadism necessary to extract them from my mind."

Esme ignored his jibe and performed the duty she had earlier forgotten. When she was done, and was certain that Raul had the sequences safely hidden from detection, she sent her mind to test the barrier that now circled Synonsis.

Returning to her body, she was pleased. "All is in readiness for the morrow," she announced.

"The morrow?" Raul questioned. "Can duty not wait another additional day?"

Esme raised her head to look at him in surprise. "Yes, of course," she allowed. "One day will make no

318

difference. But what is your reason for . . ."

She stopped speaking because Raul had wound his fingers in her hair and brought her mouth to his and closed it with his lips. Then he showed her how he planned to spend the additional time, and Esme was so easily convinced of the wisdom of his plan that she was soon suggesting still another additional day within which to fulfill it.

CHAPTER EIGHTEEN

Upon becoming aware that the barrier surrounding their planet was truly impenetrable and that the council was aboard the ship circling above the barrier, the Rebel leaders warily went aboard the cargo ship to begin negotiations.

Once they were sealed in their quarters, however, Raul gave instructions to the pilot to take the ship to Esme's Homeland.

Upon feeling the first jump, both the council and the Rebels were mightily alarmed and commenced the protest that Esme had expected. She and Raul then dutifully visited each delegation.

"Where do you take us?" the high counselor asked, much too mildly to suit those of his group who had had about all they could stand of being herded like dumb beasts wherever Esme chose to send them.

"To the place of man's origin," Esme answered calmly.

There was a moment of puzzled silence before the high counselor responded. "But, Esme, no one any longer knows where that is," he pointed out. "And even if the location of the original Earth was known, the planet was destroyed eons ago."

"What has been hidden from men for so long by He Who originated all life is about to be rediscovered," Esme said. "He wishes to remind you and those who fight you what enmity among brothers once caused. Perhaps, upon being so reminded, you will understand more fully the abomination you were about to commit."

She paused then, and added, on a note of humor, "And He also wishes you to have no distractions while you are about your negotiations."

Then she delivered the same message to the Rebels, leaving both sides confused, anxious and frustrated, a state which lasted until the arrival in orbit around the Homeland was accomplished. Then Esme brought the leaders, each in turn, to the control cabin and showed them upon the view screens the globe upon which their ancestors had been brought to life and once lived for many generations.

"But how do you know this is the original Earth?" the high counselor said in an awed tone as he looked at the spinning brown, yellow, and blue globe.

"It is my home," Esme said simply. "My people have always known. Also have we always known that there were others the Master saved when our ancestors sought to destroy one another and almost succeeded. Your people are the descendants of those others, of course."

The high counselor looked at her in puzzlement, then back at the globe. "But, Esme, it is obviously a barren planet. How could anyone live there?"

"It is barren, yes." Esme nodded, "Except for the valley the Master protected in order to support his Remnant. That valley is our destination. It is where you and the Rebels will conduct your negotiations." She looked at him gravely. "It is a fitting place for such, is it not? Where mankind once failed, the Master is now giving him the opportunity to succeed."

The high counselor let out a breath and shook his head. "Esme," he said her name, sounding overwhelmed. He shook his head again. "The Master . . ." he said quietly. "When you speak of Him, do you really mean the One certain old myths define as the Creator of all life?"

"I mean the Creator." Esme nodded. "Whatever man has ever thought, whatever he has ever believed or disbelieved, even what he has forgotten, has never made a difference to what is true. The Master was and is and will always be. He does not depend upon our acceptance for existence. Rather does our existence depend upon His acceptance."

The high counselor, thoughtful and introspective, had fallen silent then, and Esme sent him back to his quarters. Then she brought his counterpart to the control cabin, where much the same conversation was repeated, except that Finder, the Rebel leader, was less thoughtful and more belligerent.

"And how long do you plan to keep us here?" he demanded.

"Until you have done what you were brought here to do," Esme said simply, "or until you return to the dust that spawned your ancestors and then received them back again—whichever comes first. The choice is up to you and yours and the council, Finder, as it has ever been."

Finder snorted. "Choice, indeed!" he said sarcastically, and had stomped back to his quarters.

Raul came to Esme then and took her under his arm. "Finder does not seem pleased by your plan," he said lightly.

Esme shook her head. "It is not my plan, Raul," she reminded him. "And Finder, despite his disbelief that he truly has a choice in these matters, will come to know differently."

"Have you added the ability to see the future to your talents, then?" Raul asked.

"No, I am no prophet," Esme demurred. "Only do I trust that the Master does not intend His own to destroy one another again, else He would never have given me my task and brought it thus far along to fruition."

"Aye." Raul nodded. "I can believe the same."

Several hours later, the council, the Rebel leaders, and the People were all at the gathering place, listening to Esme introduce all of them to one another and explain what would now take place. Esme was sorry that Jemiah was off on one of his explorations and would not be present at this historic moment.

"My people, we have long awaited the fulfillment of the Prophecy," she said to her own. "Among you now are those others of whom the Prophecy speaks. They are here to recover their brotherhood with one another, and with us. While they attempt to come to peace among themselves, we have much to teach them about obtaining peace with He Who rules all of the universe, theirs as well as ours. And we will have much to learn from them about things that have been long forgotten among us. I ask you to shelter and feed them and aid them in whatever way occurs to you to reach the objective that concerns us all."

She turned to the council and to the Rebel leaders then, and said, gently, but very firmly, "You will live among us for as long as it takes you to learn again the meaning of the second of the Master's commandments. I suggest you do not tarry upon the completion of your task. If you wish to see again those whom you love upon your own planets and give your bodies to the soil of your own homelands when your time in the flesh is finished, you will let go of old perspectives and quickly embrace a new and better one. Otherwise, your lives have held no purpose and you will finish here, where your ancestors' lives began, and others will accomplish that which you have refused to do."

She dismissed them then, and taking Raul's arm, walked toward Baldor's cave, with the priest following behind them, as the People took their visitors home with them.

"So far from the truth have they strayed that they do not even know what the first commandment is, much less the second," she said to Raul as they walked, and her tone was amazed.

"And the first commandment is to love the Master above all else?" Raul asked, showing her that he was as ignorant of truth in some matters as were his fellows. "Is not that what you told the council when you took them hostage upon Genesis?"

Esme stopped short and looked up at him in amazement; then her eyes softened. Her beloved was, after all, a creature of his environment, and for that she could not blame him.

"Yes." She nodded. "And if you remember, the second commandment is that man is to love his neighbors as he loves himself."

"Aye," Raul said, "I have seen the first commandment in operation within you and had much trouble dealing with it, if you recall. But still, the first is probably easier to accomplish than the second."

"Yes." Esme sighed. "It is easier in some ways to love He Whom we can only know through His word, a word that calls to the best within us, even when we cannot actually see and touch and talk face to face with the Author of the word, than it is to love those whose faults and frailties are ever before us."

"True." Raul nodded. "But my people are not as ignorant of tolerance toward one another as you think. Such tolerance has ever been taught among us as a matter of basic survival."

"But have yours not recently forgotten the lesson?" Esme gently reminded him. "Else why this senseless civil war?"

"Aye," Raul admitted. "But then your people forgot some things as well recently, did they not?" He spoke of what had happened during Bazil's short reign.

Esme took the reminder well, though it caused her some minor discomfort.

Raul hid a smile and said, blandly, "As you say, it is often hard to love those whose faults and frailties are ever before us."

Esme gave him a meaningful look, then got back to the discussion at hand. "In any case, it is not just *tolerance* of one another the Master wants," she said.

"It is something more active than that. He wants us to wish for one another the same blessings we have ourselves, and not to wish anyone harm, even when they might seemingly deserve it."

Raul shook his head. "Your Master asks a lot then," he said drily, "especially when none of us, other than you, has had the benefit of seeing Him face to face and feeling personally the sort of love you say He embodies. How then do we become sure He really exists? And what example do we have to follow that is not only backed up by that assurance that He does exist, but by our personal experience of His nature?"

"I know it is hard," Esme agreed. "I did not understand fully nor truly know Him until He permitted me that face-to-face meeting. And I wish that He did not withhold such meetings from everyone. But we can believe and do, Raul, even without such a meeting. The scrolls explain everything. Then it is a matter of decision, of choice, on our part. I believed before I ever had that personal meeting with Him."

"But you are exceptional, Esme," Raul pointed out, his tone soft.

"As are you," she said with complete sincerity.

Then they were at the entrance of Baldor's cave and the high priest was asking where they wished to quarter.

"I can move out of this cave," he suggested. "You have more right to it than I in any case, Esme."

Esme shook her head and looked at Raul. "If it is agreeable with my beloved," she proposed, "I would spend upon the high meadow what little time remains before the winter snows drive the shepherds and sheep to lower pasture. I need a respite from what has occupied me for many months. I need the peace to be found in doing simple things."

Raul shrugged. "I am agreeable," he said. "I, too, could use the respite. But what of the other devices, Esme? Do you not intend to deliver them immediately to the rest of the worlds and put them into operation?"

"Not immediately." Esme shook her head. "It is only necessary that the barriers around Genesis and Synonsis be in place to stop the war while the negotiations proceed. After we have had our respite, we will see how those negotiations go. Mayhap, if they proceed apace, we can even take the council and the Rebel leaders home when we depart to dispense the other devices."

"But are you not going to oversee the negotiations personally?" Baldor asked. "What if these others begin to fight among themselves?"

Esme smiled. "They have been informed of the consequences of transferring their disagreements from verbiage to physical action," she explained. "And I or Raul will visit them from time to time, if only by mind, to check their progress."

"If peace is obtained," Raul suggested, "perhaps we do not need to put the other devices into place after all. What would be the point?"

But at that suggestion, Esme frowned and looked puzzled. "I do not know what the point will be, Raul," she said thoughtfully. "But the Master made it clear that they must be put into place regardless of what happens concerning the negotiations. But, of course, if a peace treaty is forged, they do not have to be activated."

Raul frowned then and had a thought but he did not express it. Rather he hid it behind his deepest shield while he hoped fervently that the thought was not a forerunner to reality.

"Well, then," Baldor said, "though I am sorry that you will absent yourself again from among us, I cannot argue with your desire for a time of quietude. Maza has kept your flock for you, Esme, if you wish to take up such simple duties again for a while. You know where to find him."

And within a day, Esme was a shepherdess again, and Raul was as lazily content to learn her lesser skills as he had been reluctant, at first, to learn her higher ones.

Snuggled in one another's arms among sleeping skins that first night, Esme pointed out to Raul the constellations with which she had been familiar since childhood. And she told him the dreams that had come to her upon this high meadow—dreams of traveling among the stars and of loving him before she had ever met him in the flesh.

"And all that time, I was about my calling as a warrior," Raul said, "with no thought of what awaited me on this forgotten world." He hesitated, then added, very quietly, "It makes me wonder what else is in our future that we do not at present foresee, Esme."

"I do not know, beloved," she answered, burying her head against his warm neck. "And I do not want to know. So long as I have you, I am content to live in this moment."

"Aye, I feel the same," Raul agreed. Drawing her more closely into his arms, he made their mutual contentment more complete.

As Esme attempted to herd to winter pasture a flock that was unusually skittish, perhaps because it had forgotten her and had grown used to another shepherd, she realized that the past months of tension and strain had taken more of a toll on her physical and mental resources than she'd known. For the first time ever, she grew fatigued in body and short of temper with the foolish animals she herded.

Raul laughed at her increasing frustration. "Are you that much out of practice?" he teased. "Or were you simply never that good a shepherdess in the first place?"

To Esme's and Raul's complete surprise, she then lost her temper with *him*. Though she apologized, she was unable to do so with as much sincerity as the situation required, so that there remained a coolness between them for the rest of the day.

That night, as they had their evening meal, Raul looked across the firelight consideringly at Esme.

"What is it that ails you?" he asked abruptly. "I have never seen you as prickly as this."

Esme stiffened, then relaxed and sighed. "It is just that I feel so very tired, beloved," she said with quiet weariness.

Raul's expression softened. "The last months have not been easy," he suggested. "You have been under a great deal of strain and it was not possible to relax because of the duties you faced. Perhaps, now that it is possible to relax, your system has decided to do so with a vengeance."

That last word of Raul's brought a wry smile to Esme's lips.

"You are waiting for a more sincere apology than I gave you earlier," she stated rather than asked.

Raul merely looked at her meaningfully without saying anything.

Esme set her still half-eaten meal aside, for in truth she was not at all hungry and had had to force herself to ingest as much as she had. She rose to join him. When she sat by his side, she leaned her head on his shoulder.

"I am truly sorry I was short-tempered with you, beloved," she said sincerely. "Forgive me."

Raul put his arm around her and pulled her closer. "Aye, I do," he said with quiet acceptance. "And now that I know wherein lies the trouble, I will aid in fixing it. This night, you will sleep in my arms without having first exhausted yourself performing a mate's duties."

Esme smiled. "I do not regard such as we share as a duty," she said. "You are well aware of that fact."

"Aye. Nor do I regard our mating as such, which you are aware of as well. But just the same, tonight we will forego it."

Part of Esme wanted to protest the arrangement. But she was so weary that when she and Raul at last lay together beneath the sleeping skin, and she was cradled snugly against the chill of the night in his warm arms, she slept at once, and with such heaviness that she did not dream. But in the hour before dawn, she did dream, and the dream was of a quality that she knew, even in the midst of it, that it was one of foretelling.

In the dream, a creature that resembled humanity in certain ways, but was too reptilianly hideous in others ways to be human, stood admiring his reflection in a huge mirror that dominated one whole curving wall of his private chambers.

Esme somehow knew the creature's name was Sathanas, and that his status was god-king of a vast realm in a distant galaxy called Miia. She also knew that the creature found his own reflection one of such beauty that he did not look forward to foregoing contemplating it in order to carry out his state duties.

A valet more hideous in appearance than Sathanas brought a shimmering, full-length, grayish-green cloak and respectfully draped it over Sathanas's shoulders.

Sathanas's slitted black pupils narrowed even further as he inspected the effect of the shimmering folds upon his person. It concealed too much, he decided, of his magnificent body. Thus, he threw the cloak over one shoulder and put his clawed fists on his too-narrow hips which were molded by a skintight green bodysuit. He struck a favorite pose, haughtily thrusting his receding, mottled gray-skinned chin up in a regal gesture.

Now, his round yellow eyes with the slitted black pupils held the absolutely blank expression that kept his subordinates from knowing his thoughts or feelings, and thereby kept them off guard and anxious. And just as he was about to allow himself a smile in approbation of his appearance, a voice appeared in his mind, and the smile died.

We are looking very beautiful today, the voice slithered into Sathanas's consciousness. *Very beautiful indeed. Our people will be overwhelmed.*

As always, there was the very faintest hint of contemptuous amusement underlying the power in the voice, and the source of that contemptuous amusement wiped all joy from Sathanas's heart.

Once and once only had Sathanas been allowed a vision of the one who owned the voice. But that vision, when he allowed himself to recall it, haunted him with his own inadequacies in the matter of male

331

beauty. Indeed, he had wished often that he had never been allowed the vision. But he knew that the one who controlled him, the creator of the Miian race, had granted it for the very purpose it served—to maintain control by giving Sathanas the hope that if his service was found pleasing, he might one day come to resemble the god whose beauty he envied to the depths of his soul.

I will accompany you today while you hold your audience with the generals and bureaucrats, the voice now said.

Sathanas could not stop the resentful disgruntlement inside him. It damaged his pride that the god did not trust him to hold such audiences without supervision and control.

The voice, however, was not sharp, as it sometimes was, in upbraiding him for his slight disloyalty.

The generals are dragging their feet, it explained with only a hint of harshness in its tone. *They are too soft on those they train and need to be reminded of what happens to those who do not give their all to our just cause.*

Sathanas knew all about the "just cause." The voice had explained to him that there was another God—an inferior God—who challenged his rule. The voice had also explained that he intended to use his Miian creation to make the inferior God regret His challenge by destroying all those who worshipped Him.

If you do well in the audience today, the voice then offered the reward that often accompanied his threats, *I will send you a new concubine tonight. One who is as gifted in the art of admiration as she is talented in bestowing pleasure, so that when you sleep this night, you will be almost convinced that your beauty matches mine.*

Sathanas stiffened over the reminder that his beauty was deficient, but the voice merely laughed, even as it propelled Sathanas toward the door of his chamber.

A short while later, as Sathanas paused behind the curtain that backed his throne before entering the Great Hall, where his subjects had already been painfully abject upon their knees for some time awaiting him, the voice spoke again. *After this audience, I will be absent from you for a while.*

Again, Sathanas could not control his reaction, which was one of anticipation over the prospect of being left in peace for however short a time.

But the voice knew how to deal with such disloyal thoughts. *There is another such as you whom I must needs visit*, it whispered.

Immediately, Sathanas's heart jerked in fear.

The voice laughed mockingly. *Ah, I had forgotten you fear replacement in my affections, Sathanas.*

Sathanas knew the lie for what it was. The voice forgot nothing—ever.

But why would I replace the one who bears my name? the voice continued. *Why would I have gone to such trouble as to lift you from your former state of insignificance and place you upon the throne of my kingdom, only to cast you aside when the time of fruition for my plans is coming so near? Surely, you do not think I would take all the gifts I bestowed upon you and give them to another?*

Sathanas took the voice's words in the spirit in which they had been meant, which was as a threat. The prospect of losing all that he had come to have was unbearable. Therefore, he was abject in his repentance for giving offense to the one who was the source of all he had come to require.

That is much better, the voice acknowledged Sathanas's new state of mind with dry appreciation. *You are forgiven, my son. And now, put aside your mental groveling and prepare yourself. We are about to administer some much needed discipline upon those who are slow to accomplish my objectives.*

An instant later, within Sathanas rose a surge of power. And as he stepped through the rich curtains to sit upon the throne to receive the admiration and fear from the kneeling horde in the audience chamber, his countenance was terrible to behold.

Esme came out of her dream, shuddering with horror and fear. For a long moment, she lay staring into the embers of the dying fire, fighting the thundering beat of her heart and the panic in her mind. Then, as had happened in the days when her dreams had been of a more cheerful nature upon this high meadow, the dream began to fade until she could no longer recall it clearly.

Still, she felt chilled from head to foot, and within her soul as well, and to ease that inner and outer coldness, she turned to Raul, who lay sleeping behind her.

With gratitude for the comfort of his presence, and love overfilling her heart, she gently slipped her arm around his waist and conformed her body to the contours of his back. Then she lay quietly savoring the sound of his breathing and the warmth and solidity of his body.

She felt him come half-awake and she smiled as she

listened to his thoughts. He was struggling between his desire to continue sleeping and a growing sense that she needed him in some way he did not clearly understand.

"Are you cold?" he mumbled.

"Very," Esme whispered against his broad shoulder.

He turned and enclosed her in his arms. The warmth he exuded was heavenly. The comfort of his arms around her was exactly what she needed.

"Sleep, Esme," he mumbled, his own sleepiness evident in his voice. "I will keep you warm enough to allow you to rest properly."

"I am grateful, my love," she murmured as she began to relax.

"Do not be." Raul's sleepy voice now contained a note of humor. "As always, at some point, I will require recompense for this favor."

"As always," Esme agreed, smiling, and tightened her arms around Raul's body in an affectionate hug.

They slept in one another's arms until the dawn brought with it new energy to their bodies and minds. Then Esme used that energy, despite Raul's half-hearted insistence that she needed more rest, to seal, once again, the bond between them.

CHAPTER NINETEEN

Filled with the physical and emotional contentment that was always the aftermath of Raul's loving, Esme lay savoring life.

Beneath her back was the support of the Homeland's familiar soil, sheltering the sweet scent of the life within it until spring. The sight of the familiar morning sky delighted her eyes, and the sound of her flock grazing nearby filled her ears. Her heart was at ease.

Then the summons came. Only this time, the Master summoned Raul as well as Esme.

Delighted, Esme turned her head to her mate lying quietly beside her, his eyes closed.

"We must seek the Master, Raul," she said joyfully.

Raul abruptly opened his eyes and turned to stare at her in confusion. "We?" he repeated.

Esme nodded, then sat up. "He asked for you," she said.

Raul sat up as well. "When?" he demanded, frowning.

"Just now."

Raul opened his mouth to say something further, then closed it again. But Esme took the nature of his thoughts from his expression and smiled.

"Perhaps the Master summons for rewards as well as to assign tasks," she suggested. "And we did, after all, do His will."

But the clear blue of Raul's eyes reflected doubt. "I do not recall that He has ever summoned you for such a purpose thus far," he pointed out. "And the fact that He wants me as well . . ." He shrugged.

"Let us not worry about it," Esme said, smiling up into Raul's face. "I am only happy that you will at last see why I love Him so. Once you meet Him, you will not be able to help loving Him as much as I do."

She jumped to her feet. "Come," she said excitedly. "We must herd the sheep to Maza before we set off for the mountain."

But Raul, looking at her closely, and affirming again what he had noted before since they had been re-united, shook his head.

"Not until we eat," he said firmly. "You have lost weight, Esme, and are looking frail. It is a long climb up that mountain, and you will expend much energy. Therefore, you will eat before we go."

Esme felt impatient, and her appetite was not great. But there had been no urgency in the Master's summons and Raul looked so concerned that she put aside her impatience to please him.

Later, as they herded the sheep toward where Maza normally shepherded, it was Esme's turn to laugh at Raul's sheepherding skills. He was trying to take some of the burden from her, but he was not succeeding very well.

"The trick," she said, chuckling, "is to skim their minds rather than look deeply. And while you are skimming, you plant images in their heads of ever more succulent grasses and ever sweeter water just over the next hill—in the direction you want them to go, of course."

"Aye," Raul said drily. "The strategy has merit. But even skimming the dimwitted minds of creatures who seem to prefer chaos to order makes my head ache."

"Never mind." Esme smiled. "I sense Maza ahead, so your head will not have to ache much longer."

They did not stop on the Sacred Ledge to perform the ancient ritual the People's priests had used in the past to commune with the Master. They instead pushed aside the rock door Jase's men had cut into the back wall of the ledge and entered the now empty cavern directly.

Inside, they paused to look up. The mountain was again capped. Jase had activated the controls that closed the mountaintop after the Master's device had been removed.

As they waited for the Master to come, Esme's weariness made her eyes heavy and her body tremble. The long climb up the mountain had indeed, as Raul had feared it would, taken its toll on her. And suddenly, Esme found herself frightened. If the Master did have another task for her, and she did not have time to recover her strength before it was necessary to embark upon it, she might be inadequate to perform the task and fail Him.

Esme . . . Esme . . .

The beloved rumbling voice of muted thunder that filled her with such joy and peace that she could scarcely credit the ease it brought her, echoed in her mind, gently chiding her for her worry.

In the next instant, the magnificent shimmering light that signaled the Master's presence filled the cavern, and Esme fell to her knees, tears of love and joy streaming down her face.

Raul did not kneel, and no tears traced his cheeks. But the expression on his face disclosed that he, as well as Esme, experienced the peace and wonder of the Master's presence.

"Do you not yet realize," the Master said to Esme, "that My grace is sufficient for anyone to accomplish the tasks I set them?"

He stretched out a hand from which fiery streams of light rippled, and Esme was abruptly bathed in a warmth that strengthened and renewed and refreshed her body and mind so much that she felt like a child again, so full of energy there was nothing too hard to do.

She bowed her head in gratitude. "Forgive me, Master," she said humbly. "My former weariness from accomplishing the tasks you last set me scrambled my wits and made me foolish."

"Accomplishing My tasks has not made you feel weary, Esme," the Master said gently. "I supplemented your strength to allow you to do what was needed. Your fatigue and irritability are a result of the fact that you now carry a child."

Esme's astonishment over the news was genuine.

She had felt nothing within her body to alert her to the truth. And though she had contemplated discussing with Raul his wishes in the matter of conceiving a child, she had not yet ventured upon such a discussion.

She looked at Raul, who had raised his head sharply upon hearing the Master's words. Her mate's expression wavered between joy and doubt.

Raul's joy, though tentative because of his doubt, sparked her own, and she gave herself up to her happiness.

The Master turned his attention to Raul, radiating warmth.

"Do you doubt me still, Raul?" He asked, His rumbling voice only faintly chiding. Then He lifted His hand to Raul and bathed him in light as He had Esme.

Raul, after a moment of receiving that beneficent light, said, his voice husky with emotion, "Never again."

The Master's forgiveness filled the cavern and then He began to explain the reason for His summons. "You have both done well. I am pleased with you."

His approval was like a drink of cold sweet water on a sweltering day, and both Raul and Esme basked in it.

"And now," the Master went on, "until your son has come of age, you will have another task. You must prepare Raul's people spiritually for the great battle to come."

A faint stirring of remembrance of her dream replaced Esme's happy wonderment with an uneasy chill.

"Yes, Esme," the Master confirmed. "The enemy is as active and as envious as ever. Those creatures are the flawed result of his attempt to duplicate My creation, and he commands a great force of them."

Raul was puzzled by the discussion, and the Master stopped speaking for an instant in order to fill Raul's mind with an instantaneous version of Esme's dream. Afterward, Raul's expression was grim.

"If humankind is to defeat the enemy's creatures," the Master then went on, "they must be armed with more than physical weapons. For the enemy will seek to win by use of the evil temptations he has always employed. He will attempt to set human against human by way of greed, pride, envy, lust, and hatred. And unless there are enough of you armed with My spirit, the battle will be lost. Therefore, Baldor and his priests must take the truth and sow it among the worlds."

"But will they listen?" Raul asked, frowning. He knew his own people well enough to doubt it.

"Not all," the Master said sorrowfully. "But embued with My spirit, the priests will convince enough to mount the needed defense."

"And our son?" Esme spoke up. "What role in all this will he play, Master?"

But the Master did not answer directly. "He, as you and Raul have, will serve Me," He said.

Then, to Esme's confusion, the Master turned to Raul and communed with him silently. Esme was excluded from their talk.

"I will," Raul said aloud with grim firmness at the end of the silent conversation.

Seeing in his clear blue eyes a light of fierceness Esme had only seen there in the heat of battle, she grew uneasy. But when the Master turned back to her and bathed her with His presence, her uneasiness faded abruptly to peace again, and she forgot entirely what had just happened.

"Go now," the Master blessed them both. "Set the sowing in motion. And My grace and peace go with you."

An instant later, the cavern was devoid of His light, and Raul, supporting Esme with his arm, began the journey down the mountain.

Baldor was astonished and dismayed.

"Me leave the Homeland?" he repeated faintly. "And the seekers as well?"

"Once you have brought them to full priesthood," Esme nodded.

"But . . . but . . ."

Esme smiled. "There are no 'buts,' Baldor," she said gently. "The Master cannot be gainsaid. You know that as well as we do."

At that, Baldor sighed. "That is truth," he agreed. "But judging from my discussions so far with most of those others you brought here, my priests and I are going to be in the same position upon Raul's worlds that I was during Bazil's reign—objects of ridicule. And that was not a pleasant time in my life, I assure you."

"It will not necessarily be like that," Raul interjected with a smile. "Those we brought here are accustomed to power, and the wielding of power often makes for a cynical mind. But a great number of the people on the worlds that make up the Empire are simple people, farmers, seamen, builders, and shop owners. They will most likely listen more receptively than those who negotiate here now. And besides, you and your priests will be sponsored by Esme and me, and that should lend you some clout."

"'Clout'?" Baldor was puzzled by the word.

"Respect," Esme put in, smiling.

"Ah . . ." Baldor nodded.

Then Dallia and Ana came into the main room of Baldor's cave, bearing dinner, and they left off their discussion to eat.

During the meal, Esme noticed that Ana kept studying her in a perceptive fashion, and the older woman's intense scrutiny brought a blush to her cheeks.

The blush made Ana smile with delight. "Ah, so it is true then?" she asked.

Esme nodded, her eyes luminous with joy.

"What is true?" Baldor asked, looking curiously from Ana to Esme.

"Esme bears within her the true link between the Remnant and the others," Ana said with satisfaction.

At that, Esme raised her head in startlement, gazing at Ana in a wondering fashion. She had thought *she* was that link. But had the elderly woman spoken prophecy without knowing it? she speculated. Ana did not have the expression of one who knew she spoke prophecy, but her words had struck a chord of something significant within Esme's heart, and she knew she would remember the older woman's statement.

Baldor and Dallia were ecstatic over the news and immediately turned the simple meal into a celebration.

Raul, viewing with bemused contentment the unself-conscious and completely sincere joy Baldor and Dallia and Ana displayed over his and Esme's good fortune, found himself humbled by their simple goodness. There was nothing faked about their reaction. They were as happy as if the good news was their own, and since Raul could tell that Baldor and Dallia hoped for such good news of their own soon, he hoped for them that such would be the case.

But later that night, as he held Esme in his arms while she slept deeply, exhausted by the long climb up the mountain and the trip afterwards to the Settlement, he recalled the Master's silent warning to him, and his contentment faded, replaced by grim determination.

For the one Esme and the Master termed the enemy did not wish Raul's son to be born, much less to reach the age of maturity. And the Master had made it clear it was Raul's task to keep the child safe.

Esme was not to know until after she gave birth to the child. She deserved the reward for her service to the Master of a happy, undisturbed pregnancy. And Raul had therefore tucked his secret knowledge behind the shield where she could not venture just as he tucked away his utter determination to carry out the command the Master had given him to protect the babe.

But in truth, though Raul appreciated the Master's warning, he had needed no command to protect his son. He would have done that, with every weapon he owned, regardless of instructions.

Throughout the long, cold winter, the hostility between the Rebels and the High Council waned as they began to agree. Jemiah, his explorations of the Homeland curtailed by the weather, helped in the process by providing historical background of previous such agreements reached over the centuries.

Esme increasingly left the monitoring and occasional prodding along of the negotiations to Raul. Also, though she occasionally assisted, she left most of the work of turning the seekers into full-fledged priests to Baldor.

Esme was immersed in the joy of experiencing her pregnancy.

Lying one night curled in sleeping skins, her expression was blank as she checked within her body to make sure her son fared well. Raul arrived from dining with the high counselor and Finder and settled beside her to sleep.

Upon noticing her expression, Raul sighed with both resigned amusement and a feeling of being excluded. For while he had no doubt that Esme's regard for him was as solid as ever, he was having some difficulty with the new division in her attention.

Esme came back to herself and turned into his arms, contented.

"How does he fare?" Rául asked.

Esme noted something in his tone that made her thoughtful. "He is well," she replied. "Contented and happy in his present abode."

"Good," Raul murmured, closing his eyes. He was tired.

Esme thought another moment, then said, "Would you like to visit him?"

Raul's eyes opened abruptly. "What?"

"I asked if you would like to visit our son as I am accustomed to visiting him," Esme said, hiding a smile.

Raul hesitated. "But how would such be possible?" he inquired.

Esme shrugged. "I will visit him and leave my mind open so that you might share the visit with me," she said simply.

Intrigued, Raul shifted and laid his hand upon Esme's now bulging stomach. At that moment, he felt his son move within her, and his heart leapt with joy.

"Why have we not thought of this before?" he said with satisfaction. "Yes, Esme. What you suggest pleases me."

Esme smiled ruefully, wishing she *had* thought of a solution to Raul's loneliness because of her divided attention before. But she had been too wrapped up in her own wonderment, and in any case, it was not too late.

"Attend me," she said lovingly. "I think you will find yourself much pleased by what we have created together." She sent her mind inside her body to the place where their son presently dwelled in contentment.

Raul joined his mind to Esme's open thoughts, and upon viewing the tiny, but already perfectly formed body of his son for the first time, he felt a softening of his heart so intense that tears filled his eyes.

Esme was much moved by Raul's reaction. She had felt Raul's tears only once before.

"He looks like you," she whispered.

"Aye," Raul agreed, pridefully loving. "But his eyes are closed, and I have a feeling that when they open they will be green like yours."

"I, too, have such a feeling," Esme replied, a smile in her voice.

"It will not be long now, until we are able to hold him in our arms?" Raul asked, and unconsciously his concern for the child rose in his mind before he remembered to tuck it quickly behind his shield.

Esme thought his anxiety the result of the normal concern any father felt for the safe delivery of his child. And she thought his tucking such concern behind his shield was the result of his male view that such feelings must be hidden from the world.

"Aye," she said, amused. "In the spring, we will hold him in our arms. And now let us leave him to his sleep while we go to ours. You must be as weary as I am."

She came back to herself, and was pleased by the new sense of sharing in her pregnancy that she sensed in Raul and by the new connection and love he felt for their child.

"Thank you, Esme," he said quietly.

"You are most welcome," she responded with sincerity. "I only wish I had thought to include you in such visits earlier."

He smiled. "As I wish I had thought of it." Then he yawned, and the both of them, wrapped in one another's arm, drifted peacefully to sleep.

Esme woke in pain, and for a moment she was confused. Then another shaft of pain shot through her belly, and her mood shifted from confusion to terror.

"Raul!" she cried.

The habit of sleeping lightly long engrained in him, Raul was awake and sitting up in an instant.

He did not have to ask questions. Esme's mind was open to his, and he was immediately aware that she was in labor—prematurely.

"Help me!" she begged. "It is too soon! The child cannot live outside my body!" She doubled up in agony as another pain shot through her.

347

His expression grim, Raul forced himself to shove his panic aside and think clearly and when he had, he knew why this was happening.

When Esme's pain had passed, he said with quiet force, "Esme, you must go into your own body and stop this."

But Esme's terror and the pain of another contraction prevented her from responding either verbally or with the action Raul insisted she take.

Raul then went into her mind with such force that Esme could not do other than pay him attention.

Shove your pain aside! he demanded. *Remember what you learned at Laon's hands and do it! Otherwise, the child is lost! And when you have stood aside from your pain, go into your body and help our son!* He then aided her in carrying out his instructions with the force of his own will, and his own strength.

Raul's help gave Esme the power she needed to stand aside from her pain, and then she immediately sent her mind into her body to stop the process the enemy had started. Raul's mind went with hers to continue to support her strength with his own.

Rapidly, taking care to protect the boy, who was experiencing distress, Esme worked to stop the premature contractions. When she had succeeded, she lay back on the sleeping skins, panting and exhausted, and still terrified.

Raul was no longer terrified. He was enraged.

Esme misunderstood. She thought his anger was directed at her. "I am sorry!" she wailed. "I could not help it, Raul!" She burst into tears.

Raul immediately shielded his anger and took her into his arms to comfort her. "I know it was not your fault, Esme," he soothed. "I know. I was angry at circumstances. Not at you."

He could not explain the real threat to their child even now. Esme was already distraught. The truth might rob her of the defenses she needed to counter again such an assault.

She tilted her head back, tears streaming from her eyes. "Tr–truly?" she asked.

"You know the truth," Raul said with forceful sincerity. "Take it from my mind."

Esme did, and then she collapsed into Raul's arms, her crying less violent now.

When she had calmed enough to talk, she asked, fearfully, "What if it happens again?"

"Then we will prevent it again," Raul said simply.

"But what if you are not near to help?" Esme said, her worry growing. "I panicked, Raul. If you had not been here, I could not have stopped what was about to happen."

"Then I will stay close." He shrugged. "But even if I am not close, you know now what to do, and you will do it."

His quiet certainty reassured and steadied Esme, and at last, she could not stay awake any longer. She was mentally and physically exhausted.

Raul, however, stayed awake until dawn, his mood fierce. And when first light showed at the entrance of the cave he shared with Esme, he got up to seek out Ana. He instructed her that should he be absent from Esme's side for any reason she was to be there in his stead. He also told her what to do should the premature contractions happen again.

He was reassured to see that Ana's fierce protectiveness toward Esme and the babe was well-nigh as fervent as his own.

To Raul's mystification and to his exceeding relief, by the time the first shoots of green began to appear beside the trails of the Settlement, Esme had reached the end of her pregnancy without further obstruction. He and Ana knelt in front of Esme now as she strained in the last stages of her labor.

"One last push, daughter, and it will be done!" Ana exclaimed in excitement. "I can see his head! Raul," she added quickly, shifting to the side. "If you would receive your first-born child into your own hands, you had best be ready, for the time is at hand."

Raul did not hesitate. And within a few seconds, he held the warm, wet, slippery body of his son upon his palms. He stared into two startlingly aware green eyes that were a duplicate of Esme's, except that the tiny face in which they rested held a masculine cast resembling his own.

Esme rested on her elbows. "Is he all right?" she demanded.

At the same time, Ana said, in a tone of pleased awe, "The boy does not cry. Indeed, it seems almost as though he smiles. And look how alert he is! Just as you were, Esme!"

"Let me see him!" Esme panted.

Raul, though so firmly attached to his son by now that he was reluctant to give him up, rose to his feet and brought him to his mother to put him into her arms.

"Ohhhh," Esme crooned as she stroked his small cheek with one finger. "He is beautiful!"

"Indeed, he is," Ana said proudly, reaching across

to swab the infant's wet head with a square of cloth. "And look, though he has his mother's eyes, he has his father's light hair and strong features."

Esme looked up at Raul, and they exchanged a smile of loving complicity. Neither had thought it wise to explain to anyone that they had known, before his birth, how their child would look.

"What will you call him?" Ana asked, still busily swabbing the parts of the baby she could reach as he lay cradled in his mother's arms. The child endured the cleaning without protest.

"Ian," Raul and Esme said together, then laughed together as well.

"Reflecting the Master's graciousness." Ana nodded with approval as she voiced the meaning of the babe's name. "Very appropriate. For he is, in truth, almost regally gracious. See how he allows me to clean him without cry or protest? Perhaps you should make his name 'Ian Regan,' for I confess, he puts me in mind of a little king."

"One name is enough for any child to carry." Raul shrugged then added, "Is he not likely to be chilled if we do not cover him, Ana?"

Ana and Esme exchanged a look of female amusement at Raul's fatherly protectiveness.

"I send him heat from my own body, Raul," Esme said with a smile.

"And I am going to go and prepare his first warm bath," Ana declared, straightening. "When he is clean, I will call Baldor for the blessing."

When Ana had disappeared, Raul knelt beside Esme and Ian, and while he covered his son's small back with one hand, he stroked Esme's sweat-dampened hair with the other.

"Thank you, my love," he said, his voice soft and choked with emotion. "Thank you for our son."

Esme smiled up at him, her expression radiant with love. "Thank you, my love," she echoed in the same tone. "Thank you for our son's conception, and for your help in bringing him to birth."

Raul nodded, bent to kiss her lingeringly, then bestowed another kiss on the top of Ian's damp head.

Ana bustled back, carrying a clay basin filled with warm water, and after bathing the boy, she wrapped him in soft cotton and wool. Then she gave him back to his mother, saying, "I will fetch Baldor now."

Dallia came with Baldor and stood beaming, obviously aching to get her hands on Ian, as her husband laid his hands on the boy's head. Ian stared back into the priest's eyes with a preternaturally mature expression as he received his blessing.

"May you find favor with the Master all of your days in the flesh," Baldor intoned sincerely, "and may He grant you all the blessings of His spirit . . . health, and love, and joy."

No one of the company other than Esme noticed that Baldor had somehow forgotten to add the last of the traditional blessings to his list. He had forgotten to wish Ian "peace."

But Esme pushed the sudden chill of foreboding which came into her mind as a result of the omission aside in the excitement of the well-wishing that followed the blessing. And in any case, that night, Ian's advent into the world marked an event that seemed to make the omission meaningless.

The high counselor and Finder visited the cave to view the child, to wish Esme and Raul well, and to make an announcement.

"Raul, Esme, we have concluded our negotiations," the high counselor said with a warm smile. "We are at peace."

And shortly thereafter, all those in the Settlement, at learning they had two counts upon which to make celebration, did so with joy.

CHAPTER TWENTY

SINCE RAUL WOULD NOT LEAVE THE HOMELAND UNTIL Esme and his son could travel with him, the high council and the Rebels had to wait to return home and announce the good news that the civil war was over. But since the fighting among the worlds of the Empire had ceased pending the result of the negotiations in any case, the delay made no difference, and Jemiah stepped in with a suggestion to soothe the negotiators' impatience to leave.

"Esme claims her planet . . . this planet . . . is the original Earth," he told them. "And since I have occasionally come upon some artifacts that seem to suggest there was once a much higher level of civilization here, I am beginning to give more credence to her belief than I once did. But I still have one last direction to explore. Why not accompany me on my excursion? It may be that with more hovers and more eyes than mine we'll find additional evidence this time."

The negotiators readily agreed, and the next morning, six hovers containing all of them, plus Jemiah, lifted off northwards.

Raul and Esme took the last small hover and went to the high meadow for a brief visit in order to introduce their son to Maza, as well as to the environment in which Esme had spent her early days.

Maza was as appreciative of Ian's fine qualities as any new parents could wish. After the infant grew tired of gazing happily at Esme's flock of milling sheep from the safety of Raul's arms, Maza herded them away and Esme fed her infant son. She then lay him on his belly on a sleeping skin for a nap while she and Raul stretched out beside him.

"I am going to miss the peace to be found here," Esme said drowsily.

"Aye," Raul answered, drowsy himself. "But mayhap the present peace I feel is as much from the relief of no longer being responsible for the council and the Rebel leaders as it is from the atmosphere of this meadow. Even if I am only free of them for a short while, I still feel as though a weight has been lifted from my shoulders."

Esme smiled, cuddled her head on his shoulder and yawned.

"Are the seekers ready now?" Raul asked before she could fall asleep.

"Aye. There is only the induction ceremony into the priesthood still to come," Esme answered. "Baldor has it planned for when your people return."

"Do you leave one priest behind to serve your own people?"

"Yes." Esme smiled. "The one who is least effective in persuasion. My people do not need persuading."

"Is it not interesting that there are exactly as many seekers as there are worlds to send them to?" Raul inquired, lifting an eyebrow. "And Baldor, of course, will divide his time between Genesis and Synonsis."

"It is interesting, yes," Esme answered, mumbling now. She felt very heavy with sleep, unusually so. It was as though she had been drugged, but she knew she had not been. "But not surprising . . ." were the last three words she uttered, before she was completely encompassed by blackness.

Raul asked another question, and when he got no response, he glanced down at Esme and smiled, thinking the care of their son robbed her of energy to an unusual degree. Then he, too, dozed, the usual light doze of the warrior he was, until a strong sense of danger brought him abruptly awake. Then he was on his feet in an instant for He, Esme, and Ian were completely surrounded by wolfhounds, their eyes red and malevolent, their fangs dripping with saliva.

Raul never traveled anywhere these days without his laser, and he drew it quickly as he focused on the leader of the pack, who was stalking with slow menace toward the sleeping skin upon which Ian lay sleeping.

"Esme, wake up!" Raul grated, using both mind and voice, his tone urgent. But though Esme stirred slightly, and groaned as though she sensed danger in her sleep, she did not wake.

Raul called her again, louder and more urgently, and again she stirred, but without waking. Then there was no more time. The leader of the pack of wolfhounds bounded toward Ian with a snarl.

Raul shot the animal once, taking care with his aim,

for he sensed there would be little time for mistakes. Even as the leader died and Raul quickly stepped over to straddle Ian with his legs, two more wolfhounds attacked.

The next few minutes were a blur to Raul. He shot again and again, but there were so many of the snarling, slavering creatures that he could not stop all of them using only the weapon in his hand. Even as he killed again and again with his laser, he used his mind to form a wall of force to delay the attacks of the animals behind him. But he was not as gifted as was Esme in that particular use of the mind, and his force was draining rapidly. He began to fear all was lost.

Then he heard a thud and saw an animal he had not shot rear up as though hit by something, then collapse in a heap. Again, another thud, and another animal collapsed. Raul at last realized that Maza had returned and was using his sling to aid him.

Another few minutes, and the sleeping skin was ringed with the dead bodies of wolfhounds, while Raul and Maza stood side by side, panting from their separate exertions.

"Thank the Master you came!" Raul grated as he knelt beside Esme to shake her. But she still did not wake. "As you can see, there is something wrong with Esme. She cannot seem to wake and she therefore could not help me defend Ian."

Maza was grim-faced, shaken. "I had not intended to come back," he said. "But I heard a voice in my mind commanding me with much urgency to do so. And when I arrived to see the three of you surrounded by this pack, I could not believe it at first. They normally attack only at night, and never in such numbers."

"They were sent by the one your people call the enemy," Raul said harshly, checking Ian now. He was relieved to see that his son had slept through the whole incident without stirring.

Maza frowned and then looked at Ian thoughtfully. "You say that Ian was the focus of the attack?" he asked.

"Aye." Raul nodded, sitting back on his heels. "The enemy did not wish him born, and he does not wish him to live."

"Do you know why?"

Raul shook his head. "The Master did not tell me. He merely warned me to take great care to protect Ian."

Maza smiled wryly then. "Well, you did a better job of it than any other man I know could have. Had it been me, I would be dead now, and so would Esme and the child."

At that, Raul looked up at Maza, his clear eyes blazing with relief. "And had it not been for you, so would the three of us be lying here dead, Maza. You came just in time. I owe you a debt I can never repay."

But Maza merely shrugged. "Thank the Master, not me," he said. "Had it not been for Him, I would not have come." Then he smiled, his expression serene. "And I have had my reward by hearing that voice in my head. It was worth any danger to hear."

Raul nodded. He understood what Maza meant.

"Come and see if you can help me tell what is wrong with Esme," he then said, turning back to his mate. "She seems to be unconscious, not just sleeping."

Maza moved closer and stooped beside Esme. He lifted one of her eyelids, and at that, she frowned and blinked. An instant later, her eyes opened and she stared up at Raul and Maza in a grumpy, puzzled fashion.

"What ails the two of you?" she demanded. "Why do you hover over me like a hen over her chicks?"

Raul and Maza glanced at one another. Then Raul pulled Esme up and pointed at the circle of wolf-hounds. "Look around you," he instructed.

Her skin paled, and with a gasp, she quickly crawled to Ian to check him.

"He is all right," Raul said, his tone still grim. "But for a while, it was not certain that he would be. If the Master had not sent Maza, we would all be dead."

Esme, her green eyes filled with tears, shifted her gaze to Maza and gave him an eloquent look of gratitude. But before she could say anything, Raul spoke again. "Why could you not wake, Esme? I called you with everything I had, mind and voice, and yet you lay as one dead."

Esme frowned, then shook her head in puzzlement. "I do not know," she said slowly. "I was talking to you, and then a blackness descended upon me and I knew nothing more until just now."

Raul's mood turned grimmer. If he could not count on Esme's help, the task of protecting his son was going to be much harder. But at any rate, it was time she knew what he had so far withheld from her. And quickly, deftly, he put into her mind what the Master had told him.

Esme paled again then her expression firmed and her eyes were steady and determined as she looked into Raul's.

"Should this happen again, and the enemy tries to send the blackness upon me, I will by then have worked out a way to defeat him," she vowed.

Raul studied her face, and believing her, he smiled.

Then Esme gathered her son into her arms and turned toward the hover. "Let us return to the Settlement," she said firmly. "Maza, you must come as well."

But Maza shook his head. "I have the flocks to care for," he said simply. "And with this many wolfhounds dead, I should not be in danger of an attack for a long while. Besides"—he shrugged—"it is not me the enemy wants."

Esme then turned back and lifted her face to kiss Maza's cheek. "Once again," she said, her voice quiet and gentle, "you have proved yourself to be a friend among friends. We will not forget."

"Aye," Raul echoed Esme's vow. "We will not forget." He shook Maza's hand as he would have a warrior comrade's rather than a shepherd's.

In the hover later, Esme was silent for a while, then looked at Raul, who sat at the controls, her expression strong and sure.

"We will prevail," she said with quiet calm. "We are not left alone to protect Ian. The Master watches over him as well."

"Aye." Raul nodded. But he knew the bulk of that duty still rested with himself. And he was therefore ready, later that night, when the enemy, having failed to gain his ends in one fashion, tried another.

In the wee hours of the night, Raul, who had been dozing, felt a movement. Abruptly, he opened his eyes and looked around, bewildered. He was not in the cave he shared with Esme on the Homeland. He was nowhere he recognized. He stood on a stark, forbidding plain lit by a dull, swirling light. Something about that light suggested treachery and put him on guard.

Then the light coalesced and Raul faced a being whose countenance resembled his long dead father's. But his father's face was overlaid by another, which was terrible in its beauty.

Raul hesitated between joy at seeing his sire again, and a sense that this was not really his father.

"I want the boy," the being said in a tone of command.

Raul was torn, for the tone of voice was almost an exact duplicate of his father's. While his parent had lived, Raul had respected and obeyed him without question, and he felt a compulsion to do it now. And yet. . . .

"He is mine," the being said peremptorily. "Give him to me, and in return, our family will have power such as we never dreamed existed. We will rule the Empire. The boy will be an emperor."

In a flash, Raul saw a throne suspended in the air—a glittering, bejeweled throne more glorious than he could have imagined. Upon the throne Ian sat, grown to manhood, handsome and strong, garbed in rich robes, with throngs of the Empire's citizens on their knees at his feet.

On Ian's right was Raul. On his left was Esme. And behind the throne was Raul's father, a smirk of approval on his lips.

Raul frowned. His father had never worn such an expression nor would he at the prospect of his grandson becoming an emperor. He had never been one to crave such power.

Despite Raul's growing conviction that the being's

look and tone of voice were illusions, as was the vision just granted him, his love for his sire and his desire to please him tugged at his heart. Also the prospect of giving Ian the best of everything swayed him. He did not want such power for himself, but for Ian . . .

But no, he dragged his mind away from such contemplations. The Empire did not need an emperor. That had happened once in the past, and there had been a long and costly war, in terms of human life and material destruction, to unseat the tyrant. And such power could come to corrupt Ian and cut him off from the Master.

His thinking of the Master caused the being to roar in displeasure and Raul's mind suddenly cleared completely. He knew then, whom he really faced, and his will tightened as his eyes blazed at the enemy.

"I do not want such power!" he grated. "Neither for myself nor for my son. And neither would my father want it. Not when it comes from such as you."

The vision of his father's face cleared from the enemy's abruptly, and there was only the terrible beauty left.

"Then you are a fool," he sneered. "I will have the boy anyway. But you will be left behind when he comes into his inheritance."

"If you could have him anyway, you would wish him dead," Raul stated flatly, and felt a reassurance that strengthened his will immeasurably. "And you will not succeed in killing him," he vowed. "I and Esme and the Master will see to that! Each trick you use to take my son's life will be countered, and you will fail."

At the mention of the Master, the enemy seemed to have to exert tremendous force to keep from reeling backwards. Then he laughed contemptuously.

"I do not need to kill a puling human infant," he said, shrugging his magnificent shoulders. "Such are beneath my notice."

Raul knew the lie for what it was. "Then leave him be!" he said. "For your efforts will not succeed in any case!"

The enemy was silent for a time. Then he smiled and it was a travesty of a smile, malignant and evil.

"I will leave him be," he said with silky deceitfulness. "For the present," he added, dashing Raul's hope that Ian was no longer at risk. "Instead, when the time is right, I will convert him to my cause."

"Never," Raul said with absolute certainty.

"We will see," the enemy said. "We will certainly see."

In the next instant, his presence began to fade, and his malicious laughter echoed as he disappeared.

Raul was suddenly awake, lying on his sleeping skin beside Esme. Shaken, he got up and went to check the basket where Ian lay sleeping. But Ian was not sleeping. His green eyes were awake and aware, and Raul, unable to resist, picked him up and held him close in a protective fashion.

"I do not know if he will truly cease his attempts upon your life, my son," he whispered into the tiny ear beside his mouth. "But I do know that you will be safe from such attempts. I vow it on my life. And your mother and I will make sure that when the time comes for your own temptation, you will be as ready to resist it as we have been."

After kissing the top of Ian's head, he took him to his mother and lay him by her breast. Esme stirred, and still half-asleep, opened the bodice of her sleeping gown so that the child might nurse.

And Raul, standing over the two of them watching, once again had tears in his eyes.

Esme and Raul could tell that Jemiah had news by the way he quivered with excitement when he climbed down out of the hover that had brought him back to the Settlement.

"What is it, Jemiah?" Esme asked with amused affection. "Did you find something?"

"I think so." Jemiah nodded fervently. "It will take more study, but we may have found the launch pad that was used by the saints when they left this planet, Esme. There was a metal sign there, so weathered and worn it was almost impossible to read. But if I am correct, it lists the names of the original saints and the date of their departure."

"Are you surprised, Jemiah?" Esme asked, smiling.

Jemiah took a deep breath. "Not as much as I once would have been," he admitted with a grin. Then he sobered and added, "But, Esme, if the desolation I saw on this planet was truly caused by our ancestors, I am also less philosophical now than I once was about the periodic upheavals that seem to seize our kind. And I will aid you and Raul actively now to keep the peace, rather than viewing such matters from afar with historical detachment."

Esme was touched. But she did not feel it wise to tell Jemiah, at least not for the present, that the next upheaval would not be between human warring against human, except for those humans whom the enemy succeeded in influencing. Rather would it be the enemy's creatures from Miia who would pose the next threat to humanity's survival.

"I will accept your help, Jemiah." She nodded. Then her lips tilted in a smile as she wondered how Jemiah, with his academic mind, would react to her revelation that he might help by accepting the reality of the Master and aiding others of his kind to come to the same acceptance.

Raul's family, Jemiah, the High Council, the Rebel leaders, Baldor, Dallia, and a number of newly ordained priests, who valiantly tried to hide their trepidation at being several miles above their home planet, awaited the first jump on their way back to the Empire.

Raul drew Esme apart from the others and held her in his arms, as she held Ian in hers. "You have come a long way since the day I first saw you," he said in a musing tone.

"Yes." Esme nodded. "And I still have further to go."

"As do we all," Raul agreed. "As do we all," he repeated, as he thought about what might be in his son's future. "But as long as we three are together, the journey will never be as hard as it would be if we were each alone."

"And for that, I thank the Master," Esme said with quiet gratitude.

"Aye," responded Raul, his tone matching Esme's. "As do I."

In the next instant, the jump began, and the view screen reflected a wealth of colors. And Esme once again, this time with the future in her arms, journeyed among the stars.